PRAISE FOR SUS

"I will read anything Susan Stoker puts out . . . because I know it's going to be amazing!"

—Riley Edwards, *USA Today* bestselling author

"Susan Stoker never fails to pull me out of a reading slump. With heat, action, and suspense, she weaves an incredible tale that sucks me in and doesn't let go."

—Jessica Prince, *USA Today* bestselling author

"One thing I love about Susan Stoker's books is that she knows how to deliver a perfect HEA while still making sure the villain gets what he/she deserves!"

—T.M. Frazier, *New York Times* bestselling author

"Susan Stoker's characters come alive on the page!"

—Elle James, *New York Times* bestselling author

"When you pick up a Susan Stoker book, you know exactly what you're going to get . . . a hot alpha hero and a smart, sassy heroine. I can't get enough!"

—Jessica Hawkins, *USA Today* bestselling author

"Suspenseful storytelling with characters you want as friends!"

—Meli Raine, *USA Today* bestselling author

"Susan Stoker knows what women want. A hot hero who needs to save a damsel in distress . . . even if she can save herself."

—CD Reiss, *New York Times* bestselling author

THE *Protector*

DISCOVER OTHER TITLES BY SUSAN STOKER

Game of Chance Series

The Protector

The Royal (August 2023)

The Hero (TBA)

The Lumberjack (TBA)

Silverstone Series

Trusting Skylar

Trusting Taylor

Trusting Molly

Trusting Cassidy

Mountain Mercenaries Series

Defending Allye

Defending Chloe

Defending Morgan

Defending Harlow

Defending Everly

Defending Zara

Defending Raven

Ace Security Series

Claiming Grace

Claiming Alexis

Claiming Bailey

Claiming Felicity

Claiming Sarah

The Refuge

Deserving Alaska

Deserving Henley

Deserving Reese (May 2023)

Deserving Cora (November 2023)

Deserving Lara (TBA)

Deserving Maisy (TBA)

Deserving Ryleigh (TBA)

SEAL Team Hawaii Series

Finding Elodie

Finding Lexie

Finding Kenna

Finding Monica

Finding Carly

Finding Ashlyn

Finding Jodelle (July 2023)

Eagle Point Search & Rescue

Searching for Lilly

Searching for Elsie

Searching for Bristol

Searching for Caryn (April 2023)

Searching for Finley (October 2023)

Searching for Heather (TBA)

Searching for Khloe (TBA)

Delta Force Heroes

Rescuing Rayne

Rescuing Aimee (novella)

Rescuing Emily

Rescuing Harley

Marrying Emily (novella)

Rescuing Kassie

Rescuing Bryn

Rescuing Casey

Rescuing Sadie (novella)

Rescuing Wendy

Rescuing Mary

Rescuing Macie

Rescuing Annie

Delta Team Two Series

Shielding Gillian

Shielding Kinley

Shielding Aspen

Shielding Jayme (novella)

Shielding Riley

Shielding Devyn

Shielding Ember

Shielding Sierra

Badge of Honor: Texas Heroes Series

Justice for Mackenzie

Justice for Mickie

Justice for Corrie

Justice for Laine (novella)

Shelter for Elizabeth

Justice for Boone

Shelter for Adeline

Shelter for Sophie

Justice for Erin

Justice for Milena

Shelter for Blythe

Justice for Hope

Shelter for Quinn

Shelter for Koren

Shelter for Penelope

SEAL of Protection Series

Protecting Caroline

Protecting Alabama

Protecting Fiona

Marrying Caroline (novella)

Protecting Summer

Protecting Cheyenne

Protecting Jessyka

Protecting Julie (novella)

Protecting Melody

Protecting the Future

Protecting Kiera (novella)

Protecting Alabama's Kids (novella)

Protecting Dakota

Seal of Protection: Legacy Series

Securing Caite

Securing Brenae (novella)

Securing Sidney

Securing Piper

Securing Zoey

Securing Avery

Securing Kalee

Securing Jane

Beyond Reality Series

Outback Hearts

Flaming Hearts

Frozen Hearts

Stand-Alone Novels

The Guardian Mist

Falling for the Delta

Nature's Rift

A Princess for Cale

A Moment in Time (a short story collection)

Another Moment in Time (a short story collection)

A Third Moment in Time (a short story collection)

Lambert's Lady

Written as Annie George

Stepbrother Virgin (erotic novella)

Game of Chance, Book One

SUSAN
STOKER

Published by Montlake, Seattle

www.apub.com

ISBN-13: 9781662509643 (paperback)
ISBN-13: 9781662509650 (digital)

Cover design by Hang Le
Cover photography by Michelle Lancaster
Cover image: ©by-studio / Shutterstock

Printed in the United States of America

THE *Protector*

Prologue

Jackson "JJ" Justice closed his eyes and breathed shallowly through his nose, praying the pain would lessen. But it was a futile prayer. Their captors delighted in causing as much agony as they could.

Opening his eyes, JJ squinted to see his best friends and teammates chained to the walls around him. Riggs "Chappy" Chapman had his head resting against the cinder block wall and his eyes closed. He wasn't asleep, JJ knew that without a doubt. No one slept in this hellhole. Not really.

Kendric "Bob" Evans was next to Chappy, staring over at their fourth teammate with grave concern.

Turning his attention to Callum "Cal" Redmon, JJ frowned. He had just been brought back to their cell after a "session" with their captors, and he didn't look good at all. The assholes holding them hostage were thrilled when they'd realized his identity. Cal was an actual prince.

And as Cal had often said, the title itself was actually more exciting than reality, considering a couple dozen of his relatives would have to be killed or die before he came anywhere close to becoming king.

But that didn't matter to the terrorists. They'd focused on Cal almost from the second the team had all been dragged unconscious into this cell. Currently, he was dripping from too many cuts on his body to count. He wore only a pair of boxers, making it easy to see just how horrible his latest torture session had been.

Their captors had focused on marring Cal's formerly pristine flesh, using knives, cigarettes, and who the hell knew what else to carve into his skin. They used their fists on his face but preferred various torture implements for the rest of his body.

The men who'd captured them didn't have an ounce of compassion, of course. When they'd tortured JJ, they'd laughed and jeered with every punch as their knives sliced into his skin. To their jailers, he and his teammates were less than human.

Looking around at his best friends, the three men who were literally his reason for continuing to fight to stay alive, JJ made an easy decision.

"When we get out of here, I'm done," he said fervently. His voice was low so as not to alert their captors that they were awake and talking. He knew keeping the four of them chained in the same room—so each could see the torture the others were enduring—was part of the sick mind game the assholes were playing.

Little did they know, keeping them together only strengthened his team rather than making them weaker.

When no one spoke, JJ went on. "I'm serious. We all knew this mission was doomed from the very start. We didn't have the backup we should've, the intel was practically nonexistent, and when we expressed our concerns, we were told to shut up and follow orders." He huffed a quiet laugh. "And look where those orders got us. I'm *done*. I'm out. I didn't sign up for this. To fight for my country, yes. But to sit in my own shit, getting beaten, having to watch my friends get tortured . . . and on top of it all, being filmed for the insurgents' agenda? No. Just fuckin' *no*."

JJ had never wanted to be the leader of their group. As the oldest, and not one who suffered fools easily, he kind of fell into the role. But he'd screwed up. He should've been firmer in his insistence that this mission was destined to fail. Should've pushed for more intelligence before they entered the country.

While he had no doubt the US government was working to get them released, everyone knew the policy was not to negotiate with terrorists. They were likely on their own until they could find a way to escape—which wasn't looking very promising—or one of their fellow Special Forces teams came in to bust them out.

"If you're out, I'm out too," Bob said with a grimace. "If you think I'm staying in without you, you're insane."

"Well, I'm not staying without *either* of you guys," Chappy agreed. His words were garbled from the last beating he'd received, but his support for getting out of the military was heard loud and clear.

The three men looked over at Cal.

He took a deep breath and immediately grimaced at the pain it caused. One of his eyes was swollen shut, and the man the media had once called "Prettymon" looked anything but at the moment. The terrorists had left their mark on his flesh. If he lived through this—if *any* of them lived through their captivity—he'd have visible reminders of his torture every time he looked in a mirror.

"What'll we do then?" Cal asked. His words were slow and slurring, making him hard to understand.

"Anything we fucking want," Chappy answered. "But I'm not living in a city."

"Well, I'm not living in a fucking suburb," Bob retorted.

"As long as I'm not in a cell, chained to a wall, I don't give a shit *where* we live," Cal slurred.

"Rochambeau," JJ decided.

"Huh?"

"What?"

"What the bloody hell is that?"

"Rock paper scissors. To decide where we'll live," he answered. Under the circumstances, it seemed ridiculous to decide where to put down roots once they were out of the military. Especially with a child's game. But they all needed to think about something besides how much pain they were in . . . and when their captors would be back to inflict more.

"Sounds good to me," Chappy said.

"Shouldn't we decide what we're gonna do for a living before we figure out where to live?" Bob asked.

"Nope," JJ said with a shake of his head, warming up to the idea of making plans for their future. There was probably less than a fifty percent chance they'd even *have* a future, but right now, they needed to focus on something positive. "We can't decide to be taxi drivers and then make the decision to move to some rural town with one stoplight. First, we figure out where we want to live, then we'll settle on some kind of business to open."

He waited for his friends to agree, then continued. "So, everyone think of where you want to live when we get back to the States. Somewhere you've always wanted to settle down. A place that calls to you. Then I'll Rochambeau Chappy, and Cal and Bob will play. The winner of each round plays the other. Whoever's left standing at the end decides where we live. Deal?"

Bob and Cal nodded.

A burst of laughter left Chappy's lips. "We all know this is crazy, right?" he asked. "I mean, we're about to decide on our future—a future with a high probability of never coming to fruition, considering where we are at the moment—with a game of chance."

"Why not?" Bob asked. "You got somewhere else you need to be right now? Some other plans?"

"Well, you know, I had a hot date with this chick, but I suppose I can stay and play kids' games with you guys instead."

All four men chuckled quietly at that.

JJ was well aware the odds of getting out of their current situation weren't good. But having something to look forward to could only help them in the long run. "Okay, Chappy and I will go first," JJ said. "You ready? You got a place in mind?"

"Yeah."

"Me too. Okay, on the count of three. One, two, *three*!"

JJ held his hand out flat, indicating paper, while Chappy made a fist.

"Damn," JJ said, a small grin on his face. "Paper beats rock. Guess Hawaii is out."

"Well, shit, I could've totally gotten on board with that," Cal moaned. "We've heard Mustang and his team talk about how awesome it is there often enough."

Mustang was a fellow Special Forces member they'd worked with in the past. He and his SEAL team had definitely lucked out with that duty station. The last JJ had heard, they were all settling down and starting families.

A pang hit him hard at the thought, harder than he could've imagined.

JJ had always wanted a family of his own. A woman he could protect and adore who would love him back just as much. And children . . .

He sighed. At thirty-nine, he was getting too old to think about having babies.

"Okay, Cal and Bob, your turn. On the count of three . . . one, two, *three*," JJ ordered.

Cal held up two fingers in the shape of scissors, and Bob's hand was flat.

"Scissors beat paper," JJ announced.

"Shit," Bob grumbled.

"What was your choice?" Chappy asked.

"New York City. Nothing better than the hustle and bustle of the greatest city in the world," he said fondly.

"Looks like it's you and me," JJ told Cal.

His friend's gaze was unfocused, and the pupil in the eye that wasn't swollen shut was much larger than it should've been, but since there was literally nothing JJ could do right now to help other than take Cal's mind off where they were for a few minutes, he did his best to hide his concern.

"You're goin' down, mate," Cal teased weakly.

JJ's lips twitched. They were all super competitive. It was partly why they were such good Special Forces soldiers. They didn't like to fail. Didn't like when things didn't go according to plan.

"Bring it," he taunted. "On the count of three. One, two, three!"

JJ fisted his hand while Cal held his flat.

"Damn," JJ said with a sigh.

"I was gonna go rock, but I don't think I can curl all my fingers," Cal joked.

It was true, some of his friend's fingers were mangled and most certainly broken. Hatred for their captors almost overcame JJ, but he forced the feeling down. There would be a time later to let out his anger; for now, he had to keep his cool. His teammates were relying on him to be their anchor.

"I can't believe we're letting the one guy who's not from the US pick where we live," Bob groaned.

JJ was somewhat amused about that himself, but a deal was a deal, and since Cal won the game, he'd get to decide where the four of them settled. "You win," JJ told his friend. "My choice was going to be Nashville. So . . . where are we setting up shop, Cal?"

"Maine. There's a town on the western side of the state, close to the New Hampshire border, called Newton. I saw a newsclip about it once."

"Are you shitting me?" Bob asked. "*Maine?* Please tell me Newton is a city."

Cal grinned. It was lopsided, and the movement made blood drip from his cheek down to his bare chest, but he didn't seem to notice.

"Nope. It's in the middle of nowhere. I don't think they even *have* a stoplight. There's snow on the ground for six months of the year, and the only place to shop is a Dollar General. The population is tiny, like twelve hundred or so. From what I saw on the clip, it looked like heaven."

"Fuck me," Bob groaned. "What the hell are we going to do for a living in a town like that?"

JJ sighed. It was a good question. "I know what we're *not* going to do," he blurted. "Anything to do with security. Or being a bodyguard. Or private investigations. Too many people get out of the military and do that shit anyway. I've had enough of guns. Of death. Of putting my life on the line for others. I want to do something . . . normal."

"I agree," Chappy said seriously.

"Me too," Bob said. "But seriously, what *will* we do? Let's face it, we aren't actually qualified to do much more than what we've been doing."

There was silence for a moment before JJ said, "Let's take some time to think about it. Think about Maine. Think about what you enjoy doing in your spare time—and no laughing. Yes, I realize we haven't had much spare time, ever. Maybe something you've always wanted to do but haven't had the opportunity. Then we'll Rochambeau again."

JJ had no idea if they'd actually follow through, if they'd really let a game decide their fate, but the more he thought about moving to Maine, the more the idea appealed. He'd had his fill of mankind. People were endlessly cruel. He and his men knew that firsthand. Too many people were self-centered, entitled, concerned only about themselves, and too willing to shove their beliefs down other people's throats. With every passing year, there was less tolerance for differences, for accepting people as they were.

JJ was sick of all of it. He'd happily move to a quiet, sleepy little town and eke out a living with his friends, even if it made his dream of starting a family far less likely. Finding a woman who could look beyond what he'd done in the military and love him for who and what he was would be a whole lot harder in the wilds of Maine.

Ten minutes or so went by, and it was Chappy who said, "Are we ready?"

"Let's do this," Bob replied firmly.

JJ played Bob in the first round, and Chappy played Cal. Then, it was Chappy and Bob in the final round.

Chappy made a fist and Bob held up two fingers.

"Shit! I never win this stupid game," Bob griped.

Everyone chuckled.

"So? What're we doing for the rest of our lives?" JJ asked Chappy.

"Lumberjacks," he said with a wide grin.

"You have *got* to be kidding me," Cal griped.

"Nope," Chappy said with the same shit-eating grin on his face. "I figure Maine has trees. A lot of them. I'm sure they're always falling over in people's yards and on roads and stuff. We can start a tree service. Cutting them down, pulling up stumps, things like that."

While Bob and Cal groaned, JJ nodded. "The Appalachian Trail is in Maine too. I'm not sure how close it is to Newton. Cal? Do you know? Did the show say?"

"They talked about the 'AT,' but I didn't know what that was," Cal admitted.

"Awesome. So the trails will need maintenance too. We could be trail maintainers. They're actually a real thing . . . people who're responsible for certain sections of a trail. They make sure it's clear, keep the trail markers maintained, watch over any camps in their area, and generally act as the experts on their particular section," JJ said.

"You mean we could actually hike without worrying about being stealthy or who might be following, trying to kill our asses?" Bob asked. "I'm in."

"Maybe we could even hire ourselves out as guides," Chappy said. "I mean, I'm thinking we probably wouldn't be busy nonstop with the tree stuff, so we could escort people who're unsure about the AT or who'd just feel more comfortable having someone familiar with the area leading them."

"And we could help if anyone got lost," Cal added. "I have a friend who got out of the service and now lives in Virginia. He's a search and rescue volunteer."

"Remember that woman who got lost a few years ago?" JJ asked. "Geraldine Largay?"

"Yeah. She went off trail to go to the bathroom and got turned around. There was a huge search, but her body wasn't found until two years or so later. She'd died of exposure and starvation."

They were all silent for a moment, remembering the tragedy.

"I'm in," Bob said firmly.

"Me too," Cal agreed.

"Me three," JJ said with a nod.

"Jack's Lumber," Chappy announced.

"What?" Bob questioned.

"That's what we'll call our business. As a nod to JJ, who's always been our leader. And as a play on the word 'lumberjack.'"

As the other three men discussed what services they might offer, how much they could charge, where they might want to live, JJ relaxed against the hard wall behind him, a lump in his throat. The plan to distract his friends had worked. They weren't dreading when their captors would return. Weren't thinking about how much pain they were in.

They had hope for a better future.

Now, all they needed to do was get out of this hellhole and make their plans come to fruition. It would take money—which the four of them had, since they'd had few chances to spend the cash they'd earned over the years—determination, hard work, and an open mind.

For the first time in years, and despite his current predicament, JJ realized he was excited for the future. Their captors had tried to break them. Demoralize them. Tear them down and beat them psychologically as well as physically. And there would probably be a lot more of the same coming their way. But for now, the four men had something to strive toward. A plan.

If JJ had his way, nothing and no one would keep them from getting to Newton, Maine, and starting their new lives.

Chapter One

Riggs "Chappy" Chapman smiled as he approached his cabin, instant calm descending. It was hard to believe it had been three full years since that day in a cold cell when he and his friends had decided their future. At the time, it had been a pipe dream. He was well aware JJ had been grasping at straws, desperate to help them think about anything other than their depressing situation. But the more they'd talked about Jack's Lumber and moving to Maine, the more Chappy wanted it.

And they'd done it.

They'd been rescued by a team of men from the navy and army working together. The soldiers had swarmed in like the badasses they were, killed every one of their captors, then blown up the mountain where they'd been held captive.

Their rescuers entering the country in the first place had caused a mini-international incident, but because the terrorists had gleefully shared videos of the torture Chappy and the others had been put through, the country's government couldn't exactly protest the Special Forces teams coming to their rescue.

That was his team's last mission. The paperwork for them to get out of the military was started long before their physical injuries had healed. Every one of them still dealt with the mental ramifications of what they'd been through, what they'd seen over the years, and the missions they'd participated in. But the choice to move to Maine had turned out to be just what they'd needed to soothe their souls.

Even more surprisingly, their business had taken off pretty much from the first day. If there was one thing Maine didn't lack, it was forests. And having four more men willing and able to handle the physical labor it took to deal with any kind of issue involving trees meant they were constantly busy.

So busy, they'd had to hire an administrative assistant after less than a year to keep everything straight.

Chappy had just completed his last AT guide for the season, and right on time too. A huge winter storm was approaching, projected to dump at least two feet of snow on the area.

The first winter Chappy and his friends had spent in Maine was a shock. They'd expected it to be cold and snowy—but not as cold and snowy as it actually was. Now, with only two seasons under their belts, they felt as if they were old pros at Maine winters.

Chappy chuckled to himself. He could just imagine Mother Nature sitting in a bar, reading their minds and saying "Hold my beer" to the bartender as she rolled up her sleeves.

Prior to coming to Maine, Chappy had never seen two feet of snow in person. Now, he couldn't think of a better place to experience it than the small cabin in the woods that he used when he needed some time to himself.

It wasn't big, basically one room with a small bathroom tucked in the back. He'd worked hard to get it plumbed, put in a septic tank, and set up the water system. There wasn't electricity, but he had a generator that he ran when he needed to charge his computer or heat water for a shower. It was a simple cabin, and it suited him perfectly.

The guys had bitched about him coming up here right before a huge storm, but he'd reassured them he'd be fine. Even if he was snowed in, he had plenty of food, the snow would provide water if he ran out, and he had no intention of doing anything other than relaxing.

As if thinking about his friends had somehow conjured them, the satellite phone on the passenger seat rang just as Chappy was parking his vehicle.

"It hasn't even been an hour. I'm *fine*," he said in lieu of a greeting. He didn't know which of his friends was on the other end of the line, but considering only four people in the world had the number, it was either Cal, Bob, JJ, or April . . . and he seriously doubted it was their assistant. She never called him. Or Bob or Cal for that matter.

April Hoffman was a godsend. Extremely organized and utterly unflappable. Nothing seemed to rile her—not their occasional bad moods, not stressed-out customers. She hadn't even blinked when they'd expanded her duties to include handling the reservations for their AT guide service. She'd also had a ton of great ideas in the last couple of years on how to make their jobs easier—and to make their customers happier.

Chappy was sure a large part of their success was due to April. But if she was worried about something, she'd call JJ, and he'd be the one to communicate her concerns to the team.

"I just wanted to see if you'd made it up there yet," JJ said.

"I pulled up to the cabin literally two seconds ago," Chappy said. "I haven't even had a chance to get out of my Jeep yet."

"Well, you'd better get on that because the weather guy said the storm's going to hit sooner than they'd previously predicted. And just for fun, it's going to start out with rain, then some hail, before turning to snow."

"Damn," he muttered.

"Yeah. You've still got time to come back to Newton," JJ told him.

Chappy chuckled. "Not happening."

"You okay?" JJ asked.

This was only one of the many reasons Chappy admired Jackson. He wasn't afraid to come right out and ask about their mental health. He didn't shy away from his PTSD, or his team's, and he was especially concerned about Cal. Out of the four of them, Cal had come out of captivity with the most scars. Not to mention, because he had royal blood, he'd gotten the most media attention.

It ate at him, they all knew that, but he always kept his cool and never let anyone know his experiences had taken a part of his soul . . . except JJ. Their leader could always break through the ice that seemed to surround Cal and get him to open up and admit when he was struggling.

"I'm good," Chappy reassured him. "Just ready for this break."

"That last group you took on the AT was a handful, huh?"

Chappy huffed out a breath. "That's one way to describe them." He'd taken three college girls on a two-night trip down the Appalachian Trail, and they'd done nothing but complain the entire time. Their feet hurt, their backs ached, their bags were too heavy, they were hungry, the coffee sucked, the shelters they'd stayed in were too cold . . . the complaints went on and on.

By the time Chappy had waved goodbye as they were picked up at a designated stopping point, he was utterly relieved to be by himself. He took his time during the two-day hike back the way he'd come, making notes on which trail markers needed to be repainted and which trees would probably fall across the trail during the upcoming winter, needing to be chopped and cleared come spring. When he finally returned to Newton, he was ready for some down time.

"Well, if you need anything, call. I'll be pissed if you don't," JJ said sternly. "You need extraction, we've got your back."

"The roads up here are going to be unpassable, and you know it," Chappy told him.

"Don't care. You need help, we'll be there. Besides, you know it'll give Bob a thrill to have a chance to take his truck out with that new plow."

Chappy laughed. JJ wasn't wrong. Of their small team, Bob was the most comfortable in nature, which was somewhat humorous since he'd wanted to live in New York City. He'd taken to life in Maine as if he were born to it. He volunteered for the longest AT guide jobs and was always the one who wanted to shimmy up a tree to get to the highest branches that needed trimming.

"I appreciate it," Chappy told JJ.

"And I know I don't need to say it, but I'm going to anyway . . . the rain before the snow is gonna make the snowpack unstable. Just because there hasn't been an avalanche out this way in a long time doesn't mean there won't be again."

"Let me guess, April cornered you and filled your head with statistics on avalanches and how many there have been in the state and what the ideal conditions are for them to occur," Chappy said with a smile.

"Got it in one. But she has a good point. There was one over at Baxter State Park only a couple of years ago. And you being at the base of Baldpate Mountain doesn't give me the warm fuzzies."

"I'll be fine, Mom," Chappy teased.

"I'm being serious," JJ argued, sounding grumpy.

"I know. But this cabin is about a mile away from where the slides are most likely to occur, if they happen at all."

"Right. Well, enjoy your time away from the hustle and bustle of Newton."

Chappy laughed outright at that. "Uh-huh. You gonna tattle to April if I don't check in every other day?"

It was JJ's turn to chuckle. "Don't need to tattle. She's gonna be on my case, wanting to know if I've talked to you and if you're all right. You don't check in, she'll probably find a way to get up there to see for herself that you're in one piece."

"She would too, wouldn't she?" Chappy mused.

"Yes. So hunker down, enjoy the solitude, and call me so I can reassure her that you're fine and don't need to be rescued."

Chappy smiled. He and the others might bitch about April being like a mother hen, but the truth was, it felt good. He wasn't close to his biological family. Couldn't even remember the last time he'd talked to his own mother.

"I will. Talk to you soon."

"Later."

Chappy clicked off the phone and climbed out of his Jeep. He had a good bit of work to get done before the worst of the weather moved in.

As soon as he had the thought, a drop of rain hit his nose. JJ wasn't wrong, the weather was moving in *way* faster than forecasted. Looking up, he saw the tops of the trees blowing in the high wind. He frowned and mentally calculated which trees needed pruning. It was too late now, of course, so he'd just have to hope they held up under the weight of the coming snow. It would suck to have one of the large trees fall onto his cabin.

Taking a deep breath, and trying not to borrow trouble, Chappy turned back to his Jeep. He needed to get his supplies inside, make sure the generator was filled and operational, ensure there was enough firewood stacked on the porch to last awhile, and what seemed like a hundred other little chores.

He had three new books to read, along with the dozens he'd hauled up here over the last two years that were sitting on bookshelves inside. He was looking forward to a nice, relaxing, boring two weeks before he headed back down to Newton to pull his weight with Jack's Lumber.

It was official.

Carlise Edwards was lost.

She'd started driving the day before yesterday, her only goal to get away. To get out of Cleveland. Away from whoever was stalking her.

She was pretty sure it was her ex-boyfriend.

At first, Tommy seemed like everything she'd been looking for in a man . . . but before long, he'd turned possessive and jealous. Violent.

And if there was one thing she wouldn't tolerate, it was an abusive boyfriend.

She'd already watched her mom struggle to make Carlise's father happy, to no avail. The man had beaten her more times than Carlise could count—and her mom had made excuses for him for the longest time.

So when Tommy got angry after arriving home after work to find she didn't have dinner waiting for him, shoving her hard enough for Carlise to stumble and fall, knocking her head on the counter before slumping to the floor, she was done. She knew how things would go. He'd apologize, promise he didn't mean to hurt her, swear it would never happen again . . . until it did. His behavior would likely escalate until Carlise was hiding bruises and making up excuses for broken bones.

Wasn't going to happen. She'd dumped him without hesitation.

He hadn't taken it well. At first, he'd begged her to give him another chance, but when that didn't work, he became obsessed. Following her everywhere she went, showing up at her apartment, calling and texting at all hours of the day and night. His behavior was alarming, and it went on for weeks.

Then he turned destructive, painting the word "Bitch" on her front door and slashing all four of her tires. At least, she *assumed* the vandalism had been Tommy. She couldn't be certain, since she'd never caught him in the act. He'd also started harassing her from a number and an email address she didn't recognize, as if suddenly realizing an electronic trail wasn't so smart.

But it wasn't as if she didn't have all the other texts and emails with his name attached, and she couldn't imagine anyone else in her life wanting to damage her property.

His initial calls and texts, following her . . . all of that had been scary enough, but after the vandalism, she'd *really* started to worry. She'd shared her concerns with her mom and her best friend, Susie.

Though they warned her to be careful, neither could offer much beyond a sympathetic ear.

She'd also gone to the police and taken out a temporary restraining order but suspected a piece of paper wouldn't keep Tommy from continuing his harassment. And she was right. Even nastier texts and emails followed.

Ultimately, Carlise had decided to leave town for a while. Maybe if she wasn't around, Tommy would finally move on with his life. Forget all about her.

Thankfully, she had a job that she could do from anywhere. She translated books from French into English. She'd hated the language when she'd first started taking it in middle school, but eventually she learned to love it, realizing she had a natural affinity for speaking and writing French. And of course, the year she'd spent in France while in college was the best thing she could've done to really learn the language.

She'd kind of fallen into the translation gig. She'd seen a post on social media from a French author, wanting to know if someone would read an excerpt from her book and make sure she had the English right—she didn't—and that had slowly turned into a career, translating books from French to English. She wouldn't have minded translating the other way as well, but most translators converting text to French were native speakers.

She'd just downloaded a new manuscript, so she wouldn't need the internet for a while, although eventually she'd have to log on and manage new requests for translations and check her email. Carlise had been a little reluctant to get online for the last few days, just in case Tommy could somehow track her. She knew it was highly unlikely, and Carlise didn't think he was smart enough to figure out how to do such a thing, but she didn't want to take any chances.

She just needed a break. She'd become reluctant to leave her apartment, nervous to go to the store . . . to go *anywhere*, really, for fear of running into him. After the tire incident, she was worried his threats would escalate, with Tommy taking his frustration and anger out on her in even more dangerous ways.

She wouldn't put it past him to burn her entire building down with Carlise inside.

So she'd hit the road without a word to anyone but her mom, though she *didn't* tell her where she was heading because, well . . . she didn't *know* where she was going. She didn't have a destination in mind, her only plan to get out of town and hunker down somewhere.

She'd left Cleveland before sunrise two days ago. And clearly, she should have given her plan more thought. She'd changed her direction more than once, first heading south, then meandering east, and finally north.

The problem was, she didn't know if she'd be safe from Tommy *anywhere.*

And worse, the more she drove, the more she couldn't help feeling like everything happening was somehow partly *her* fault. Which was crazy. All she wanted was to find a man who loved her as much as she loved him. Not someone who would fly off the handle for something stupid and hurt her.

This morning, she'd found herself in Maine, and Carlise suddenly felt as if she could breathe for the first time in weeks. Fully charmed by all the small towns on her route, she decided to find one with a hotel, maybe a cute downtown area she could explore, and make that her home base for a couple of weeks before heading back to Ohio. Hopeful that, by then, the whole Tommy mess would have gone away.

She'd happily taken various back roads, enjoying the serene forests and quiet roads . . . until she'd realized she hadn't passed a sign or even any other cars for quite some time. She'd briefly consulted her phone, but cell service was sporadic at best in the heavily wooded area. Her GPS app was useless.

If that wasn't bad enough, the weather had gotten nasty—fast. At first it was cold rain, which quickly turned into sleet. Now it was snowing so hard, Carlise couldn't see more than a few feet in front of her vehicle.

She couldn't go back the way she'd come because she knew there was nothing behind her for miles. She hadn't passed a town in a good while—no restaurants, no gas stations. She'd just been driving around, attempting to find some sort of civilization. In desperation, she'd turned onto an access road of sorts—little more than a wide track, really—thinking surely it existed for a reason. Had to lead to maybe a village or even just some random houses.

Looking at the seat next to her, she grimaced. She had half a bottle of water, a Snickers bar, some trail mix, and two mini doughnuts, all left over from the last time she'd stopped for gas hours ago. Her sweet tooth had gotten the better of her, and she'd happily munched as she drove, not concerned about dinner or where she might next find something to eat.

Now here she was, lost somewhere in Maine, driving blindly through a snowstorm . . . and scared out of her mind. She'd messed up. Bad. At least she was wearing hiking boots and had a suitcase full of warm clothing in the cargo area of her CR-V. The vehicle was pretty good in most bad weather, but this storm was proving too much for the small SUV to handle.

As soon as she had that thought, a tree suddenly appeared in front of her.

The road must have curved, but thanks to the near-zero visibility, she hadn't noticed. Instead, she'd driven straight into the woods.

Carlise slammed her foot on the brake instinctively, the car continuing to slide forward in the wet snow. Her front bumper hit the tree, and her body slammed forward. Carlise hit her head on the steering wheel hard enough to see stars.

"Crappity, crap, crap!" she muttered, taking a deep breath and putting a hand to her forehead. She wasn't bleeding, thank goodness, but she probably had a huge bump on her head now. The car's engine shut off when she hit the tree, and even though she had a feeling it would be useless, Carlise reached for the key in the ignition.

The usually reliable SUV didn't start.

Closing her eyes, Carlise did her best not to cry. She was in big trouble here, and she knew it. It was getting dark outside, and she was lost. Not only that, but the wind had picked up, and the snow was blowing so hard, she knew the second she stepped away from her vehicle, she'd be hopelessly lost in the blinding whiteness.

Taking a deep breath, Carlise opened her eyes. She couldn't stay here. She had to find *somewhere* to take shelter. She'd seen the rare cabin tucked into the trees as she'd driven along, hoping to come across some sort of town. None had looked occupied, and a couple seemed dilapidated . . . but hunkering down in an abandoned cabin was better than being buried in her car.

Carlise generally wasn't a pessimistic kind of woman. She did what needed to be done, even if it was unpleasant . . . like breaking up with Tommy. Not wanting to remember that day—and how pissed he'd been—she unfastened her seat belt and turned to crawl into the back seat. She needed to get into her suitcase, put on as many layers of clothes as possible, then start walking.

By the time she was as ready as she was going to be, Carlise felt nauseous. Partly from the knock on the head she'd taken, but also because there was a good chance she wouldn't find a cabin in which to wait out the storm. She might've survived Tommy's harassment, but that seemed like nothing compared to attempting to find shelter in a Maine blizzard.

She shrugged on her backpack, regretting her decision to take her computer and iPad because they only weighed her down. But she'd procrastinated long enough. If she was going to leave, it had to be now.

Taking a deep breath, Carlise pushed open the door and stepped into a blinding-white hell.

The cold wind immediately stole her breath and made her eyes water. Of course, that didn't help her vision, as the tears froze as soon as they formed in her eyes. Blinking quickly, Carlise used her gloved hands to adjust the scarf over her face, pulling it tighter against her skin before forcing herself to take a step away from the car. Then another. And another.

She found the road, at least what she assumed was the road, and felt a spark of hope. She'd just follow it. Either someone would come along, or she'd pass another one of those sporadic cabins.

Refusing to think about the fact that she couldn't see more than five feet in front of her—let alone a cabin tucked into the trees that were thick all around her—Carlise ducked her head into the wind and trudged forward.

Chapter Two

Chappy groaned. He felt like shit.

He felt fine when he'd arrived at the cabin. It wasn't until he was carrying the last of the firewood he'd chopped during his previous visit onto the long covered porch, stacking it neatly at one end in preparation for the storm, that he'd felt the first indication something was wrong.

His throat hurt when he swallowed, and his muscles ached as if he'd been climbing along a precarious mountain ridge in Afghanistan for hours, like one of the many he'd traversed while on missions in the country.

He hated being sick. *Hated* it. And the last thing he wanted was to be sick now. He had plans. Books to read. Snowfall to watch. Relaxation to experience. He didn't want to feel like crap while on vacation.

Sighing, he built a fire in the fireplace and snuggled under a mound of blankets.

He loved his blankets. The guys all made fun of him, but Chappy didn't care. The softer and fluffier the material, the better. There was nothing as comforting as being warm and cozy under a blanket, with a fire crackling and a book in his hand.

Except his head hurt, his muscles throbbed, and his throat felt as if he'd been swallowing glass instead of water.

"Damn flu," he muttered.

Seconds later, as he willed himself to fall asleep, hoping rest would help . . . something caught his attention. He sat up on the couch and tilted his head.

A sound from the yard in front of his cabin . . . ?

No. On the porch.

Figuring it was probably a wild animal trying to escape the wind and snow, Chappy ignored it. Until he heard it again. Scraping.

If it was a bear, he needed to scare it away so it wouldn't attempt to get inside the cabin. He hadn't seen too many bears up here, but they were around, even in the winter.

Throwing off the blanket, Chappy stood and swayed on his feet for a moment.

Cursing how weak he felt, he went to the window at the front of the cabin and peered out. He couldn't see anything but whiteness. He went to the coatrack by the door and pulled on his parka, shoved his feet into the boots he'd taken off earlier, and grabbed the shotgun he kept nearby just in case. He wasn't going to shoot the bear, or whatever animal was on his porch, but he could shoot into the air to scare it away.

He cautiously opened the door a crack, and the cold wind made him shiver violently. Holding the shotgun at the ready, Chappy peered outside.

At first, he didn't spot anything. Then he glimpsed the most pitiful-looking dog he'd ever seen in his life. He couldn't believe the thing was still alive. He could see it was a male and so skinny that Chappy could see the ribs along his sides. His hip bones were sticking out obscenely, and his head was huge. It had to make up at least half his body weight at the moment.

It was a pit bull mix of some kind. Black. Its fur stood out against the white snow. It didn't make a noise. Didn't growl. Didn't bark. Simply stood in the storm as if he didn't even notice it raging around him.

"Where did you come from?" Chappy asked, his voice sounding deeper and more growly than normal.

Of course, he didn't get an answer.

"You want to come in?" he asked, holding the door open a little wider.

In response, the dog took a step backward, but didn't lose eye contact with Chappy.

He didn't want to leave the dog in the storm. There was no way it would survive, considering its current condition. But he also couldn't stand on his porch for hours with his door open, trying to earn the dog's trust.

"Come on," he coaxed. "I'm not going to hurt you. It's warm inside. I've got some food and water. You can stay on one side, and I'll stay on the couch."

The dog took a step toward him, and Chappy's hopes rose. But then the beast turned his head and looked out into the storm, then back at Chappy before whining.

"This is ridiculous," he muttered under his breath. He was sick with the flu and felt like crap, for God's sake.

Still, there was something about the dog that wouldn't let him go back inside and forget about him. Something about his mannerisms that sparked a long-forgotten memory inside Chappy. A mission from years ago.

They'd been deployed with a group of men and women from the Royal Australian Air Force. The group had K9s and were using them to find unexploded IEDs in the desert. He'd been fascinated by the way the dogs communicated with their handlers. It was an awe-inspiring sight, and seeing how much trust the handlers had in their dogs, and vice versa, was eye-opening.

What struck Chappy at the moment was how the stray, starving and probably freezing, was acting exactly like one of those professional military dogs. As if he was trying to communicate something to Chappy.

"What is it, boy?" he asked. "Got something you want me to see? Maybe a mama dog out there with puppies?"

The dog woofed. Sort of. It was an odd sound, really, not much like a bark at all, but Chappy knew he couldn't ignore it. If there actually was a litter of pups, they definitely wouldn't make it through the storm. The snow was falling hard and would continue to accumulate. They were in for at least another foot and a half of the heavy stuff.

"Damn it," Chappy muttered as he leaned over and placed his shotgun on the floorboards of the porch, then began to tie his boot laces securely. "Give me a second, and we'll see what you have to show me." He stood, grabbing the shotgun as he did, taking a moment to brace himself against the wall of the cabin before heading back inside.

Chappy propped the weapon near the door, went to a dresser against the wall, quickly ripped off his jacket, and pulled a sweatshirt over the long-sleeved shirt he already had on. He grabbed his hat and scarf, then put his coat back on. When he was as bundled up as he could be, Chappy went back to the door.

A part of him was hoping the dog would be gone. That he'd be off the hook in trying to figure out what the animal was trying to tell him. But when he opened his cabin door and shone a flashlight into the storm, the dog was sitting right where he'd last seen him.

As soon as Chappy stepped off the porch, the dog turned and started walking in the direction of the road. Which wasn't a road, per se, so much as a meandering dirt two-track that connected to a rural road in one direction and dead-ended in the other.

Chappy's cabin was well off the beaten path, which was how he liked it. In all the time he'd been up there, he hadn't had one visitor except for his friends, and he didn't count them as visitors. . . they were family. No one had accidentally stumbled onto the cabin asking for directions.

Shivering, and cursing his body and the flu virus raging within him, Chappy trudged after the dog. "Ten minutes," he muttered. "That's all you're getting, dog. Because this is crazy."

Not even five minutes later, the snow making every step an effort, Chappy was ready to turn around and go back to his cabin when, surprisingly, he thought he saw something in the distance.

He stopped in his tracks and blinked. The dog was standing in the middle of Chappy's long driveway. They were almost at the end of it, where the path met what the map called a road. As he stood there, the shape in the distance slowly got closer.

It was a person.

Chappy couldn't have been more shocked. What the hell was a person doing out here in this storm? It made no sense. Just as it made no sense that the dog had led Chappy right to him. If he'd ignored the dog or waited a little longer to see what kind of animal was making the noise or if he'd taken a few extra minutes to put on more clothes, the person probably would've walked right by the driveway to his cabin.

The chances that Chappy was here, at the exact moment when some stranger in distress was about to pass, had to be astronomical.

The person had yet to look up, keeping his head tucked to his chest and looking down at his feet while he walked. He was shuffling more than walking, really, as he followed the weak path of the flashlight in his hand, barely illuminating more than a foot in front of him. The snow was around six inches deep now and falling faster and harder than before.

It wasn't until the person was about six feet away that he finally looked up.

Chappy saw huge blue eyes in a pale white face.

"Oh!" the person exclaimed in surprise.

"What the hell are you doing?" he nearly growled. He hadn't given any thought to what he might say to this stranger, but his surprise and unease at seeing *anyone* out in this storm had taken over.

"Um . . . walking?" the person said.

Two things hit Chappy at once. The person in front of him was female—and the dog who had literally led him to her was nowhere to be seen.

"What are *you* doing?" she retorted when he didn't respond.

The question sounded just as stupid coming from her as it probably had coming from his own lips. Shaking his head a little, Chappy said, "Come on, we need to get inside."

To his surprise, the woman didn't move and, instead, simply stared at him.

"What?" he asked.

"I don't know you."

Chappy wanted to laugh. "I don't know you either. You could be a serial killer who chops off my head as soon as we get inside my cabin. But at the moment, I'm willing to take that chance. It's freezing out here, I feel like crap, and we haven't even seen the worst of this storm. You coming, or do you want to die out here?" he asked grumpily.

He was amazed when she still hesitated for a beat before saying, "I'm Carlise. Most people mispronounce my name when they see it because they add an extra L that isn't there."

Chappy blinked. "What?" he asked inanely.

"C-a-r-l-i-s-e. That's how it's spelled. Car-leese."

Chappy couldn't believe they were standing in the middle of a damn blizzard introducing themselves, but he simply shrugged. "I'm Riggs."

He had no idea why he'd told her his given name instead of his nickname. He could tell her that literally everyone called him Chappy, but this wasn't the time or place to go into more detail.

"It's nice to meet you, Riggs. You said your cabin is near here?"

"At the end of this path," he said, turning and pointing back the way he had come. Of course, neither of them could see anything but snowflakes swirling in the beam of his flashlight.

"I would be very grateful if you'd allow me to take shelter for a while," Carlise said stiffly and formally. "And I promise I'm not a serial killer. Are you?"

"What would you do if I said yes?" Chappy asked.

She shrugged. "Keep walking, following my dog friend until I got to another cabin."

"There isn't another cabin out here. I'm the end of the line."

"Oh."

That was it. All she said. Just *Oh.* Chappy sighed. "I'm not a serial killer either," he told her. "You'll be safe with me."

He could see her shoulders sag with relief. She was far too trusting. Or maybe just too desperate to question anything he said at the moment.

Chappy was suddenly angry, but not with her. More with the situation. He didn't know how she'd come to be wandering around out here in the middle of nowhere, but just as he couldn't shut his door on the dog, he couldn't leave a woman stranded in a storm. She'd probably be dead in under an hour.

"Come on," he said a little more gruffly than he intended. "I don't know about you, but I'm freezing." Chappy started walking, looking over his shoulder to see her following as he headed back toward the cabin.

"Where'd the dog go?" she asked after a couple of minutes.

"Don't know."

"Is it yours?"

"I've never seen him before tonight," Chappy told her. "And there's no way I'd let any pet of mine get as skinny as he is."

"Do you think he'll be okay?"

He didn't know that either. And Chappy couldn't help but be worried himself. He hadn't seen the mutt since he'd started talking to Carlise. It didn't sit well with him that the dog would be out by himself in the storm. "I hope so," he said softly, not sure what else to say to her question.

They walked in silence the rest of the way toward the cabin, and Chappy found himself both grateful and confused. Why wasn't she asking more questions? She should be trying to figure out where she was, asking more about him, wanting to know when she could get out of here, asking for a phone . . . *something*. But instead, she simply walked behind him, using his footsteps to help her tromp through the snow, and kept her mouth shut.

By the time Chappy saw his cabin, he was more than thankful and less concerned about the woman's lack of conversation. He was shivering violently and couldn't think about much beyond getting inside and in front of the fire to warm up.

He stepped up onto the porch and sighed in relief. He heard Carlise coming up behind him as he jerked open the door.

"You didn't lock it?" she asked.

Chappy snorted. "It's not as if someone was going to steal anything while I was gone," he said a little sarcastically as he stepped inside. The warmth of the cabin felt like heaven. And the roaring in his ears from the wind abruptly ceased as he shut the door behind Carlise.

She hadn't moved, except to step out of his way so he could shut the door. She looked around with wary eyes. His cabin was one room. There was a queen-size bed along one wall, a couch in the middle of the room facing a large fireplace, a small kitchen along the wall opposite the bed, and a door to the bathroom in the back wall.

Besides the couch and the bed, there was a bookcase, a dresser, a small side table next to the couch, a two-person table near the kitchen, and a large rectangular rug on the floor in front of the fireplace. That was it. The log walls were bare of any decorations, and there weren't any pictures or other knickknacks to mess up the place.

It was exactly how Chappy liked it—sparse, clean, and decidedly uncluttered, except for the multitude of blankets on most available surfaces.

Another shiver shook his frame, and he turned to the coatrack. He took off his jacket and hung it up, along with his hat and scarf. He had a feeling his hair was sticking up, but he didn't care. He'd never been the kind of guy to worry about his looks . . . it wasn't as if anyone cared what he looked like while on a mission, or during a sweaty hike in the woods.

Running a hand over his face, Chappy wondered what Carlise was thinking. Of him. Of his space. But then he mentally shrugged. It didn't matter, really. She was stuck here until the snow stopped. He assumed she had a car somewhere and hadn't just materialized out of thin air. He'd deal with that later.

Right now, all he wanted was to get warm.

Carlise stood stock still and watched Riggs take off his coat and wander over to the fireplace. He picked up two logs, which were sitting on the floor nearby, and threw them onto the flames.

He turned to her and said, "If the fire gets low or if you're chilly, feel free to throw more logs on. I've stacked a ton of wood on the porch, so we'll be good for as long as the storm continues. There's a bathroom over there." He gestured to a door on the far side of the room with his head. "Get warm. If your clothes are wet, you're welcome to wear some of mine until yours are dry. I've got shirts and sweats in the dresser over there. I've got water and food too. Just don't go outside. Don't want you getting turned around and lost."

He closed his eyes briefly, and it seemed to Carlise that he swayed on his feet.

"I'm sorry, I wouldn't normally leave you to fend for yourself, but I don't feel so good. I think I'm getting the flu or something. Don't get too close because the last thing we need is *both* of us being sick. I'm sure I'll feel better soon enough. I'm gonna stay here on the couch. Make yourself at home."

Then he sat on the sofa, leaned over and took off his boots, threw them to the side closer to the fire, and pulled what looked like a heavy blanket over his lap. He tugged it up to his chin, leaned back, and rested his head on the couch cushion behind him before closing his eyes again.

It was as if she wasn't there, which confused Carlise. She didn't expect to be treated like a friend or even a welcomed guest—she was neither. But it was kind of odd that he was ignoring her entirely.

A shiver went through her frame, and she forced herself to move. She shrugged off her backpack and left it where it fell against the wall. Then she leaned over and fumbled with the laces of her boots. They were soaking wet, caked with snow, and difficult to untie. When she finally got them untied and the boots off, she looked over at Riggs.

He hadn't moved. His eyes were still closed and, if she wasn't mistaken, his cheeks were flushed. She took off her coat, hung it up on the rack next to his, and hesitatingly walked toward the couch.

She needed to get warm but remembered that he'd mentioned being sick. She felt a pang of remorse that he'd been out in the storm because of her.

Carlise looked around. She hadn't missed the fact that his cabin was essentially just one room. It was a relief that it had a bathroom, at least, so she wouldn't have to go back into the storm to find an outhouse. There were no lights on in the cabin, but the light from the fire was enough to illuminate the space.

It was . . . cozy. Carlise liked it a lot. This was no tourist destination. No bear or moose motifs decorated the comforter on the bed, and from what she could see, the kitchen looked sparse but functional. There were no light fixtures hanging from the ceiling. In fact, she doubted the place even had electricity, as she couldn't see any appliances or lamps that would need to be plugged in.

The warmth from the fire drew her closer, and Carlise sat on the floor in front of the dancing flames, holding her hands out gratefully. She'd get up in a bit and see about finding something dry and warm to put on.

She'd almost died out there.

She knew that. Riggs probably knew it as well.

If he hadn't found her, she wouldn't have been able to walk for much longer. She had no idea what he'd been doing out in the storm, but she was grateful.

Carlise spared a thought for the dog. He had appeared out of nowhere. The longer she'd failed to find any sort of shelter, the more frustrated, depressed, and terrified she had become. At one point, nearly delirious from the cold, she'd even considered stopping. Just lying down, letting herself fall asleep and die. That's when she'd spotted the dog.

She was scared to death at first, thinking maybe he'd attack. But instead, he simply joined her, walking slowly several feet away. Every time she stopped, too tired and cold to take another step, he was there. Encouraging her. She didn't know where she was going, but she followed the dog because she had no other choice, really.

He was extremely skinny, with a few small scars on his face, but he wouldn't come closer to her no matter how much she cajoled and sweet-talked the thing. And now that she was alive and warming up, she couldn't stop thinking about him.

Where was he? Was he okay? Was he cold?

That was a stupid question. Of course he was cold. There was a freaking blizzard outside.

Carlise looked over at Riggs. His mouth was open a little, and he was snoring lightly. He'd fallen asleep.

Standing, she looked around and picked up two of what looked like the oldest blankets she could find. She really hoped Riggs wouldn't be mad when he woke up and realized what she'd done.

She walked back to the door, took a deep breath, and opened it.

Once again, the cold seemed to blow right through her, but she couldn't in good conscience leave the dog to fend for himself. He'd saved her life. The least she could do was try to help him.

Looking around, she didn't see any sign of the dog. Of course, she couldn't see more than a few feet from the door because of the dark and the snow.

A noise to her right caught her attention. Carlise turned and saw a dark shape at the end of the porch. The dog had wedged himself behind a tall stack of wood. Her heart nearly broke as she took a step toward him, and he whimpered.

"Thank goodness you're here. I'm not going to hurt you. I'd invite you in, but I don't think you'd come inside anyway, even though it's much warmer. But I brought you some blankets. They'll help keep you warm."

She kept her voice low and even as she went to her knees. She moved slowly, shivering as she pushed the blankets toward the dog. He backed up as far as he could get and trembled as he stared at her.

Carlise wanted to kill whoever had owned this dog. He'd obviously been abused. She felt an affinity with the creature. She continued to murmur, reassuring him that she wasn't going to hurt him, that he was safe, thanking him for rescuing her, for bringing her to this cabin.

Eventually, she got the blankets close enough to the dog that he could reach them. Then she backed up. "I'll be right back," she told him before heading into the cabin.

She was still shivering, but she couldn't rest until she'd taken care of the dog.

She went into the small kitchen and began to open cabinets. Thrilled with how much food she found—and relieved that she likely wouldn't be putting a burden on Riggs with her presence—she found a large plastic bowl and emptied two cans of shredded chicken, a can of carrots, a can of green beans, and a can of chickpeas inside before stirring it all together. Then she got another bowl and filled it with water before heading back to the front door.

Carlise looked over at Riggs, who was still sleeping. She frowned. She didn't know the man, but it seemed odd to her that he'd fallen asleep so easily after inviting a stranger into his home, sick or not.

Shrugging, she headed back outside and kneeled once more on the wood planks of the porch. She put the bowls down and scooted them as close as she could to the dog. She was pleased to see he'd dragged the blankets behind the logs and had obviously scrunched them around himself as best he could while she was inside.

"Good boy," she said softly. "I bet it feels much better to have some warm blankets around you, huh? I brought you some food. And water, although I'm guessing the water will freeze pretty quickly, so you should drink it soon. And don't eat too fast, as it'll make you throw up. I'll be back in the morning to bring you more. You look like you need all the calories you can get. I promise to look after you, since you looked after me when I needed it most."

She wanted to stay there, wanted to hug the dog. Watch to make sure he ate and drank, but she hadn't put her coat on in her haste to help the animal, and her fingers were quickly going numb.

Praying the dog would be okay, Carlise scooted backward. "I'll see you in the morning, yeah? Please be okay. *Please*."

Then she turned, tears in her eyes, and headed back inside.

It was silly, but Carlise couldn't help but turn the lock on the door. It was highly unlikely anyone would show up at the cabin with the intent to do her or Riggs harm, but she was from the city, and locking her door was as natural as breathing.

Not to mention, Tommy could be out there. The chances of him knowing where she was or even getting to her when there was a raging blizzard outside, were slim to none, but old habits were hard to break. There was no way she was staying in any house without a locked door.

She made her way back to the fire, not hungry in the least. Her first concern was getting warm. She'd worry about everything else later.

~

"Where is she? The bitch must've left town. I *know* she did. She thinks she's so fucking sneaky, but she's wrong. She'll never get away! I just have to be patient. I just have to wait. She'll slip up. She's too stupid not to. Not nearly as smart as she thinks she is!"

The words were fast, bitter, as the pacing resumed, back and forth, over and over—and Carlise's phone went straight to voice mail. *Again.*

"You think you can hide from me? I'm going to find you—and you'll regret everything!"

Ideas. Plans. Plans on how to find Carlise . . . beginning to form. The bitch would get a few more days to show herself, then alternative plans would have to be made.

And if that happened, Carlise would suffer so much worse than she had already.

"I'll find you. There's *nowhere* you can go to get away from me!" This time, the words were firm, angry, and spoken without any doubt whatsoever.

Chapter Three

"No! Bob, duck! Shit, it's gonna blow!"

Carlise sighed and rolled off the couch, standing slowly in a tired daze.

It was late—or early, depending on how she looked at it. Pitch black outside, sometime after midnight during her third evening in the cabin. And since that first night, Riggs's illness had only gotten worse.

Throughout today, he'd seemed delirious from his fever, mumbling frequently in his sleep. She was certain now that he'd already been sick before going out into the storm, but being out there in the cold couldn't have done him any favors.

The night she'd arrived—after taking care of the dog, changing into a pair of sweats she'd found in the dresser, and warming up by the fire—she'd tried to wake him, but he'd been completely zonked on the couch. It felt weird to be in a stranger's house. She wasn't even sure if he remembered she was there. Hungry, Carlise had fixed herself a peanut butter and jelly sandwich. She let Riggs sleep for another hour, then tried to wake him again.

He roused enough to shuffle to the bathroom, then fell facedown on the bed in the corner of the room. Not knowing what else to do, Carlise had covered him up with another of the many soft and fluffy blankets sitting neatly around the cabin.

Eventually, she fell asleep on the couch. She woke up several times throughout the night to hear the wind howling outside the windows. Hearing the storm made her even more thankful that Riggs, and the dog, had found her.

Yesterday, Carlise had spent most of her time trying to get Riggs to eat and drink something, encouraging him to swallow some Tylenol, helping him to the bathroom, and attempting to befriend the dog who was still hunkered down in the blankets on the front porch. Once more, she'd slept on the couch, startling awake with every little sound outside and from the man on the bed.

It was almost surreal that two days ago she'd nearly died, and now she was living in a stranger's house, taking care of him while he tossed and turned with a fever.

She'd been sleeping in fits again this evening, waking up because she was in a strange place, because of the storm . . . because she wanted to check on Riggs. She didn't know him, hadn't talked to him much at all, but for some reason, she felt responsible for his well-being.

And, oddly, she was drawn to the man.

It was probably because he'd rescued her, and she felt extremely grateful. Of course, there was also the fact that he was gorgeous. She wasn't the kind of woman who chose a man solely based on how he looked, but she couldn't deny that he was easy on the eyes. But then again, Tommy was a good-looking man too, and he'd turned out to be an abusive asshole.

There was no telling what kind of personality Riggs had, since he hadn't been conscious for most of the time she'd known him. He could be just like Tommy. Could be the kind of man who took advantage of a woman who needed a safe, warm place to hunker down in a storm . . . when he wasn't passed out from the flu.

But deep down, she didn't think he was. Even when he was sick and about to pass out, he'd told her to help herself to his clothes and food.

He'd been worried about her going back out into the storm. That small glimpse of concern was . . . encouraging.

The cabin was also very tidy. Which she supposed might not mean much, but the fact that he wasn't a slob and could clean up after himself indicated he didn't need a woman to do such things. She thought back to Tommy yet again and shook her head. He didn't like to do *anything* around the house, insisting that, since she worked from home, she should clean the place and have dinner waiting when he got off work.

Not wanting to think about her ex, Carlise sighed and ran a hand over her face. At the moment, she was safe from whoever was stalking her. Even though she was exhausted, she wasn't worried about what she might find when she opened the door or what messages she might wake up to.

She hadn't turned her phone on once in the last two days, and it felt oddly freeing. There wasn't any electricity to charge it, and she had a feeling she wouldn't get a signal up here in the middle of nowhere anyway. She hadn't realized *exactly* how stressful it had been to read the harassing emails and text messages on a daily basis until she literally couldn't.

"No! Leave him alone! Cal! Are you all right?"

Carlise padded over to the bed where Riggs was thrashing jerkily, obviously having some sort of nightmare. She didn't know who Cal was or the Bob person he'd mentioned earlier, but she guessed they were people he cared about, otherwise he wouldn't sound so concerned.

"It's okay," she soothed, feeling a little awkward. It was weird trying to calm someone she didn't even know. Her appreciation for nurses all over the world skyrocketed.

"JJ! Where the hell is JJ?" Riggs asked, bolting upright in bed and staring sightlessly into nothing.

"He's fine. Lie back down, Riggs," she begged quietly.

But instead, the man turned his gaze on her, and his amber eyes seemed to see straight into her soul. "Who're you?" he barked.

They'd been through this a few times since yesterday, so Carlise didn't take offense. "I'm Carlise. Carlise Edwards. I'm a friend. Lie down, Riggs."

"Where're the others? JJ? Bob? Cal? What'd you do to them?" he demanded.

His brown hair liberally sprinkled with blondish streaks was sticking up in disarray on his head. He had creases on his cheek where his face had been pressed into the pillow, and he was wearing nothing more than a T-shirt and a pair of boxers. The day before, Carlise had wrestled his sweats off him before leading him into the bathroom, and it was too much of a chore to try to get them back on him when he fell back into bed.

"We're in your cabin. In Maine," she reminded him. "There's a storm outside, but we're safe here. Your friends are at their houses. They're okay."

Of course, she didn't know if that was true or not, but she had to assume the men were safe wherever they were.

"They're hurting Cal," he cried in a tortured tone. "We have to find him!"

Carlise's heart hurt for Riggs. She had no idea who Cal was or what he'd been through, but it was obvious Riggs was extremely worried for his safety. She put her hand on his arm. "He'll be okay. Please lie down, Riggs."

She wasn't prepared for how fast he moved.

One second she was leaning over him slightly and the next she was on the bed, lying *under* him. He stared down at her with fever-glazed eyes. "It hurts!" he moaned. "When will the torture stop? Why are they doing this?"

Her heart beating a hundred miles a minute, Carlise reached up and put her palm on his heated cheek. She should be terrified. But even though Riggs was looming over her—and clearly much stronger than her, even in his weakened state—he wasn't hurting her at all. He had his weight propped on his elbows as he caged her beneath him.

"You're safe now. You're here in Maine. In your cabin. You aren't there . . . they can't hurt you anymore." She had no idea what she was saying, just knew that she wanted to soothe his obvious pain and fear.

"You have a nice voice . . . soothing. I'll keep you safe. I swear I won't let them hurt you!"

Carlise's heart turned over. Riggs sounded so earnest. "We're safe here," she told him.

But it was as if he didn't hear her. "When they come back, stay still. Maybe they won't see you. I'll distract them, turn their attention on me. You can have my rations. We're gonna get out of here. We just have to wait for someone to rescue us. In the meantime, I'll kill *anyone* who tries to touch you!"

A tear leaked from Carlise's eye. This man, who didn't know her, was vowing to do whatever it took to protect her from his nightmare enemies. "Okay," she whispered, not sure what else she should do or say right now.

He stared at her, meeting her gaze directly and with what looked like complete clarity, but she knew he was still lost in his fever-induced hallucination.

Then, without warning, Riggs's arms collapsed.

He shifted enough at the last minute that he didn't land directly on top of her. The bulk of his weight was resting on the mattress, but she was still trapped beneath him, his arm across her body and his legs tangled with hers. The heat coming off him was almost scalding. She needed to get up, get more cool water from the bathroom, and use the washcloth to try to bring his temperature down.

But surprisingly . . . Carlise didn't want to move. The bed was much more comfortable than the couch she'd been napping on between taking care of Riggs. And the last few days were finally catching up with her.

The fear when she'd made the decision to leave Cleveland, the aimless driving, getting lost, walking through the snow. The terror, then relief, when Riggs appeared out of nowhere. Feeding the dog on the porch and trying, without luck, to coax him inside, and then the stress of trying to get Riggs to eat and drink while figuring out what to make without electricity so she could also feed herself.

Carlise sighed. Maybe she'd just lie here for a minute or two. It wasn't as if either of them had anywhere they needed to be or anything that needed doing at the moment. In fact, it almost felt as if they were the only two people on the planet.

All her worries seemed to fade away as she lay under Riggs. She counted his breaths, and when he violently twitched next to her, she whispered, "Shhhhh."

Amazingly, he quieted at the sound of her voice.

She felt completely safe at the moment. Susie would probably tell her she was crazy, that she was trapped in a cabin with a stranger who outweighed her and could hurt her without even trying. But even though Carlise hadn't spoken more than two dozen words to this man, she wasn't scared of him. He'd done everything he could to protect her. From the storm, the cold, and from the memories of bad men in his past.

If this was Tommy, she'd be on edge at all times, worried about doing or saying the wrong thing—and having him punish her for it.

Riggs wouldn't hurt her. She knew that instinctively. As well as she knew her own name.

The fire crackled in the small room and the wind howled outside. She was more than warm enough lying half under Riggs, and she couldn't deny she was exhausted.

Carlise's eyes closed as she relaxed, and before she knew it, she'd fallen into a deep sleep.

When she woke, it took her a moment to remember where she was. It was still dark, indicating the sun had yet to rise, so she couldn't have been asleep for more than a few hours. But she and Riggs had clearly been restless. They'd both moved in their sleep, and he was now behind her. One of his arms was wrapped around her waist, her head resting on his bicep.

He was basically curled around her. She could feel every inch of his body against hers, and instead of feeling threatened or nervous that they were so close, she felt . . . good.

Maybe it was because she'd been taking care of him while he was vulnerable. Maybe because he'd saved her life. Maybe it was simply because she was so tired. Whatever the reason, Carlise had never felt as content as she did right at that moment, in this stranger's arms.

It was that thought that got her moving. Riggs *was* a stranger. He probably wouldn't be happy to know he was spooning an equally strange woman who was living in his cabin, eating his food. Nor would he like being completely vulnerable to whatever she might do to him.

Riggs grunted as she slid out from under his arm. She stood next to his bed for a moment, watching him frown and fidget restlessly, as if looking for her now that she wasn't in his arms.

"Fire," she muttered to herself, realizing the room was chilly because the fire had died down while they were sleeping. Forcing herself to turn away from Riggs, she wandered over to the fireplace and added three more logs to the burning coals. Within seconds, they caught and the flames once more danced and crackled.

Carlise turned and walked back to the bed to check on Riggs. She hoped his fever had finally broken . . . but when she put a hand on his forehead, she realized he was just as hot as he'd been for the last two days.

"Damn," she whispered. For the first time, she started to get truly worried. She'd assumed he had a twenty-four-hour bug or something. That the fever would break, and he'd be up and around in no time. But the longer this fever lasted, the more concerned Carlise got. It wasn't as if she could call for an ambulance. Or even drive him to a hospital or clinic. She was on her own here, and it was a scary feeling.

She went to the bathroom, relieved herself, brushed her hair and teeth using the toiletries she'd had in her backpack, then took a deep breath before heading back into the main room. When it was light enough, she needed to check on the dog, get him—and herself—something to eat, bring in more logs from the front porch.

But first, she'd see if she could get Riggs to drink something and take more Tylenol. Then she'd tackle everything else before maybe reading one of the many books Riggs had on the shelves in the corner of the room.

Anything to keep her mind off the surreal situation she'd found herself in.

~

Chappy hurt.

All over.

There was only one other time he could remember being this miserable.

For a moment, he wondered if he was back there. In that cell. Chained to the wall with his buddies hurting all around him.

"Cal?" he called out.

But got no answer.

Agitated now, Chappy tried to open his eyes, but they were so heavy. He couldn't do it.

"JJ? Bob?"

"Shhhhh, they're fine," a quiet voice soothed from nearby.

Chappy froze. That was new. There hadn't been any women around that hellhole that he could remember.

The mattress dipped as if someone had sat beside him. A soft hand touched his face, and he turned into it. When was the last time he'd been touched? He couldn't remember. And by a woman? It had been years.

"Drink this," the melodic voice ordered. Chappy wanted to ask what it was, but he didn't get the chance before he felt his head being propped up and something touch his lips.

He was leery until she said, "It's just water, Riggs. I promise."

He trusted her. He didn't know why, but he did. So he opened his mouth and drank.

The water was cool, soothing his throat, which felt as if it were on fire.

"Easy. Don't drink too fast or it'll make you sick."

Chappy felt as weak as a newborn, and he hated it. Again, the only other time he'd felt so helpless was when he'd been a hostage.

And just like that, he stiffened at the memory.

"No, you're okay. You're here in Maine, in your cabin. You're safe, Riggs. I swear."

He was still worried and on edge, but that instinctive trust filled him once more. A name left his lips without thought. "Carlise."

"That's right. I'm Carlise, and you're safe. I'll be right back." The mattress shifted as she stood, and his hand shot out, grabbing her arm and keeping her from leaving.

"Stay," he croaked.

"I need to put some more wood on the fire. I'm not going anywhere. Not that I could, even if I wanted to."

"Stay! Please!" he begged once more.

"I'll be right back, Riggs."

"Promise?" he asked.

"I promise. You're okay. Your friends are okay. You're just sick, Riggs. You'll be better soon . . . I hope."

Confusion swam in his veins, but Chappy let go of her arm. She said she'd be back, and he trusted her to keep her word.

He didn't know how much time had passed before he felt the mattress next to him sag again.

"I'm here," she said.

"Are you okay?" he asked.

He thought he heard her chuckle before she said, "Yes. You're the one who's sick."

"Did you eat? Are you cold? I can . . ." He made a move to get up, but she stopped him by putting a hand on his shoulder.

"I'm good, Riggs. Promise."

Chappy frowned. He didn't like feeling so helpless. He was confused about where he was and what was happening, but deep down he knew something wasn't right. He couldn't put his finger on what might be wrong, but he wanted to protect Carlise. Make sure she was warm, fed, comfortable. At the moment, however, he couldn't even sit up.

Needing to be closer to the woman, to keep her by his side and make sure nothing happened to her, that she wouldn't get lost again, Chappy turned and threw his arm out . . . over her lap? It felt like she was sitting on the bed right beside him. He tightened his hold and snuggled against her leg.

He felt gentle fingers running through his hair, and he sighed in contentment. He felt like shit, his body hurt, but with the woman next to him, somehow his discomfort faded away.

A couple of hours later, Carlise could feel her panic building. Riggs managed short bouts of sleep, but every time she tried to move, he'd start calling for his friends and thrashing on the bed. The only way he seemed to remain calm was if she stayed right where she was, letting him hold her.

She felt guilty about that. He was sick. Practically unconscious . . . and she enjoyed being in his arms more than she wanted to admit. When his fever finally broke and he came back to his senses, he'd most certainly be horrified over his actions. Not that she'd tell him.

She hadn't expected or wanted to play nursemaid to a man she didn't know, though she no longer found the experience nearly as awkward as she had the first night. And the concern went both ways. Even though he wasn't fully conscious, he was worried about her. Was she eating? Was she warm? Was she okay?

She suspected his true self came out while he was delirious. And if he was that protective and concerned about her when he was semiconscious, she had a feeling he'd be even more so when he was fully awake and aware.

For her part, it was a heady feeling, knowing she could soothe him when he was unconsciously afraid. And being held in his arms was . . . heaven.

Hence the guilt. He was delirious. Out of his mind with a fever. Hurting. Terrified as he relived whatever awful experience he'd been through in his past. And all the while, she was enjoying being close to him. There had to be something wrong with her for liking it as much as she did.

But it had been so long since she'd felt wanted or needed. Tommy didn't cuddle. Ever. He was the sort who got himself off, then rolled over and immediately started snoring. Riggs held her as if he never wanted to let her go.

Of course, he was very likely imagining she was someone else. That had to be the reason he clung to her so tightly, why he'd calm so quickly at her touch. Dreaming of a woman from his past.

When she'd gotten out of bed minutes ago, finally too hungry to remain, Riggs's brows furrowed, and he'd grunted in displeasure. Carlise had smiled a little at his reaction. He was like a kid who'd had a favorite toy taken away.

But Riggs was no boy. He was all man, and it was disconcerting and confusing to realize how much she was attracted to him. She didn't know anything about the man.

Okay, that wasn't true. She'd been living in his space for three days now. She knew what kind of books he liked to read—thrillers and science fiction—and that he was a neat freak. He had an unnatural affinity for the color black, since most of his T-shirts were that color. He probably didn't drink much alcohol, if any, since she hadn't found a drop in the cabin, and he preferred crunchy peanut butter over smooth.

She also knew that he was extremely protective and loyal. Whoever JJ, Cal, and Bob were, they were lucky to have someone who cared about them as much as Riggs did. And he was clearly a hard worker—there were lots of logs out on the porch that he must've spent hours chopping and stacking.

Thinking about the front porch made her think about the dog again. She'd been feeding him every day and was immensely relieved he hadn't died or wandered off. Every time she went to check on the pooch, Carlise ached to bring him inside where it was warm. But he was still extremely skittish, cowering in his blanket fort when she got near him with food and water. He needed time to learn she wouldn't hurt him, but it was stressful leaving him out in the howling wind and swirling snow.

A noise from the bed made Carlise look in that direction, and she was startled to see Riggs staring at her. He'd propped himself up on an elbow and was blinking in confusion.

"Riggs?" she asked.

"Bathroom," he muttered.

Putting down the knife she'd been using to make herself another peanut butter sandwich—if she never ate another in her life after this, it would be too soon—Carlise quickly hurried to his side.

The second she touched him, every muscle in her body sagged in relief. His T-shirt was soaking wet, and she could see sweat glistening on his forehead, but his fever had broken. *Finally.*

She helped him to his feet, and they shuffled toward the bathroom. Thankful that she hadn't had to help him pee while he was sick, she said, "I'll be right here, outside the door, when you're done."

He nodded and slowly headed for the toilet.

Carlise blushed as she heard him using the bathroom. Which was ridiculous. It wasn't as if he was doing anything every person on the planet didn't do. But somehow, listening felt too intimate.

His gaze had been a little clearer than in the last three days, but he hadn't asked who she was or what she was doing there, so she assumed he was still a little confused.

She heard the water running and couldn't stop the small grin from forming on her face. He was sick, still weak as hell, and yet he was washing his hands after using the bathroom. This was definitely a man she could like.

Wait. No. No, no, *no*. She couldn't like him. He lived in the middle of nowhere. There wasn't any electricity in his house. He was clearly a hermit. She was from the city. She liked going out for dinner now and then. *Really* liked hot showers.

And Tommy would *not* be happy if she started dating someone else.

She couldn't like this man—

Her inner monologue was cut short when the door opened, and she barely caught Riggs before he fell flat on his face. She wrapped an arm around his waist, and he leaned heavily on her as she led him back to the bed.

He lay back as soon as his ass hit the mattress, closing his eyes. Carlise shifted his legs and got him under the covers once more.

After getting a wet washcloth from the bathroom, she returned to the bed and sat next to him as she gently wiped his face. It couldn't be comfortable to have all that dried sweat on his body.

Deep down, Carlise knew she wasn't helping him *solely* for his comfort. This was probably her last chance to be close to him. Now that his fever had broken, he'd remember what happened and they'd go back to being two strangers. Holding her in his arms, calming when she spoke to him, relying on her for . . . well . . . *everything*, would end.

Things might be awkward and uncomfortable, and of course, he'd want to know what the hell she was doing out in the storm in the first place. She was dreading that conversation. It wasn't that she didn't want to warn him about her stalker. She'd just enjoyed not having to think too much about Tommy or worry about him finding her.

Being here, with no electricity, was so . . . elemental. All the bullshit waiting for her in the real world had been taken away. Despite her worry for Riggs, she'd felt relaxed and needed for the first time in ages.

Sighing, Carlise forced herself to stand. Riggs was sleeping again, she could tell by his even breaths and his slight snoring. She probably should've gotten him to drink some more water before he fell asleep, but going to the bathroom had exhausted him.

She went back into the kitchen and picked up the knife to finish making a sandwich for breakfast. She'd been eating them for the last three days because it was the easiest thing to make. There were a ton of canned goods in the pantry, as well as pasta and rice, but she had no idea how to cook them without electricity. She supposed Riggs must use the fire, but she wasn't exactly sure how to go about it. So PB&J it was.

She'd just finished eating when she heard a strange noise. It was especially noticeable over the now-familiar sounds of the fire and the continuing storm. It was a steady beeping. Electronic.

Frowning, she glanced around the kitchen and didn't see anything that might account for the noise.

Before she could find the source, the sound stopped.

Only to start up again a minute later.

Curious now, and determined to find where it was coming from, Carlise began hunting in earnest. It could be some sort of alarm, like a battery-operated carbon monoxide detector. The last thing she wanted to do was ignore whatever it was, especially if it meant she and Riggs could be in danger.

She followed the noise to the dresser along one of the walls and frowned when she didn't see any kind of device sitting on top of the wood. She didn't want to go through his things; that just didn't seem right. Yes, she'd had to open the drawers while searching for something dry to wear, but that was different.

When the sound stopped, then started a third time, she realized she was going to have to invade his privacy.

Opening the first drawer, all Carlise saw were boxers.

Blushing, she shut the drawer. It was silly to be embarrassed about seeing his underwear. He'd been walking around in nothing but boxers and a T-shirt for the last two days. Not to mention, she'd been plastered against said boxers while sleeping.

She opened another drawer—socks. Then another. Bingo. There was a phone nestled among what looked like shorts, and she picked it up. It wasn't like any phone she'd ever seen. It looked like something she recognized from pictures of phones in the nineties. The big, bulky things people used before cell phones became more mainstream.

For a moment, Carlise considered ignoring the ringing, now that she knew it wasn't some type of alarm. Answering Riggs's phone seemed even more wrong than going through his drawers. But the caller was clearly insistent. He or she had called back three times, and she had a feeling they weren't going to stop until someone answered.

Looking over at the bed, she thought about waking Riggs so he could talk to whoever was calling, but he was still out of it. The noise hadn't even made him stir.

Making her decision, Carlise clicked on the green button on the front and brought it up to her ear. "Hello?"

There was a tense pause before a very pissed-off-sounding man said, "Who the hell is this and where's Chappy? You better put him on the phone in two seconds or there's gonna be a shitload of trouble."

Swallowing hard at the anger in the man's voice and realizing her entire body had tensed as if preparing to protect itself, Carlise couldn't speak for a moment.

"I'm serious. Who are you, and why are you answering Chappy's phone? Where is he?"

Carlise frowned. "Who's Chappy?" she blurted.

"Who's Chappy?" the man echoed. "Shit. I'll ask again. Who the hell are *you*, and why do you have my friend's phone?"

"I'm Carlise. Is your friend Riggs?"

There was yet another beat of silence on the other end of the line before the man asked, "Riggs?"

"Yeah. That's what he told me his name was."

"Wow. Okay. No one calls him that. But you still haven't said what you're doing there and why you're answering the phone instead of him."

"He's sick. Or he was. He's getting better now," Carlise told the mystery man. The longer they spoke, the less her voice shook. She wasn't sure, but considering the man was so concerned about Riggs, it made her think he might be one of the three guys Riggs had been calling for when he was delirious.

"He's sick? What's wrong with him?"

"He had a fever for a few days. But it finally broke just this afternoon. Are you . . . Cal, Bob, or JJ?" she asked hesitatingly.

"JJ. How'd you know my name? Or the others?"

"Riggs was calling for you. During his fever, he had nightmares. He'd wake up and cry out, wanting to make sure you were safe. I just assumed . . ."

"Put him on the phone," the man ordered.

"Um . . . ," Carlise hedged, looking at the bed where Riggs was sleeping. His mouth was open slightly and his limbs were starfished, so he took up nearly the entire mattress.

"I mean it. Put him on *right now*, or I'm coming up there—with Cal and Bob—and we'll find out firsthand who the hell you are and what you've done to our friend."

"I haven't done *anything* to him," Carlise protested. "He's fine. Well, he will be now, I think. And it's still snowing."

"I don't care if there's an alien invasion and the Earth is burning from an apocalypse. If you've hurt Chappy, or done anything to incapacitate him, there's *nowhere* you can hide. We'll fucking find you. Do you hear me?"

Damn. This guy was intense! Despite his threats, a tendril of jealousy swam through Carlise's veins. To have someone that loyal, that concerned about her well-being, wasn't a concept she was familiar with.

Yes, her mom loved her, but she was fairly meek when it came to speaking her mind or sticking up for herself and others. Of course, the abuse she'd suffered for years had made her that way. Still, there'd been many times in her life when Carlise had wished her mom was more assertive.

Her best friend, Susie, was someone Carlise could count on. She'd been her rock ever since the stuff with Tommy had begun . . . but she still couldn't imagine her being as forceful as JJ in wanting to talk to his friend.

"He's sleeping," she told the man as she stepped toward the bed. "But I'll try to wake him up."

"There'd better not be any *try* about it," the man said under his breath.

"Riggs?" Carlise said as she sat on the mattress.

The second her fingers touched his shoulder, Riggs moved, rolling until he'd thrown his arm over her lap, one of his legs over hers, and buried his face against her hip, as he'd done a few times in the last couple of days.

As much as she loved how he immediately turned to her, she really needed him to wake up and talk to his friend. She had no doubt JJ would somehow make his way up to the cabin if he needed to, if only to make sure Riggs wasn't being held hostage and tortured.

"Riggs!" she said, louder this time, trying to rouse him.

"Ummmm," he sighed.

Carlise froze as his hand eased up her thigh to her hip—then under the shirt she wore.

He'd never done *that* before. His hand seemed huge on her waist, and his thumb brushed against the sensitive skin of her side in a slow caress.

It felt good. Better than good. Her nipples immediately hardened, and the sudden longing for his hand to move higher was almost a physical ache.

"Riggs, JJ is on the phone. He wants to talk to you."

His hand stopped moving as her words sank in. His head tilted back, and he stared up at her. They stayed frozen for a heartbeat, his warm hand on her bare skin, his leg pressing against her own, his gaze suddenly piercing in its intensity.

"What?" he asked in a croak.

"Your friend. JJ. He's on the phone. He's worried about you. You've been sick for days, and he wants to make sure I haven't gone all *Misery* on you and tied you to the bed or something. He's threatening to come up here if he doesn't get to talk to you. And trust me, that wouldn't be safe. The storm is still crazy out there, and there's at least two feet of snow on the ground. The drifts are probably double that. I'm not sure he could make it if he tried . . . although I'm guessing that wouldn't stop him. Please, can you wake up enough to reassure him that you're okay, and I'm not holding you hostage or something?"

Carlise knew she was babbling, and that JJ could hear every word she was saying, but she was more nervous about the way she felt with Riggs wrapped around her than she was about this JJ person's opinion of her.

Taking a deep breath, Riggs removed his hand from under her shirt and rolled over onto his back, breaking their physical contact.

Carlise felt almost cold when he held out his hand for the phone.

This was it. The beginning of their end. Not that there'd ever been anything between them, actually. Not really. He'd been delirious, for God's sake. It was immoral and ridiculous to think there'd been any kind of connection while the guy was out of his mind.

She was starting to scoot off the bed, to give Riggs as much privacy as she could in the one-room cabin—maybe she'd go into the bathroom—when his hand shot out and wrapped around her thigh, holding her in place.

Carlise froze, a frown on her face as she stared down at her leg, where Riggs was holding her. Vaguely, she knew she could break his grip, but she was so startled that she simply sat still.

"JJ?" Riggs said in a husky voice after he'd brought the phone up to his ear.

Carlise couldn't hear his friend's side of the conversation, but she held her breath, hoping both men would be reassured after speaking with each other.

"Yeah . . . I feel like crap . . . uh-huh . . . I don't know . . . what day is it? Seriously? Damn. Yeah, I felt it coming on when I heard something on my porch. Went out to investigate and saw a pathetic dog. It wanted me to follow it. I did, and that's when I found Carlise."

He met her gaze, and Carlise inhaled deeply. She'd been wondering what in the world had brought a very sick Riggs out into the storm. It seemed the dog truly *had* saved her. He'd led Riggs right to her.

She was extremely relieved that he seemed to remember. Glad she wouldn't have to explain who she was and why she was in his cabin in the middle of a storm.

Riggs listened to something JJ was saying, then continued speaking. "I know, man. I have no idea, but I'm good. Yeah, promise." He looked around the cabin, then locked eyes with Carlise again. "It looks like she's got everything under control. I'm weak as hell. I'm not going anywhere for a few days at least."

He frowned slightly, then, "No, it's fine. JJ, she's at least fifty pounds lighter than I am, a few inches shorter, and if she wanted to do something to me, she's had three days to do it. We're *fine*. Okay . . . yes, if I need anything, I'll let you know. Right. I haven't asked, but I'm assuming she has a car out there somewhere, which is probably buried by now. Uh-huh. Right. I'd appreciate that. The last thing I need is Cal or Bob showing up on my doorstep. Thanks. No . . . Why? What're you going to say to her? Fine. But don't scare her. I mean it."

Then Riggs held the phone out and said, "JJ wants to talk to you again."

Carlise stared at the phone for a moment before accepting it. She expected Riggs's hand to move, but it didn't. It stayed clamped on her leg.

"Hello?" she said tentatively into the phone.

"I'm sorry," JJ said without hesitation. "Chappy is one of my best friends, and he's never had anyone up at that cabin except for me and our other friends. When you answered his phone, I panicked. I'm truly sorry if I scared you."

"It's okay," she said softly.

"It's not. But I'll do what I can to make up for it. You drive up there?"

"Uh . . . yeah. I got lost. When the snow got really bad, I drove off the road into a tree and got stuck."

"You're lucky Chappy found you."

"I know."

"What kind of car?"

"What?"

"What kind of car do you have?"

"A Honda CR-V."

"Four-wheel drive?"

"Yeah."

"That's something, at least. Okay, when the weather calms down, I'll see what I can do to find it for you."

"Oh, um, thanks."

"It's the least I can do after what you've done for Chappy. He's really been out of it for three whole days?"

"Almost."

"And you've taken care of him?"

"There wasn't anyone else here to do it," she reasoned.

"We're all in your debt," JJ said seriously.

"No, really. It's okay."

"You sayin' no doesn't make it not true. This storm isn't over yet. They're calling it the storm of the century, which is ridiculous because this is Maine and there's bound to be another just like it in the not-too-distant future. But more importantly, the snow on the slopes isn't stable. When the sun does come out, it's going to make the situation a lot worse, so just stay hunkered down there."

"Wait, what slopes? Are you talking about an avalanche?"

"You're smack dab in the area surrounding the base of Baldpate Mountain. I'm not sayin' it'll happen, but the people who know about these things *are* saying the conditions are right. Chappy's cabin is protected, it's not in the danger zone for any avalanches, but a mile or so in any direction is another story. Just stay put. That's all I'm tryin' to say."

"I wasn't planning on going on a pleasure hike," Carlise couldn't help retorting.

JJ chuckled. "Right. Anyway, I'm gonna be a pain in Chappy's ass and call every day. I'd appreciate it if you make sure he answers when I do."

"Why wouldn't he?" Carlise asked.

"Because he's stubborn. And doesn't like to be fussed over," JJ said. "Thanks again, Carlise. And I'll apologize again in person when I see you. Later."

When he hung up, Carlise stared down at the phone in confusion. She didn't want to look at Riggs, but she couldn't stare at the phone forever, so she sucked it up and lifted her gaze.

His amber eyes were locked on her face, and he looked worried. "You okay?" he asked.

"I should be asking *you* that. How do you feel?"

"Awful. My muscles hurt, my throat is still scratchy, and I'm weak as hell. But I'm guessing, since JJ said it's been three days since the storm hit, that I have you to thank for not feeling worse than I do right now."

Uncomfortable with his attention and praise, Carlise shrugged.

They sat in silence for a moment, with Riggs's hand still on her thigh, and neither of them moving.

Then, to Carlise's surprise, his thumb moved in a soothing caress, just for a few seconds, before he dropped his hand.

"I'm sure you're hungry. And thirsty. And you need some more Tylenol. I'll get it for you. Just rest." Carlise popped up off the bed, feeling weird about sitting near him for the first time in three days. She placed the phone on the mattress and headed to the kitchen.

Riggs didn't say anything, but she could feel his gaze on her.

She didn't know what to say either. Things felt awkward now, and she hated it. This was his home, and she felt like an interloper. Was he wondering how she knew where everything was in the kitchen? How she knew where the plates were? The paper towels? The silverware?

God. Of course he wasn't. He wasn't stupid. He knew she'd been there for three days while he was out of it with a fever. But it still felt wrong, going through his cupboards.

She heard blankets rustling and turned around, only to see him getting out of bed. "Where are you going?" she asked without thinking.

He gave her an amused smile from the side of the bed. "Not outside to run a few miles, I can assure you. Just to the bathroom."

"Oh, right. Of course. Sorry."

He gave her a look she couldn't interpret before shuffling toward the door on the other side of the room. Carlise resisted the urge to go to his side to help him. To make sure he didn't fall. It was one thing to assist when he was sick, but he was obviously on the mend and completely aware of his surroundings. He also seemed steady on his feet. He didn't need her help anymore.

Why that thought made her sad, Carlise didn't know. She tried to shrug it off. Things would change now, and she wasn't sure if that was a good or bad thing.

"Please don't let him be an asshole," she whispered before turning her attention back to the sandwich she was making. It would be better for him to have soup or something, but she wasn't sure he'd like to eat it cold, and she wasn't up to using the fireplace to heat anything just yet. Maybe when he felt better, he'd show her how to do it.

Though, it wasn't like she was going to be there long enough to really master the art of fireplace cooking.

That thought made her sad all over again, but she pushed the emotion down. She was relieved Riggs was better. He'd scared her there for a while. All she had to do was wait for the snow to stop and she could be on her way.

She still didn't know where she was going, ultimately, but she couldn't hide out from Tommy forever. While she was here, she'd just enjoy the feeling of being safe for now.

Chapter Four

Chappy stared at his reflection in the mirror and grimaced.

He felt awful. Grimy. He needed a shower in the worst way, but before that could happen, he'd need to go outside and start the generator so there would be hot water. He had a feeling going out into the storm wouldn't do him any favors right now. He'd gone longer than this without showering in the past. He'd survive.

But he took his time using a washcloth to try to get as much of the dried sweat off his body as possible. He brushed his teeth, used his beard trimmer to shape up his beard, and put on a bit of deodorant. When he was done, he felt a little better. His face was still pale and his head a little woozy, but he hoped eating something would help.

Leaning heavily on the counter, Chappy stared at the mirror again, but his mind wasn't on his looks . . . it was on the woman in his cabin. Carlise.

He didn't remember much of the last three days, just a few blips. But one thing he *did* remember was waking up, disoriented, and holding her tightly against him. They'd slept as close as longtime lovers, and a sense of comfort and contentedness had filled him before he fell back to sleep.

Chappy wasn't a man to trust easily. But for some reason, he instinctively trusted Carlise. Maybe it was because she literally could've done anything while he'd been out of it. She could've robbed him blind, put drugs in his water to kill him, or completely left him to deal with his sickness on his own. She hadn't done any of those things.

She'd taken care of him.

He hated being sick, hated feeling helpless, and this woman, a stranger, had stepped up and done what was necessary to make sure he didn't die.

Not that Chappy thought he would've kicked the bucket, but he definitely would've been in trouble if she hadn't been there. She'd kept the cabin warm by stoking the fire, she'd helped him to the bathroom when he'd needed it, made him drink as much as possible and take meds.

In short . . . she'd gone above and beyond to help a stranger.

Chappy straightened too quickly—and had to throw out a hand against the wall to keep himself from falling over. "No sudden moves," he muttered before reaching for the door handle. He wanted to see Carlise. Talk to her. Get to know her. And hanging out in the bathroom wasn't going to get him the answers he needed. He wanted to know everything about the woman in the other room. Where she was from. What she did for a living.

Why the hell she'd been driving around on the back roads of Maine in the middle of a storm.

He opened the door and headed straight for his dresser. With his back to the kitchen, he tore off the T-shirt he'd been wearing for way too long and replaced it with a clean one. Then without really thinking—because he hadn't ever had an overnight guest in his cabin before—he pushed his boxers down his legs and bent over to put on a clean pair.

He heard a slight gasp from the direction of the kitchen, and grimaced.

"Sorry," he muttered, not turning around as he fumbled with one of the drawers and looked for a pair of sweats. "I forgot you were there."

That was far from the truth. An undercurrent of awareness swam through his bloodstream. In the past, he'd felt edgy and uncomfortable when he knew someone was watching him . . . but Carlise's gaze caused more of a buzzing feeling than an alarming one.

"It's okay," she said quietly.

Chappy finished dressing, then picked up his dirty clothes and added them to the hamper next to the dresser. He took a deep breath and finally turned to face his guest. He ignored the bed for now—he'd been laid up there for too long—and headed for the small table. His legs shook slightly, and he cursed his weakness.

"I made you a sandwich," she said as she placed a plate in front of him on the table. "I wanted to make you some soup or something, but I didn't think you'd want to eat it cold."

Chappy looked up at her with a frown. "Why would I eat it cold?"

"Well, because you don't have electricity, and if I tried to heat it on the fire, I'd probably burn it, or my hand, and ruin your pan in the process."

"The stove is gas," he said softly.

"What?"

"The stove. It runs on propane. I have a small tank under the sink that it's hooked up to. I can heat water, sauté stuff, make pasta and rice, and anything else you can make with a pan on the stove top."

Carlise stared at him for a long moment. "Oh," she finally muttered.

"There's also an icebox on the side of the porch. I use it in the winter because it's more economical than plugging in the small fridge I have out in the storage building. I've got meat, milk, and cheese out there. Eggs, too, but they're probably frozen solid. Hell, most likely everything is."

"Wait, you have a fridge you can plug in? I didn't think there was any electricity here," she said.

She hadn't sat down, was still standing next to the table staring at him. Chappy wanted to reach out and pull her into the other seat, but he also didn't want to freak her out by touching her without permission. Yes, they'd slept wrapped around each other, and she hadn't freaked out when he'd put his hand on her thigh earlier, but he didn't want to push his luck.

"I have a generator outside. When I need to charge my electronics or use the few electrical appliances I have here and there, I can start it up and get some juice for a while. I don't use it a lot, as the generator is loud, and I like the peace and quiet of the place." He sighed. "I'm so sorry," he said, shaking his head.

"For what?"

"For not giving you a tour, for not explaining how stuff around here works before I passed out on you."

"It's not like you did it on purpose," she said with a small shrug. "I should've figured out the stove. That was stupid of me."

Chappy didn't like hearing her disparage herself. "You aren't stupid. You managed to keep the fire going. You took care of me. You did what you needed to do in order to survive. Just because you didn't know about the stove or the generator doesn't make you stupid."

She shrugged again.

"Will you sit with me while I eat?" Chappy asked.

She glanced at the sandwich she'd made for him and winced as she reached for the plate. "Let me heat you some soup. You don't have to eat that."

Chappy reacted without thought. He grabbed her wrist to prevent her from picking up the plate. "Peanut butter and jelly is one of my favorite foods in the world," he told her, completely seriously. "Why do you think I have so many jars of the stuff?"

His thumb caressed her wrist as she studied him, probably trying to decide whether to press the issue or not. Her skin was remarkably smooth, and he could feel her pulse hammering in her wrist. He wasn't sure if it was because she was scared or if it was his touch that made her breathe faster.

It was the uncertainty that made him let go. The last thing he wanted was to make her uncomfortable.

He might not have invited her here, but she *was* here now, and with the way the storm outside sounded, she wasn't leaving anytime soon. He didn't want to make her stay awkward or uncomfortable. Especially after what she'd done for him.

Chappy couldn't remember the last time someone had taken care of him without any expectations. After he and his friends had been rescued, they'd been taken to a military hospital in Germany, where nurses and doctors had looked after them and done what they could to heal their injuries, but that had been their job. Women had fawned all over him when he'd first returned to the States, but Chappy knew it was because he and his friends were all over the media after everything that had happened. The last thing he wanted was someone dating him out of a desire to be with someone "famous."

Chappy was pretty sure the woman standing next to his kitchen table, looking adorably mussed, had no idea what had happened to him. She hadn't made sure he was warm, fed, and hydrated because she'd seen his face on the news. She'd done it out of the goodness of her heart. Yes, she was essentially trapped in the cabin with him because of the storm, but if she truly hadn't cared about his well-being, she could've done the bare minimum.

"Please sit, Carlise," Chappy requested again.

To his relief, she pulled out the chair next to him and slowly lowered herself onto it.

Chappy held out his hand as he said, "Maybe we can start over. I'm Riggs Chapman. My friends call me Chappy."

"Carlise Edwards," she said somewhat shyly, putting her hand in his.

"It's nice to meet you," he said with a smile. "Welcome to my home away from home."

He saw the question in her eyes as she shook his hand. He didn't want to let go, but he did anyway. "I have an apartment in Newton. It's the closest town to here. My friends and I own a tree service company called Jack's Lumber, which is based out of there."

"Who's Jack?" she asked with a slight frown.

"Right . . . so, maybe I should go back a bit. My friends and I were all in the military together. When we got out, we decided to go into business."

"Cal, Bob, and JJ, right?" she asked.

"Yup. Callum 'Cal' Redmon, Kendric 'Bob' Evans, and Jackson 'JJ' Justice are my best friends. We could've called the business Lumberjacks, but I think JJ would've had a hissy fit."

Carlise giggled.

The sound made Chappy grin. "Anyway, we cut and trim trees, pull up stumps, help the emergency rescue folks when there are trees down across roads. We also do maintenance on the Appalachian Trail, making sure it's clear, the trail markers are visible and haven't been worn away, and accompany people who're unsure about hiking through the Maine part of the AT by themselves."

"Wow. I'm guessing you're pretty busy then."

"In the warmer months, yes. Not as much in the winter, which is okay by all of us. I bought this cabin and fixed it up so I'd have a place to go to unwind when I needed it."

Carlise nodded as if she understood perfectly, though he knew most people would probably laugh. It wasn't as if Newton was a huge metropolis or his job was all that stressful. Still, there were times when Chappy just needed to be alone.

The thought startled him. He should be upset that his retreat from the world, from the crap that sometimes swirled in his head, had been intruded upon by a stranger. Oddly, Carlise didn't *feel* like a stranger.

He opened his mouth to say something else, he wasn't sure what, when she gasped and bolted up from the chair.

Chappy stood just as abruptly, slight dizziness assailing him as he looked around to see what had startled her. When he didn't spot anything, he watched as she frantically sorted through the cans in his pantry.

"What's wrong?" he asked urgently.

"I almost forgot Baxter!"

"Baxter?" Chappy asked. "Who's that?"

She turned to him. "The dog who found me."

"The pit bull?" Chappy asked in surprise.

"Yeah."

"He's here?" He looked around again, trying to find the dog. It wasn't as if the cabin was all that large; he should've spotted the big mutt right away.

"He wouldn't come inside. Believe me, I tried. He's on the porch. I hope you don't mind, but I took out a couple of the blankets you had around here. Not the newer-looking fluffy ones. There's a space between the cabin and the logs you stacked on the porch where he's made himself a little home with the blankets. It's still really cold, but no matter how hard I try, I can't get him to budge from his nest. I've been feeding him, though."

"I don't have any dog food," Chappy said unnecessarily. She obviously knew that.

"I've been using the stuff you have handy. Chickpeas, green beans, canned tuna and chicken . . . things like that. But now that I know I can use the stove, I can cook some rice and include that too. I bet he'd really like something warm in his belly."

She stopped as suddenly as she'd started and looked over at him. Her cheeks flushed bright red as he watched. "I mean . . . if it's okay with you? It's your food. You might not want me using it to feed a stray. I'm so sorry, I didn't really think about that."

Chappy couldn't stop himself from approaching. She was now standing outside the pantry he'd built to hold all his canned and dry goods. All his friends had laughed at the amount of food he kept at his cabin, but he wanted to be prepared at all times.

He stepped close and lifted his hand, stopping himself when he was inches away from her face. "May I?" he asked softly, gaze flicking to his hand.

She looked confused for a second, then seemed to understand that he was asking permission to touch her. She nodded once.

Chappy slowly ran the backs of his fingers down her cheek before resting his hand on the side of her neck. His thumb caressed the underside of her jaw. He shook his head slightly as he said, "I'm in awe of you, Carlise."

Her brows furrowed once again in confusion.

"You could've died. Were probably frozen to the bone. And yet when I saw you that first time, I could see the determination in your eyes, in the way you continued to put one foot in front of the other. You weren't going to stop until you were safe. Of course, you couldn't know there was literally nothing in the direction you were going. Nothing but my cabin. The road you were on eventually dead-ends, with only trees and wilderness for miles and miles.

"But by some miracle, I found you. Led you here . . . and then promptly passed out on you." He smiled slightly. "You did what you needed to do in order to keep both of us safe and warm. Not only that, but you didn't forget about the poor dog."

"He saved my life," she whispered.

"He did," Chappy agreed, his gaze tracking over every part of her face. He liked this. Liked being close to her. Touching her. She was looking at him with big blue eyes, and he felt good about what he saw in her gaze—relief. Trust.

And an attraction that Chappy was feeling down to his toes.

"Why Baxter?" he asked.

"I thought of all sorts of other names . . . I've had a lot of time to think about it, after all. But nothing felt right. Then Baxter just kind of popped into my head, and it seemed to fit."

"I like it. So he's been eating?"

Carlise nodded. "Last night was the first time he ate while I was out there with him."

"You've been sitting out there with him? It's freezing," Chappy said with a frown.

"I know, but I've been talking to him. Wanting him to get used to my voice. I hate that he's out there in the cold and we're in here. It's not right."

It *wasn't* right. But until the dog trusted her, trusted both of them, he wouldn't come inside. "How about we make some rice and add it to his food?"

"Won't it take a while to make? I mean, it's already past the time I usually feed him. I don't want him to think I forgot about him."

Chappy's lips quirked. "He won't think you forgot him."

"You don't know that."

"That dog's not going anywhere. He's probably warmer than he's been in quite a while, and you're his food source. He's not going to risk losing either of those things. Besides, I've got some minute rice, the stuff that doesn't take long to cook. Do you think he'll eat if I go out there with you?"

Carlise thought about it for a moment. "I don't know. Not about Baxter, but about you going outside. You're still a little flushed. And you were delirious not too long ago. It's probably not a good idea for you to be out in the cold."

Her concern felt good. "We won't stay out there long. Besides, I need to get more logs for the fire anyway."

"I can do it."

"I know you can. And I appreciate it. But now that I'm awake and aware of what's going on, you won't."

She frowned. "Why not?"

"Because."

"That's not an answer," she said, rolling her eyes.

God, she was cute. Although Chappy knew better than to call her that to her face. He wasn't an expert when it came to relationships, but he'd called a woman cute once in his distant past, and she'd made it very clear that she found the adjective offensive. He wasn't sure why, maybe she'd had some sort of bad experience. He had a feeling it was probably more *her* problem than an issue for women in general. But he'd been very careful not to use the word to describe future girlfriends.

"Because you've been taking care of me for three days," he said after a short pause. "You didn't have to. I didn't expect you to. But you did. If I thought Baxter would react positively to me, I'd ask you to stay inside and let me feed him. But he's used to you now, and I don't want to risk him running off if I go out there by myself.

"But . . . I'm a protector, Carlise. It's who I am. When my friends and I got out of the army, we didn't want to go into any kind of profession that involved weapons . . . security or bodyguarding, that sort of thing . . . but it's in my DNA to try to make sure those around me are protected and cared for. I'm uncomfortable with the fact that you had to tend to my every need these last few days, though I'm so very relieved, grateful, and touched that you did."

Chappy didn't know where he was going with all this, but he couldn't seem to shut up.

"You could hurt your hands on the wood. Get a splinter. Hurt your back because some of those logs are damn heavy. And I don't like to think of you hurting in any way. It's not a big deal for me to grab the logs because I've been doing it for years. And I chopped all of them in the first place."

Carlise put a hand on his chest and said, "Okay."

That finally stopped his word vomiting. "Okay?"

She nodded. "Yes. I'd be stupid to argue with you. I mean, you can probably carry more than I could at one time anyway . . . even though you've had a fever for three days. But can you try to take them from the far end of the stack, away from where Baxter's holed up?"

"Of course. When the wind and snow die down, maybe I can make him a proper doghouse."

Her eyes got wide. "You'd do that?"

"Absolutely. That dog saved you. He got my attention and made me go out in the storm to see what he was so worked up about. If he hadn't done that, you might not be here right now. I have a feeling I'd do *anything* for that dog."

She smiled.

Chappy stood there in his kitchen, his hand on her neck, her own resting on his chest, and simply absorbed the feelings coursing through him. Feelings he couldn't recall having often. Contentedness. Gratitude.

A rightness that this was where he was supposed to be. Right here with Carlise.

He didn't want to move, but Baxter needed to be fed. "I'll start the rice, if you want to get the rest of the food mixed."

"Okay."

Neither moved.

Chappy didn't want to be the first to break their physical contact, but it had to be done. Reluctantly, he dropped his hand and stepped back, surprised when it felt painful to do so.

Chapter Five

"It's okay. That's Riggs. I told you about him. He's good. Remember? You came and got him so he could find me. It's his food you've been eating and his blankets you're using. They're warm, huh?"

Carlise spoke calmly and gently to the dog, who was cowering as far back as he could get in his little hidey-hole. While he seemed scared, she was encouraged by the fact that he hadn't bolted off the porch. He could've. He could've backed out of his nest and escaped off the side of the porch. But instead, he kept his huge brown eyes peeled on both her and Riggs.

Speaking of the man, he'd insisted she put on two of his long-sleeved shirts, two pairs of his socks, and his galoshes, as well as her coat, hat, scarf, and gloves. She was so bundled up, she felt like Ralphie's little brother in the movie *A Christmas Story*.

Then again, he'd come right out and told her he was a protector. That he was concerned about her well-being, so she wasn't surprised about the excess of clothing. It had been a long time since anyone had cared about her so much. Her thoughts turned to Tommy, but she immediately cut them off. She didn't want to think about her ex right now. She was safe, and it had been such a relief not to have to deal with any kind of harassment or stalking for the last few days.

She turned and saw Riggs hunkered down on the balls of his feet by the door to the cabin. He'd grabbed some logs earlier and now was simply hovering behind her, watching.

"We have a surprise for you today," she told Baxter as she slid the bowl of food closer. "Rice. I think you're gonna like it. It'll warm you from the inside out. Although I'm not sure you should get used to this kind of gourmet food. Regular dog food probably has a better balance of nutrients for you. Then again, this probably tastes a lot better. But who knows what you've been eating before you found us, huh? It's okay. You can eat. It's safe. You're safe."

She started to scoot back but was stopped by Riggs's hand on her back.

"Keep talking to him. He needs to get used to your presence. He'll eat, just give him a moment," he said softly.

Every other time she'd been out here, Carlise had backed up and given Baxter space to eat. The last thing she wanted to do was scare the dog so he wouldn't touch the food. But she trusted Riggs, so she did as he requested.

"I'm sorry I didn't have rice before now. I didn't know the stove had gas. How silly is that? I mean, I should've, but in my defense, I'm not much of a cook. Sometimes a bowl of cereal is just as satisfying as a four-course meal, ya know? But I bet you wouldn't think so, huh? You're looking like you've put on some weight . . . of course, that could just be wishful thinking on my part. You were so skinny. I can't believe you've survived this long on your own. But you aren't alone anymore, Bax. If you can learn to trust me, I'll take you back to Cleveland when—um . . . when I'm sure it's safe. Go on, eat up, boy. It's good for you. Promise."

She hadn't meant to say that part about being safe, but the last thing she wanted was to take this dog back home, only to have her stalker decide to take out his anger on the defenseless animal. Baxter had been through enough. She didn't want to risk him suffering through any more abuse.

She prayed Riggs hadn't heard what she'd said . . . but she had a feeling he didn't miss much.

"Good boy," she murmured as Baxter sniffed the bowl she'd pushed under his nose. "That's it. Eat it all up."

The first time she saw the dog eat, she'd been surprised he hadn't scarfed up the food in a couple of bites. As skinny as he was, she'd assumed he would be desperate for any kind of meal. But then, as now, he ate slowly, as if he knew inhaling the food might make it come back up.

"It's good, huh?" she asked.

Baxter looked at her as if he understood what she was saying and licked his chops. Then his head dropped back into the bowl.

"He does look better than the last time I remember seeing him," Riggs said softly.

Goose bumps immediately rose on her arms as his breath wafted over the sensitive skin of her neck. Riggs was crouched right behind her now, with his hand on her back and his mouth at her ear, and it took everything within Carlise not to lean back and curl into the man.

Delirious and out cold, he was handsome. Upright, conscious, and whispering to her in that low, sexy voice . . . he was lethal.

Carlise was a practical woman. She didn't believe in love at first sight. She was wary of men in general. Their motives and their hidden intentions. But this man was getting under her skin without even trying. Maybe it was the way he'd asked for permission to touch her in the kitchen. Maybe it was how he'd said, without any embarrassment or ego, that he was a protector. Or perhaps it was because he'd insisted on making sure she was completely bundled up before going outside.

Whatever the reason, Carlise had a feeling this man would either be a dream come true or break her heart into a million pieces.

She nodded in response to Riggs's comment and kept her eyes on Baxter. But the man behind her didn't move away. He simply stayed where he was, the hand on her back never moving.

The wind didn't seem to be howling quite as badly as it had the last few days, but the snow was still falling, and visibility continued to be extremely limited. She, Riggs, and Baxter could've been the only three beings on the planet. They were in their own little bubble.

"I think he needs some more blankets," Riggs said after a moment. "I've got one inside that will be better than those. I got it in South Korea when I was there. It's called a mink blanket, but it's not real mink. I don't know *what* it is, actually, but it's thick and soft as hell. Maybe we can drape it over the logs so it'll block more of the wind."

Carlise's heart melted. He sounded genuinely concerned about the dog. She turned to tell him she didn't think he needed to sacrifice what sounded like a hard-to-replace blanket, but he was already moving away from her.

Baxter stopped eating and watched cautiously as Riggs backed toward the cabin door.

"It's okay," Carlise soothed. "He's just going to get you another blanket."

Within seconds, Riggs was back. "Here, I brought two. One we can put over the logs, and we'll use a few to hold it down; the other he can have in his little nest for more warmth. I think it's better if you do it, though. He doesn't trust me as much as he does you."

"I'll put the one over the logs, but you push the other toward him. He needs to know you've got his best interests at heart too. And that you won't hurt him. But let's wait until he's done eating."

It seemed intimate, sitting there on the porch watching Baxter eat. Riggs sat behind her, one of his gloved hands resting on the wood planks of the porch, beside her hip, and the other curled around her waist, holding her against him. His body blocked some of the wind, and even though they were both bundled up so much there was no way she could feel his body heat, it still felt as if she was warmer against him.

Eventually, Baxter finished the food Carlise had made for him. He licked every inch of the bowl clean before looking up at her and Riggs.

"I wonder where he came from," Riggs mused. "I mean, there isn't any other cabin around for miles."

"Someone probably dumped him," Carlise said.

"Yeah, you're most likely right," he agreed. He shifted against her. "Okay, let's do this. I'll push this blanket toward him first, then you can attempt to drape the other one over the logs."

Baxter trembled as they moved slowly, but he didn't bolt, which Carlise was grateful for. By the time they were done, the dog's hideaway was a lot more protected. "I should've thought about doing this three days ago," Carlise said sadly as she stood by the cabin door with Riggs.

Baxter was busy scrunching the new blanket, turning in tight circles as he attempted to make his nest as perfect as his doggy paws could make it.

"What you did was perfect," Riggs told her. "Come on, let's get inside and I'll make us some tea to warm up."

Carlise was more than ready to go inside. It was damn cold. As soon as they entered the cabin, Riggs went over to the fireplace and added a log before coming back to the door and taking off his jacket and hanging it on the coatrack.

His cheeks were flushed red, and Carlise didn't give it a thought before stepping toward him and placing a hand on his forehead. "You feel a little warm," she noted.

Riggs shrugged. "I think I still have a slight fever, but it's nothing like before. I'll be okay."

"Maybe I should make the tea," Carlise suggested.

"I've got it. Go sit on the couch and get warm. It'll take a bit for the water to boil."

"But you'll sit and relax once it does?" she asked.

He looked at her for a long moment before nodding. "Yeah."

"Okay."

It seemed to her that he wanted to say something more, but he simply gestured to the couch with his head before turning to the kitchen.

After the last three days, it felt weird for Carlise to simply sit there while Riggs waited on her, but now that they'd taken care of Baxter, and Riggs was on the mend, she realized just how tired she was. She'd slept here and there over the last few days, but never deeply. She'd jerked awake with every unfamiliar noise and anytime Riggs moved restlessly in his sleep.

She hadn't admitted it to herself at the time, but she'd been terrified that he'd die on her.

She dozed off while waiting for Riggs to return with the tea.

When she felt something touch her shoulder, her knee-jerk reaction kicked in. She ducked and rolled off the couch at the same time, covering her head with her arms, protecting herself from the blows she was sure would come.

When nothing happened after a long minute, she tilted her head and looked up, only to find Riggs sitting on the couch, frowning in concern.

"I didn't mean to scare you. You're safe here, Carlise. I won't hurt you. I'm sorry I touched you without permission, but I swear I'd never do *anything* to cause you pain. If I gave you any other impression, I'm so sorry."

Embarrassed by her over-the-top reaction, Carlise took a deep breath and moved to her knees, then stood and moved back to the couch. She sat next to Riggs and shrugged a little sheepishly. "No, *I'm* sorry. I mean, you did startle me, but I know you won't hurt me. You've had chances to do so already, and we both know I wouldn't be strong enough to stop you."

"You obviously *don't* know that, if your reaction was any indication," Riggs said in a heavy tone.

Carlise reached out and put a hand on his knee. She didn't like that he thought she was scared of him. She truly wasn't. Even though he was essentially a stranger, deep down, she knew he'd never hurt her. She wasn't sure *how* she knew . . . she just did.

"My mom was in an abusive relationship for years," she blurted. "We had to watch everything we did or said around my dad, for fear of him turning on us. She took the brunt of his anger for a long time, but when I got a little older, he turned on me too. He often came into my room and woke me up by hitting me. My reaction just now was instinctual. I'm sorry."

Riggs's jaw ticced as he stared at her.

For some reason, maybe in an attempt to calm him, Carlise went on. "I vowed never to stay with a man who hit me. I didn't want to be like my mom. She's a good woman, but she wasn't strong enough to leave him until it was almost too late. He eventually hurt her so badly that she was in the hospital for weeks. Finally, with my urging—or begging, really—she got up the courage to say enough was enough.

"Then, in *my* last relationship . . . Well, I thought Tommy was a good man. That he loved me. Until he showed his true colors. I left that very day."

Riggs took a deep breath, putting his hand atop hers on his knee. "I swear on my honor, I will never hit you. I will never belittle you. Never make you feel as if you can't trust me. I may not have known you for long, but it's clear to me that you're an amazing person, Carlise. Strong. I already said it, but I'll say it again—not many people would've done what you did. Would've helped me like you did. Would've had the inner fortitude to make it through that storm."

Carlise wasn't sure what to say. She simply stared at him.

"I want to know why you were out there, Carlise. Why you were lost in my backyard. What's put that wary look in your eyes. Why, with every howl of the wind, you look as if someone's going to storm in here and hurt you . . . despite being nowhere near Cleveland."

Shit. She was right. This man *didn't* miss much.

"But now's not the time. I feel as if I've known you forever, but in actuality it's only been a few hours since I've been conscious enough to know where I am and what's going on." He grinned slightly. "And you don't trust me yet. I can wait until you do. I want you to talk to me, to let me help you, but I want *you* to want that too. Not just tell me what's going on in your life because you feel as if you have no choice. So for now, how about we warm up, and we talk about less threatening stuff?"

Carlise sighed in relief. She wasn't ready to talk to Riggs about Tommy. About how scared she'd been of her stalker . . . that he'd escalate from petty vandalism and threats to something more physical. "Like what?"

"How old you are. Where you grew up. What you do for a living. That kind of thing." He turned to the small table next to the couch and handed her a mug of steaming tea.

Carlise had no problem sharing more general things about herself. Mostly because she was just as curious about the man sitting next to her. Now that he was coherent, she wanted to learn more about him. More than the fact that he had scars all over his body and a cute beauty spot on the side of his neck, just under his ear.

She cupped the mug and inhaled the scent of cinnamon and apple before saying, "I'm thirty. Grew up in Birmingham, Alabama, and I translate books from French into English."

Riggs turned and grabbed a blanket from the back of the couch, shaking it out before turning to her. "May I?" he asked, gesturing with the blanket.

Carlise nodded, and Riggs gently placed the blanket over her lap, tucking it in tightly.

"You warm enough?"

"Perfect," she told him. And she was. She felt more relaxed right this second than she'd been in days. Weeks.

"I'm thirty-four, but there are days I feel decades older. I grew up in Macon, Georgia, and you know that I'm a tree guy."

"What branch of the military were you and your friends in?" Carlise asked as she took a sip of the delicious tea.

"Army. We were Special Forces."

Her eyes widened. "You were? Like a SEAL?"

He chuckled. "Well, SEALs are navy."

"I knew that," Carlise said quickly.

"Yes, like that, but for the army." Riggs sighed and reached for another blanket. He covered himself, then settled into the other corner of the couch. Carlise felt his foot brush against hers on the cushion, but instead of pulling away, she pressed her foot harder against his own.

He smiled slightly, then sobered. "On our last mission, everything went wrong. Our intel was bad, the soldiers with us panicked when shit hit the fan, and in the end, my team and I were captured."

Carlise gasped. "Oh no!"

"Yeah. It wasn't a good time. That's when we decided we were done. That when we got home—*if* we got home—we were going to go into business together."

"I . . . were you hurt?"

Riggs nodded. "Yes."

"Your scars," she said quietly.

"Yeah, they aren't pretty. But we all got off pretty lucky compared to Cal."

"Wait . . . Callum Redmon, you said? Why does that name sound familiar?" she asked.

"He's originally from Liechtenstein, and yes, that's a real country. We all gave him a rash of shit about making up the name of some fictional country, but it turns out it's legit. He grew up mostly in England, even has the English accent, but he's fluent in German—that's what his people speak—and also knows a bit of French. He's the fourth son of the fourth son in line for the crown . . . or something like that. I can never keep it straight," Riggs said.

"Holy crap, I remember now! There were videos on the internet of him being tortured." She gasped and her eyes got huge. "Wait—you were there too?"

"Yeah. Our captors loved that they had royalty in their clutches. He got the worst of their attention."

Without hesitation, Carlise leaned over and put her mug of tea on the floor, then moved toward Riggs. She hugged him, resting her head on his chest and clutching him tightly in her arms. "I'm *so* sorry."

Riggs shifted until his feet were on the floor, back against the cushions of the couch, and effortlessly maneuvered Carlise until she was sitting on his lap. He clamped an arm across her upper thighs, the other around her back, holding her against him. "It wasn't so bad."

Carlise snorted.

"Okay, it was. It was awful. But I'm here, as are my friends. Alive and thankful for every day I've got on this Earth."

"But he's okay? Your friend? Cal?"

"Yeah. He has his bad days, but he's getting better."

"You mentioned him and your other friends . . . you know, when you were sick? You yelled out for them in your sleep. Were worried about them."

Riggs shrugged. "Not surprised. I'd do anything for those guys. We've been to hell and back together."

"I'm glad you have them," she murmured. Carlise had hugged him impulsively, unable *not* to offer him comfort, but now she didn't want to move. He was extremely comfortable and so warm. Her eyes drooped.

"You don't have any close friends?" he asked.

"I do," she said. "Susie. I met her when I moved to Cleveland. She lives in my apartment complex. We got close pretty fast, just sort of clicked. But . . ." Her voice trailed off.

"But?" Riggs prompted when she didn't say anything for a few minutes.

"I don't know. Lately it feels as if we're drifting apart. I mean, I work from home, so I don't go out a lot, and she used to be able to coax me to a bar with her on the weekends. We had a lot of fun, but I always say no when she asks now. I can tell it frustrates her. But . . . I just don't want to go out anymore." She didn't want to tell Riggs why. That she didn't feel safe, not knowing where or when Tommy might show up. "We still go to lunch, talk and text all the time, and we hang out at each other's apartments, but I know she wishes things were the way they used to be."

"People change," Riggs said.

Carlise loved how rumbly and deep his voice was. With her cheek on his chest, she could feel his words reverberating throughout her body. "Yeah. She's still my best friend, and I don't know what I would've done without her these last couple of months."

Riggs stiffened under her slightly. "Does she know where you are?"

"No. I called my mom before I left Cleveland. Told her I needed to get away for a while, but I didn't think it was safe to tell anyone else, even my best friend. I was afraid if she knew, she'd demand to come with me. And normally, I'd love a road trip with her. She's a lot of fun. But I just needed to get away from everything that's been going on for a while. I was going to call her once I was settled somewhere and safe."

"I can tell you're half-asleep. So I'm going to ask you what *everything* and *safe* refers to later," Riggs warned.

Carlise was too comfortable, too warm, too sleepy to protest. "Okay."

"You need to call either of them to reassure them you're good? You've been here a few days."

Carlise shook her head. "My phone's probably dead. And I'm guessing there's no cell service up here."

"There isn't. But I have my satellite phone. And we can charge your phone if you need to look up their numbers."

"That's right. I already forgot that JJ called you."

"He feels bad for jumping down your throat."

Carlise shrugged. "He was worried about you. I can't be upset about that."

"Well, when you want to call either Susie or your mom, just let me know and we'll get that done."

"Thanks."

"What about your job?" Riggs asked.

Carlise's head felt fuzzy. She was *so* damn tired. "What about it?"

"You need to call your boss or anything? I don't know a damn thing about translating books."

"I'm my own boss," she said. "I can work from anywhere. Now that I know you have electricity and I can charge my laptop, I should probably get some work done."

"I'll go out soon and fire up the generator so you can make sure your phone and laptop are charged. It'll also be good to shower."

Carlise perked up at that. "Shower?"

Riggs chuckled. "Yeah, with the generator running, we can have hot water."

"Oh, that sounds like heaven."

"You saying I stink?" Riggs joked.

In response, Carlise turned her head and inhaled deeply. He smelled like smoke and man, with a hint of laundry detergent. "No," she said with a small sigh.

She thought she felt Riggs sniff her hair, but she had to be mistaken. "You're tired," he said after a moment. "You should sleep."

Carlise yawned. "But it's not even noon yet."

"So? You've had a hard few days."

"So have you."

"We can both nap then."

"Okay." Carlise started to get up, but Riggs's arms tightened around her.

"Stay. I'm comfortable," he said.

Carlise leaned her head back and looked up at him. "I'm not too heavy?"

"No."

"We're strangers."

"No we aren't," he said without hesitation. "You do *not* feel like a stranger to me. Not in any way, shape, or form. But if I'm making you uncomfortable . . ." His voice trailed off.

Carlise immediately shook her head. "No. You feel good. Warm."

"I remember this," he said quietly, after she'd put her head back down on his chest.

"What?"

"Holding you. It feels familiar. Right."

He wasn't wrong. Carlise sighed again in contentment.

Susie would tell her she was acting way too impulsively and would warn her to be careful, not to let her heart overpower her head. Her mom would probably sigh wistfully and say it was a sign that she and Riggs were meant to be. The truth was probably somewhere between the two opinions.

But at the moment, Carlise couldn't muster up the energy to think on it further. To suggest that Riggs should nap on his bed while she took the couch. She felt too comfortable right where she was. So she threw caution to the wind and snuggled even closer to the man under her. His arms tightened for a moment, and she felt him lift the blanket she'd been using over her shoulders, covering both of them.

"Sleep, Carlise."

She could've sworn she felt him kiss her temple, but she had to be imagining the tender touch. Before she could dwell on it, her eyes closed, and she was out.

Chapter Six

Chappy puttered around the kitchen, preparing a hearty dinner for himself and his guest. He'd browned some ground beef, added taco seasoning and Ro-Tel tomatoes, and had just dumped some noodles into a second pot. The cheesy taco noodle dish was a favorite of his, and he was sure Carlise would enjoy the warm meal. He hated that she'd been eating PB&J sandwiches for three days, but her no-nonsense attitude about the situation she'd found herself in only increased his admiration for her.

She was still sleeping soundly on his couch. Her blonde hair was in disarray, and she looked exhausted. He'd woken up about an hour after they'd dozed off and couldn't get back to sleep. He'd been resting for three days, and his body was telling him it was more than enough. So he'd slipped out from under her . . . then simply watched her for an embarrassingly long time.

When he finally tore himself away, he visited the bathroom, read a little, checked on Baxter, made himself a snack . . . and still Carlise slept. Chappy knew he should probably wake her, otherwise she might not sleep through the night, but he didn't have the heart. She was clearly exhausted from the stress of looking after him for days.

But also from whatever had chased her out of Cleveland. All the way to his out-of-the-way cabin in the first place.

She'd said enough for him to assume her ex—possibly the one who'd hurt her—was causing her problems. He could only further assume she was running from the asshole . . . which was infuriating. Chappy hated to think about anyone hurting Carlise.

While the noodles boiled, he went outside and started the generator so he could check his cameras. It wasn't that he didn't trust her; he didn't think for a minute that she'd searched through his cabin for valuables she could steal. He was more curious about what he'd said in his delirium.

His friends told him he was paranoid, that having cameras *inside* his cabin as well as outside was going too far. But Chappy didn't care. After being kidnapped and tortured, he needed the reassurance the cameras gave him that all was right in the cabin when he wasn't there.

There were two tiny cameras set up on opposite ends of the main space, allowing him to see everything that went on. They were connected to an app on his cell phone, which luckily still had enough charge for him to download. He also had satellite internet at the cabin that worked when the generator was on, allowing him to get texts and emails. It was often unreliable, especially during high winds or any sort of weather event. He'd been meaning to install a booster, a better antenna, but hadn't done so before the snowstorm hit.

He held his breath, hoping he'd have enough of a signal to download the videos from the hard drive. Thankfully he did, but it was super slow. In the past, that usually meant the internet would peter out completely. The fact that he was able to download the footage from the last few days was a minor miracle in itself.

After the videos downloaded, he turned off the generator and went back inside, leaning against the counter in the kitchen and bringing up the app on his phone. Nothing he saw in the videos made him change his mind about Carlise.

Scrubbing through the footage, he watched her help him to the bathroom and back to bed several times, help him into a clean T-shirt, fret over him as she tried to get him to drink water or eat.

And he couldn't stop watching, over and over, the moment when she'd sat on his bed to soothe him when he'd called out in his sleep. The way he'd reached for her, even in his delirium.

The way their bodies naturally wrapped around each other as they slept.

It was no wonder she'd felt so familiar in his arms when she'd been on his lap. She fit against him perfectly, curvy in all the right places, and he particularly enjoyed how touchy-feely the woman was, how her first reaction to his nightmares was to try to make him feel better.

The truth of the matter was, it had worked. When she shushed him, touched him . . . when he was holding her, all the shit in his head quieted down, giving him rare and blessed peace.

There was something special about Carlise Edwards, and while watching those videos, Chappy decided he couldn't let her slip away.

Maybe he was desperate. Maybe he just hadn't had a woman's attention for far too long. But he didn't think so. If he'd met Carlise on the streets of Cleveland, he had no doubt he'd feel the same draw toward her as he did out here in the wilds of Maine. He'd been prepared to take care of her, to nurse *her* back to health after finding her in that storm, but the roles had been switched. She'd taken care of him perfectly.

And based on the videos, she'd apparently done it without an ounce of disgust or exasperation. She'd done what she needed to do for his well-being, and her own.

That was the kind of woman Chappy wanted. Someone who didn't freak out when shit hit the fan. Who rolled with the punches. She'd managed for three days without electricity or any way to heat the food she'd found in his pantry. She eventually would've figured out either the stove or how to heat something over the fire. In the meantime, she didn't bitch about the circumstances she'd found herself in. Carlise merely adapted.

Chappy also couldn't deny the way she acted with the dog went a long way toward endearing her to him, as well. He had a soft spot for abused animals, and Baxter was as abused as any dog he'd seen in a long time. He'd literally saved Carlise's life, and Chappy was relieved she'd gone out of her way to give Bax a safe space, to make sure he was fed.

Yes, all in all, Carlise was *exactly* the kind of woman he'd dreamed about . . . back when he still thought he had a chance for a true relationship. Being held captive had changed him, changed his outlook. Since then, all he'd wanted was to be left alone.

Until Carlise appeared in his life. Now, he already couldn't imagine her leaving.

Chappy felt a little bad about the cameras, but he'd tell her when she woke up. He didn't want her to think he was spying. They were just there for security reasons when he wasn't at the cabin.

A noise from the living area drew his attention, and Chappy turned to see Carlise sitting up on the couch. Her eyes were unfocused, her hair was a mess, and her T-shirt was twisted around her so tightly, he could see every delicious curve.

"What time is it?" she asked groggily.

"I've made us a warm meal," he said instead of answering her question directly.

"It smells good. Although I think at this point anything other than PB&J would taste like heaven."

Chappy smiled at her. "It'll be ready when you are. I'll start up the generator later, but I've heated some water on the stove that you can use to wash up if you want."

"Oh, I'd love that," she said, sounding and looking a little more awake.

"I'll just move this pot into the bathroom for you then," Chappy told her.

Carlise stood and her brows furrowed. "Should you be doing that? How do you feel? Do you still have a fever? Did you take any Tylenol today?"

Chappy couldn't help but grin. "I'm fine," he told her. "My fever is gone, and yes, I took some meds."

"Okay. I just . . . I spent three days trying to get you better, and it would suck if you had a relapse while I was sleeping," she said with a small shrug.

Chappy couldn't stop himself from going to the woman who'd appeared out of nowhere and was quickly becoming an obsession. He walked right into her personal space and wrapped her in his arms.

To his relief, she didn't pull away in alarm. Instead, she snuggled into him as they stood next to his couch.

Chappy rested his cheek on her temple and sighed in contentment. "Thank you," he said fervently. "I can't remember the last time anyone did something as selfless as you did for me."

He expected her reaction. She shook her head against him, then pulled back and looked up to meet his gaze. "I wasn't going to just let you fend for yourself, Riggs. You were the one who went out into the storm, while you were *sick*, to find me. If you hadn't followed Baxter . . ." Her voice trailed off and she shivered.

"But I did. And you're fine. And I'm good," he reassured her.

"Yeah," she agreed.

The last thing Chappy wanted to do was let go, but he forced himself to drop his arms from around her and take a step back. "Three days ago, we were strangers, and now I feel as if I've known you forever." He shrugged. "I don't understand it, but I've learned over the years to not question things like this."

"Same," she said, making Chappy almost sag in relief. "But I know intense situations can sometimes make people feel closer than they might otherwise."

Chappy shook his head. "I have a feeling no matter where or when I met you, I'd feel the same way I do right now." He wanted to say more. Wanted to tell her that he wouldn't force her into any kind of relationship if she didn't want it. But it was way too soon for that kind of conversation . . . wasn't it?

He cleared his throat and stepped backward toward the kitchen. "I'll move the pot into the bathroom for you. The water isn't boiling anymore, but the pot will still be hot to the touch. Just be careful, okay?"

"I will," she said with a small nod.

She stood next to the couch as he carried the large pot into the bathroom.

"Take your time. The meal's not going anywhere."

"Okay. Thanks," Carlise said, giving him a small smile before walking over to her backpack, which was sitting against the wall. Chappy had seen it earlier but left it alone. She hadn't gone through his drawers and personal items while he'd been unconscious—although, honestly, if he'd been in her situation, he totally would've. Still, he didn't want to repay her thoughtfulness and unselfishness by pawing through her things.

She pulled out a change of clothes, then headed to the bathroom and closed the door.

Chappy let out a long breath. He was somewhat shocked to realize how empty the cabin felt without her in sight. Which was ridiculous, but he still couldn't shake the feeling. She didn't take long in the bathroom, and when she reemerged, the hair around her face was wet, letting him know she'd taken advantage of the warm water to wash her face.

Immediately, he wondered if she'd washed other parts of her body as well.

Feeling like a pervert, he did his best to shut down that line of thinking. If he thought about her standing naked in his bathroom, using one of his washcloths to caress her luscious curves . . .

No . . . he wasn't going there.

Chappy cleared his throat. "All good?" he asked.

Carlise nodded. "The warm water felt great. Thank you."

"Again, I'll get the generator fired up tomorrow, and we can both take a shower. There won't be a ton of hot water, but it'll be enough for a quick wash. We can also run a load of laundry."

"I'll never take hot water or electricity for granted again," she said with a small smile. She dropped a bundle of dirty clothes next to her backpack, then wandered over to the kitchen. "What can I do to help?"

"Nothing," Chappy told her. "It's all done. Just have a seat. What can I get you to drink?"

"Water's fine," she said.

He felt her anxious gaze on him as he dished out two plates of the ooey-gooey pasta dish.

"What?" he asked, unable to *not* ask. "What's wrong?"

"Nothing."

"Don't do that," he said quietly, catching her gaze. "Don't say nothing's wrong when I can tell you're worried about something. You can ask me anything. Say anything. I'm not going to get mad. I'm not going to punish you for thinking a certain way. Things between us have gone from zero to a hundred in lightning-fast speed, but I don't want you to feel as if you can't express a concern or tell me what's on your mind."

"I'm just not used to sitting around and letting someone wait on me," she replied. "Tommy always expected me to do everything. Cook, clean, get him a beer. And, of course, it also feels weird to just be sitting here after doing everything the last few days."

Not for the first time, Chappy wanted to kick her ex's ass. He brought their full plates over to the table and set them down before going back into the kitchen and grabbing the two glasses of water, two forks, and two paper towels.

He set everything down on the table, sat, then took a breath before turning to her. "I'm thirty-four years old. I've been cooking for myself for at least the last decade and a half. I've done my own laundry, paid my own bills, cleaned my own dishes, floors, bathrooms, and everything else. I don't expect you—or anyone else, for that matter—to do that stuff for me. In fact, it would feel extremely weird for *me* to sit around and let *you* do all that stuff.

"I also don't like the thought of you having to do everything around here while I was sick. Don't get me wrong, I'm appreciative, and I can't remember the last time anyone has gone out of their way to do so much for me . . . but I don't expect or want that dynamic in any kind of relationship I have, whether platonic or romantic."

Carlise was staring at him so raptly, Chappy wished he could read her mind and know what she was thinking. When she didn't comment, he kept talking.

"I have to admit, it feels good to cook for someone other than myself. I always make too much and have to eat leftovers for days. I usually get sick of eating the same thing but feel guilty if I throw perfectly good food out. So you're really doing me a favor."

Her lips twitched, and she rolled her eyes. "Me letting you wait on me hand and foot is doing you a favor?"

"Yup," he said with a grin.

"Whatever," she muttered and reached for her fork.

Chappy knew the taco pasta was good, but he still held his breath as she took her first bite. Her eyes widened as she chewed. After she swallowed, she grinned at him. "Holy crap, Riggs. This is . . . it's *so* good!"

He chuckled. "I'm not sure how much of a compliment that is since you've had nothing but PB&J for the last three days."

"No, I'm serious. It's really, really good," she said enthusiastically.

"Well, there's plenty, so dig in," he returned, pleasure blooming in his chest. It was silly. It was only food. But as they sat there, and she ate a meal he'd prepared for her, Chappy's protectiveness for this woman grew. He knew it wasn't just about the food. It was a sense of satisfaction deep in his soul for providing for her.

He hadn't lied earlier when he'd told her he was a protector. He enjoyed being needed, doing things for others. But this felt so different.

Different from helping out his friends or a neighbor. Assisting a tourist on the AT. Different from just wanting to return the favor after she'd taken care of him.

He was already falling for Carlise.

It wasn't like him. He'd met his share of women over the years, and none of them had made him feel like he did right that moment, sitting at the table in his humble cabin, so proud of sharing a meal he'd made. No one had even come close.

He might not know many details about her life, but he knew Carlise was the kind of person who would do whatever was necessary to take care of a fellow human, even if she didn't know them. She was the kind who worried about a stray dog. Who'd feed him and make sure he was warm and safe from a storm.

She was the kind of woman who wouldn't put up with a man abusing her, who'd left the first time he raised his fists. Who'd refused to pry into a man's personal life and belongings even when he'd been delirious and wouldn't have ever known. The kind of woman who found pleasure in something as simple as warm water.

Okay, maybe he knew a lot more about Carlise than he'd thought. And every single thing made him want to know more.

"You're awfully quiet over there. I think you talked more when you were delirious," Carlise said, sounding a little nervous.

"Sorry, I'm not used to having guests," Chappy said.

She grimaced. "No, *I'm* sorry. As soon as I can, I'll be out of your hair."

"That's not what I was insinuating," he told her, instant panic welling up inside him. "I just . . . I'm not the best conversationalist. I was just enjoying sitting here with you and trying to remember the last time I'd been this content. Usually I eat standing up in the kitchen, snarfing my food down quickly."

"Me too. Somehow it feels even more lonely to sit at a table by yourself, doesn't it?" she asked.

Relief filled Chappy. She understood. He shouldn't have been surprised. "Yeah," he agreed. "So . . . tell me about this translation thing you do. What kind of books do you translate? How did you learn French well enough to be able to do that? I'm assuming it pays all right since you've made it your profession."

Carlise's face lit up. She began to tell him all about what she did, and Chappy heard only half of the words. He was more fascinated by how passionate she was about her job, how animated she became while describing it.

When she'd wound down, she gave him a sheepish grin. "Sorry. That was probably way more than you were interested in hearing."

"No," he said immediately. "It's fascinating. I guess I hadn't ever thought about it before, but it's great that books by French-speaking authors can be made available in other languages for others to read as well. I don't know what I'd do without books."

"Isn't it the best when you can lose yourself in a story? When you're sad because you've finished a book? One of the greatest things about my job is that I get to communicate with authors directly. I mean, sometimes I'm hired by publishers to translate, but most of my business is with authors themselves. I have to pinch myself when they actually have a conversation with me via email."

"That's definitely cool," Chappy said, leaning his elbow on the table and resting his chin on his hand as he stared at her.

"It really is," she agreed.

"You haven't been able to work much the last few days. Is that going to put you behind?" he asked.

Carlise shrugged. "Not too much. I mean, I should probably get back to work soon, but I always build in plenty of wiggle room for each translation. The last thing I want is to deliver a book late to an author and mess up their publication schedule."

Considerate. Another trait Chappy added to Carlise's plus column.

They were quiet for a moment, then she tilted her head and said, "Listen—do you hear that?"

Tensing, Chappy strained to hear what had caught her attention. "No, what?"

"It's quiet," she whispered. "I'd gotten so used to the wind howling outside that it sounds weird *not* to hear it."

"You're right," Chappy said. "Hopefully that means the storm has finally decided to move on."

"It's about time for Baxter's dinner," she said. "Do you think we could mix some of this delicious pasta in with his dinner? It would be warm, which I know he'd like. And it's cheese . . . all dogs like cheese and beef."

Chappy chuckled. "I'm sure. It's light on the spices, and I made a ton. Like I said, when I cook, I tend to overdo it."

"Well, I'm glad. Because I can totally eat this for breakfast, lunch, and dinner and not get sick of it."

"So says the woman who ate peanut butter and jelly for three days straight."

Carlise grinned and shrugged.

"Come on, I'll clean up while you get Baxter's food ready. Then we'll head out and make sure he's good."

"I can—"

"No."

Carlise huffed. "You don't know what I was going to say."

"You were going to say that you could help me clean up. I've got it. If you helped me with the dishes and packaging up the leftovers, it would just take longer for Baxter to get his meal."

"That's devious," Carlise said, but she was smiling, so Chappy knew she wasn't really upset.

"Nope, it's practical. Now, how much do you think you want to add to Baxter's food tonight?"

It felt comfortable to work side by side with Carlise in the kitchen. The space wasn't terribly large, so they constantly bumped into each other. It felt intimate and not awkward at all. It was crazy how content Chappy was with this woman in his space.

It didn't take long for him to hand-wash the plates and other dishes he'd used in prepping their meal and for Carlise to get Baxter's bowl ready. He explained that he collected his recyclables and brought them into Newton when he went home and that he burned any trash he could. In the summer, he also had a compost pile. It was important to Chappy to make the smallest impact possible on the environment and live as naturally as he could while at the cabin.

They both got bundled up to head out to the porch with Baxter's dinner, and Chappy held his breath as they went outside, praying the dog was still there.

He was.

As soon as the door opened, Baxter's head popped up from the nest of blankets he'd made. There were paw prints that led down the porch into the yard, so it was obvious the dog had done his business, then returned to the warmth of his little den.

"Hey, Bax," Carlise said softly. "How're you doin'? You look comfortable. Although it would be so much warmer and nicer inside with Riggs and me. We won't hurt you, I promise. The storm seems to have stopped, which is good news. Without the wind, you should be much warmer. I brought you some more food and water. And tonight you're in for a treat . . . Riggs made cheesy taco noodles! They're sooooo good.

You're going to think you've died and gone to heaven. I mixed in some green beans and chickpeas, because you need the nutrients, but I'm thinking you won't even notice them with the cheesy beefy goodness you're about to scarf down."

Chappy had a huge smile on his face. She was adorable, talking to the dog as if he could understand what she said. But then again, maybe he did. Baxter was watching her with his head tilted as if he was fixated on every word.

Carlise put the bowls on the wooden boards of the porch and scooted them forward, toward the dog. When she started to move backward, Chappy said, "No, stay close to him again. And keep talking. He needs regular reminders that you aren't going to hurt him. That you aren't going to give him food, then take it away."

"I'd never do that," she said, sounding scandalized, but she did as he suggested and slowly sat on her butt, closer than she'd ever sat near him before.

"Good boy. I know I'm close, but I won't hurt you. That food's all yours. I ate my fill—more than my fill, if you must know," she told the dog in a quiet tone. "And there's lots of leftovers. I'll see if I can control myself so you can have some tomorrow, but no guarantees. I might wake up in the middle of the night and sneak out here to the icebox thing and eat the rest myself."

She continued to talk nonsense to the dog, and eventually the lure of food won out, and Baxter crept forward just enough to reach the bowl. Like he had before, he didn't gulp the food down as fast as he could. He seemed to be savoring each bite, as if he was afraid he'd never get any again and needed to enjoy the experience while he could.

Chappy could relate. When he and his friends had been POWs, they hadn't exactly been fed regularly. And when they were, it was disgusting, watered-down oatmeal or something that had no flavor whatsoever.

The first meal he'd had at the hospital in Germany had tasted better than anything he could ever remember eating in his life. It had taken him twenty minutes to finish a simple bowl of chicken soup. Not because his stomach had shrunk, but because he was savoring every bite.

"He's eating," Carlise said in the same tone she'd been using to talk to the dog.

"Reach down and put your hand near the dish. Don't try to touch him, just rest your hand there," Chappy suggested.

"I don't want to scare him," she argued.

"That's why you aren't going to try to touch him," he returned calmly.

Without any more protests, Carlise moved slowly, once more talking to Baxter in that calm tone as she placed her hand near the bowl.

Baxter stopped eating for a moment, looked at her, then at her hand, then turned his attention back to the bowl.

"He's ignoring me!" Carlise said happily.

Chappy would've chuckled if he didn't think it would scare the dog.

They both watched as Baxter licked the bowl clean of every single morsel of food. Then, to their surprise and delight, he licked Carlise's fingers, just once, before backing up into the little den he'd made on the porch.

Carlise turned and smiled at Chappy—and it was all he could do not to pull her into his arms and kiss her senseless.

"He licked me!" she exclaimed happily. "Did you see that, Riggs? He licked me!"

"I saw it, sweetheart." The term of endearment popped out without thought. Now that the dog had finished eating and was curled back into the blankets, Chappy crouched on the balls of his feet next to Carlise. He balanced himself by putting a hand on her shoulder and the other on the wall next to her.

"Hey, boy. You did good," he praised the dog. "Thank you for coming to get me and leading me to Carlise." His friends would laugh their heads off at the sight of him talking to a dog, but he hadn't had a chance to show his appreciation to the mutt yet and figured this was a good time to talk and not scare him, when his belly was full, and he was hopefully feeling mellow.

Carlise leaned against him, and the three of them stayed like that for a long moment. Then a small gust of wind whipped under the roof of the porch, and Chappy felt Carlise shiver.

"Time to go back in," he said firmly as he stood.

Carlise didn't complain, simply reached over and grabbed the now-empty dog bowl, pushed the fresh water closer to Baxter's bed, then stretched her hand up so he could help her stand. When she was on her feet once more, Chappy wrapped his arm around her waist, leading her back to the door.

She looked back at Baxter and said, "Good night, boy. We'll see you in the morning. Stay warm and safe, okay?"

Of course the dog didn't respond, but his big brown eyes stayed fixed on them as they headed back into the cabin.

Chapter Seven

Carlise sat on one end of the couch with her computer on her lap. After they'd fed Baxter, Riggs had suggested she get some work done. He was reading a book on his end of the sofa, and she couldn't help but look over at him every now and then.

He looked a lot better than he had for the last three days. She much preferred him to be up and moving around than lying so still and sick. It was crazy how he'd gone from being completely out of it to seeming like he hadn't been sick at all in mere hours. But she was more than relieved he was on the mend.

Of course, now that he was conscious, she felt a little awkward. She was an unwanted guest. And she'd been living in his space for three days. Granted, he hadn't exactly been aware of her, but still.

She'd slept all afternoon, which she never did, and now she wasn't tired in the least. Which was probably a good thing because she wasn't looking forward to discussing the sleeping arrangements. She hadn't thought twice about sleeping next to him in the bed while he was sick. He'd clearly wanted her close, and he wasn't in any shape to do anything inappropriate. But now that he was awake and aware . . . it wasn't as if she could just climb into bed with him again.

But she wanted to.

God, how she wanted to.

She'd never felt safer than when Riggs held her in his arms. Never felt as content.

Which was crazy. Stupid. Ridiculous.

Riggs Chapman was a stranger. She didn't know him. He could suddenly decide she should thank him for saving her in a physical way. He could force himself on her, and there wouldn't be anything she could do about it since he was far stronger. And she couldn't leave . . . She was stuck here at the moment.

Just the thought of anyone taking something she didn't want to give, then having no choice but to share tight living quarters afterward, made her almost physically sick.

"You okay?" Riggs asked.

Looking up at him in surprise, she nodded.

He stared at her for a long moment before returning her nod and turning his attention back to the book in his hands.

Carlise calmed herself. Riggs wouldn't force himself on *anyone.* It was true that she didn't know him all that well, but he'd had plenty of chances today to become aggressive, to hurt her if he wished, and he hadn't. He'd made her dinner, opened up about being lonely, sat with her while she'd fed Baxter.

Carlise *knew* Riggs was one of the good guys.

She still itched to call Susie. To get her opinion. Her friend was honest to a fault and could be counted on for good advice. But no. She was enjoying the break from her real life even more. And she didn't think Tommy could trace her calls, but she wasn't going to risk it. Not yet. She wanted a few more days of feeling completely safe before she had to worry about harassment from her stalker starting up again.

Taking a deep breath, Carlise turned her attention back to the book she was translating. It was one of her favorite genres, romantic suspense. With a heroine in trouble . . . and in need of the man in her life to help her out of it. She always wished she was like the heroines in those books. Strong. Resilient. Brave.

She'd never felt like that. Ever. Hell, at the first sign of a threat, what did she do? Run.

But the heroines in the books she translated weren't like her. Most of the time, they met danger head-on. Even when everything went wrong, they still fought, not willing to give up.

For a moment, Carlise daydreamed about what she'd do if Tommy showed up at the cabin. Would she be like one of the heroines in the books she loved and stand up to him? Tell him off and be prepared to protect herself?

Probably not. She'd be a mess. Her first instinct would be to hide. To get away . . . if Tommy didn't drag her off first and do whatever he wanted.

Hating the thought of her ex following through with all the threats he'd sent via email and text—it had to be him; who else would it be?—Carlise shivered.

Riggs suddenly moved, standing and going over to the bed and grabbing one of the fluffy blankets folded up at the foot, bringing it back to the couch. Without a word, he shook it out, then motioned for her to move her laptop.

Lifting it up, Carlise let Riggs spread the blanket over her lap, on top of the one that was already there. Then he turned to the fire and added another log, making the flames dance with renewed vigor.

Finally, he sat again. "Better?"

Carlise belatedly realized that he'd seen her shiver and thought she was cold.

She suddenly wanted to cry. He was so in tune with her needs. So eager to give her whatever he thought she wanted. Had Tommy *ever* been that way? Not really. And her dad had definitely never cared that much for her mom.

"Much. Thanks," she said.

Riggs smiled, then turned his attention back to his book.

Shoot. She was falling for the man.

In one day, he'd been more of a boyfriend to her than Tommy or any other guy she'd ever dated. And it seemed to come naturally to Riggs. He wasn't going overboard just to schmooze her. Wasn't fawning or making obnoxious, overt moves. Everything he did was simply part of who he was.

And she liked him. A lot.

But she had no idea what he thought of *her*. She was an unexpected guest. Someone forced on him, because a man like Riggs would never turn away someone in need. And who knew how much longer they'd be stuck in his cabin together? The poor man had come up here for some peace and quiet.

If she was being honest, however, he didn't seem all that perturbed. He'd even said how much he enjoyed having someone to cook for and eat with.

Deciding she just needed to chill, Carlise tried once again to focus on the words on the screen in front of her. The storm had ended, which meant hopefully she'd soon be able to get back to her car, get back on the road, and get on with her life.

The thought of leaving the cabin, leaving Riggs, made her belly clench. She had a feeling that when she left, she'd be walking away from something amazing. Something life changing. But what other choice did she have? It wasn't as if Riggs was going to declare his undying devotion and beg her not to go.

But a small part, deep down—the romantic who believed in happily ever after and true love—wanted just that. She had a job she could do from anywhere. Why couldn't she do it from here? Or from his apartment in Newton?

Starting over fresh actually sounded perfect. Tommy would eventually get over his obsession, or whatever his issue was. Her mom would probably think she was making a big decision too quickly, but she'd ultimately understand. And she and Susie could still be best friends . . . they had email, texts, and phone calls. They could still gossip and laugh together.

Hell, Susie would probably love Maine. She believed in things like Bigfoot and alien abductions, and this area was a hotbed for fans of both.

For a moment, she daydreamed about moving here. About meeting Riggs's friends, greeting him when he came home from leading a trip on the AT or after going out in the middle of the night to cut down a tree that had fallen across a road or on a house.

Then her brows furrowed. She was being ridiculous again. At best, maybe Riggs would attempt to stay in contact after she left, mostly because he'd want to make sure she was safe. But eventually they'd lose touch and get on with their lives.

"It's not going well?" Riggs asked.

Carlise jerked in surprise and looked at him. "What?"

"You're sitting there staring at the screen and not typing. Is the translation not going well?"

Carlise felt her cheeks get hot. Shit. She'd been daydreaming about living with the man next to her instead of working. "No. It's fine. I mean . . . I'm just thinking."

"About?"

Yeah, there was no way she was going to tell him the truth. That she'd dreamed up a full-blown fantasy about greeting him when he got home and the two of them falling into bed together. "Just life. What I'm going to do next now that the storm has stopped."

"Well, there's no rush. It'll still be quite a while before we're able to get out of here safely. It's not as if the plows come out this way. JJ will see what he can do, but the priority will be the main roads."

Carlise couldn't tell if Riggs was upset that he was going to be trapped here for a while longer or not. "I know you weren't expecting a houseguest—" she started, but Riggs immediately interrupted.

"I wasn't. But I'm not upset that you're here, Carlise. Maybe if you were a bitch, if you complained about the lack of electricity, about how we're in the middle of nowhere, or were a general pain in the ass, I might be. But I think you fit here perfectly."

His words settled into her soul. "I actually love the peacefulness out here."

"Me too. Although I don't think I could live here full time," he said with a shrug. "I mean, I love coming out here to recharge, to reconnect with nature, to get away from annoying people. But eventually, I miss being able to pop down to the grocery store to grab something I need or to get a fast-food hamburger or something."

"They have fast food in Newton?" she teased.

Riggs grinned. "Better. Granny's Burgers," he said. "It's a hole-in-the-wall, family-owned restaurant, and they make the best burgers I've ever tasted. And french fries. Lord, they're so good."

Carlise grinned.

"Anyway, I'm just sayin', I love this cabin, but *Little House on the Prairie* isn't the life I want full time."

"What do you know about *Little House on the Prairie*?" she asked.

Suddenly, a tinge of red filled his cheeks. "I told you I like to read," he said a little sheepishly.

"You've read the books?"

"Yeah. I was only going to read one . . . but they sucked me in. I couldn't stop. I love a good series."

"Me too," she told him.

"Authors are cruel, making us love all the characters they dream up. It's usually impossible *not* to pick up the next book in a series."

"Right? And when they introduce a character in book one that we *have* to have a story for, only to learn we don't get it until book eight? So mean," Carlise agreed.

Riggs chuckled. "Anyway, I was just sayin' that while I love it out here, I have no plans to make this my permanent residence."

Carlise stared at him for a long moment. Eventually, she nodded.

"Right, I'll stop talking now so you can get some work done. You want to set up at the table? Will that make it easier?"

"No. I'm good here. Thanks, though."

"Okay. If you need anything, let me know."

Carlise nodded again and watched as Riggs looked back down at the book in his hand. She took a deep breath. She needed to get some work done. She wasn't behind, yet, but she would be if she took too many days off.

Thankfully, she was soon engrossed in the story, and the translation began to come fairly quickly. It was always easier when she enjoyed the book she was translating. Luckily, she wasn't too picky and loved reading just about every genre, so disliking a story didn't happen very often.

The familiarity of her job kicked in, and Carlise lost herself in making the French words sound seamless and just as meaningful in English.

~

Chappy couldn't keep his gaze from straying to Carlise. He had no idea what he was reading, hadn't turned a page in quite a while. He was too fascinated by the woman next to him. It had taken her a while to start working, but now that she had, she made him smile.

She'd frown, furrow her brow, type a few words, tilt her head as she thought, then type once more. The process of translating a foreign book into English was incredibly interesting. And the woman doing it even more so.

He wondered what she'd been thinking about so hard before focusing on her work. Yes, he'd surreptitiously watched her then, too . . . and he'd seen so many emotions flit over her face. The more he was around her, the more he wanted to get inside her head.

Chappy certainly didn't want her to feel as if she was invading his space, and it was clear she was worried about just that. He liked having her there. Was so damn relieved and grateful to Baxter for leading him to the stranger walking on the road. The alternative made him feel physically sick all over again. Her body would've been buried in the snow by now. He never would've seen her smile. Heard her laugh. Seen her compassion toward Baxter or himself.

The world would've been a dimmer place without her in it.

Never knowing her seemed impossible now. He felt as if he'd known her for years. He would've definitely missed out if she hadn't stumbled into his life.

Eventually, Chappy was able to turn his attention back to his book. It was a spy thriller, and he still had no idea who the bad guy was, for which he gave major props to the author. He was usually able to figure that kind of thing out fairly early in a story. But not this time.

He didn't know how many hours had passed by the time he'd finished the book, but when he looked over at Carlise, he saw her head was resting on the cushion behind her, and she was fast asleep. Her fingers were still resting on the keyboard, and he wondered how many times she'd conked out in the middle of working in the past.

Moving slowly so as not to wake her, Chappy stood. He put another couple of logs on the fire, then gently pulled the laptop out of Carlise's grip, touching the mouse pad to bring up the document she was working on. Thankful she didn't have it password protected, he hit save, just in case, and closed the computer before placing it on the small kitchen table.

Then, without a second thought, he leaned over and put his arms under Carlise's legs and around her back. He lifted her easily and carried her toward the bed.

This moment had been in the back of his mind all night. Their sleeping arrangements. He wanted her in his bed. Wanted to be in it *with* her. They'd slept curled together when he'd been sick, but his gut said she'd feel awkward about doing so now, when he was no longer out of his skull with fever. If he were a gentleman, he'd put her in his bed, then go sleep on the couch.

But he didn't want to do that.

"Riggs?" she mumbled into his chest. Her arm had curled around his neck as he'd carried her the short distance, and he held his breath as he eased her onto the mattress.

"Yeah?" he asked quietly.

"I'm cold."

The blankets she'd been buried under had fallen off when he'd picked her up, and Chappy quickly got her legs under the blankets on the bed and pulled them over her.

"Better?" he asked.

"Ummmmm." She was obviously still mostly asleep.

Chappy stared down at Carlise for a long moment, internally arguing with himself. He should turn and go back to the couch. Sleep there. It would be presumptuous to do otherwise, and she'd probably freak out if she woke up in his arms.

But his feet wouldn't move. He felt rooted to the spot. Indecision tore at him. Stay or go?

When she shivered under the covers, his decision was made.

Earlier, Chappy had pulled on a pair of jeans and a long-sleeved shirt, and while he usually slept in nothing more than a pair of boxers, he lifted the comforter and lay down on the mattress fully clothed without hesitation.

Carlise was cold, and she'd be warmer with him next to her. But with his clothes on, he'd hopefully avoid making her uncomfortable in the morning. Skin on skin would be more effective in keeping them both warm, but he wasn't willing to do anything to make her think he was taking advantage. Keeping his clothes on wasn't a difficult choice.

The second he curled himself around her, a memory flashed through his head of lying with her just like this, his bare legs entangled with hers. Of slipping his hand under her shirt and resting it on her soft skin.

To Chappy's surprise, his cock twitched.

He forced himself to think about something else. About going out in the cold to start the generator in the morning. Shoveling snow. Calling JJ eventually and asking him to come up to help him with Carlise's car.

The thought of her driving away instantly killed any lust he felt.

With every minute he spent in her presence, he wanted ten times more. That sort of attachment didn't happen to him. Usually, people annoyed him. Quickly. Even his friends sometimes. He liked being by himself. Was a natural introvert. But he was extremely comfortable with Carlise.

She mumbled something, then turned in his arms, burying her face in the crook of his neck. Her nose was chilly, and she wiggled against him, pushing both hands under his shirt to rest on the bare skin of his chest.

Chappy smiled, even as he sucked in a breath at her cold fingers against his skin.

"You're warm," she mumbled sleepily.

"Shhh," he replied, resting his chin on top of her head.

One of her legs pushed between his, so she was now snuggled against him as tightly as she could get.

Chappy had never felt more relaxed. They were both fully dressed, but the moment still felt intimate. Carlise wiggled against him a bit longer, then finally sighed in what he had to believe was contentment.

For a moment, he still worried about what the morning would bring. Wondered if she'd be angry that they were in bed together. If they'd still be as intertwined as they were now. If she'd be scared of him because he'd very clearly chosen to sleep next to her.

But the longer he lay with Carlise in his arms, the more his worry faded away. He'd deal with her reaction in the morning. He'd convince her there was nothing wrong with what they were doing. They were merely sharing body heat. The cabin got chilly at night as the fire died down. It was the logical thing to do.

And she was safe with him. Completely, one hundred percent safe. He'd never hurt her. Would hunt down anyone who tried.

Chappy was perfectly comfortable with the direction his thoughts had taken. This woman was his. He knew it instinctively. Felt it in his bones. She'd been led straight to his door for a reason. And he wasn't going to let her go without a fight.

Luckily, he had a bit more time to convince her he wasn't insane, and that they belonged together. He had no idea how he was going to do so, but he'd figure it out. He had to. In his mind, there was no alternative.

Chapter Eight

Carlise woke up the next morning with sunlight shining in her eyes. She frowned and blinked in surprise. She hadn't seen the sun in days.

"Sorry," Riggs's deep voice said, and she felt movement before the light dimmed behind her lids.

She opened her eyes and realized Riggs was lying next to her—*right* next to her—and hovering, blocking the rays of the sun with his head.

She tensed and tried to read what he was thinking and feeling by looking into his eyes . . . with no luck.

"Sleep okay?"

She nodded.

"You weren't cold?"

Carlise shook her head.

"You're sleepy in the morning."

She shrugged. "Without coffee, it takes me longer to wake up."

"I'm going to go out and start the generator in a moment. I'll get the coffee maker out and fire it up."

"You have a coffee maker?" she asked incredulously.

"Yup."

Carlise closed her eyes in ecstasy. "Be still, my heart," she joked.

When Riggs laughed, she felt it in her torso. Which brought her back to their current positions. She was on her side, one of her legs between his, and her hand was under his T-shirt, resting against his chest. The other was clutching his forearm. She was holding on as if she never wanted to let go . . . and she realized she didn't.

"Um . . . we slept together." She winced as soon as the words left her mouth.

But Riggs didn't seem fazed in the least. "Yup. You fell asleep working, and I didn't have the heart to wake you up. I could've slept on the couch . . . but honestly? I didn't want to. I wanted to be here. Next to you. I vaguely remember that we slept this way when I was sick, and I have to say, it's much better now that I'm not out of my head with a fever." He studied her for a moment, then added, "I'm not sorry, Carlise . . . but I don't want *you* to worry or freak out about it. Are you okay?"

Was she okay with this gorgeous man wanting to sleep by her side all night? Um . . . hell yes! But she kept her excitement to herself and simply said, "Yes."

"Good. And you'll be okay tonight? When it's time for bed and we do it again?"

Tingles shot through Carlise as arousal swam in her veins. He wasn't actually saying anything would happen beyond sleep, but her body had other ideas. "Yes," she repeated.

Riggs sighed. "Thank God," he murmured.

Then, to her surprise, he leaned down and kissed her forehead. "Close your eyes, sweetheart. I'm about to move, and the sun is going to be right in your eyes again."

She did as he suggested and felt the rays against her lids as he shifted off her. Cold air infiltrated the warm cocoon they'd been in, and she immediately burrowed into the blankets to try to preserve Riggs's body heat.

"I'll put some more logs on the fire. It'll warm up soon. Just stay in bed for now," he said.

Carlise opened her eyes and watched as a fully dressed Riggs headed for the fireplace. Knowing that they'd both remained clothed, that he obviously hadn't taken advantage of her the night before, made her estimation of him rise even higher than it already was.

Her instincts had been right. He was an honorable man. He wouldn't hurt her. He wasn't going to attack or rape her as soon as her guard was down.

Yet, a tiny part of her, the part that had always been let down by the men in her life, cautioned that she still didn't know Riggs that well. Didn't know if there were parts of himself that he kept buried away.

She watched as he puttered around the cabin, pulling an ancient coffee maker from the back of one of the cabinets, one she hadn't bothered to look into. Eventually he glanced over at her. "You want to feed Baxter this morning? Or do you want to stay in bed and let me give it a shot when I go out to start up the generator?"

Carlise wanted to check on the dog, but she could hear Riggs's desire to befriend Baxter in his tone. "You can do it, if it's not too much trouble."

"Never," he told her with a small smile.

She watched from across the room as he emptied two cans of shredded chicken into a bowl, along with a can of green beans. "You're spoiling him," she called out.

"Hey, this is the first time you won't be there feeding him. I need to give him incentive not to bolt," Riggs said. "I'll scoop in some of the cheesy pasta when I get out there and get it from the icebox. I'll be right back."

Carlise had to smile at that. Where else was he going to go?

Fifteen minutes or so passed while Carlise dozed, waiting for Riggs to return. When she heard the creak of the door, she opened her eyes and saw Riggs enter with a huge smile on his face and an empty bowl.

"He ate?" she asked unnecessarily.

"Yeah. He's coming around," Riggs said. "It's only a matter of time before we'll be able to get him inside. He's going to love sleeping in front of the fire. I got the generator started too. It's kind of loud, but as soon as we're done doing what we need to do with the electricity, I'll shut it off."

Now that she was more aware, Carlise could indeed hear the hum of the generator outside. After the silence of the forest, it did sound a little out of place.

"You can shower first," he said. "It'll take another ten minutes or so for the water to heat, but I'll get the coffee started and plug in your laptop so it'll be fully charged. You want me to charge your phone too?"

Carlise forced herself to sit up. The air in the cabin wasn't nearly as cold as it had been when Riggs got up. She thought about his question for a moment, then shook her head.

"You sure?"

"Can I even get service?"

Riggs shrugged. "Probably not."

Carlise shook her head again. "My mom will be okay for a few more days. The last time I talked to her, I told her I was going offline for a while."

"If you're sure."

"I'm sure," Carlise told him. She wasn't ready for real life to intrude. She wanted to pretend she was simply on vacation.

Well . . . the truth was, she was scared to death that when she turned on her phone, she'd have dozens of scary messages and texts from her stalker. She wasn't ready to deal with that yet. Wanted to live in a fantasyland with Riggs for a little longer.

"Okay. Whenever you're ready, just let me know. I thought maybe we could take a walk today."

Carlise stared at him with a frown. "Um, there's, like, two feet or more of snow out there, Riggs."

"I know," he said with a smile. "But I'd like to check out the area, see if there are any trees down that I need to deal with. And the sun is out. It's probably at least twenty degrees warmer without the wind blowing. It'll be fun."

"So says the man used to Maine winters," Carlise muttered.

"Yup," Riggs said without any hint of embarrassment. "I'm thinking Baxter will like the chance to stretch his legs too."

"You think he'll follow us?"

"I think anywhere you go, he'll go," he said with a nod.

"I don't know about that. He's used to being on his own," Carlise said, although pleasure bloomed at the thought of Baxter liking her enough to want to follow her around.

"There's an old saying that goes something like, 'If you save a life, you're then responsible for it.' He saved you, so he feels as if you're his now. Besides, you gave him food when he was starving, blankets when he was freezing, and you've talked to him in a soothing, loving tone. I have a feeling that dog would do anything for you."

The pleasure at the thought of Baxter liking her faded as she thought about what would happen once she left.

"What? What's wrong?" Riggs asked, stepping closer to the bed.

"I just . . . I've never had a dog. I don't know what to do with one. He'd be better off attaching himself to you."

"Too late, sweetheart. Don't borrow trouble. Things will work out."

He sounded so sure. Carlise had a million questions but didn't want to be a pest, not after all the nice things he'd said about her the night before. "Okay."

"Okay. If you get up and get me the things you want washed, I'll get a load ready for after our showers. By the time you brush your teeth and stuff, the water should be ready for you."

For the first time, Carlise realized that she'd be naked behind the bathroom door. And she didn't remember seeing a lock on it. Riggs could burst in while she was in the shower and—

No.

He wouldn't do that. She knew that down to her toes. She forced herself to push back the comforter and climb out of the warm sheets. She went to her backpack and took out the last clean outfit she had.

She'd loved wearing Riggs's sweats, but now that he was awake and aware, it felt too intimate, so she'd gone back to wearing her own things.

She was relieved her clothes could be washed but felt a little weird about handing over her underwear to Riggs. Of course, he didn't even blink at the bundle of clothes. He simply dumped them into the hamper she'd seen him use earlier before picking it up and heading over to a wide closet she hadn't bothered to investigate.

He pulled back the pocket door, and Carlise saw a small stacked washer and dryer. The appliances almost seemed out of place in the cabin, especially after all the days of only using the fireplace as a source of light. "I'll add the clothes you've got on after you shower," he said as he leaned over to grab a bunch of clothes to put into the washer.

Carlise couldn't help but stare at his ass. It was a thing of beauty. Round. Tight. And her fingers itched to touch.

At that thought, she spun and headed for the bathroom. Being around Riggs was hell on her libido. But the last thing she wanted was to make him uncomfortable. Women had to hit on him all the time. He was that beautiful. And she didn't want to do anything that would make him regret letting her stay here.

She glanced at the doorknob as she brushed her teeth and saw she was right. There was no lock. But she didn't feel any fear. After brushing her teeth, she turned on the shower and was delighted with how fast the water warmed. She stripped her clothes off as fast as she could and was under the warm spray before she had a chance to even worry about being naked with only a flimsy door between her and Riggs.

A shower had never felt so good, and she swore once again to never take electricity or hot water for granted again.

~

Chappy gritted his teeth as the water in the bathroom came on. Carlise was on the other side of the door. Naked. Soapy. In *his* shower.

His cock hardened, and this time he didn't immediately think about something else to make it go down. It had taken every bit of willpower to leave her in the bed earlier. She hadn't panicked when she'd woken up in his arms. She'd taken it in stride, just as she had everything else since they'd met.

He hadn't been able to stop himself from making it clear that he wanted to sleep with her again tonight, surprised and relieved when she hadn't protested. He hadn't missed the look of lust in her gaze, nor the way she'd shifted subtly under him. She'd been aroused at the thought of sleeping with him again—and Chappy had never been more thrilled in his life.

"Slow, Chap. You have to go slow," he muttered. "You can't jump on the woman like a wild animal."

But that was how he felt. He'd never wanted a woman as much as he did Carlise Edwards. That was actually part of the reason why he'd suggested they take a walk. He needed to take his mind off the feelings she stirred in him. If he sat in this cabin with her all day, he'd probably do something he regretted. He didn't want to scare her. To let his desire for her mess up the connection they had.

He'd never been the kind of man to *need* sex, but the more time he spent around Carlise, the more he thought he'd go crazy with want.

He wanted to see her looking up at him with sleepy eyes, run his hands over her naked body, and feel her tremble under and around his cock as he took her over the edge.

"Damn," he swore, running a hand through his hair. It was time to think about something else. His cock throbbed in his pants. His balls were pulled up tight, as if they were ready to release their load at just the thought of being inside the woman in his shower.

He could go in there right now. Strip. Join her under the water and have her coming on his hands, his tongue, in minutes. He was that sure of their connection. But he wouldn't do anything that might make her lose the trust they were building.

And that was why he needed to get outside. To expel some of this crackling energy. He was feeling fine, as if he'd never been sick. Without Carlise, he would've been in a lot worse shape, he had no doubt. But now he was more than ready to do something physical . . . something that didn't include getting naked and indulging in a marathon sex session with his gorgeous houseguest.

Damn it. There he went again. He had to get himself together. When it was his turn in the shower, he'd masturbate. That should take the edge off.

Deep down, Chappy knew he was fooling himself. Yes, jacking off might make him feel better in the short run, but as soon as he laid eyes on Carlise, his cock would be raring to go again.

Sighing, he did his best to concentrate on getting the coffee made. He was just as ready to have a cup of joe as Carlise. He leaned against the kitchen counter and listened to the water in the bathroom shut off as the coffee percolated. He tortured himself by imagining Carlise running a towel over her wet body, bending over to put on her underwear, reaching behind her back to fasten her bra.

God! His mind literally wouldn't give him a break! Wouldn't stop thinking about how luscious Carlise would look spread out on his sheets. Naked.

By the time she opened the bathroom door, Chappy was so hard, he was surprised he hadn't come in his pants. Carlise smiled at him, and it was all Chappy could do to say, "Coffee's ready. I'll be out soon," before brushing past her toward the bathroom. The scent of his soap on her skin, the sight of her long hair making her shirt wet, made a burst of precome leak out of his dick. He barely got the door shut before he was stripping off his clothes and heading for the shower.

The water hadn't had time to completely warm back up yet, but that was fine. A cold shower would probably do him some good. He'd been abrupt with her, and he knew that, but he hadn't wanted Carlise to see his hard-on. It was either be a little short or potentially make that beautiful blue gaze turn fearful. The latter wasn't acceptable.

Chappy took hold of his cock the second he stepped under the water, hissing in pleasure as he began to stroke himself. It didn't take long. He didn't even have a chance to pour soap in his hand to help him jack off. He'd barely taken hold of his balls with one hand and squeezed his cock with the other before he was coming. Hard.

White ropes of come hit the plastic wall of the shower, and Chappy could picture how Carlise would look with his release on her tits. She'd smile at him and rub his ejaculate into her skin . . .

Shit. His cock twitched again, and another spurt of come coated his hand. The water at his back was lukewarm, and Chappy turned and let it hit his face, forcing himself to think about all the things he needed to do today.

After a minute or so, he was able to grab the soap and clean himself up. Although using the washcloth on his cock was almost painful. His balls were still sensitive as he washed between his legs, and he let out a small chuckle. The fact that he thought he'd feel better once he'd masturbated was almost hilarious. He didn't feel better. He felt even more wired.

He needed Carlise Edwards in a way that continually shocked him. And not just for sex. He needed her smiles. Her calmness. Her caring nature. The woman had gotten so far under his skin, so fast, that he should've been terrified. But instead, all he felt was an anxiety that he wouldn't be able to convince her to give him a shot.

Then he thought about the look on her face when he'd suggested charging her phone. She'd been . . . nervous? Scared? Of what, he wasn't totally sure, but Chappy didn't like it. If anyone dared put a hand on her ever again, they'd regret it. She might not know it, but she had a ready champion. He hadn't spent all those years in the military without learning how to take down an enemy.

The water went from lukewarm to freezing in a heartbeat, but Chappy stood under the spray for a moment longer, hoping against hope that it would help his cock behave once he got dressed and went back out into the cabin. He wanted Carlise in his bed, under him, wanted to be inside her, but he wanted her to trust him, to feel safe, even more.

And if she never got to the point where she was comfortable making love with him, he'd respect that. Respect *her*. He'd still protect her. Let her go if that was what she wanted. It might kill him, but he'd do it. He'd never take more than she was willing to give.

In a lot of ways, she was like Baxter. Wanting to be loved. Wanting desperately to be safe. But unable to fully trust those who were willing to help.

Yet.

He'd give Carlise space and time. He'd let her see that she could trust him with her secrets, her body, her everything. And once she opened up, let him know what she was running from, he'd get with JJ, Cal, and Bob to take care of the threat.

Then it was only a matter of convincing her to move to Newton. With him.

Chappy snorted. Right. He had a feeling nothing about Carlise would be easy. But she'd be worth the fight. He knew that without a doubt.

~

Something was different about Riggs, but Carlise couldn't put her finger on what it was. He was still his usual friendly and protective self, but she'd caught him staring at her more than usual. And after yesterday, that was saying something. It wasn't alarming, not really, but she was aware that he was scrutinizing her even more than he had the day before.

She'd been a little reluctant to go for a walk, but once she was outside, she realized how much she'd needed to get out of the cabin. She loved it, but it was small, and she'd been stressing over her constant thoughts of Riggs. Now, being outside in the sun felt amazing.

Baxter obviously felt the same. At first, she'd been worried the dog would run off and get lost, but Riggs had reassured her that he wasn't going to lose them, not when they were feeding him and he had a warm place to sleep on the cabin's porch.

He was still skinny, too skinny, but amazingly, even after only a few days of full meals, he'd actually filled out a little. His hip bones and ribs didn't stick out quite as much as they had before, and currently, the dog frolicked around them. That was the only word Carlise could think of to describe it. Baxter bounded through the snow like a jackrabbit. It even looked as if he was smiling as he played in the tall drifts. He wasn't getting close enough to be petted, but he was very definitely keeping his eye on them both, not letting them get too far ahead or behind.

The air was cold, Carlise could see her breath as she exhaled, but it didn't feel as cold as it had previously. The wind wasn't nearly as strong now, but it was still making the trees sway above their heads.

As she slowly trudged through the deep snow, Riggs reached for her hand. It felt natural, as if they walked like this every day.

A small smile formed on Carlise's face. She caught Riggs staring at her out of the corner of her eye—again—so she turned to look at him as they walked. "What?"

He shrugged. "You look content."

"Truth?"

"Always."

"I am," Carlise told him. "I mean, I'm not exactly a nature girl. I've always lived in a city. But it's so peaceful walking around out here, in the middle of nowhere. Being the first people to make tracks in the fresh snow. It makes my problems seem not quite so insurmountable."

"I love it out here. When my friends and I were being held hostage, I was pretty sure I'd never get a chance to do something like this again. I try not to take it for granted."

Carlise squeezed his hand. She hated to think about him being a POW. It seemed inconceivable. He was so strong, so capable.

After a long moment, she asked, "Are we going anywhere in particular?"

"Yup. I thought about heading to the road to see about your car but decided to go this way instead to show you something."

"What?"

He grinned. "You'll have to wait and see when we get there."

"You're mean," Carlise pouted. "I hate surprises."

"You'll like this one," he said mysteriously.

The truth was, Carlise used to love surprises, but for a long while now, she hadn't gotten very many good ones, and she'd become wary.

They walked for a while, probably around thirty minutes or so, frequently stopping to admire the scenery or check on Baxter, before Riggs turned to her. The walking hadn't been easy with all the snow, and Carlise felt a bead of sweat drip down the side of her face. She was bundled up, and at first, she'd been cold, but now she was feeling a little overly warm. The temperature was probably well below freezing, but she'd been exerting a lot of energy.

"You ready?" Riggs asked.

"Yup."

"Okay, close your eyes."

Without thought, Carlise did as he asked.

"Stay here. Keep your hand on this tree. And no peeking, no matter what you hear. Okay?"

She was getting more and more intrigued. They'd been walking through the woods, and everything around her looked the same. She wasn't sure how Riggs knew where they were going, but he was obviously in his element out here. She had no doubt in his navigation skills.

"Okay," she belatedly reassured him.

He left her side, and it was actually harder than she thought it would be to keep her eyes shut. The second he stepped away, it felt as if she was alone out here in the wilderness. She could hear his subtle sounds nearby, but it somehow wasn't enough.

"Riggs?" she called out, hating that her voice wobbled.

She heard his footsteps as he came closer.

"What's wrong?" he asked.

The second his gloved hands touched her face, Carlise relaxed. And immediately felt stupid. "Sorry. It's nothing."

"Look at me," he ordered.

She opened her eyes. He'd tilted her head up so when her lids lifted, all she saw was him.

"What's wrong? What happened?"

"I just . . . got worried for a second."

"About what?"

"That you'd leave me here. That you might think it was funny to play a joke or something."

In response, Riggs's jaw tightened as he inched closer. "I'd never do that. That wouldn't be funny in the least."

"I know," she whispered.

"Why would you even think something like that?"

Now that her eyes were open and she saw how affected Riggs was by her thoughts, Carlise felt awful. "I don't know."

"Yes, you do," he countered. "Talk to me, sweetheart."

"My ex . . . he thought it was funny to scare me. He'd jump out from around corners and behind doors, just to hear me scream. Tell me he needed to grab something from another aisle in a store, then go outside and move the car, making me think he'd left me. He *loved* to prank me by calling late at night and not saying anything when I answered, just breathing heavily." She shook her head, trying to dislodge all the thoughts of Tommy. "Leaving me standing here while he went and hid is something he would've gotten a huge kick out of. He always said I couldn't take a joke."

"None of that's funny," Riggs said tightly. "Scaring people isn't something I do as a prank, and it's not cool. I'd never do anything like that to you. Ever."

Carlise's muscles relaxed at his response, both his verbal one and the way his entire body seemed to go taut with anger. But it wasn't aimed at her. "I'm sorry I doubted you."

"Don't be," Riggs said with a shake of his head. "We're still getting to know each other. And your past has taught you to be wary. But you can lower your shield around me, Carlise. I hope to show you in time that *I* can be your shield. I can protect you from the assholes in the world. From the crap life likes to throw at people from time to time."

His words were everything. Carlise was used to no one standing up for her. Starting with her mom when she was a kid, unable to protect Carlise from her father. Riggs vowing to protect her didn't automatically make the past go away, but looking into his serious gaze, she felt the wall around her heart crack a bit.

It took a moment, but eventually, Riggs relaxed. She felt his thumb caress the underside of her jaw. "You okay now?"

She nodded. "I think so."

"Would it make you feel better to keep your eyes open, but to turn your back to me instead?"

More relief flowed through Carlise. "Yeah."

"Okay." He moved his hands so they were on her shoulders and physically turned her around. But he didn't let go. Instead, Riggs leaned in and rested his chin on her shoulder. Their faces were a hairbreadth apart, and if she turned, their lips would touch.

One hand moved to her hip, and he held her against him for a moment. "Look at Baxter. He's having a ball."

Carlise immediately saw the black pit bull against the snowy wonderland of the woods. He was throwing a stick in the air, then pouncing on it when it landed, throwing snow up all around him as he played.

She grinned at the joy the dog was expressing.

"He knew you were upset, you know," Riggs told her.

"What?" Carlise asked.

"He was waiting to see what I'd do. Standing close enough that he could protect you from me if he needed to. But when you relaxed, so did he."

Carlise stared at the dog playing in front of her. "I didn't see him."

"I know. You only saw me."

He wasn't wrong. When she was looking into Riggs's eyes, he was the only thing she could think about. He filled her senses, in a good way.

"I'll be right back. I won't be long, and you'll be in my sight the entire time. You're safe with me, Carlise. I give you my word."

She nodded, knowing she couldn't say anything at that moment if she tried.

Riggs moved away from her, and she felt the cold wind blowing around her once more. She hugged herself and leaned against the tree Riggs had left her beside. She watched as Baxter played in the snow as if he hadn't a care in the world. The dog had been starved, abused, and abandoned, and yet after a bit of love, he couldn't be happier.

She could learn a lot from the dog, Carlise thought. She'd had a tough childhood, and yet she always knew her mom loved her with all her heart, despite being too weak and frightened to get herself and Carlise away from her dad. When Carlise had eventually moved to a new city to start her life over, everything was a bit better. Her neighbors were friendly, she had a job she enjoyed and was very good at, and she'd found a close friend in Susie. Her mom was moving on with her life as well, happy for the first time in years.

After various failed dates over the years, Carlise's one remaining issue was loneliness . . . a longing for someone to love, who loved her back. And she'd thought Tommy was that man. Instead, he'd become the biggest mistake of her life.

After the restraining order, when the "anonymous" texts and emails got more vicious, she'd confronted him just once. Tommy claimed he didn't know what she was talking about. Denied any contact beyond those first few weeks after the breakup.

Yet, the harassment continued. In her mind, there was literally no one else it could be. Then the more tangible violence, culminating in her slashed tires . . . So she'd run. It was cowardly, but Carlise didn't want to see what he'd do next.

Now . . . she was kind of like Baxter. Looking for her place in the world. A place where she could be safe.

And she'd found Riggs.

Movement to her right caught her attention, and Carlise turned to see Riggs standing quietly a few feet away, staring at her.

She blinked. "Sorry, I didn't hear you."

"I didn't say anything. And I didn't want to touch you when you were lost in thought, potentially scaring you . . . so I was just waiting. It's not exactly a hardship to stand here looking at you," he said with a small shrug.

Another brick in the wall around her heart fell away with his words. "Is my surprise ready?" she asked.

He looked sheepish. "Yeah, but now I'm thinking it's kind of stupid. It's not terribly exciting, and I probably got your hopes up too high."

Carlise thought it was cute he was so worried. "Riggs, you could lead me here and tell me you wanted to show me your favorite tree in the entire forest, and I'd be thrilled. Anything you want to share with me, I want to see."

For a moment, a look so intense crossed his face, Carlise was startled, but then his expression cleared, and he grinned at her. She wasn't sure what it was about her words that had affected him so much.

He held out a hand. "Come 'ere, honey."

She hadn't missed the terms of endearment he'd been letting slip. Warmth spread through her with each one. Surely he didn't mean anything by them, so she couldn't get her hopes up. He'd probably run screaming if he knew how much those simple pet names meant to her. She needed to tread carefully. Keep her feelings to herself.

She closed the distance between them and put her gloved hand in his. He squeezed her fingers before turning and walking toward a copse of trees.

"This place is easy to find because of this particular bunch of pine trees. They're the only ones around as far as you can see," he said as they walked toward where the snow had been disturbed in front of the trees he'd pointed out.

Carlise realized he was right. She hadn't even noticed the pines were somewhat out of place in the middle of all the spruce and maple around them.

"I'm guessing someone planted them as a kind of marker," Riggs went on. "We're about a mile from my cabin, and at one point, there used to be another cabin out here, not too far from where we're standing."

"What happened to it?" Carlise asked, looking around and seeing no sign of any kind of structure.

"Avalanche."

She stopped and stared at him in disbelief. "Seriously?"

"Yes. Most people don't think of Maine as avalanche central, but see that mountain?" Riggs asked, pointing behind the pine trees.

Carlise saw the huge mountain looming. A shiver went down her spine.

"We're safe," Riggs soothed as if he could read her mind. "It's still cold enough that the snow on the slopes is stable. As the weather warms, and the snow shifts up there, it'll be a different story."

"Is your cabin in danger of being buried?" Carlise asked.

"No. I made sure to build it out of the slide zone. But I'm thinking whoever was here before me didn't. I haven't looked into the archives of the area, but after seeing for myself what I'm about to show you, I looked around a bit and discovered what was left of a foundation nearby. An avalanche took out the cabin, and whoever was here decided to move elsewhere afterward. If they'd only built their cabin a mile or so to the west, where I am now, they would've been safe."

Carlise shivered again.

"We're good," Riggs said. "I wouldn't have brought you out here if I thought differently. But I've made you nervous, and that wasn't my intention. So I'll show you what I brought you out here to see, then we'll go back to the cabin. Okay?"

She nodded eagerly. Now she couldn't get the image out of her mind of snow burying both of them.

Riggs pulled her forward and pointed to the ground. "I'm guessing the previous owners were preppers of some sort because of this."

Looking down, Carlise realized Riggs had cleared the snow in a small area in front of the pines. She saw a small open door with a ladder leading into the ground. "What the heck?" she asked in confusion.

Riggs chuckled. "When I bought the property up here, the realtor told me about this place. It's a doomsday bunker, as far as I can tell. It's not huge, just enough for a couple of people. There are metal shelves, which were stocked with some old military MREs and some jugs filled with water. My friends and I cleaned it out, so it's empty now."

Her curiosity piqued, Carlise stepped toward the hole. When shut, the door would be flush to the ground, and she assumed it would blend in with the dirt in the summer. Inspecting the door, she saw a large ring on the outside, obviously to open it, and there was what looked like some sort of hydraulic system attached to the underside.

"Can I go down there?" she asked.

"Of course. Be careful going down the ladder. It's not that deep, but it would still hurt if you fell."

"Are you coming too?" she asked.

For the first time, Riggs looked uncomfortable. "I don't do so well in enclosed spaces," he said with a small shrug.

Carlise felt awful for him. "I'm sorry."

"Don't be. It's not your fault. I've been in there but would rather not go in again unless I have to."

She nodded. "I can just look from up here."

"No," he said firmly. "My phobias aren't yours. I can see you're curious, and it's why I brought you here. I had a feeling you'd be intrigued. Go on, I'll be fine up here."

"Is there a chance I could be locked in?" she asked.

"No. No way. It actually only locks from the inside. So once in, you can keep others out but not the other way around. That's why I figured it was a doomsday kind of bunker. Those inside would want to keep the rest of humanity out."

Carlise nodded. She walked closer to the hole in the ground and looked down. It was dark in the bunker, and before she could have second thoughts or ask Riggs if he had a flashlight, his hand appeared with exactly what she needed.

"Here, it's a strong light. You can put it on the floor once you're inside, and it should light up the entire interior."

Smiling at him, Carlise sat in the snow at the edge of the hole and put her feet on the ladder rungs. She quickly descended into the bunker and looked around in fascination after putting the flashlight on the floor. The beam illuminated the space exactly as Riggs had said it would. Looking up, she saw him squatting at the entrance.

"It's so cool," she said with a smile.

"We left the shelves in there because it would've been a pain in the ass to take them out. I'm assuming the previous owner built them while down there because they won't fit through the door as they are now. The back corner held a chemical toilet, and if you look really close in the back left-hand side, you can see a hole in the ceiling that's been filled in."

Carlise walked deeper into the bunker and looked at where Riggs was directing. Sure enough, there was a small hole.

"That's the air hole. Cal thinks there was probably some sort of fan attached to suck air down, or up, if needed. We covered it up, though, so no critters could get in and then get stuck."

There was what looked like the remnants of a metal cot in the space as well. There wasn't a mattress on it anymore, though. Looking around, Carlise could just imagine a family sitting in here as the world raged above their heads. She'd translated a few apocalypse and alien invasion books and could clearly picture a group of people hunkered underground, trying to survive in a world turned upside down.

She walked back to the hole, where Riggs was still crouched. "This really *is* cool."

"Yeah," Riggs said. "I couldn't bring myself to have it removed. Not many people know about it, so I'm not really worried about anyone using it for nefarious purposes. And it's not like someone would just stumble onto it. No one comes out here except for me and the occasional hunter, but it's kind of hard to find unless you know what you're looking for."

Carlise picked up the flashlight and took one last look around the bunker before she grabbed hold of the ladder. The container was just tall enough for her to stand upright. She had a feeling Riggs would have to stoop a bit when he was inside. There were only about eight rungs to the top, and as soon as she got high enough, Riggs's hand went under her elbow to assist her out.

Carlise gave him the flashlight, and he put it into one of the deep pockets of his jacket.

"You want to close it up?" he asked.

Carlise grinned. "Yes!" She couldn't help but be enthralled by the bunker and how it worked. Before shutting it, Riggs showed her the locking mechanism. It was a simple dead bolt, which slid into place to prevent the door from being opened from the outside.

To her surprise, the heavy-looking steel door was easy to close. The hydraulic contraption kept it from slamming shut, but it wasn't slow either. Carlise supposed if you were running for your life and an alien was on your heels, you wouldn't want to have to strain to get inside, and you'd want the door to shut fairly quickly as well.

"I can see the wheels turning in your head," Riggs said with a small smile once the bunker door was secured.

"I was just picturing someone trying to get away from an alien invasion and coming here to hide out," she told him.

"You ever thought about writing your own books?" he asked.

Carlise blinked in surprise. "What?"

"You translate others' words. Have you ever wanted to write your own?"

"Oh, I'm not an author," she protested. "I just translate for other people."

Riggs stared at her for a long moment, and it felt as if he could read her mind. "I bet you could do it."

"Do what?" But she knew what.

"Write a book."

"Why would you think that? You just met me," she said a little defensively.

"I have a feeling you can do whatever you set your mind to," he said without hesitation.

His belief in her, the way he sounded so damn sure, made her belly flip-flop.

"Besides, from what it sounds like, you've translated a lot of books. I'm sure you've gotten your own ideas from doing what you do."

Carlise nodded reluctantly.

"What's holding you back?"

She shrugged. "I don't know."

"Well, I think you should go for it. Even if it's just for yourself. Maybe you can write an alien romance. The heroine hides out from the evil aliens in a bunker in the woods. Then a benevolent alien finds her and reassures her that he's there to help. Help *all* the humans. He earns her trust. They spend some sexy time in the bunker, then come out and kick evil alien butt. She goes back to his planet because it turns out he's the king of his people and can't stay on Earth forever, and she lives happily at his side as his queen."

Carlise stared at Riggs in disbelief.

"What?" he asked with a grin.

"I . . . you . . . *what the heck*?"

"I may or may not have read an alien romance or two in my time," he said, laughing.

"Seriously?"

"Yup."

Carlise shook her head. "You never fail to surprise me."

"Good. Want to keep you on your toes," Riggs told her, stepping into her personal space.

She had to tilt her head back to maintain eye contact. That intense expression was back.

"What are you doing to me?" he murmured.

Carlise swallowed hard. She wanted to ask him the same question. She felt rooted in place. Frozen. Had his head lowered? It had. God, was he going to kiss her? She wanted him to. More than she wanted to breathe.

She tilted her chin up, letting him know she wanted this. Wanted *him.*

"May I?" he whispered, still holding her gaze.

Goose bumps rose on her arms under her long-sleeved shirt and jacket. The way he always asked for permission to touch her was one of the many things that she adored about him. "Yes. Please."

Instantly, his lips were on hers.

They were cold from being outside for so long but quickly warmed. The kiss started out sweet and soft, two pairs of lips caressing, learning each other. But before long, the chaste touch turned into more.

Carlise suddenly felt as if she couldn't get close enough to Riggs. Her hands gripped his jacket tightly, and she held on. One of his hands went to her back to hold her against him, the other to the back of her head. He held her still as he devoured her mouth.

She'd never been kissed like this before. As if he needed her to breathe. Their tongues swirled around each other, he bit and sucked on her bottom lip before diving back into her warmth.

The way he held her against him might have made Carlise uncomfortable if she was with any other man. But this was Riggs. He held her tightly, but she had no doubt if she made the slightest move to back off, he'd let her go in a heartbeat. But she didn't want to back off. She wanted more.

A groan moved from his throat to her mouth, and immediately Carlise's pussy wept. Knowing Riggs was just as turned on made her want him all the more. Their kiss had gone from zero to four hundred and twenty-two in seconds, and as she kissed him more urgently still, Carlise cursed the fact that they were in the middle of the woods instead of inside his cabin.

She wanted this man. It didn't matter that it had been less than a week since she'd met him. It didn't matter that she wasn't the kind of woman who engaged in flings. This felt like anything *but* a fling. She needed this man more than she needed air.

It was Riggs who finally pulled away, but he didn't let go. He kept his hands right where they were and stared into her eyes as they both panted, trying to regain their equilibrium.

"Holy hell," he whispered after a moment.

Carlise grinned. "Yeah."

"I want you, Carlise," he said baldly. "I don't think I've *ever* wanted a woman as badly as I want you. But not for a one-night stand. There's something about you that's gotten under my skin. I can't stop thinking about you. Wondering what I did right in my life to have you appear as if out of nowhere."

"I shouldn't have been on that road," she whispered. "My plan was to stay on Route 2 to Bangor."

"But you didn't. You drove to me. To my mountain. My cabin."

"Yes."

This was an important moment. Carlise could feel it. She wasn't sure what it meant, if things with her and Riggs could ever work out, but she wanted them to. So damn bad.

"We aren't making love today," he said finally.

Carlise frowned as she stared up at him.

"I want to. You have no idea how much. But I want to prove that you're more than a passing fancy. I want you to get to know me. I need you to be sure, because once you let me have you . . . that's it. There's no going back, Carlise. Do you understand?"

She did. As much as she wanted to be with Riggs, a tiny part of her was worried that once they made love, he'd want her gone. Taking time to get to know each other better was the smart thing to do. The adult thing. But it still kind of sucked. Because damn, the man could kiss. And if he could kiss as well as he did, she had no doubt making love with him would rock her world. "Yes."

"Yes what?" he asked.

"We should wait. I don't want to, but it's probably smart."

"And the other? I was serious, Carlise. Once you let me inside your body, you're mine. Just as I'm yours. I need you to understand that."

The thought of this man being hers made longing course through her veins. "Yes."

He stared at her for a beat before taking a long breath in through his nose. "Okay."

"Okay," she echoed. After a minute or two, she smiled. "So, are we gonna stand out here all day or go back to the cabin?"

"I can't move," he admitted with a small frown.

"What? Why not? Are you all right?" Carlise asked in concern.

He huffed out a breath. "I'm fine. I just don't want to let go of you. And for the record, just because we aren't making love doesn't mean you aren't sleeping in my bed, in my arms. That still stands."

Carlise smiled again. "Good. Because your bed is really comfy."

Riggs growled. "That's the only reason you like it?"

He was fun to tease. "Maaaaaybe. I also like the way your sheets smell."

"And?"

"Your pillows are awesome. And I've never met a man with an obsession for blankets like you have."

"And?" he asked again, yanking her against him roughly. She could feel his erection against her belly. Desire shot through her once more.

"And sleeping with a man has never made me feel as safe as when I'm in your arms," she admitted softly.

He smiled gently. "Damn straight. When you're with me, you *are* safe." He took a deep breath, then let his hand fall from the back of her head.

Carlise immediately missed his touch.

But he made it better when he turned and wrapped an arm around her waist, keeping her locked against his side. "Let's get you back and warmed up."

"You were the one who was sick, not me," she reminded him.

"And I don't *want* you to get sick," he retorted. "It's no fun, believe me. Although I did have the best nurse."

Carlise smiled all the way back to the cabin. Things had changed between her and Riggs out at that bunker . . . and she was thrilled. Susie would tell her she was completely crazy and moving way too fast, that she needed to slow the hell down, that she didn't even know the man. But Susie would be wrong.

Riggs treated her better than anyone ever had, and she knew deep in her bones that he was exactly the kind of man he'd shown her so far. Honorable. Good. Protective. Safe.

At some point, she was going to have to deal with the reason she'd left Ohio in the first place, but she was too busy living in her own romance story at the moment. Maybe she'd write a book about a heroine who gets lost in the Maine wilderness and ends up at a mountain man's cabin and lives happily ever after.

Butterflies swam in Carlise's belly. She felt giddy. Excited. Happy.

And it had been a long time since she'd felt any of those emotions. Lately, she'd been filled with apprehension, fear, worry. It was a nice change. A great change.

Her attention was caught by Baxter when he chased some small animal ahead of them as they walked, but he didn't run off. It didn't seem as if he wanted to get more than twenty or so feet away from the humans he'd apparently claimed as his own.

"How does salmon sound for lunch?" Riggs asked. "I've got some in the icebox that I could cook up."

"Sounds good. I could make a green-bean casserole to go with it?" Carlise asked.

"Perfect," Riggs said.

Glancing at him, Carlise saw he was staring at her as he said that word, and somehow, she had a feeling he wasn't talking about the food.

She returned his smile and snuggled into his side. She was the luckiest woman in the world. She'd go through all the crap she'd experienced in her life all over again if it meant ending up right here at Riggs's side.

Chapter Nine

The last three days had been both heaven and hell for Chappy. Heaven because he'd never gotten along with a woman so well. Hell because he wanted her so damn badly, and he was doing his best to be a gentleman. To give them both time to be completely sure before he claimed her.

Carlise was funny and smart. She laughed a lot and made him laugh as well. She was also beautiful, she smelled amazing, and she kissed like she was starving for him. He wished they were in a tropical locale so he could see more of her curvy body, but then again, having her curl into him on the couch under one of his blankets was almost as wonderful.

There was something electric about the steadily building anticipation and sexual tension in the cabin. It was an incredible turn-on. Chappy masturbated every time he showered, although it barely touched the lust he felt coursing through his veins.

Yesterday morning, he'd also heard Carlise moaning quietly in the shower, and it took every ounce of his control to keep from joining her in the bathroom.

When they did finally make love, it was going to change his life. Chappy knew it. Carlise was going to ruin him for any other woman—and he was all in for that.

As much as he enjoyed sitting on the couch and reading while Carlise worked on one of her translations, enjoyed talking with her about nothing and everything, Chappy was a little relieved his friends were coming up to the cabin today. They claimed it was to make sure he was truly all right after being so sick, but he knew they wanted to check out Carlise.

They were his best friends, and he couldn't be upset that they wanted to make sure she was good enough for him. That she wasn't some user or gold digger. He wouldn't have the privacy he needed to promise his friends that Carlise wasn't anything like some of the bitches they'd met during and after their days in the military.

He was actually eager for them to meet her because he knew without a doubt that within minutes of being in her presence, they'd know he was one lucky son of a bitch.

Chappy could tell that Carlise was a little uneasy to meet his friends, though. He'd tried to reassure her that they'd love her, but knew she'd just have to see for herself how down-to-earth JJ, Cal, and Bob were. The plan was for them to try to find her CR-V on their way to the cabin and see if they could dig it out. They'd also grab the suitcase she'd left in the back and bring it up to the cabin.

As for the car itself, the battery could be shot from the cold weather, or there might be damage to the engine from the tree she'd hit. They'd check it out and pass on the info when they arrived. The sun had been out for the last three days, but it was still cold, and the snow hadn't melted at all. The two feet of snow might've been too much for the small SUV to handle, but it didn't matter. If Carlise needed to go to town, he'd take her there in his Jeep.

"What time do you think they'll be here again?" Carlise asked nervously.

"I'm not sure. Probably around lunchtime," he told her. "Bob has a plow on the front of his pickup, but ultimately the condition of the roads will determine when they arrive."

"Okay. I hope Baxter doesn't freak."

"He won't," Chappy reassured her.

"You don't know that."

"I do. He's been so much better around us. He's getting used to us and realizing that not all people are bad. Just yesterday he almost came into the cabin when you left the door open. If nothing else, I think he'll stick around, if only to make sure you're okay."

"He is kind of protective, isn't he?" Carlise asked with a small smile.

"Yup. I about crapped my pants when he barked yesterday when I was tickling you on the couch, and he heard you shrieking through the door. I'm sure he thought I was hurting you."

"You wouldn't hurt me," Carlise said firmly.

He loved that she sounded so sure. "Of course I wouldn't. But Baxter doesn't know that. He'll learn, though."

"Do you think Cal will remember to bring the bag of dog food? I mean, as much as I'm sure Bax is enjoying the human food, it's probably better to wean him off it sooner rather than later."

"He'll remember."

"I can't believe I'm going to meet Callum Redmon. He's famous!"

Chappy chuckled. "Whatever you do, don't bow or call him Your Highness. He hates that."

"Oh my God, I wouldn't do that. That would be . . . weird or something."

"It would."

"But that doesn't mean I'm not thinking it," she said with a small laugh.

"I know I don't need to tell you this, because I trust you, but I'm going to anyway. Please don't stare at his scars. He went through hell when we were POWs, and he got the brunt of the torture from our captors."

"I won't. Scars don't make the man, it's what's inside that I care about. The prettiest men are sometimes the biggest assholes, while the ones who don't fit society's mold of what's masculine or handsome often have the biggest hearts and are the kindest people."

"That's very true. He's just had a lot of crap said about him because of his royal status and the scars. It takes a toll."

"Well, he's safe here," Carlise said. "I'd never do anything intentionally to upset your friends."

"And they won't do anything to upset you," Chappy returned.

"It's . . . we've . . ." She paused. "I think they're going to be concerned about how fast things have moved with us."

"They won't."

"Of course they will. I mean, it *has* been fast, Riggs."

"Does it feel wrong to you?"

"Well, no, but—"

"Then screw what anyone else thinks," he said firmly. But Chappy knew where this was coming from. She had yet to call her best friend or her mom because she was afraid they'd judge her, just as she thought his friends would.

"Yeah."

They were standing in the kitchen, and he cupped her cheek as he urged her to look at him. He loved putting his hands on her. Touching her in any way he could. Her skin was dewy soft, and she was so fragile looking, but he knew she had a spine of steel.

"If Susie tells you that you're making a mistake, will you believe her? Or trust in what you feel building between us?" Chappy hadn't really meant to ask the question, but he was a little concerned about how stressed she seemed over the speed of their relationship. As far as he was concerned, they were perfect together, but if she didn't feel the same way, he'd wait as long as it took for her to realize this was meant to be.

"You don't understand," she whispered, dropping her gaze—and not answering his question.

Chappy's stomach churned. They hadn't talked about what had brought her to Maine in the first place, but it was there between them, like a boulder they'd eventually have to get around. He was trying to be patient, to let her tell him the details when she felt comfortable.

"Then talk to me," he said, hearing the pleading tone of his words.

"I . . . I'm scared."

"Of me?" Chappy asked.

"No! Not of you. Never of you."

"Then what?"

She opened her mouth to respond but stopped when a sound from outside caught their attention.

Mentally cursing his friends' bad timing, Chappy leaned down and kissed Carlise gently. "We'll talk later. But in the meantime, know this: Whatever happened. Whatever you're afraid of . . . we'll figure out *together* how to move past it. A few skeletons in your past aren't going to scare me away, sweetheart."

She gave him a brave smile and nodded.

It would have to do for now. But later, when they were alone, Chappy was determined to hear her story. To let her get it off her chest. Instinctively, he knew they couldn't move forward until they dealt with whatever she was running from.

"Come meet my friends. They're going to love you."

Chappy helped her put on her coat, and they headed out onto the porch. Baxter was in his little den under the firewood but was keeping his eyes on both Carlise and the newcomers.

He was a great dog and an amazing protector. Chappy couldn't be happier with how in tune he was with Carlise.

Cal, Bob, and JJ got out of Bob's Chevy Silverado, which had a huge plow on the front—the only reason they were able to get to his cabin—and Chappy was surprised to see their admin assistant, April, exit the truck as well.

"Hey!" Bob said with a grin as he walked toward the cabin, carrying a large suitcase. JJ hovered near April, making sure she didn't fall in the deep snow, and Cal followed behind.

Before Chappy could respond, Baxter came out of his makeshift doghouse and growled low in his throat as he stood near Carlise.

"Whoa. Okay, not coming any closer," Bob said, stopping where he was at the bottom of the three steps leading up to the porch.

"It's okay, Baxter," Carlise said, immediately going to her knees on the porch near the clearly unsettled dog. "They're friends. They aren't going to hurt you."

"I think he's more worried about them hurting *you*, honey," Chappy told her.

She looked up at him, then back to the dog. "They aren't going to hurt me either," she added.

"Holy crap, that is the skinniest dog I've ever seen," JJ commented.

"Actually, he's gained weight over the last week or so since we first saw him," Chappy told his friends with a shrug. To his surprise, Baxter was close enough to Carlise for her to touch him. Her hand gently touched his neck, and he could see the dog's body shaking.

"I'm not sure that's the best idea," he said warily.

But Carlise ignored his warning. "It's okay. He's just nervous. This is probably the first time he's seen people other than us in a long time. You're okay, right, Bax? These are Chappy's friends. They're just here to visit. They're good people. They won't hurt you."

Her voice was a little singsongy—and Chappy had a flash of what she'd sound like talking to their baby. It was totally nuts, but nevertheless, a longing hit him so intensely, it almost brought him to his knees.

"I'll bring you an extra-large dinner to reward you for being so brave," Carlise went on, oblivious to Chappy's visceral response to her sweet-talking the dog. "Go on, get cuddled back up in your nest. It's still cold out here, and until you put on some more weight, you're gonna feel it more."

To his surprise, Baxter took one more look at the four new humans, as if to give them a nonverbal warning not to hurt his favorite person, then turned and padded back to the space behind the firewood that he'd made his own.

Carlise stood and grinned at his friends. "Hi. Sorry about that. We think he was abused terribly by someone. He doesn't trust easily. That was actually the first time he's let me get close enough to touch him."

Chappy could tell how excited Carlise was, and for a moment, he resented his friends being there, since he couldn't share in her joy in the way he preferred—which would've involved his lips on hers. Then again, if they hadn't arrived, Baxter wouldn't have had a reason to be so protective, and who knows how much longer it would've taken for him to get up the courage to let Carlise pet him.

"You look pretty good for someone who was sick not too long ago," Bob said as he climbed onto the porch and gave Chappy a typical man hug—one armed, with lots of back slapping.

"I had an exceptional nurse," he said, smiling at Carlise. Her cheeks turned pink, as if she wasn't used to anyone giving her compliments.

"I'm Bob," his friend said, holding out a hand to Carlise. She shook it, her hand engulfed in Bob's large one.

"And I'm JJ. This is April," JJ said, shaking Carlise's hand after Bob had stepped back.

"I tried to keep everyone from coming up at the same time and overwhelming you, but they wouldn't listen," April said in an exasperated tone.

"We wanted to check on our friend," Bob protested.

April rolled her eyes, and Carlise bit her lip to keep from laughing out loud.

"I seem to remember a job where Chappy was hit in the head by a flying piece of wood and bleeding like a stuck pig, but none of you felt the need to stop what you were doing to check on him. You just told him to slap some bandages on his head and get back to work."

Chappy chuckled. April wasn't wrong. *She* was the one who'd briefly stopped by his apartment after work to make sure he was all right.

"He's got a hard head," Bob muttered defensively.

"Nothing's gonna get through that large melon of his," JJ agreed.

"He's hardy," Cal added.

Carlise giggled.

April rolled her eyes again.

"Do you guys want to come in?"

Everyone nodded, and Chappy held his door open for his friends as they all filed inside. Cal, still bringing up the rear, stopped before he entered and asked quietly, "You really all right, mate?"

Chappy nodded. "Yeah. I feel fine. Was a little weak until my fever broke, but I'm good."

Cal nodded. "And it seems *she's* good for you."

"What?"

"She's good for you," Cal repeated. "You look relaxed. Your eyes aren't constantly on the move, looking for trouble, waiting for someone to leap out from behind a tree."

He was right but wrong at the same time. When they went for their walk, Chappy had been very aware of where they were and the sounds around them, but it was to protect Carlise. Not because he was afraid there were hidden IEDs beneath the snow or rogue terrorists hiding in the trees.

Cal slapped him on the back, not giving him a chance to respond, and entered the house, carrying a huge bag of dog food.

Chappy looked back at Baxter and said, "Good boy." Then he went inside and shut the door.

Bob was putting another log on the fire, Cal was headed for the bathroom, and JJ was standing near the couch, where April and Carlise were sitting and talking as if they were long-lost friends rather than two women who'd just met minutes ago.

It was a cozy scene. With four extra people in his small cabin, it should've felt packed. Almost claustrophobic. But having his friends come up to make sure he was all right, and to get a read on the woman who'd appeared out of nowhere, filled him with gratitude.

"You guys hungry?" he asked the room in general.

"Naw, we're good."

"Nope."

"No, thank you."

"I could eat something."

That last comment came from JJ. Before Chappy could head into the kitchen to see what he could offer his friend, April spoke.

"Jack, you just ate before we came up here. You can't be hungry already."

"I'm a growing boy," he told April with a smirk.

She turned to Carlise. "You would be shocked at how much of the company's budget goes toward food. We have a packed fridge at the office, as well as very full cabinets. I swear they're *always* eating."

Carlise smiled at her. "I'm sure they burn a lot of calories chopping down trees and stuff."

April nodded. "True, but still."

"Carlise could make you a PB&J. She got really good at that while I was sick," Chappy said with a chuckle. "I pretty much passed out as soon as we got back to the cabin after I found her wandering around on the road. I didn't get a chance to explain anything about the place. She didn't know the stove ran on gas, and of course the generator wasn't on, so there wasn't any electricity."

"Oh no! You ate peanut butter and jelly for three days?" April asked.

"Yeah. But it wasn't awful. I mean, I was more worried about Riggs than eating much."

"Riggs. Man, I haven't heard anyone call you that in years," Cal said as he reentered the room.

"Right?"

"It's what he told me his name was before he passed out," Carlise said a little defensively. "It's hard to use another name after calling him Riggs in my head for three days while he was out of it."

"It's more than fine," Chappy said, not wanting her to think he didn't like his given name coming from her lips. "So . . . I'm assuming by the suitcase Bob brought in, you guys found her car," he said, wanting to take the attention off Carlise.

She gave him a relieved smile.

"Yup. Stopped on our way up. It's buried, man," Bob said. He was leaning against the wall of the cabin, now that he'd built the fire to his satisfaction.

"I figured," Chappy sighed.

"Yeah, we were able to open the back hatch to get into the cargo area, but it looks like she went straight where the road has that almost-ninety-degree bend. The bumper's covered, and the snow's up over the tires," Cal added. "From what we could see, there's a pretty good dent in the front where she hit the tree. Won't know exactly what the damage is until the snow melts a bit."

"We can dig it out, but it'll take some work," JJ agreed. "The weather's supposed to warm up this coming week. I'm thinking if we give it a bit of time, let the sun do its thing, it'll be easier to get free and see what we're working with."

Chappy looked at Carlise. His first reaction was to protest them digging out her car at all. But it wasn't as if she could stay here forever . . . could she?

They stared at each other for a long moment before she turned her attention to Bob. "Thank you for grabbing my suitcase. I appreciate it. And I'm okay with waiting for a little longer," she said slowly. "I just don't want to outstay my welcome."

"You can stay as long as you want," Chappy blurted.

She gave him another small smile. It felt as if they were the only two people in the room.

"You need to get ahold of someone? Let them know where you are? A boss? Family? Boyfriend? Husband?" Bob asked.

Anger rose instantly at his friend's insinuation. Chappy glared at him.

"I should probably call my friend soon, and my mom. But there's no one else. I have my own business that I can do remotely, so I don't need to worry about that," Carlise said calmly.

"Really? Can I ask what you do? Or is that being too nosy?" April asked.

"It's not. I'm a translator. I take French books and turn them into English ones, basically, so authors and publishers can sell them here."

"That's so cool!"

Bob wandered toward him, but Chappy kept his gaze on Carlise. She seemed comfortable enough, and he was glad April had accompanied his friends. He had a feeling her presence was making this meeting easier. JJ and Cal seemed relaxed, but he knew without a doubt they were listening to—and analyzing—every word Carlise said.

In any other circumstance, he'd be pleased they had his back. But at the moment, especially after Bob's question, he was a little annoyed that they didn't fully trust his judgment.

"I had to ask," Bob muttered when he approached Chappy.

"That wasn't cool," he told him. "Do you seriously think I wouldn't already know whether she was single or not?"

But Bob didn't look the least bit chagrined. "Sorry," he said, not really sounding all that contrite. "You obviously like her."

"I do," Chappy agreed without hesitation.

"Is it because she took care of you? Because she's trapped here? Do you feel an obligation to her until she can deal with her car? Because we have enough room in the truck to take her to Newton, leave you to the peace and quiet we all know you need now and then."

"No!" he exclaimed.

At his outburst, Carlise turned to look at him with a concerned expression. He gave her a tight smile and a chin lift to let her know all was well. She nodded slightly, then turned her attention back to the woman sitting next to her.

"That, however, *was* cool," Bob observed, mimicking Chappy's earlier words.

"What?"

"You had a whole conversation without saying a word."

They had. Chappy shrugged. "I'll be honest, I may not understand the connection we have, but it's real. It's not because she's trapped here or anything. It's because of who she is. She was thrown into an uncomfortable situation. She was responsible for taking care of a stranger right after she herself had just been through something harrowing. And she didn't even hesitate. She did what she needed to do, without complaint. She didn't rifle through my things, didn't look for valuables to stuff into her bag. When she wasn't caring for me or eating PB&J, she read. Or napped. Or simply sat on the couch and stared at the fire. Pretty much everything I do when I'm here by myself."

"You tell her about the cameras?" Bob asked quietly.

Chappy winced. "No."

"You had sex yet?"

Chappy did his best not to get pissed at his friend all over again.

Bob held up his hands. "I'm just asking because if you haven't told her about the cameras and you two were intimate, she's not going to be happy to learn that it's been caught on video. That *definitely* wouldn't be cool, man. Not at all."

Crap. Chappy hadn't even thought about that. The cameras were there for his peace of mind. His eyes only. But *no* woman would be happy to hear that she'd been recorded in bed without her knowledge. "I'll tell her before we go there."

Bob nodded. "For what it's worth . . . I like her. I don't know her, of course, but just seeing her with the mutt outside and how she keeps one eye on you even while talking with April . . . I like that for you, Chappy."

He liked it for him too. "Thanks."

Cal wandered over to join them. "I know JJ told you about the weather warming up . . . that means the risk of slides is going to increase," he warned.

"I know," Chappy said with a nod. "We'll stick close to the cabin until the risk has passed."

"You're cutting it a bit close for comfort," Cal said. "You'd be safer if you came back down to Newton."

Chappy knew that. But he wasn't ready. It was hard enough to share Carlise with his friends for a short visit. He was enjoying being alone with her. He didn't want to think about taking her to town just yet. He was being selfish, but for once, he didn't care. "We'll be okay here. The cabin's not in the danger zone from any slides on the higher grades of the mountain."

"If nothing else, a slide could mean they're trapped here even longer," Bob joked.

Chappy's lips quirked upward.

"And he seems perfectly okay with that," Cal said. "Just be careful," he said, sobering.

"I will."

"With the weather *and* with her," Cal warned.

"Not you too," Chappy said with a sigh.

"What do you really know about her? About her family? Her background? Her financial situation? She could be seeing you as a convenient way out of some problem she has."

Chappy didn't like that his friends were so cynical. And distrusting. But those feelings warred with the satisfaction he felt that they gave a shit. And he couldn't deny, he'd have wondered all the same things just a week ago, had his friends been in his shoes.

"She *is* hiding something," he finally admitted.

Bob's and Cal's brows rose in unison at his admission. He went on before they could comment.

"She's mentioned an abusive ex. She hasn't told me how she ended up on my road, except to say she got lost. She was headed for Bangor from Cleveland. She's close with her mom and her best friend, but other than that, I don't think she has many people she can depend on. I'm trying not to rush her. She'll tell me more as we get to know each other. I'm not worried about how she ended up here, though. She doesn't have a dishonest bone in her body, guys. I'm sure of it."

"She on the run?" Cal asked.

"Did her ex hurt her?" Bob growled.

This. *This* was why he put up with his friends' nosiness and over-protectiveness. They hated to hear about anyone being abused or hurt as much as he did.

"I'm not completely sure. She's not the kind of person to quit when life gets hard. But in this case, I think she's scared of something . . . or *someone*."

"You need anything, you let us know," Cal said in a low tone.

"Yeah, we might be washed-up military bums, but we're more than capable of protecting one of our own," Bob agreed.

Warmth spread through Chappy. These men were his best friends, like brothers. They'd fought together and saved each other's lives more times than he could count. Their willingness to go to bat for Carlise, a woman they didn't even know, meant the world to him.

"Thanks," he told them. "When I find out more, and with her permission, I'll share, and we can figure out a game plan, if that turns out to be necessary."

Both Bob and Cal nodded.

"You guys look serious over there. Everything okay?" Carlise asked nervously from her seat on the couch.

"We're good," Chappy said immediately, wanting to reassure her.

"Yeah, we're just talking about which one of us is going to Old Man Smith's house tomorrow."

"Old Man Smith?" Carlise asked.

"He's not that old," April said with a sigh. "And he's not that bad."

"Last time I was there, he insisted I stay for lunch and served some sort of meat that he'd probably had in his freezer for twenty-five years," JJ said. "He also insisted there are people watching him, and that someone's out to get him because he was a government spy forty years ago."

"Was he?" Carlise asked with wide eyes.

"No," JJ said with an amused shake of his head.

"He's lonely," April insisted. "And it's no big deal for you to sit with him for an hour or so after you reassure him the trees in his yard aren't going to fall on the house."

Looking chastised, JJ nodded.

"Now that we've seen for ourselves that Chappy isn't at death's door, I need to get back to Newton," Bob announced suddenly.

"Yeah, there's a show on the telly I've been meaning to watch," Cal agreed.

"And since Chappy didn't feed me, and I'm starving, we might as well go," JJ added.

Chappy didn't argue with his friends. Didn't try to get them to stay longer. In fact, he'd owe Bob big time for being the first to suggest they leave. He might not fully understand or trust what was going on between Chappy and Carlise, but Bob trusted him enough to get out of his hair and let him do his thing.

"Oh, but I'm sure we could make something for everyone," Carlise protested as she stood.

"Nope, we wouldn't want to put you guys out. Besides, we know Chappy likes his solitude. It's why he comes up here, to hide out and be alone," Bob said.

Chappy saw Carlise frown, and he could've kicked his friend for not knowing when to shut up. It was obvious she was now worrying about intruding—again.

"Maybe I should—"

"I'm going to write down my number for you," April interrupted. "I'll give you the number to Jack's Lumber, as well. The service up here is nonexistent, but I'm sure you could use Chappy's satellite phone. You need anything, just give me a yell. I'll get one of the guys to bring it to you. Or if you just want to chat . . . you know, hear a friendly female voice . . . I'm just a phone call away."

"Oh . . . thanks," Carlise said. "I'll give you mine too."

Thankful to April for the distraction, Chappy sighed as the guys went to grab their coats off the rack by the door. He hovered behind April and Carlise as they exchanged info. He wasn't surprised when Carlise leaned in and hugged the other woman. April looked surprised for a moment, but then a smile took over her face.

Chappy liked April, always had. She was the glue that held their business together, and he usually thought of her as one of the guys. But now he realized he didn't know all that much about the woman. Anything about her family, how she spent her free time, if she had friends.

He'd always just assumed she had people to hang out with when she wasn't at the office. But seeing how quickly she and Carlise had clicked, and her obvious pleasure over a simple hug, he wondered if he'd assumed incorrectly.

But he didn't have time to do much more than smile at her before she was striding out the front door behind the guys. JJ was holding the door open, standing between them and Baxter. The dog seemed content to stay huddled in his nest, keeping his eyes on all the strangers.

At one point, April slipped on the snow and would've fallen on her ass, but JJ was close enough to catch her. He pulled her close, holding her against his side until she had her feet under her again.

As he observed his friend holding April, Chappy had the sudden realization that JJ was looking at their assistant the way Chappy probably looked at Carlise. As if she were the sun and the moon at the same time.

As he watched, JJ's face cleared of all expression, and he stepped away from April. "You good?"

She blushed but nodded. "I'm clumsy. I could trip over air."

JJ didn't comment, but Chappy noticed that he stayed close to April as they continued toward the truck.

He stood on the porch as the group got into the truck. Everyone rolled down their windows as they prepared to pull away. The sun was out, but it wasn't doing much to cut the chill in the air. The upcoming week would bring warmer weather, but for now, it was still quite cold.

Without thought, Chappy moved behind Carlise and wrapped his arms around her, pulling her against his chest to keep her warm.

"Glad you aren't dead," Bob called out.

April shook her head and smacked him on the arm. "That was rude," she scolded loudly from the back seat.

Bob merely grinned, not sorry in the least for his macabre humor.

"Call if you need anything," JJ ordered.

"We'll be in touch if we hear anything about the avalanche warnings," Cal added.

Chappy felt Carlise stiffen against him, and he frowned at his friend.

"But I'm sure it'll be fine," Cal added belatedly, prompted by Chappy's unhappy look.

"If you need help with her car, let us know," JJ told them. "We'll come back up."

"Thanks!" Chappy called.

He and Carlise watched as Bob pulled his truck around and they made their way back toward the road. The big plow pushing snow out of the way as they went made it all the more obvious how much they'd gotten in the storm. Even with a plow, it had to be difficult making it to his cabin, though Chappy wasn't too surprised. His friends were stubborn as hell, and there was no way they were letting a bit of snow get in the way of having his back.

"Come on, let's get you inside," Chappy said, turning Carlise toward the door.

To his surprise, Baxter had come out from his spot against the house and was sitting next to them. So close he could reach out and almost touch the dog's head.

"Oh! Hi, Baxter. You want to come inside too?" Carlise asked in the same singsong voice she'd used earlier. "It's nice and warm in there. I'll make you a comfy bed next to the fire. You'll love it. I promise."

She opened the door—and to Chappy's shock, Baxter walked in as if he'd spent his entire life as a house dog.

"Riggs! Look! He's inside!" Carlise breathed.

"I see, sweetheart."

"I'm so . . ." She trailed off, then quickly turned to him and buried her face in his chest.

Chappy got them both inside and the door shut, then wrapped his arms around her and let her cry against him.

She got herself under control in minutes, raising her head to look at him with bloodshot eyes. "I'm so happy," she whispered.

He chuckled. "Forgive me for saying so, but you don't look it."

She gave him a lopsided smile. "I am." She wiped her eyes with her hands, then rested them on his chest and leaned into him. "Have you ever been so happy that it freaks you out because you're waiting for things to go to hell again?"

Chappy frowned and tightened his arms around her. "Yeah."

She nodded. "I just . . . You. Baxter. My job . . . Everything's so perfect right now. And I'm scared to death that it's all going to disappear in a puff of smoke. Like maybe I'm dreaming or something. That I'll wake up and it'll all be gone. Different."

"You aren't dreaming. And I'm not going anywhere. Baxter's inside now, and I have a feeling he's not gonna want to sleep outside again anytime soon. You're good, sweetheart."

"The past always has a way of sneaking up on you when you least expect it," she muttered.

Chappy held his breath, hoping she was on the verge of opening up to him.

But instead, she sighed. "I'm being morose. I'm good," she said. "I'm not usually so emotional."

He mentally echoed her sigh. She was right there. Whatever was bothering her was on the tip of her tongue. He would've pushed, but since Baxter coming inside was a happy, momentous thing, he didn't want to bring the mood down. "You can be as emotional as you want. I can handle it. I can handle *anything* you want to tell me. You're safe with me. Period."

She smiled and brought a hand up to his cheek. "I know."

"Do you?" he couldn't help but ask.

She nodded immediately.

"Good. Because it's true. Are you really okay with staying up here with me for another week or so until we can get your car out?"

"Are *you* all right with me being here? You've told me you like your solitude, and your friend confirmed it. I really *don't* want to intrude."

Chappy mentally swore. She'd obviously taken Bob's words to heart. "You aren't intruding. While I do like my solitude, I've also been lonely. Since you've been here, I haven't felt that way in the least."

"Me either."

"Good. It's settled. You can stay as long as you want. How about we get Baxter comfortable and decide what we want to make for lunch? I'm starving."

She chuckled. "You and JJ both."

"Yup. You haven't seen that guy eat, though. He would've eaten us out of house and home."

Carlise giggled, and the sound wrapped around his heart and wouldn't let go. He hadn't lied, he could handle her being emotional, but he much preferred her laughter to her tears. Even if they were happy ones.

Later, with Baxter snuggled into a mound of blankets in front of the fireplace, his belly full, Chappy sat on the couch with his arm around Carlise. She'd snuggled into him and opened a paperback book from his shelf. They'd been reading like that, cuddled up together under another fluffy blanket, for at least an hour.

It was taking all of Chappy's self-control not to rip the book out of her hands and throw her down on the cushions to have his wicked way with her. But Bob had been right—he needed to tell her about the cameras.

"I have to tell you something," Chappy blurted.

She closed her book and looked up at him. "It sounds serious," she said, her brow furrowed.

"It's not. I mean, I don't think it's a big deal . . . but you might."

"What is it?"

"I have cameras," he said bluntly. "For protection."

Carlise nodded. "That's probably smart. This cabin isn't exactly on the beaten path, and if someone wanted to break in, it's not as if any neighbors would see and call the police."

"Exactly. There's nothing here that I'd care too much about if it was stolen. When I'm not here, I don't leave any firearms or anything else that could be used to hurt someone else. But I don't like the thought of someone in my space. This cabin is a refuge for me, and if someone were to break in, I would want to know about it."

"I can understand that."

"The thing is . . . the cameras aren't just outside. They're in here too." Chappy held his breath as he waited for Carlise to freak out. He could see her processing what he'd just said.

She bit her lip.

"They aren't connected to any service or anything, just an app on my phone. I'm the only one who can access them. I've set up a ton of security protocols, so the likelihood of someone hacking in and watching the footage is slim to none. The app holds recordings for thirty days before they're deleted." He was speaking fast, but he wanted her to know that he wasn't hoarding hundreds of hours of videos or anything.

"Bob said I needed to tell you. That I'd be a dick if I didn't. So I'm letting you know."

She lifted her chin at that. "You aren't a dick," she said.

Chappy huffed out a breath. "That's all you have to say?" he asked. "I tell you that your every move for the last week, except when you were in the bathroom, is on video and you're more concerned about my friend calling me names?"

"Well . . . first, I'm not that surprised about the cameras. You did tell me that you're protective. I assumed that meant protective about your stuff as well as your friends. If I'm completely honest, I'm not thrilled about being on film. But I trust you, Riggs. If you say that no one will see it but you, I believe you."

Chappy could only stare at her for a long moment. How the hell had he gotten so lucky?

"Where are they?" she asked, looking around the room.

"One's there," he said, pointing to the corner across from them. "And the other's in the corner of the kitchen, pointing into the room."

She turned to meet his gaze once more. "Did you watch the ones from when you were sick?"

He wouldn't lie to her, though he didn't go into detail about how he was able to download them in order to watch. "I scanned through them. But it was more to make sure I didn't hurt you in any way than to spy on you."

"I didn't take anything. Or look through your stuff."

"I know." They stared at each other for a long moment. "I'll turn them off for the rest of the time you're here," he told her, surprising himself with the offer.

She studied him for a moment, then said, "You have them for a reason. To make you feel safe. I'm assuming your need for them is related to what happened to you."

As usual, her insight was dead on. He shrugged. "Being held captive took away my trust in humankind for a long time. I didn't trust *anyone*. The other drivers on the road, people I passed on the street, the hikers along the AT. It ate at me. I wondered who might be out to get me, what they'd take from me. Our captors stole the security I'd always took for granted. I hate them for that," he admitted quietly.

"Don't turn them off," she said firmly.

"What?"

"Leave them on. I'd never want to do anything to make you feel like you did when you were a POW."

"It's not that I don't trust you—" he began, but she put her hand over his mouth and shook her head.

"I know. If you need them to feel comfortable here in your safe place, then they stay on."

Chappy pulled her hand off his mouth and kissed the palm. "I watched us. Sleeping," he clarified. "You climbing onto the bed when I was sick . . . grabbing you and not letting go. You didn't freak out, didn't try to get away. You just talked me down. And when you fell asleep, I couldn't take my eyes away from the sight of you in my arms."

Carlise swallowed hard.

"If I don't turn those cameras off . . . when we make love, it'll be on film," he reminded her. "But no one—and I mean *no one*—will ever see it. That's between us. I'm not sharing what you give to me with anyone else. If that makes you uncomfortable even a little, I'll turn them off before we go to bed and turn them back on in the morning."

"Can I see them?"

"What? The videos?"

"Yeah. Of us sleeping. When you were sick."

"Of course. They won't be deleted for another few weeks or so." When she didn't respond, he asked, "Oh, you mean now?"

"If that's okay?"

Chappy nodded. His heart was in his throat. She'd said she didn't mind the cameras, but that might change once she saw the videos.

He disentangled himself from her and got out from under the blanket, then went to the kitchen where his cell phone was sitting on the counter. He'd charged it earlier, when the generator was running. The phone itself didn't work for calls, but the satellite internet, when it was working properly, had enough power to run the apps. And since the videos had downloaded onto the hard drive when he'd turned on the generator that first time, they could be viewed.

He went back to the couch and sat next to her. Chappy was relieved when she cuddled into him once again. He pulled up the app on the phone and rewound to when she'd first arrived.

He handed the phone to her and showed her how to scrub through the videos. He watched over her shoulder as she scanned the footage.

Ten full minutes went by before she turned off the phone, reached over him, and placed it on the small table next to the couch.

Then she shocked the shit out of him by straddling his lap. The blanket fell off her shoulders, but Chappy barely noticed. His hands went to her waist as he stared into her eyes.

"Can we save clips from the videos?" she asked.

Chappy frowned and nodded. "Yeah."

"Good. When you download today's footage, I want the one of Baxter walking into the cabin for the first time today. And maybe one of you cooking, because you're hot when you're holding a spatula, Riggs Chapman," she teased.

For the first time since he'd brought up the cameras, Chappy's muscles fully relaxed. He hadn't realized how tense he'd been. "You aren't freaked out by the cameras?" he asked.

She shrugged. "I didn't do anything I'm ashamed of. And it's not like you've got one in the bathroom or anything . . . because that would've been a completely different thing. I trust you, Riggs. But . . . maybe you could delete the videos of us making love before the thirty days are up?" she asked tentatively.

"They'll be gone as soon as I can download the footage," he vowed.

She smiled then. A sexy smile that made his cock twitch in his pants. "Well . . . maybe not immediately. I've never been one to watch porn, but this might be a good time to start. I mean, maybe watching *us* together won't be so bad." This time, her smile was shy.

Chappy's brain felt as if it was going to explode. "Damn, woman," he sighed.

"Too weird?" she asked with a grimace.

"No! You're perfect."

She shook her head. "I'm not. I have flaws, Riggs. Don't put me on some pedestal."

"Fine. Then you're perfect for *me*," he told her.

The frown remained on her face. Chappy grasped the back of her neck and encouraged her to lean against him. She collapsed onto his chest, her arms between them, curled up as she let him take her body weight.

"Talk to me," he whispered. "There's nothing you can tell me that will make me change my mind about having you here. About making love to you. About *anything*."

"I will. But not tonight. Is that okay? Tonight, I just want to sit here and try to pretend that everything in my life is happy and fine."

"Okay, sweetheart," Chappy said. He was disappointed, but if she needed more time, he'd give it to her. Because she'd finally confirmed that there *was* something going on in her life that wasn't good. And she'd said she'd share with him. He just needed to be patient.

"Thank you. Riggs?"

"Yeah, honey?"

"Please don't hurt me. I don't think I could handle it. Not after everything else."

"I won't. Not physically, mentally, *or* emotionally. I promise."

She sighed, then shifted so she was even closer. Her arms came out from between them, and she pushed one behind his back. The other went to the nape of his neck, where she caressed the hair there.

Goose bumps rose on his arms at her touch. This woman could break him, but he somehow knew she wouldn't. She'd treat him with care, just as he'd treat her. He'd slay all her dragons, simply for the right to end each day exactly like this. With her in his arms, warm and trusting.

Clothes went flying across the room as they were flung out of dresser drawers. Next, the dresses and shirts hanging in Carlise's closet were ripped off their hangers.

"Where are you, bitch? Where *are* you?"

Each word was accompanied by the thrust of a knife as Carlise's clothes and bedding were slashed over and over again in frustration and rage.

Every nook and cranny in the apartment had been searched. All the mail opened, the papers in Carlise's desk rifled through . . . and yet there was still no sign of where the cunt had gone! She'd truly up and disappeared without a trace.

Panting with exertion, the intruder stood in the middle of Carlise's bedroom and stared at the dozens of ripped shirts and panties, broken pictures and knickknacks, mind racing to figure out what to do next. How to figure out where she might have gone.

This was unacceptable! Carlise obviously assumed leaving would make everything go away, but she was wrong. *Dead* wrong. When her location was discovered, she'd pay for vanishing without a word. Pay for getting that fucking restraining order. Pay for *everything*!

Then—a thought occurred.

Her mother.

Of course! She was the key.

Carlise *had* to have told her mom where she was going or, at the very least, called her by now. Her mother would know exactly where she went. And she'd spill the beans, especially if a little . . . *persuasion* was used to coax out the information. The old loser was weak. Just like her daughter.

The intruder smirked and headed for the front door of the apartment, ignoring all the destruction left behind.

"I'm gonna find you, bitch. And when I do, you'll regret all the lies . . . all the pain you've caused. Mark my damn words."

Chapter Ten

Thirty-six hours had passed since Riggs's admission about the cameras, and Carlise was more than surprised that she wasn't bothered by knowing he was taping every single thing they did or said inside the cabin.

If it had been Tommy, she would've completely freaked. It would've felt like a huge invasion of privacy, and she wouldn't have been able to trust he'd keep the footage to himself. But since she and Riggs were together every minute of every day, both being filmed at all times—not to mention the important fact that she trusted him in a way she could never trust her ex—she couldn't bring herself to care.

Another surprise in the last day and a half—Baxter had taken to being an inside dog super easily. It confirmed Carlise's thought that he'd once been someone's pet. He hadn't had an accident in the house and even went to the door and scratched at it, letting her and Riggs know he wanted to go outside. He didn't get close enough to be petted, preferring his spot near the fire in his blankets, but Carlise was confident that with time, he'd relax even more. He kept his gaze on them no matter where they went in the cabin, always on alert.

Carlise and Riggs had slept together almost every night since she'd arrived, and she had never felt safer or more content. When she and Tommy slept together, she was always tense. On alert, and therefore never fully able to rest.

She should've left him long before she did. She'd stayed partly because she was ashamed that she'd somehow found herself in the kind of relationship she swore she'd never get into after growing up in an abusive household. But also because she'd made excuses for him for so long. He worked too hard, he was stressed out, was worried about providing for her . . .

She'd kept what was happening from Susie and especially from her mom, not wanting them to worry. But when Tommy had finally gone from merely cruel or threatening to shoving her so hard she'd hit that counter and hurt herself, she'd finally opened her eyes.

Having no inkling of Carlise's unhappiness, both her mom and Susie had asked why she'd suddenly decided to leave him. When she'd fessed up, it prompted Susie to wonder if the abuse was a one-time thing . . . if maybe Carlise should give him another chance. Not surprising, since he excelled at charming anyone who didn't know him well. From the outside looking in, Tommy was a catch, and their relationship was great. Carlise knew that was all on her.

She didn't bother trying to explain that men like Tommy didn't change, that their apologies were hollow, and it wouldn't be long before he fell into a pattern of beatings and false regret. Carlise knew Susie would never fully understand. She'd never been in an abusive relationship. Hadn't grown up wondering what kind of mood her dad would be in when he got home. If he'd be happy, or if he'd immediately start swinging his fists, not caring who he hurt.

Her mom understood all too well, of course.

Her best friend had been more supportive after Carlise started receiving threats. She'd been outraged, in fact . . . even as she'd tentatively questioned whether it could be someone other than Tommy. And she had a point. Slashing tires, painting her door, leaving notes . . . none of that was really his style. He was more the in-your-face, confrontational type. The type who'd come right up to her door and ring the bell and tell her in person that she was a bitch.

But if it wasn't Tommy harassing her, she had no idea who else it could be. She couldn't think of anyone who hated her enough to want to make her life as miserable as it had been before she'd left Cleveland.

There was that woman at the grocery store who'd gone over-the-top crazy when Carlise had taken the last pint of Thin Mint ice cream, following her to the register, then all the way out to her car, screeching the entire time. Despite the woman's irrational display, Carlise couldn't imagine anyone stalking her over ice cream.

Maybe it was the author who'd claimed her translation was terrible. It wasn't; the woman just didn't want to pay for the work Carlise had done.

The possibility that it could be her dad was always in the back of her mind. He'd seemed relieved enough to wash his hands of both his wife and daughter . . . but then again, maybe when he'd learned how well they were both doing, his ego couldn't handle it. And Carlise *had* been the one who'd continually begged her mom to leave the man.

"What time is it?" Riggs mumbled from next to her.

It was still dark outside. She was snuggled against Riggs the same way she went to sleep every night. One of her legs between his, her head on his chest, her arm across his body, and holding him almost as tightly as he held her. She wore one of his T-shirts and a pair of panties, but the shirt had ridden up in the night.

One of his hands rested on her lower back, fingers brushing against the elastic of her underwear. The other was on the arm over his chest, as if making sure she didn't move from his side.

"Not time to get up yet," she whispered back.

"Can't sleep?" he asked.

Carlise shook her head. "I'm thinking."

"About what?"

This was it. She needed to tell him about her stalker. About the reason she'd fled Cleveland, and why she'd ended up in his cabin in the middle of a freaking snowstorm. He deserved to know that if they stayed together, it was possible he might be in danger. That someone might find this cabin and defile it in some way. Ransack it, burn it to the ground.

The latter thought had her shivering against him.

"Carlise? What's wrong? Talk to me."

"I have a stalker," she blurted.

The relief that swept through her body at the quick admission was immense. She hadn't realized just how much it had been weighing on her to keep that secret.

To her surprise, he didn't tense under her. "Do you know who it is?" he asked.

She lifted her head and tried to see his face in the dark. "You aren't upset?"

"Oh, I'm pissed," he said calmly. "But I need information in order to fix it. And the last thing you need right now is me leaping up and ranting and raving and pacing the room. Baxter wouldn't like that either. I'm just thrilled that you're finally trusting me enough to tell me what brought you here. So I'm staying calm, trying to gather intel, so I can pass it on to JJ and the others, and we can end the threat to you. And so we can get on with our lives."

That was the sweetest, most loving thing anyone had ever said to her. Which was probably messed up, but whatever.

"I'm pretty sure it's my ex . . . He wasn't happy when I broke up with him. And he was even madder the next day, after he discovered I'd packed up all the clothes and stuff I'd brought to his house while he was at work. He begged me to give him another chance. Followed me everywhere I went—even during his workday. Came to my apartment, called me dozens of times a day for weeks. He also texted me over and over. I never answered the phone or the door.

"At first, his voice mails and texts were all sweet and apologetic. Then they turned threatening, mixed in with random pleas. After a while, he stopped trying to contact me altogether, and I thought he'd finally given up. But . . . it wasn't too long after that when the weird stuff started happening."

"Weird stuff?" he asked.

Carlise nodded and took a deep breath. "Creepy things. Notes left on my car, both at my apartment complex and when I was out doing random errands. My tires were slashed. The word 'Bitch' was painted on my door. Emails and texts from unknown numbers and accounts."

"What'd they say?"

"Nothing good," Carlise said with a wrinkle of her nose.

When Riggs didn't comment, she sighed. "Whoever it was said I was an idiot. A stupid bitch. A horrible human being. That I didn't know how good my life was. That kind of thing."

"Did you go to the cops?" Riggs asked.

Carlise could tell he was upset, but his thumb brushed back and forth on her arm soothingly. It meant a lot that he wasn't leaping up and being over-the-top pissed about the situation. "Yes, and I got a protection order, based on all the calls and texts from his phone. But there wasn't much else they could do, since I can't prove who's leaving the notes or who vandalized my car or door. I don't have any cameras at my apartment.

"They told me I could probably hire someone to see if the emails or texts can be traced, but honestly, while I make enough money to live on, I don't have endless funds to hire specialists. It seemed easier to just get out of town for a while and hope it blows over rather than pay someone to *maybe* track down whoever's harassing me."

Riggs was silent for a long while. Carlise had a feeling he didn't agree with her decision, but she appreciated him not harassing her about it.

"Who else could it be, other than your ex?" he finally asked.

She told him about the author who wasn't happy with her work. About the woman in the grocery store. She named every single person she might have upset even mildly in the weeks before the harassment started.

Riggs shook his head, and Carlise leaned up to look at him. "What?"

"Carlise, people don't do the sort of things you've endured because you wouldn't let them into your lane in a construction zone. Or because you took the last tub of ice cream. Or because you disagreed with them in a social media post."

"People are crazy, Riggs," she said softly. "I swear, everyone's skin has gotten a lot thinner over the last decade or so. The smallest thing can send someone off the deep end."

"I realize that," he said calmly, "but I still don't think those things would make someone so mad they'd track down where you live and slash your tires. Not to mention send you all those emails and texts."

"Yeah," she agreed with a sigh as she put her head back down on his chest. "The only other person I can think of is my dad."

Riggs stilled. "Your dad knows where you live? When was the last time you had any interaction with him?"

"Yes, and about four months ago. He came to Cleveland wanting to see my mom. She had moved to Ohio at my urging. I missed her, and she's been doing really well there. Anyway . . . my dad calls every so often. Tries to get Mom to go back to him. She always says no, but when he came to Cleveland several months ago, she actually agreed to have lunch.

"I was *so* upset when she told me after the fact. I made her promise to tell me if and when he contacted her again. Surprisingly, she did. He returned to Cleveland just a couple of months later. I begged her to let me meet with him instead, and she agreed."

"Please tell me you didn't go meet this abusive asshole by yourself," Riggs growled.

"No way!" Carlise said fervently. "I asked Tommy to go with me, but he said he was busy. So I called Susie, and she went. Nothing happened," she said soothingly, bringing her hand up to the side of Riggs's neck and running her thumb over his jaw. "I told him in no uncertain terms that Mom was done with him. That we were lucky to no longer have him in our lives.

"He tried to tell me that he'd changed, but I knew better. He's always going to be an asshole. He wasn't thrilled when I wouldn't back down. His jaw started ticcing, just like it used to right before he lashed out at Mom or me. But since we were in a public place, he couldn't do anything. He simply got up and left."

"That's not good," Riggs said.

"I know. The tire thing is something I could totally see him doing, but I don't know how he would've gotten my email or phone number. It's not like I gave them to him."

"That kind of info isn't hard to find," Riggs told her. "Have you had any messages since you've been here?"

"Honestly?"

"Of course."

"I'm scared to turn my phone on. I know I should. I need to call my mom and Susie . . . but I just don't want to see if being gone has made him back off or pissed him off more," Carlise admitted.

"You want me to do it? To turn it on the first time? I mean, I won't delete anything that might have come in because we'll need the messages for proof of the harassment for the police, but just hearing all those dings and vibrations when you first turn your phone on can be stressful."

Carlise moved without thought. She rolled until she was lying on top of him. They were plastered together from hips to chest. She propped herself up slightly and looked down at his handsome face. His hands shifted to her hips to hold her steady. "You'd do that for me?"

"I'd do anything for you, Carlise. Haven't you figured that out yet?"

"I'm starting to. This is . . . I haven't ever had someone who's been as considerate as you have, Riggs. I don't know what to do with it."

"You don't have to do anything. Except go with it and accept it as your due."

"I want to thank you."

"For what?" he asked.

"For not freaking out. For not leaping out of bed and stomping around the room. Anger scares me. I know why; it doesn't take a rocket scientist to figure out that my father's actions when I was a kid still affect me even today. And being with Tommy didn't help. Even when I know someone's anger isn't directed at me, I still get nervous. So I appreciate you not reacting when I told you about Tommy. You weren't happy—I could tell by how tense you were. But you didn't do anything that made me uneasy."

"I abhor violence," Riggs told her, not taking his gaze from hers. "Which is pretty ridiculous, considering what I did for a living before moving to Maine. But after being a POW and seeing my friends get the crap beaten out of them for absolutely no purpose, after seeing the torture that Cal went through simply because our captors thought it was fun to hurt a royal, I can't stomach it. I can't promise to never get angry in the future, but now that I know how strongly it affects you, I'll do my best to keep it in check."

"You don't have to—"

"I'll keep it in check," Riggs interrupted firmly. "I'll never give you a reason to be afraid of me. *Never.*"

Carlise swallowed hard and blinked to try to keep her tears at bay. "Thank you," she whispered.

"We can turn on your phone to check it, but honestly, even though the storm is done, I'm not sure the Wi-Fi will work. I've got satellite internet, and it's super temperamental. I need to check the antenna and probably upgrade it. It's been going out more and more lately. If it doesn't work, I'll have to drive down the road a bit to pick up a signal.

"When we get up, I'll let you use my satellite phone to call your mom and Susie. I'm sure they're worried sick by now. You need to reassure them that you're okay and make sure *they're* doing all right. Then maybe we'll take a walk with Baxter, do some laundry, read, play checkers . . . you can get some work done on the book you're translating. Then we'll make dinner together. Okay?"

His plans for the day sounded wonderful. Because they'd be doing most of those things together. "Okay."

"What I find on your phone will determine how soon you should contact the police here in Newton. They aren't a huge force, but the police chief is a good man. He'll take your concerns seriously, honey. He's not going to tolerate anyone in his jurisdiction being harassed."

"But we don't know who's messaging me."

"He'll find out. He might need to take your phone for a while, to give it to the state cyberforensics people to analyze, but we'll figure it out. We'll get you a new one when we get to town, so you can still communicate with your mom and Susie."

Carlise stared down at the man under her. The sun was just beginning to peek over the horizon, giving the room a slight glow. "Riggs," she whispered.

"This is normal," he said with a small shake of his head and a serious expression. "This is what a man does for his woman. He protects her. He goes out of his way to make sure she's happy and safe. He looks after her. Just as she does for him.

"You haven't had a good example of what a relationship should look like, but I've got you, Carlise. If you're hungry, I'll feed you. If you're cold, I'll bring you some blankets. If you're scared, I'll keep you safe, and if you're happy, I'll do whatever I can to keep you that way."

Carlise couldn't speak at that moment if her life depended on it. She was overwhelmed, in a good way. How the hell had she found this man? The odds were astronomical. And yet, here she was, in his bed, in his arms.

She lowered her head without thought. Without hesitation. Without any doubts.

Her lips touched his, and he immediately opened for her. She kissed him almost desperately, expressing with her lips the words she couldn't get past the lump in her throat.

The kiss turned passionate in seconds. What had started as a way to say thank you turned into something infinitely deeper in a heartbeat. Riggs rolled until she was under him. One leg was between hers, and she could feel his erection pulsing against her core. All that separated them was their underwear. And that was suddenly too much.

"I want you," she panted when he pulled back to take a deep breath. His lips were swollen and wet from their kiss. Even as she watched, his tongue came out to swipe his bottom lip, and it was all Carlise could do not to pull his head back down to hers.

"Are you sure?"

"I've never been more sure of anything in my life," she replied.

In response, Riggs leaned over and reached for the small table next to the bed. He yanked the drawer open, swearing when he used too much strength and it ended up on the floor. He shifted off her and fumbled on the floor for a moment.

Carlise giggled and held on to his waist so he wouldn't fall off the bed.

When he righted himself and hovered over her body, he had a condom in his hand. They'd never discussed protection, but she appreciated his willingness to glove up. Tommy had bitched and moaned about having to wear one. Though, she already knew she couldn't compare the two men in any way. Riggs would come out on top every single time.

"I bought them to keep the end of my shotgun dry if I have to go out in the rain or snow," he told her seriously. "Not because I've ever had a reason to use them before now."

Carlise believed him. How could she not? He was going out of his way to reassure her, to make sure she was safe. She had no reason to doubt him. She nodded and licked her bottom lip, wanting him more than was probably normal.

His amber eyes bore into hers as he placed the condom next to the pillow, then lifted off her onto his knees and reached for his T-shirt. He pulled it over his head, and Carlise took in all that was Riggs as he knelt over her. He was gorgeous. She hated seeing the scars on his torso because she knew now how he'd gotten them, but they didn't detract from his beauty in any way, shape, or form.

Her hands lifted without thought, and she placed them flat on his pecs, running them slowly up and down his body. Riggs didn't move. Was still as a statue, in fact, and Carlise began to get worried. "Riggs?"

"Yeah?" he asked through clenched teeth.

She stilled and stared up at him. He really didn't look like he was enjoying her touch. She lifted her hands uncertainly. "Do you not like me touching you?" she whispered.

"Not like it?" he asked as his brows drew down in confusion. "I've literally thought about nothing but your hands on me for the last week. I've masturbated in the shower every day as I dreamed about how you'd feel against me. I'm harder than I've been in years, and it'll be a miracle if I can last long enough to put this condom on and get inside you. Not like you touching me? Impossible."

His words made Carlise feel better, although she was still confused. "Then why aren't you doing anything? Touching me back?"

"Because I don't think I can move," he admitted. "I'm afraid I'm going to lose it if I do."

Carlise smiled and put her hands back on his chest. "That'll just mean you'll last longer when we get down to business then," she reassured him.

He stared at her for a heartbeat before climbing off the bed, dislodging her hands. He shoved his boxers over his hips and kicked them off before straddling her once more.

Carlise couldn't help but blush. She wasn't a virgin. Had seen her share of penises. But his was . . . God, it was stunning. And daunting. He was big. Not much longer than normal but thicker than anyone she'd been with. And even as she stared at him—because there was no way she could look anywhere but between his legs—a bead of precome leaked out of the slit in the mushroomed head and dripped down his hard shaft.

"Fuck, woman, your eyes on me alone are enough to make me blow," he admitted.

Slowly, Carlise brought a hand to his erection and ran one finger down the side. He twitched instantly, as if her touch were electrified.

Riggs groaned and gripped the base of his dick and squeezed hard. "Touch me again," he pleaded. "Please. I need your hands on me."

Smiling, loving that even though he was kneeling over her, she seemed to have all the power at the moment, Carlise returned her hand to his throbbing cock. She grasped him tightly, amazed when her thumb and finger didn't touch, and stroked upward.

He hadn't let go of the grip he had on the base, and he threw his head back as he groaned.

Delighted, Carlise began to stroke him slowly. Men's cocks were so amazing. Hard as steel, and yet the skin was so soft. His head fell forward, and he pierced her with his intense gaze. It surprised Carlise that he was staring at *her*, and not at her hand on his cock. She alternated looking up at him and down at what she was doing.

"I hope you weren't just being nice when you said what you did earlier," he growled in a low, tortured voice.

"About what?" she asked, fascinated at how much precome was leaking out of his dick as she stroked him.

"About you being all right with me coming first."

"I wasn't just being nice," she reassured him. Seeing how aroused he was, how much he wanted her, was a huge turn-on. She didn't think she'd ever had a man look at her the way Riggs was right at that moment. As if she was the light of his world. As if she made the world itself turn.

She removed her hand and wiggled under him, trying to sit up slightly.

Riggs straightened to his knees, giving her room to move. "Am I hurting you?" he asked in concern.

She didn't reply, just grabbed the hem of the shirt she wore and pulled upward, arching her back so she could get the material over her head. She threw the shirt to the side and lay back down. "I don't want to get your shirt dirty," she said coyly as she smiled at him.

"Shit," he swore as his gaze fixed on her chest. "You're perfect. Look at you, woman. Your tits are . . . damn . . ."

His reaction was all she could hope for and more. Carlise arched her back, even as she reached for his cock.

"*Yes* . . . God, your hand feels so good. So soft. More, harder, please . . . just like that! I'm gonna come."

And he did. Without warning, a burst of come flew out of his cock, hitting her chest. She laughed when another spurt came out. Then another. Her hand was slippery from his orgasm, and the look on his face was almost one of pain rather than pleasure. She had ropes of come on her chest and probably on her face, too, but Carlise didn't care.

She'd never felt so desirable before. Riggs hadn't even lasted thirty seconds after she'd gotten naked. There was no better sign that he was attracted to her than that.

She expected him to collapse on top of her, but she should've known he wouldn't do anything she thought other men would do. His hands reached out, and he touched her reverently. His palms flattened on her chest, and he began to massage his release into her skin. The scent of him, musky and earthy, filled the air.

"I hope you're comfortable," he said almost conversationally.

"What? Why?"

"Because we're going to be here awhile. Now that you took the edge off, I can take my time. Find out what you like . . . what makes you squirm, what makes you squeal, what makes you lose control. The good thing about living out here in the middle of nowhere is that there are very few distractions. I'm gonna take my time and show you how amazing sex can be."

His little speech was a bit conceited. He was assuming she didn't already know that sex could be good. But Carlise had a feeling any experiences she'd had in the past would pale in comparison to what this man could do to her, so he might have a reason to be conceited.

In response, she arched into his touch. "What are you waiting for then?"

"Your permission. Your consent. Your assurance that you want me as badly as I want you. I want all of you, Carlise. Your trust, your body, your heart."

She stilled under him.

"I'm in love with you," he said without a trace of hesitation. "I don't know how it happened so fast, or why, but I *know* you're it for me. The last woman I'll ever want. The last I'll ever have. You're the woman I've been looking for my entire life. And suddenly there you were, practically on my doorstep. I'm a lucky son of a bitch, and I'm going to do whatever it takes to make sure you never want to leave me."

Her mouth was dry, and her throat was tight. Was this man for real?

Her life had been a whirlwind lately, but from the second she'd seen him passed out on his bed from a fever . . . she'd known. Even if she wasn't ready or able to admit it at the time. He was hers.

Deep down, she suspected that was why she so willingly took care of him for three days. Why she wasn't freaked out to sleep next to him when he was still a stranger. Why she'd trusted him so quickly.

"Carlise?" he asked, his hands stilling. He was palming both her breasts, and it seemed as if every muscle in his body was frozen in time.

"Yes. Touch me, Riggs. You have my permission and consent. I've wanted you from the moment I saw you. I'm yours. All of me. I . . . I love you too."

Passion bloomed in his eyes. "I hope you aren't just saying that to be nice," he said somewhat desperately.

Carlise couldn't help but laugh. "I may not like conflict, but I'd never agree to a man touching me, making love to me, just to be nice."

Riggs's hands began moving again. He kneaded her breasts before leaning down and taking one of her nipples into his mouth and sucking hard. He didn't ease into it. Didn't let her get used to his touch, he simply went for it with gusto right out of the gate.

Carlise's pussy wept for him, and she arched into his mouth, grabbing hold of his head and fisting his hair in an iron grip. "Yessssss," she hissed.

His other hand moved to her hip, clutching her underwear. Lifting up, Carlise assisted as best she could to get them off, all while writhing in pleasure under the ministrations of his tongue and the suction of his mouth.

When she kicked the scrap of material off the bed, Riggs went up on his knees again, adjusting to kneel between her thighs, then stared down at her. This time, his gaze wasn't on her face, instead roaming over her chest and torso before zeroing in on her pussy.

"Damn, woman."

Carlise grinned, thankful she'd taken the time to trim herself in the shower the day before. She didn't like to go bare because it was a pain to maintain, and she didn't like looking like a kid down there, but she kept the hair trimmed short on her mons and shaved bare on her labia.

Feeling sexy as hell, his words still reverberating in her head, Carlise bent her knees and slowly spread her legs as far as she could.

Riggs licked his lips as he watched, the hunger easy to see in his gaze. Amazingly, his cock was hard again, and every time he moved, she felt it brush against her thigh, her lower belly. The thought of taking him inside her was becoming an obsession.

"Touch me, Riggs," she said firmly.

"Where?" he whispered.

"Everywhere."

His eyes came back up to her face, and he grinned. "Hold on, sweetheart. This is gonna be intense." Then he moved.

Chapter Eleven

Chappy felt as if he'd stuck his finger in a socket. Electricity buzzed through his system. The orgasm he'd had minutes earlier felt like it was days ago. His cock was hard and ready to go once again, which was almost a normal state when he was around Carlise.

Except now she was under him. Gloriously naked. And he'd never seen anything, anyone, as beautiful. She was all woman. She wasn't stick thin, had curves in all the right places. Her tits were more than handfuls—and he had big hands. Her stomach had an adorable little pooch that he couldn't wait to explore. Her thighs were thick . . . but it was her pussy that currently had his attention.

He scooted down her body and lowered his head, needing to inhale her essence. He shoved his shoulders between her thighs and grabbed her ass, tilting her up to meet him. Inhaling deeply, Chappy felt his cock twitch hard. It knew where it wanted to be. Buried deep inside her body. But it would have to wait. Chappy's mouth wanted a turn with her pussy first.

He took a moment to look up, past the hills and valleys of her torso and into her eyes. Carlise had propped herself on her elbows and was staring back at him. He loved that she wanted to watch what he was doing.

Who was he kidding? He loved *everything* about her.

The way her eyes had sparkled when he'd come on her tits wasn't something he was going to forget anytime soon. She'd loved it. Not all women enjoyed that kind of thing. But messy sex was Chappy's favorite. And like he'd told her—she was it for him. Period. If things didn't work out—a thought that had his heart rate increasing—he suspected he'd never have sex with anyone else. No one could replace her; he had no doubt whatsoever.

"Riggs?" she asked with a small smile. "Are you going to do something down there or just stare at me?"

"Oh, I'm going to do something. I'm just prolonging the moment. The anticipation of tasting your sweet pussy for the first time."

Redness bloomed in her cheeks, which Chappy thought was adorable.

"Hang on," he warned.

"To what?" she said with a laugh.

"Me." Then he lowered his head once more. He ran his tongue between her inner folds, her musky flavor bursting on his tastebuds, making him desperate for more. He felt her hands brush through his hair and smiled before getting back to work.

Within moments, she was writhing in his hold as he sucked and licked, paying special attention to her clit. It wasn't long before the small bundle of nerves emerged from behind its protective hood, giving him better access to drive her crazy. Her juices were soon covering his face, and Chappy almost came again, just knowing how turned on she was.

Pulling back, he slowly impaled her with one of his fingers, marveling at the sight of her muscles squeezing him as she clenched around his digit. She was tight, and hot, and so damn slick, he had no doubt she'd be able to take him without any issues.

He pulled his finger out and couldn't resist bringing it to his lips to lick it clean. "Delicious," he moaned before slowly inserting it back into her body. He finger-fucked her gently, fascinated by how easily her body opened up for him.

She groaned above him. "Riggs," she pleaded.

"Yeah?" he asked distractedly.

"Inside me. I want you inside me."

"I am," he said calmly, adding a second finger to the first.

"More! I want your cock."

The appendage in question jerked again. If he hadn't been pressed up against the mattress, Chappy had a feeling he'd be in jeopardy of coming right then and there. Hearing Carlise talk dirty drove him wild.

"You're going to get it, sweetheart. But you aren't quite ready yet."

"I am," she insisted.

"I don't want to hurt you," Chappy said. "I need you wetter. I need you to come first."

To his surprise, one of her hands flew down between her legs. "Fine. Then I'll come," she panted before she began to strum her clit.

Seeing her masturbate up close and personal was more of a turn-on than Chappy had ever thought it could be. His fingers were still inside her, and he could feel her pulsing around him as Carlise brought herself closer and closer to orgasm.

Her scent changed slightly as she neared the edge, and Chappy held his fingers still as he memorized the way she was touching herself. Making notes for the future. Her legs widened and her hips thrust upward as she came, and Chappy's heart was beating just as fast as it had earlier, when he'd had his own orgasm.

She immediately removed her fingers from her clit, but Chappy wanted—no, *needed*—more. He twisted his fingers and searched for that little spongy spot inside her body, even as he took her clit into his mouth and sucked.

Carlise shrieked and grabbed hold of his hair so hard it hurt, but Chappy could only smile through the slight pain as he prolonged her orgasm.

Her leg muscles shook uncontrollably, and he felt her abs tense. She was so beautiful in the throes of her pleasure, it was all Chappy could do not to come right then and there himself. Except he needed to be inside her when he orgasmed again. There was nothing he wanted more than to feel her muscles squeezing his cock the way they were gripping his fingers.

When she whimpered, he eased off. There would be a time and place to push her over the edge again and again, forcing her to come for him repeatedly, but this wasn't it. He needed to become one with this woman. Show her how much she meant to him. Treasure her.

Moving quickly, not letting her come all the way down from her orgasm, Chappy reached for the condom he'd placed on the edge of the mattress earlier. He swore when he tried to tear it open, because his fingers were slick with her juices, and he couldn't get a good grip on the foil. Eventually he used his teeth to rip it open, and he quickly rolled the condom onto his cock. Then he draped her knees in the crooks of his elbows, spreading her wide.

He looked down at her pussy, which was gaping and glistening. *He'd* done that. He'd prepared her to take his cock.

He looked from her pussy to her hard nipples to her face. She was breathing hard and staring up at him in awe. He saw the love in her eyes, and it almost made him lose it before he got anywhere close to being inside her.

"Yes?" he couldn't help but ask again. He wanted to be certain she wanted him. He'd never take a woman without her permission.

"Yes!" she practically shouted.

Grinning, Chappy lined up his rock-hard cock with her pussy and began to push inside. He didn't need to guide himself into her body; he was hard enough not to need any assistance whatsoever. His smile fell into a moan as the head of his cock was engulfed in the hottest, wettest pussy he'd ever had the pleasure to enter.

Precome spurted inside the condom, and he gritted his teeth. He wasn't going to last. This felt too good. Too much like coming home.

But then Carlise's hands moved to his ass, and she gripped him hard, pulling him closer. "More! I want all of you."

That was it. Her words were all it took for him to be completely and totally hers.

He pushed all the way inside her body without stopping, until his pubic hair meshed with hers. Then he shifted, wanting to be even deeper. His cock throbbed almost painfully. The pleasure that swam up the small of his back, up his spine, down his arms, making them shake, was almost too much for him to handle.

His balls were pulled up so close to his body, it was a wonder he hadn't lost it yet.

"You feel so good. I'm so full. I love this, Riggs. You have no idea."

Her words were hot against his ear. He hadn't even realized he'd dropped his torso to bury his face in her neck. Lifting his head, he stared at her, wanting to make sure she wasn't hurting as he slowly moved his hips backward, then slid home once again.

He saw no pain on her face, only pleasure.

"*Yes*. Riggs! More. Move! Faster, please."

He was happy to oblige. He kept a steady pace—in and out, in and out—loving the way her body moved under his. She wasn't lying there passively; her hips were undulating, the pace increasing quickly, as if that would make Chappy move faster in turn.

He still held her knees in his arms, so she was almost folded in half under him. Every thrust made her tits jiggle, and his mouth watered with the need to eat at her nipples as he fucked her. But he wasn't a contortionist, couldn't quite reach them while he was inside her. There would be time later for him to feast.

One moment he was enjoying the feel of being balls deep inside her for the first time, and the next, the base of his spine tingled, letting him know he was seconds away from coming.

He hated for their first time to end so quickly, there was nowhere he'd rather be than buried deep inside her cunt, but he had to move faster. Gritting his teeth, he kept his eyes on her face as he fucked her. Hard.

She inhaled sharply, and her eyes closed halfway in pleasure as he pounded into her body. It wasn't long before he was done. He shoved inside her as far as he could get, regretting for the first time in his life that he wouldn't be able to bathe a woman's womb with his come, before he exploded.

Chappy saw stars. The world went black for a moment as the most intense pleasure he'd ever experienced swamped him. When he came to, he still had Carlise bent almost double, but her hands were running up and down his back soothingly.

Screw soothing. He wanted her as inside out as he felt. Moving, Chappy lowered her legs, but pulled her lower body closer as he knelt back on his heels.

"Riggs?"

"I need you to come again. On my cock this time."

"How can you still be hard?" she asked incredulously.

"I'm not completely hard, but how could I *not* be, looking down at this beautiful body that's all mine?" he asked. He brought a hand to her clit and began rubbing her, hard and fast, just the way he'd watched her do earlier.

Reaching between them, he scooped some of the juices that had leaked out of her body and used them to lubricate her clit. "Come for me, sweetheart. Let me feel you squeeze my cock."

She jerked against him, and he smiled. Dirty talk really did turn her on.

"Riggs, that's . . . oh crap!"

Her hips began to shake once again, as well as her thighs, and this time, instead of watching her face, Chappy couldn't help but look down to where they were still connected. The sight of his cock buried inside her body was erotic and sexier than anything he'd seen in his life.

He couldn't help but think of the time in the hopefully not-too-distant future when he'd be able to enter her bare. When he'd be able to fill her with his come and watch her belly grow round with their baby.

Damn. They hadn't talked about children or anything close to what would happen after they left his cabin, but now that he'd had the thought, he couldn't shake it. She'd be an excellent mother. Would be a beautiful pregnant woman. Their kids could run amok up here at the cabin, enjoying nature as much as he did. He'd have to expand, give them more rooms, but he could do that without a problem.

His thoughts were brought back to the present when Carlise cried out with her release. The feel of her rippling around his cock was indescribable. He was awestruck by this woman. She'd impressed him with her willingness to go with the flow, her adaptability, her kindness toward his friends . . . but now that they'd been as close as two people could be? She blew him away.

As soon as she finished shaking, Chappy reluctantly pulled out of her body. His cock was shiny with her juices, and it was almost painful to remove the condom. He left the bed to discard it but was back before she'd moved an inch. Smiling at the way she was sprawled on the mattress, Chappy straightened the blankets that had gotten tossed with their lovemaking and pulled her against his body after he joined her under the covers.

She immediately burrowed into him, one leg resting over his and an arm over his chest, pulling him close.

"Holy crap, Riggs. I'm boneless."

He couldn't help the satisfied smile that crept over his lips. "Same, honey."

"I have some bad news for you, though," she said nonchalantly.

He stiffened. "What?"

"I'm not going outside to start the generator so we can shower."

Relaxing, Chappy chuckled. "I won't ever ask you to, so you're safe. I'll do it."

"Thank goodness."

They lay together in lazy satisfaction for several minutes before Carlise propped her chin on his chest and looked up at him.

"What?" he asked when she didn't say anything.

"I just . . . I don't ever want to leave here. I want to live in this happy bubble forever."

"Now you see why I like to come up here."

"Yeah. It's so quiet and peaceful."

"As much as I want to keep you right here, in my bed, so I can make love to you every day, we can't stay here forever," he said gently.

"I know," she said. "You have a life and a job you have to do in town. I just . . . I don't want the real world to intrude on how happy I am right this second."

"It won't," Chappy said firmly.

Carlise sighed. "As soon as you turn on my phone, it will."

But he shook his head. "Nope. I'm gonna take care of that for you. No one's gonna touch you, if I have anything to say about it."

"You can't promise that," she said soberly. "I'm a pragmatic person. I can't be with you every second of every day, no matter how much I might enjoy just that. Bad stuff happens. I've seen and lived it firsthand. But just knowing you *want* to keep me safe means the world to me."

Chappy knew she was right. When he was leading groups on the AT, he was away from home for several days and nights at a time. And he could be on a tree job for hours. But luckily, this wasn't the time of year when he had any trail hikes. He had time to figure out who the hell was stalking her and make sure they knew she was off limits from here on out. "You've got a good head on your shoulders. When things got too intense, you got yourself out of the situation," he said after a moment.

"You mean I ran," she said dryly.

"Yes. And put space between you and whoever was harassing you. It was the smart thing to do, Carlise. I mean that."

She sighed. "I hope so. I hoped if he couldn't find me, he'd lose interest."

"Well, we'll see if it worked in a little while. But first, I want to lie here and revel in the mellowness I'm feeling right now."

"Two orgasms will do that to you," she said, the satisfaction and pride easy to hear in her tone.

Chappy chuckled. "Yup. And for the record . . . that's never happened before."

"What? You having an orgasm?" she sassed.

He dug his fingers into her waist, tickling her, loving how she squealed and squirmed against him. Feeling her nipples against his bare skin, the brush of her pubic hair against his thigh . . . It was so intimate, and he couldn't love her any more than he did right at that moment.

"No, smartass," he said when they'd both settled again. "Me coming twice within such a short period of time. I'm addicted to you. Maybe in a year—or five or ten—I'll have had you enough times to not feel so desperate that I have an immediate urge to come."

She giggled against him. "Honestly, Riggs, it's a compliment. I've never felt as sexy as I did with you kneeling over me, unable to hold back and having to come right then and there."

"You *are* sexy," he reassured her.

"I love you," she whispered against his skin. "I know people aren't going to understand how or why things between us have moved so fast, and I can't explain it either. I just know that I was meant to be yours."

Her words made Chappy's eyes close in relief. And gratitude. "Same, sweetheart. Same."

He started to roll on top of her again when something made him stop. He felt as if he was being watched. It wasn't a feeling he'd ever discount, not after his military training and all that he'd been through.

Turning his head—he blinked.

Baxter was sitting next to the bed, staring at him with huge brown eyes.

"Crap," Chappy swore.

"What? What's wrong?" Carlise asked, sounding a little worried.

"Don't panic. Nothing's wrong. But your dog is staring at us."

Carlise turned her head to look to the side of the bed, and he felt her chuckle against him. "Oh, so he's *my* dog when he wants out?" she sassed.

"Nope. He's always been your dog. He found you walking on that road, led you in the right direction, came and got me, and led me to you. He's your dog, lock, stock, and barrel."

"You think he wants out? Or is he some kind of voyeur?" she asked with a grin.

"I'm thinking out," Chappy said with a chuckle.

"Well, I'm not ready to get out of this warm bed yet."

Chappy leaned over and kissed her. "I wasn't going to ask you to. I'm just getting up the energy and nerve to pry myself away from your delectable body, out from under the warm covers, get dressed, put a log or two on the fire, take him out, then start up the generator so we can have a hot shower, coffee, and a warm breakfast."

"I'll get up while you're outside and do the coffee thing," she offered.

But Chappy shook his head. "No. Stay put. I want to see you lying in my bed, naked and happy, when I come back. I can't tell you how many times I've fantasized about just that in the last few days."

She blushed. "You're going to spoil me," she scolded.

"That's my goal," Chappy told her without hesitation. He turned to the dog. "I'm comin', boy. Give me a second."

As if Baxter could understand him, he turned and walked to the front of the cabin. Then he sat, facing the door, as if giving him privacy.

"So *now* he turns his head," Chappy said with a shake of his own and a low laugh before climbing out from under the covers. He leaned over and kissed Carlise gently. "I love you. So much. I'll be back."

Then he turned, not embarrassed in the least by his nudity, and bent to pick up their discarded clothes. He could feel Carlise's gaze on him, and it made him smile. She could look all she wanted, he didn't mind. Every inch of him belonged to her.

He went to the dresser and pulled on a pair of boxers, pants, and a long-sleeved shirt, then turned to the bed once more. Just as he'd thought, Carlise's eyes were glued to him. "Enjoy the show?" he teased.

"More than you know," she replied with a huge smile.

Knowing if he went over to the bed, he'd crawl back under the covers and Baxter wouldn't get to go outside anytime soon, Chappy forced himself to head to the bathroom instead. He hadn't expected the morning to go how it had, but he was beyond thrilled. He'd wanted Carlise ever since he'd first become aware of her presence.

He could picture them being together for years and years, but first he needed to make sure whoever was harassing her was taken care of. Once that was done, they could both relax and move on with their lives . . . hopefully together.

Chapter Twelve

Carlise couldn't remember a better start to a day than what she and Riggs had shared. The sex was . . . better than she ever thought it could be. Riggs was a generous lover. And he didn't treat her with kid gloves, which she adored. She hadn't known that about herself, how much she'd like it when Riggs was forceful. Not in a way that hurt, but he easily held her still when she tried to squirm, forced her orgasm to continue in a way that had been almost painful, but ultimately so damn good. And he took her hard and fast, rough.

Everything he'd done felt amazing—and she couldn't wait to do it again.

But after he let Baxter out and fired up the generator, he refused to join her back in bed, ordering her to relax. Since she didn't want him to wait on her, she didn't listen. She'd gotten up, showered, helped him make eggs, bacon, and toast for breakfast, and fed Baxter.

She knew he was waiting for her to grab her phone, and so she stalled, trying to think of anything and everything to talk about besides her stalker. She had a feeling he knew what she was doing, but he didn't call her out on it.

It wasn't until the dishes were done, Baxter was snoring back in his bed next to the fire, and she'd rambled on about the plot of the book she was translating and who she thought the villain was that he walked up to her and pulled her against his chest.

One of his hands palmed the back of her neck, and the other was firm around her waist. "It's time, sweetheart."

Carlise sighed against him and nodded.

"It's going to be fine. I promise."

She wasn't so sure about that, but she nodded again anyway. The last thing she wanted was her real life to intrude on their current happiness. But he was right, ignoring the problem wasn't going to make it go away. She needed to find out one way or another if the harassment had stopped, now that she was no longer within easy reach of whoever was stalking her.

Riggs pulled back but didn't let go. "Do you trust me?" he asked.

"Yes." Carlise didn't even need to think twice about her answer to that question.

"Good. Go grab your phone while I go outside and turn the generator back on. I'll get it going and see if we get lucky and the Wi-Fi works, so we can find out what we're dealing with. Okay?"

"Okay." Nausea swam in her belly as she turned to head to her backpack, where she'd stashed the phone so she wouldn't have to see it. She prayed Riggs wouldn't decide her problems were too big and he didn't want to deal with them. With *her*.

It didn't take him long to go outside and get the generator running. She was waiting for him with her cell in her hand when he returned and handed it over without meeting his eyes.

"This changes nothing," he said firmly.

Carlise looked up at him tentatively.

"No matter what he's sent or not sent, nothing changes about my feelings for you. I love you, Carlise. Better or worse, isn't that how the saying goes? I'm in this for the long haul, and even if we're dealing with this asshole for years to come, I'm not going anywhere. All right?"

Relief swamped her. She nodded, too choked up to speak.

"Good." He kissed her forehead, then turned his attention to the phone.

Holding her breath, Carlise stared at him with apprehension as he powered up the device.

Nothing happened. No dings. No vibrations. Nothing.

"Is it dead?" she asked.

"No. It looks like it's got about a twenty-percent charge," Riggs said.

"So the Wi-Fi isn't working?" she asked.

"Unfortunately, it doesn't look like it," Riggs said calmly. "I never really cared much about Wi-Fi while I was up here before since I use this cabin as a place to get away from everything. I'll definitely be looking into upgrading the equipment and making it more stable since you need it for your job. I'm going to head down the road a ways to a place where I think it'll pick up."

She felt all warm and fuzzy inside that he wanted to upgrade his internet system because of her. But now wasn't the time to think about that. "Let me get my coat, and I'll go with you," Carlise said, turning toward the door.

Riggs caught her hand in his before she could take a step. "I'm thinking you should stay here. I'll take my Jeep down the road, stop by your car while I'm out. I'll check out the notifications, then come back."

Carlise knew she should protest. Should insist this was her problem, and he shouldn't have to deal with it. But a bigger part of her was relieved. It felt good—*really* good—to have someone looking out for her. The bottom line was, she didn't know how she'd react if a flood of notifications came in the second she turned on her phone.

"Please? Let me do this for you, honey," he said.

She nodded.

The relief that came over his face made her realize he *needed* to do this. She had a feeling if she'd insisted, he would've let her come with him, but the fact that he wanted to shield her from a possible onslaught of vitriol when he turned her phone on felt good.

"Stay here with Baxter. I won't be long," he promised.

"Okay."

He studied her for a moment before nodding. She was glad he wasn't hesitating, was going to get this done right now, even as a small part of her still wanted to postpone it for a little while longer. But she was a grown woman. And she needed to know one way or another.

She walked with him to the door and kissed him hard before he walked out with her phone and his keys. She watched through the window as he went to the small detached garage that obviously held his vehicle. He exited a moment later in a Jeep, waved at the cabin as if he knew she'd be watching, then powered down the path Bob's truck had plowed when his friends had been here.

Taking a deep breath, Carlise turned, only to see Baxter standing three feet from her, studying her with a tilt of his head, as if he knew she was stressed.

"Hey, Bax," she said softly. "He'll be back soon."

He didn't move, just continued to stare at her with that all-knowing gaze of his.

Carlise walked around the dog, giving him plenty of space, and headed for the couch. She sat, not really wanting to read, and she didn't bother to reach for her laptop. She wouldn't be able to concentrate right now anyway.

To her surprise, Baxter walked around the couch and jumped up onto the cushion next to her.

He turned in a circle, then sat, his butt against her thigh.

Shocked and delighted, as she'd only been able to touch him once so far, Carlise very slowly ran her hand down his back. His spine wasn't protruding nearly as much as it had when she'd first met him, and satisfaction swam through her veins.

Amazingly, she found herself relaxing. Whatever Riggs found when he turned on her phone, they'd deal with it. She was more excited that Baxter finally seemed to fully trust her. Either that, or he was trying to comfort her. She had a feeling it was a combination of both.

Whatever the dog's reason for jumping up next to her, he'd taken Carlise's thoughts away from the messages that might be on her phone. She couldn't wait for Riggs to get back so he could see Baxter. As she continued to pet him, she smiled, which was the last thing she thought she'd be doing right now.

~

Chappy frowned at the phone in his hand. He'd expected to find some messages and texts, but he hadn't expected to see *hundreds* of them. Carlise's escape from Cleveland had not only *not* made her stalker back off, but it had also apparently escalated the situation.

His entire body tense, Chappy scrolled through the messages. They'd gotten more and more angry as the days went by. Whoever Carlise's stalker was, he was pissed that he couldn't find her. That she wasn't responding to his messages. That she was apparently beyond his reach.

His stomach rolled. Carlise definitely needed to go into Newton and talk to the chief of police.

Alfred Rutkey had lived in Maine his entire life, was somewhat of a good ol' boy, but Chappy respected him. He didn't put up with shenanigans in his town, and he never hesitated to send help when someone was hurt or lost on the AT. Some small-town chiefs didn't like to spend their hard-earned, somewhat-scarce budgets on what many assumed were wild goose chases, but Chief Rutkey wasn't one of them.

Chappy was more relieved than he could say that Carlise wasn't currently dealing with all these awful messages. As he scrolled through the texts, his anger continued to rise. How *dare* someone treat another human being this way? How dare he feel as if Carlise owed him something?

The latest texts were the most concerning.

Unknown: Where are you, bitch?

Unknown: You think you can hide from me? There's nowhere you can go that I won't find you.

Unknown: Eventually you'll have to come back, and when you do, I'll still be here. Waiting. Watching.

Unknown: How's your mom doing? She looked pretty relaxed at the library. Too bad about that flat tire she got the other day.

Unknown: Women were made to obey. To be subservient to men. The problem with the world is people like YOU. You haven't gotten it through your thick skull that you're nothing without a man telling you what to do.

Unknown: Where the fuck are you?! You're going to pay big time when I find you!

There were also several rambling emails that didn't even make much sense. But the threats were clear. Carlise was in danger, and possibly her mother, too, if the stalker really had been following her like he'd insinuated . . . had somehow caused her flat tire.

If it was up to Chappy, Carlise would never go back to Cleveland and her mom would move to Newton.

He sighed. He'd so wanted to tell Carlise that all was well, that there were no messages, so she wouldn't stress. But he wouldn't lie to her. First, that would be a dick thing to do; second, he didn't want her to let down her guard. And she needed to warn her mom to be careful as well.

He respected women. They were no more supposed to "obey" a man than men were supposed to expect subservience. As far as he was concerned, women made the world go round.

He sat in his Jeep on the side of the road, contemplating what his next steps should be. He'd need to talk to Carlise when he got back to the cabin, make sure she understood that whoever her stalker was, he wasn't going away anytime soon. Then he'd talk to Chief Rutkey, get him to look into her ex, Tommy. He wanted to discuss everything with his friends, make sure they were aware of the situation. They'd help keep Carlise safe; he had no doubt.

The truth of the matter was, even though they'd decided to go into the tree business and not do anything clichéd for former Special Forces soldiers, like security or bodyguard work, Chappy still felt a deep-seated need to keep others safe. He kept a close eye on the men and women he led on hikes on the Appalachian Trail. He and his friends were all very protective of April, not only because she was their employee but also because she didn't seem to have anyone else to rely on. Chappy didn't know her story, none of them did, but they'd gotten the impression that whatever it was, it wasn't great.

Chappy had no doubt that when Bob, Cal, and JJ heard about Carlise's situation, they'd do whatever it took to make sure her stalker didn't get anywhere near her.

Sighing, he forwarded the emails she'd received to his own inbox, then made a folder called Yucky Stuff in her email program. He couldn't delete them since they were evidence, but he didn't want her to have to see them either. He opened the emails she'd received from her mom and Susie but didn't read them. He only wanted Carlise to be able to read them without cell service or Wi-Fi when he got back to the cabin.

He was in a quandary as to what to do about the hateful texts she'd received from her stalker. In the end, he left them because he knew they were more evidence, but he'd at least ask Carlise not to read them to avoid additional fear and stress. To trust him to take care of the situation.

He loved her. More than he ever thought possible after little more than a week. And it scared the hell out of him. Now that he'd had a glimpse of what it meant to find his person, to be loved by her, and what life could be like with Carlise at his side, he was terrified of losing her.

Looking at his watch, Chappy swore. He'd been gone longer than he'd thought. Especially with a stalker out there, pissed off at Carlise for some reason he hadn't been able to ascertain. As far as he could tell, she'd done nothing more than break up with a man who was abusing her and was now trying to move on with her life. Not only that, but also none of the emails or texts actually talked about wanting to get Carlise back . . . or any mention of the breakup or their relationship.

If the stalker was Tommy, wouldn't he at least reference their time together?

That was just one of the things that was so confusing about Carlise's stalker. From what he could tell, she wasn't the kind of person who would incite such . . . fury from someone else. She'd broken up with Tommy and moved on. Chappy didn't know if *Tommy* had moved on, but whoever was sending the messages obviously hated Carlise.

Whoever this stalker was, they were less than stable. That much was obvious. Many men had the mindset that if they couldn't be with a woman, no one else could either. He'd never understood that kind of thinking. If a woman didn't want to be with him, why the hell would he ever fight to keep her? It made no sense.

His mind swirled with all the things he needed to do, but first and foremost was getting back to Carlise. It was an odd feeling, being so desperate to be by someone's side. To want to know what they were doing at all times. Not because he was being overbearing or possessive, but because he wanted to make sure she had everything she needed or wanted.

Before stopping to turn on her phone, Chappy had also checked her CR-V. She'd been extremely lucky when she'd driven off the road. Yes, she'd hit a tree head-on, but it was clear she hadn't been moving too fast at the time. There were also two other trees close by that were twice as big and would've messed up her car even worse, no matter the speed.

Still, the small SUV would need some fixing before she'd be able to drive it. As he'd suspected, the battery was dead. And from the way the car was leaning, he had a feeling she had one, maybe two, flat tires.

Carlise may not like it, but Chappy wanted to tow the car into town to have someone look it over. Maybe put some snow tires on, give it a tune-up . . . things like that. Maine was extremely tough on vehicles, and he wanted to make sure she was safe. Carlise was now the most important person in his life, and he'd do whatever was necessary to keep her healthy and alive for years to come. Including making sure her car was in tip-top shape . . . and ending the threat from her stalker.

He drove slowly back toward his cabin. Toward Carlise. Bob's plow had done a great job of clearing the two-track to his place. It wasn't perfect, hence the need to drive slowly, but he was a confident driver, and his Jeep had navigated worse conditions.

Still, when he pulled into the small one-car detached garage he'd built near his cabin, Chappy let out a sigh of relief. If something had happened to him while he was out and about, it would have left Carlise by herself in his cabin, which was unacceptable. He'd left her his satellite phone, just in case, but he was relieved to be back.

Looking around the property as he walked toward the cabin, he made mental notes about expanding the garage to fit her CR-V. It was unlikely they'd take two vehicles up here, but just in case, he wanted to be sure to have a place to shelter both cars at the same time.

He walked into the cabin and opened his mouth to call out a greeting but stopped himself in the nick of time.

Instead, he stared at Carlise, who was sleeping on the couch. Her head was resting against the back cushion, her mouth open slightly . . . and she had one hand resting on Baxter's head. The dog was sitting next to her, curled into a ball.

His eyes were open, watching Chappy, but he didn't move from Carlise's side, which Chappy fully approved of.

"Hey, boy. It's comfy up there, isn't it?" he asked quietly as he put Carlise's phone on the counter. He couldn't keep himself from going to her, as if she was some kind of magnet, pulling him in.

He walked slowly, not wanting to alarm Baxter, but the dog looked perfectly content to stay where he was. Chappy knelt at Carlise's feet, balancing on his haunches as he stared at her.

He was a lucky son of a bitch, and he knew it. She was so beautiful. He took in her long blonde hair in disarray around her face, remembered running his hands through it while she slept in his arms, how it looked against his pillow. She was a dream come true. *His* dream come true.

As if she could sense his intense gaze, her eyes fluttered, then opened. She blinked in confusion for a moment before her lips curled in a lazy, sleepy smile. "Hey," she greeted him.

"Hey," he returned.

When he didn't say anything else, she asked, "Is everything okay?"

"Everything's good," he reassured her. "I just got back. You tired?"

Carlise shook her head. "Not really. But I sat down, and Baxter joined me"—she smiled at the dog at her side—"and I didn't want to disturb him by getting up to get my laptop. I guess I fell asleep. Someone tired me out this morning," she said with a shy grin.

Chappy smiled hard. This was what he'd always dreamed about, but never thought he'd have. Coming home and finding the woman he loved waiting, smiling at him happily.

"You want me to grab your laptop for you? Do you want something to drink? Are you hungry?"

She shook her head. "No, I'm fine. What time is it anyway? How long were you gone? Oh! Did he message?"

It was obvious she'd just remembered where he had been and why. Chappy mourned the loss of his sleepy, oblivious woman.

"I wasn't gone that long. Maybe an hour. And yeah . . . he messaged," he told her.

"Was it . . ." She paused, then said in a rush, "Was it bad?"

"Let's just say leaving didn't make your stalker forget about you," he said grimly.

Carlise's shoulders slumped, and she looked down at her lap.

Chappy put a finger under her chin and gently lifted so she had no choice but to look at him. "We're going to get to the bottom of this," he said firmly.

"I don't even know what I did to piss him off so much," she whispered. "I mean, I'm just *me.* I'm hardly a model. I'm nobody special. Why is he doing this?"

Chappy moved slowly so he wouldn't disturb Baxter, sitting on her other side. His hand slid from her chin to her nape, the other gripping her waist. "You *are* special," he insisted. "You're smart and funny and beautiful and so damn sexy, it's all I can do to keep my hands off you pretty much at all times.

"You just being *you* is the reason I fell in love so fast. I know without a shred of doubt that without you, I was only half the man I could be. Since leaving the service, I was just existing. Now? I feel as if I have a renewed purpose in life. Like all the things I've seen and done, that time I was held hostage . . . it was all worth something. I've made it through because it was my destiny to meet *you.*

"Honestly? I have a feeling this guy's stalking you because he knows he let a good thing slip through his fingers. He screwed up, and he's desperate to get you back, to have you under his thumb. But it's not going to happen. I won't let him snuff out your light . . . because it's *mine* now. And I don't mean that in a weird, psycho way. It's mine to protect. To keep safe. To help you shine."

Carlise's eyes teared up as he spoke.

Chappy had no idea where the words were coming from—he wasn't exactly known for having much of a romantic soul—but somehow, she brought it out in him.

"Riggs," she murmured.

"We were meant to be," he said simply. "I can't imagine that some higher power led you to Baxter, who led you to *me*, only for you to disappear from my life now. We'll talk to the police chief in Newton. We'll tell my friends what's going on. We'll tell your mom and Susie to be careful, that someone out there might try to use them to get you to come back to Cleveland. We'll do whatever it takes to make sure you're safe, and the people you care about are safe, so we can live happily ever after."

"You think he'll go after my mom or Susie?" Carlise asked, alarmed.

Shit. He hadn't meant to scare her. "I wish I could say no, but I honestly don't know *what* this guy'll do." Chappy didn't want to bring up the fact that he suspected her stalker was watching her mom. Not when she was so worried already. "I swear we'll figure it out. We'll bring your best friend and your mom out here to Newton if we have to. I'll hire bodyguards for them both. We'll send them on a monthlong cruise. Whatever they want. But I'll do what it takes to make sure they're safe because it's the right thing to do, and because I know you'll worry and will blame yourself if anything happens to them."

With a sigh, Carlise closed her eyes and leaned into him. "I'm so tired."

"Then sleep," he said immediately.

Her eyes opened, and she shook her head. "No, I mean, I'm just tired of all this. Of worrying. Stressing. Tired of wondering when and where he might show up. I'm not sorry I left Cleveland because it led me to you . . . but what next? Will he find me here, and I'll have to leave again? Then what? Where will I go? Where will I be safe?"

"With me. You'll be safe with me," Chappy said firmly. "I'm not going to let anything happen to you."

"You can't prevent it," Carlise said sadly. "Eventually, he'll find me. Will he hurt *you* for being with me? Or your friends? Or April? Or Baxter? I just . . . I can't let anything happen to you, Riggs. I *can't.* I'll do whatever it takes to keep you from being sucked into my drama."

"You know what you can do?" he asked.

"What?"

"Fight. For me. For you. For *us*. You're right that I can't be by your side all the time. But I don't want you to give up on us. Don't run. Stay here in Maine. With me. Fight for what we have. It's unique, Carlise. I've never felt this way before, and I don't care how fast things happened. We were made for each other, and no stalker is going to take that away."

"I can do that. Fight, I mean," she said softly.

"Good. Now, do you want to see the messages from your mom and Susie?" he asked, needing to change the subject. Just thinking about Carlise having to fight off her stalker, to fight for her life, made him nauseous.

"Oh, I can see them? I thought since the Wi-Fi wasn't working, I wouldn't be able to," she said excitedly.

"I downloaded the emails to your phone's hard drive by opening them. I didn't read them," he said quickly.

"I wouldn't mind if you did. I trust you, Riggs."

Once again, this woman brought him to his proverbial knees with her words.

"I forwarded the emails from your stalker to myself, then put them in a folder called Yucky Stuff on your account—I know it'll be tough, but I'd prefer if you didn't read them. They'll just upset you, and I'm going to deal with them—but I couldn't do anything about the texts. So I'm also asking you to please not read those either. At least none from the unknown account. You can read the texts from your friend and mom, but it would make me feel a lot better if you left the others for now," Chappy told her.

Carlise nodded. "I feel like I'm being a wuss because I'm relieved I don't have to see what he wrote."

"You aren't," he countered without hesitation.

"Thank you," she said on a sigh. "I don't know what I would've done if you hadn't been here."

Chappy really didn't want to think about that. Because if he hadn't decided to come up to the cabin to get away from life for a while, she probably would've died out here in the wilderness. Her car would've been found without her in it. Her body might not have been discovered until the spring thaw. He shivered at the thought.

To hide his distress, he leaned forward and kissed her forehead. "But I *was* here, and you *did* find me," he said firmly, his lips brushing against her skin with every word.

She nodded against him, then whispered, "Baxter *got on the couch* with me! He's letting me touch him!"

Chappy smiled. "I see."

"He's scared, but he trusted me not to hurt him. That's how I feel about you, Riggs. I'm a little nervous about how much I love you, how fast this is happening. But I trust you not to hurt me. To treat me well. And when I freak out in the future about stuff that seems small or stupid because it reminds me of something from my past, I'm trusting you to go with it. To know that it's not you, it's my memories that I'm fighting."

Chappy stared into her eyes and nodded. "I couldn't have said the words better myself, sweetheart. My captors took a part of me. They stole a slice of my soul. And sometimes I wondered if I'd ever get it back. But with you by my side, I have a feeling I will. Be patient with me, too, honey. If I do or say something that makes you rethink being with me, please give me a chance to make it right."

"I will. And we're going to make it," she said firmly. "I know it."

Chappy breathed out a sigh of relief. "I think so too. Stay put. You and Bax look too comfortable to move. I'll grab your phone and let you read your emails and messages. There are a couple there from people who I'm assuming are clients. I'll go outside and crank up the generator, see if the Wi-Fi is working, so you can respond if you need to."

He kissed her briefly and started to stand, but she stopped him by putting a hand on his arm. "Riggs?"

"Yeah, sweetheart?"

"I love you."

God, he'd never get tired of hearing those words from her mouth. "I love you too," he returned. "I'll be right back."

He wanted to reach over and give Baxter a pet but didn't want to scare the mutt. So he stood and headed for where he'd left her phone. "You want caprese pasta for lunch?" he asked. "Tomatoes, pasta, and mozzarella cheese?"

"Sounds delicious, although I would've been fine with a PB&J," she joked.

Five minutes later, as he was puttering around the kitchen, Chappy looked over and saw Carlise focused on her phone. Her hair was behind one ear, and she was absently petting Baxter with her free hand.

She filled up his home simply by existing. She occupied all the empty spaces in his heart in the same way. She might not know it, but Chappy's new mission in life was to do everything in his power to make her happy.

Carlise's stalker watched her mom with narrowed eyes. It would be so easy to sneak up behind her as she fumbled with the keys to her townhouse. So easy to push her inside and knock her down, tie her up. So easy to get her to admit where Carlise was.

The weak bitch wouldn't last through two minutes of torture before she broke.

Before returning home, the old broad had pushed a grocery cart around the supermarket as if she didn't have a care in the world. It was infuriating. Nearly rage-inducing. Because there was no fucking way she'd be so unconcerned, humming to herself in the damn produce section, if she *didn't* know where Carlise was. She'd clearly been in contact with her daughter.

Well, one way to get Carlise back to Cleveland was for something awful to happen to her mother. If the dumb slut wouldn't get her ass back here on her own, despite being warned time and time again, then drastic measures would have to be taken.

Either the old woman would spill the beans about where Carlise was hiding, or she'd suffer in her daughter's place.

One way or another, Carlise was going to pay for being a complete and utter bitch.

Chapter Thirteen

"I'm going out to chop some more firewood while you talk to your mom and Susie," Riggs said as he headed toward the door. He stopped to put on his boots and jacket.

"I don't want to kick you out of the house. It's okay if you stay while I talk to them," Carlise said with a frown.

"It's fine. I want you to be able to say whatever you need or want to without worrying about me overhearing."

She'd read her mom's messages, then the emails from her clients but hadn't gotten to Susie's before Riggs served lunch. Afterward, he'd suggested she call her loved ones with his satellite phone to reassure them that she was okay. Perhaps tell them to be extra careful until they could get to Newton and talk with Chief Rutkey about the situation.

"Overhearing what? I have no secrets from you, Riggs," she told him.

He winked, and Carlise almost swooned right then and there at the sexy move.

"Oh, you know . . . how cute I am and how you can't keep your hands off me."

He wasn't wrong, but Carlise still rolled her eyes. "I'm thinking it's *you* who can't keep your hands to yourself, mister."

"True," he said without any trace of embarrassment. He stalked toward her—that was the only word she could think of to explain the way he approached—and Carlise backed up until she was trapped against the counter.

Riggs's hands went to her waist, and he yanked her against him.

She giggled and put her hands on his chest, giving him her weight without any concerns about his intentions. If Tommy had grabbed her so aggressively, she would've tried to get out of his hold.

"You, woman, are lethal. I swear, all I have to do is look at you and I want you. Again. I can't get enough. But it's not just about sex. It's talking to you. Watching you work. Seeing you with Baxter and the trust he has for you. Listening to your laugh when I do something stupid. It's everything."

"You have it wrong, it's *you* who's dangerous. I had no idea I could be this . . . this fixated on sex."

"As long as it's only with me, I'm okay with that," Riggs said with a smirk.

"Oh, there's no doubt. You're the only man I want, Riggs," Carlise told him seriously.

"Good. Now kiss me before I go out and get all hot and sweaty. And probably sore. I'm sure I'll need a massage when I get back inside."

"Right. Of course you will. But only after a shower," she teased.

Riggs grinned, then his head was dropping. Carlise went up on tiptoes to meet him halfway. She'd wanted to kiss him again ever since the last time, just before eating lunch, when he'd swung her around and planted one on her eager lips.

The kiss immediately turned carnal. By the time he pulled away, her shirt was askew, his jacket had been unzipped, and one of her hands was under his shirt on his bare skin. The other was in his hair, which stuck up in all directions from her clenching and pulling.

"Lethal," he muttered before kissing her hard once more. Then he pulled back, straightened her shirt, and zipped his coat.

"The cold'll do me good," he said. Then he turned to Baxter. "You want to go outside with me, Bax?"

The dog didn't make a sound, just trotted to the door, then turned back to look at him as if saying, "Well? Let's go already."

Carlise chuckled along with Riggs. Then she couldn't stop herself from saying, "Be careful."

She immediately winced. She was a worrywart. She couldn't help it. She'd always said that to Tommy when he went anywhere, and he'd hated it. Told her she was being ridiculous, that it wasn't as if he was going to be intentionally reckless.

But Riggs smiled at her and said, "Always. Take your time with the calls. I'll be a while."

"Okay." He got to the door and had it open before Carlise added, "Riggs?"

"Yeah?" he asked in the doorway.

"Love you."

Seeing the smile cross his face was the highlight of her day.

"Love you too. Later."

Then he was gone.

Carlise took a deep breath, then grabbed his satellite phone and went to the couch. She pulled a blanket over her lap and dialed her mom's number.

She answered after three rings.

"Hello?"

"Hi, Mom, it's Carlise."

"Leese! Where are you? Are you okay? You haven't answered any of my messages or texts. I've been so worried!"

"I'm fine, Mom."

There was a short pause on the other end of the phone. "You actually *do* sound fine. Especially considering the last time we spoke, you were pretty much panicking."

Carlise winced. She'd called her mom when she was on her way out of Cleveland. At the time, she was stressed out, had no idea where she was going or when she'd be back, and of course, she had no idea who was stalking her.

"Where are you?" her mom asked.

"Maine," Carlise said with a small smile.

"What? Seriously? Maine? Wait, didn't they just have a huge blizzard or something?" she asked.

"As a matter of fact, yes. So, to make a long story short, I got lost and ran off the road just as that blizzard was starting and was found by a dog, who literally saved my life."

"Carlise Renee Edwards, you had better start talking faster! What the heck happened?" her mom asked, sounding completely rattled.

"Calm down, Mom. I'm *safe*. And even better . . . I'm happy. I met someone."

There was a much longer pause this time. Then her mom said, "Oh, honey," in a tone that clearly communicated she wasn't thrilled about this development.

"He's amazing, Mom. I promise. He's nothing like Tommy . . . or Dad. He has this cabin, and it's so cute. The dog I told you about, Baxter, led me straight to him. He was sick when I got here, and I had to take care of him for three days while the storm raged outside. When he woke, I was worried that things were about to get scary, but he went out of his way to make sure I felt comfortable and not threatened. His name is Riggs. He was in the military, was held as a POW with his friends, and I've met them too. They came up to make sure he was all right after learning he'd been sick and there was a strange woman in his cabin, and I love him."

Carlise was aware her words were running together, and she was babbling on as if she were eight years old, but she wanted to get everything out before her mom told her she was making a mistake, that she was rushing things. That she didn't approve.

When there was nothing but silence on the other end of the line, Carlise said in a worried tone, "Mom?"

"I'm here," she said, sounding remarkably calm.

"Say something," Carlise begged. "You're freaking me out."

"The mom part of me wants to tell you that you're moving way too fast. That there's no way you can love a man you just met."

"But?" Carlise said, practically holding her breath as she waited for her mom to speak her piece.

"But . . . I hear something in your voice that I've never heard before. Certainly not when you spoke about Tommy. Does this man treat you well?"

"So good, Mom. He's different from anyone I've ever met. It was as if I knew him before he even opened his mouth and said one word."

There was sniffing on the other end of the line.

"Mom? What's wrong? Are you crying?"

"Nothing's wrong. I'm just happy for you."

Carlise blinked in surprise. "I thought you'd be upset. Or at least warn me to slow down or something."

"Honey, I knew before I even walked down the aisle with your father that I shouldn't do it. But I didn't have the guts to back out. There were too many people at the church, too much money had been spent. And then it took me way too many years to extricate myself . . . and you. I'm ashamed that I stayed with him for as long as I did. You've had some very bad examples of what love is. How a partner is supposed to act.

"But that also made you wary and very aware of how a man *should* treat you. If you say you love this man, and he treats you well, then I say go for it. There's nothing like living on top of each other for days on end to tell you immediately what kind of man he is. It's happened very fast, yes . . . but if anyone deserves to be happy, it's you. You've suffered through too much of your life already."

Relief swept through Carlise, and it was her turn to get teary-eyed. She already knew she loved Riggs, but having her mom's support meant the world to her. "You're going to love him. He's super protective."

"That's good. But is he hot? Please tell me he's a lumberjack!"

Carlise burst out laughing. "Actually, he and his three friends own a company called Jack's Lumber . . . they run a tree service."

Her mom joined her in laughter. "And his looks?"

"Oh, Mom," Carlise breathed. "He's so handsome."

"When do I get to meet him?" she asked. "When are you coming home? Will you bring him with you?"

This was the tricky part. "Well . . . I can't come home just yet," Carlise hedged.

"Tommy's still harassing you, isn't he?" her mom guessed immediately.

"Yeah. He's not happy that he can't find me. Riggs checked my messages—he had to drive down the road a ways since there's no cell service at the cabin, I'm using his satellite phone to talk to you—and there are even more messages and texts than I had before I left. So I'm going to stay here for a while. And pray Tommy gets over his obsession sooner rather than later."

Her mom sighed. "I understand, but I hate this for you."

"I know. And you need to be careful. I guess he . . . he hinted that he'd go after you if he couldn't find me."

"I can take care of myself. You know that," her mom said firmly. "I may have stayed with your father way too long, but I learned a lot from that. I'm a different person now. I'm just sorry that it took me so long. That you had to suffer because of my decisions."

"I don't blame you. I understand. If I'd had a child with Tommy, it would've been much harder to leave. And I know that you're tough, but if anything happened to you because of me, I'd never forgive myself."

"None of that. I'll be fine. You stay put. Keep on getting to know your man. It sounds like he's well aware of what's going on, and hopefully he'll keep you safe."

"He will," Carlise said without a shadow of a doubt.

"Good. Thank you for calling, sweetie. I was really so worried."

"I'm sorry. I don't know when I'll call again, but please know that I'm safe."

"Okay. I'm going to want to meet your Riggs at some point."

"You will. I love you, Mom."

"I love you, too, sweetie. Take care and be safe. We'll talk soon."

"We will. Bye."

"Bye."

Carlise hung up, feeling a ton better. She'd been worried about what her mom would think of her loving a man after just days. But she was right, Carlise knew what a relationship should be—and what it shouldn't—and so far, Riggs had far exceeded her every dream.

She stood up and wandered over to the window. The sun was out, and it was the first day since she'd arrived that it would warm up to above freezing. It was still chilly, but the sun shining made it look almost balmy.

A snowball flew past the window, followed by Baxter, who jumped and caught it in midair. Of course it disintegrated as soon as he chomped down on the lightly packed snow, but that didn't stop the silly dog from leaping about in victory as if he'd vanquished a villain.

Carlise looked to the right, where the snowball had come from—and nearly swallowed her tongue. Riggs had stripped down to a T-shirt, and the muscles in his arms rippled as he swung an axe and split a log in two.

She watched for a few minutes, noting the sweat at his temples as he labored to cut the wood for the fireplace. He would swing the axe, cut a log, then throw a snowball for Baxter. His actions were mesmerizing, comforting, and it wasn't until Riggs paused to run an arm over his forehead and wipe away sweat that he looked in her direction, and she realized she'd actually been staring at him for quite a while.

"You okay?" he mouthed, his brow furrowed as he stared back.

She smiled and nodded. He gave her a chin lift and went back to chopping, this time with a small grin on his lips. Carlise swore he was flexing a bit more than he had before, simply because he was now aware she was watching.

She chuckled. It was extremely difficult not to put down the phone and go outside to join him. She was drawn to Riggs in a way she couldn't understand. When she was around him, she was content, and this morning, when he'd left to check her phone, she'd missed him the moment he was gone. It was a strange feeling, but not a bad one.

Carlise vaguely wondered if it was merely a result of them sharing such a small space and being around each other for essentially twenty-four hours a day. All she knew was that the more time she spent in his presence, the more she *wanted* to be around him. Which was a new thing for her.

Honestly, she was relieved the call to her mom was done. She'd called her first because she'd wanted to get it over with, sure her mom would try to convince her to come home. It had gone so much better than she'd expected.

After one more lingering glance at Riggs, she turned back to the room. Returning to the couch, she dialed Susie's number, the only other one she knew by heart, looking forward to some girl talk with her bestie.

"Hello?"

"Hey, Suz, it's Carlise," she said when her friend answered.

The ear-splitting screech that came through the phone line was so loud, Carlise winced, even as she smiled.

"Oh my God! I've been trying to get ahold of you for almost two weeks!" Susie exclaimed.

"I know. I'm sorry! There was a huge storm here, and I don't have any cell signal where I've been staying."

"Where *are* you? I've been so worried!"

"You aren't going to believe everything that's happened."

"Well, you've only been gone about a week and a half," Susie said. "Now that I know you're alive—thank God—what could've happened in such a short time?"

"I wrecked my car, I almost froze to death, was saved by a dog, and found the man of my dreams," Carlise said simply.

"What?" Susie asked, shrieking again. "Start at the beginning and don't leave anything out!"

Carlise laughed and did just that. She told her friend everything about her adventure, which really only took about ten minutes. Susie didn't interrupt, simply letting her talk.

When she was done, Carlise waited a minute or so before asking, "So? Why aren't you saying anything?"

After a beat, Susie sighed. "I'm honestly not sure *what* to say. Now I'm even *more* worried about you, Car."

"What? Why?"

"Because this isn't like you. First you leave town without telling anyone where you're going, worrying your mom and me, and now you're shacking up with some lumberjack you met a week ago as if you're going to live happily ever after? That's just . . . that's not how life works."

Carlise frowned. She'd expected this exact argument from her mom, actually, but she'd hoped her friend would be happy for her. "Who says we *aren't* going to get an HEA?" she asked a little shortly.

"Look . . . I know you're in the throes of this new relationship, and you think you're happy, but you're in *Maine*. In some backwoods cabin. You don't like bugs, you're a city girl, and you said you'd never rush into another relationship after what happened with Tommy. It sounds to me like you've done just that."

"You don't understand—" Carlise began, but Susie interrupted.

"Then explain it in a way I *can* understand. Because all I know is that my best friend is on the run from one man and most likely now in a similar dysfunctional relationship with another and headed down the same road."

"That's not fair," Carlise told her. "Riggs isn't Tommy. Other than the three days he was unconscious, everything he's done has been with my happiness and safety in mind."

"Honey, you were just as happy with Tommy in the beginning," Susie reminded her gently.

Carlise was getting frustrated. Riggs was *nothing* like her ex, and it irritated her that her friend was being so hardheaded . . . even if she reluctantly admitted her arguments were valid. If their positions were reversed, she might say the same things to Susie.

She took a deep breath, then did as her friend requested—explained in a way she might understand.

"Two days ago, I was working on a translation and had lost track of time, like usual. The next thing I knew, Riggs placed a plate with a sandwich on it next to me. Then he kissed the top of my head and walked away. Tommy always got irritated when I worked when he was around. He didn't like not being the center of attention—and he never, not once, made me something to eat.

"Another time, we were in the kitchen cooking dinner—*together*—and I dropped a fork on the floor. I leaned over to pick it up, and when I stood, I noticed he'd moved and put his hand over the corner of the counter. I asked what he was doing, and he just shrugged and said he wanted to make sure I didn't hit my head on the corner when I stood up.

"I could give you twenty more stories like that, Susie. Situations where Riggs has looked out for me, done sweet things solely for my well-being, or when he could've gotten upset for one reason or another but didn't. And all of it in just the week since his fever broke. I've never met a man like Riggs. The more I'm around him, the more I *want* to be around him."

"I love that he's treating you so well, but don't *all* men do that when they first start dating? I don't like that your mom and I don't know this guy or where he's keeping you," Susie said. "Tell me where his cabin is. What towns are nearby. At least give us a *chance* to find you if you suddenly drop off the radar again. He could murder you tonight and bury you in the wilderness, and no one would ever find your body!"

With a deep sigh, she finished, "I'm your best friend, Car. I wouldn't be a very good one if I wasn't trying to be the voice of reason here."

Without hesitation, Carlise said, "The closest town is Newton. I'm told it's pretty small. I was on State Route 2, headed toward Bangor, and I guess I pulled off at the wrong exit and headed north on a smaller road called 26. The next thing I knew, I was seeing signs for Baldpate Mountain, and I took some other road. It was storming really hard, and I knew I needed to turn around, but there wasn't a good place. And then I ran off the road, and Baxter found me . . . and led me to Riggs."

There was silence for an uncomfortably long moment.

"God, I don't like this," Susie said.

Carlise sighed in frustration. "I want you to be happy for me. Is that so hard?"

"Honestly? Yes. Remember, I was with you when you first met Tommy, and you said similar things to what you're saying now. You gushed over how great he was and everything he did for you. Then things turned bad, and now you have a stalker. Wait—have you gotten any notes or messages from him since you've been there?"

"There's no cell service here and the Wi-Fi is buggy, but Riggs checked my phone and said that yes, he's still leaving me awful messages."

"Wait, wait, wait! You haven't seen them for yourself? *Seriously?* Car, you're being extremely dumb right now!"

Susie sounded pissed, and Carlise wasn't sure why. "I trust him, Susie."

"It's been a week and a half! You don't even know him!" she yelled.

"I do!" Carlise retorted, her own voice rising.

"You've fucked him, haven't you?" she asked abruptly, as if just realizing that was a possibility. "That's why you're acting like this. He's mesmerized you with his magic cock, and you're in some sex haze."

Now *Carlise* was pissed. "I have. And it was *awesome.* The best I've ever had. He actually cares about my pleasure—unlike Tommy, who only wanted to stick his dick inside me and get off, then go to sleep. I've never been with a man who wants me as much as Riggs does."

"Of *course* he does. He's living in the middle of nowhere. How many women just show up on his doorstep during a storm? Seems awfully convenient that you're stuck there if you ask me. God, he could have an STD or something."

"Now you're just being a bitch," Carlise seethed.

"And *you're* being reckless and ridiculous. You need to come home. *Now.* Before he manages to drain your bank account or convince you that he wants to get married and have fourteen babies."

Carlise's stomach tightened, and she put a hand on her belly. Babies with Riggs. That sounded heavenly.

She knew Susie was trying to shock her into seeing the situation from the outside, but she'd actually achieved the opposite. Carlise *longed* to give Riggs children. They could come up to the cabin in the summers, and their kids could run around safely to their hearts' content. They'd sit by the fire at night and read books and simply enjoy spending time together as a family.

"Carlise? Are you listening to me?"

"No," she told her best friend calmly. "When you meet Riggs, you'll see how wrong you are. He's one of the good guys, Suz. I promise."

She sighed heavily. "What are you doing about your stalker then? Have you even read my emails? You know I've been getting weird gifts, right? Since he can't find you, he's apparently trying to get to you through *me*."

"Oh no," Carlise breathed, her stomach now twisting for a different reason. Tears pricked her eyes. "Suz, you need to be careful."

"No shit," she retorted. "What I *need* is for you to get back here and make this stop."

"And how do I do that?" Carlise asked, completely seriously.

"I don't know! But hiding out in Maine and pretending you're in love with this Riggs person isn't helping."

"I know running didn't help anything," Carlise said with a sigh. "But I'm not pretending. I really do love him."

"You're killin' me," Susie said sadly. "I miss you, Car. I miss talking to you, laughing, having my best friend around to tell all my good news to."

"I miss you too," Carlise reassured her. "And good news?" she asked, wanting to lighten the mood of the call.

"Yeah. I have a new boyfriend."

"You do? That's awesome! Who is it? Someone I know? Where'd you meet him?"

"Yeah," she said, sounding almost shy. "He's great. Loves me so much that he hates when someone looks at me wrong. He's possessive but in a good way."

Carlise wasn't sure she liked the sound of that. Tommy had been possessive, too, and at first, she'd thought it was flattering. It soon turned stifling, and he was scary when he confronted people who'd simply said hello to her.

But after finally calming her friend, she was unwilling to upset her again or rain on her parade.

"I'm happy for you," Carlise said. And she really was.

"Thanks. I'm happy too . . . except for my best friend not telling me where she was going or not being able to get in touch with her for the last week and a half."

"I'm sorry. I'll be better at staying in touch from here on out."

"Good. I really do appreciate you calling, Car. And I'm sorry I flipped out. Will I talk to you again soon?"

"Yeah, you will," Carlise reassured her. "And please don't be mad at me," she pleaded. She was uncomfortable with a lot of their conversation, but Susie was still her best friend. Things would calm down, and she'd realize once she met Riggs that she had nothing to worry about.

"I'm not," Susie said with a sigh. "I'm just worried about you."

"I'm good. I promise," Carlise said.

"How would you feel about me coming out there to see for myself?" Susie asked.

"Seriously? Yes!" Carlise exclaimed.

"I want to meet this Riggs character and make sure he's good enough for my best friend."

"I'd love that. I promise to keep in touch better than I have, and we'll figure out a good time for you to come. I mean, Newton isn't exactly on the beaten path, so I'll have to give you specific directions," she teased with a laugh.

"Okay. Stay safe," Susie said softly.

"You too. If you see Tommy anywhere around, just go in the other direction. Riggs said he was going to help me end this stalker stuff. He's going to get his friends involved and the local Newton police."

"That's a relief, at least," Susie said.

"Yeah."

"Okay, I'll talk to you soon."

"Love you, Suz."

"Love you too. Bye."

Carlise hung up, not sure how to feel about the conversation with her best friend. She and Susie had always been brutally honest with each other, but all her worry aside, today she seemed . . . weird. She couldn't put her finger on exactly why, but the feeling persisted. Maybe it was because Susie seemed almost more angry than concerned.

She hated that her friend couldn't be supportive of her relationship with Riggs, but she knew Susie had good reason to be wary, considering Carlise's last relationship. And she probably hadn't said anything that wasn't expected. But she also didn't know Riggs. Once she met him, she'd see that he was nothing like Tommy. That his feelings for Carlise were genuine.

It wasn't until she got up and put the phone back on the kitchen counter that she realized Susie hadn't told her anything about her new boyfriend. She'd neatly changed the subject.

Mentally shrugging, Carlise decided that would be the first thing she asked when she talked to Susie next. She wanted to know all about the new man in her life.

At the moment, though, she needed to see Riggs. Talk to him. Reassure herself that he was the man she thought he was and not the monster Susie seemed to assume he could be.

She put on her boots and jacket and stepped outside. Baxter saw her and immediately ran in her direction. He came close enough for her to just brush her fingers over his head before he bolted away and grabbed a mouthful of snow, throwing it up in the air.

Laughing, Carlise turned toward Riggs . . . and stilled. He was headed in her direction with a look she couldn't interpret on his face. If she had to guess, she'd say he looked upset.

"What's wrong?" she asked with a frown as she stepped off the porch.

"That's what I was going to ask *you*. Were you not able to get ahold of your mom or Susie? Are they sick? Do we need to get you to town or back to Ohio? We can probably be there within a day if we drive, or we could head up to Bangor and catch a flight to Cleveland."

Carlise stared at him in surprise. "Are you even real?" she blurted.

"What?" he asked, looking completely confused.

"I didn't know men like you existed. You don't even know if anything's wrong, yet you're talking about taking me to Ohio because you think I might need to see my loved ones."

"So they're okay? Then what's wrong?"

Carlise shook her head. This man. Susie was so wrong about him. This right here was reason number five hundred and sixteen that proved it.

She stepped close and put her arms around his neck. Riggs immediately pulled her flush against him. Then he put a finger under her chin and tilted her head up so he could see her eyes.

"Are you okay?"

"Yes."

"Is your mom okay?"

"Yes."

"Susie?"

Carlise nodded.

Every muscle in Riggs's body relaxed. "Talk to me, sweetheart. Based on your expression when you came outside, I'm imagining the worst here."

"My mom was thrilled for me. Said she can't wait to meet you."

"I want to meet her too," Riggs said with a small nod.

"Susie . . . She's not so sure. She thinks I'm insane, actually. That there's no way I can love you. She's basically worried. Wants me to come home before you steal all my money and knock me up with one of the fourteen babies she's sure you must want."

"Four," Riggs said immediately.

"What?"

"I'd like four kids. I've always wanted a big family, and four kids seems like it would be perfect. They'd always have a friend and someone to play with, someone to have their backs in school, and someone they can lean on for the rest of their lives. I don't care if they're boys or girls, just that they're healthy."

Carlise swallowed hard.

"What about you? You want kids?"

She nodded.

"Am I freaking you out with the four kids thing?"

Carlise shook her head slowly. "When I was little, I used to tell my mom I wished I had brothers or sisters. I thought that maybe if there were more of us, we could've protected Mom better. Or Dad wouldn't have been so mean. I don't know. But actually . . . I always thought four would be perfect." She practically whispered that last part.

"Really?"

She nodded.

Riggs grinned. Huge. "We were meant to be, honey. That's just another sign."

Carlise had to agree. "You about done out here?"

"Not yet."

"Oh," she said with an exaggerated pout. "I thought maybe you might be too cold. Or hot. Or sweaty. That maybe a shower would sound good right about now."

"I've got about twenty more minutes to—oh. Right. Yeah, now that you mention it, a break would be great. I wouldn't want to get overheated."

Carlise grinned, happy he'd picked up on her meaning. "Exactly. And it wasn't too long ago that you were sick. Maybe I should assist you in the shower. You know, so you don't fall and hit your head or anything."

"You want me?" Riggs growled.

Carlise's cheeks felt hot, but she smiled and nodded anyway.

"You want me, all you have to do is say the word. Because I will *never* pass up the chance to get inside you."

His words were blunt, but he somehow made them sound romantic at the same time.

"I want you," she told him.

Without a word, Riggs turned and grabbed hold of her hand and headed for the cabin.

Baxter barked, as if to ask where they were going.

"We'll be back, boy. Go on and explore. Make sure things around here are safe. I'll come back out and finish my chopping and throw more snowballs in a while."

"Do you think he'll be okay out here alone?" Carlise asked worriedly, looking back at the dog, who'd already gone back to rolling in the snow.

"He'll be fine," Riggs told her as he pulled her up the porch steps.

The second they were inside and the door closed behind them, Riggs's hands got busy peeling off her coat, and Carlise wasn't thinking about Baxter or her mom or Susie anymore.

Riggs picked her up and carried her toward the bed. He dropped her on the mattress, and she giggled as she bounced.

"You have ten seconds to get naked," Riggs warned.

"Or what?"

"Or I'll do it for you."

Carlise grinned and threw her arms above her head, smirking up at Riggs. "If you think that's a threat, you're wrong."

He whipped his T-shirt over his head, and Carlise practically drooled. The man was gorgeous, and he was all hers.

He leaned over, unlaced his boots, kicked them and his socks off, shoved his pants and underwear down his muscular legs, then climbed onto the bed.

She and Riggs didn't get back outside to play with Baxter for an hour and a half. They also didn't get the shower she'd suggested. But she wasn't complaining.

No, she had not one complaint about Riggs making her feel like the most beautiful and desirable woman in the entire universe.

Chapter Fourteen

"Are you sure you don't want to come with me?" Chappy asked for the hundredth time.

"Positive," Carlise told him with a smile. "I'm behind on this translation because *someone* keeps distracting me by taking their clothes off and being too damn sexy."

Chappy chuckled and pulled her into him. They were in the kitchen after a morning spent in bed. He'd woken up with her mouth on his cock, and he honestly thought he was going to die with pleasure. She'd ended up making him come that way, which was actually a blessing because it gave him enough control to thoroughly pleasure her before he needed to be inside her again. She'd come twice—once on his face and again on his fingers—before he'd pushed his way inside her and orgasmed a second time.

Chappy couldn't stop thinking about having a child with Carlise. She was beautiful now, but she'd be even more so round with their baby. He had a feeling the first time he came inside her without a condom, he'd knock her up. Of course, life didn't always work that way, but with how lucky they'd been so far, he was pretty sure they wouldn't have any problems conceiving.

It was uncanny how well they fit together. From their desire to have four children to her love of the same kinds of books he liked to the way they were both perfectly happy hanging out at the cabin without a phone, internet, or TV. She was made for him, and he'd do everything in his power to treat her so well, she'd never want to leave him.

Four days had passed since she'd reached out to her mom and best friend, and as much as he wanted to continue to hide away from the world, the messages on her phone were constantly in the back of his mind. He needed to get the ball rolling on figuring out who was stalking her and make sure it stopped. Make sure both Carlise and her loved ones were safe.

"Riggs?" she asked. "Is everything all right?"

He forced himself to concentrate on the here and now. "Everything's fine. I'll probably be gone for at least five hours. Will that be okay?"

"I'll be fine. And I don't want you spending a ton of money on my car. I can pay for whatever needs to be done."

Chappy nodded, but in his head, he was already making plans. She wasn't paying for the repairs on her car. He didn't want or need her money. If she wanted to spend it on Baxter or their kids or their friends, he had no problem with that, but the neanderthal inside him wanted to provide for her. Wanted to give her everything she wanted or needed.

"You're totally ignoring me, aren't you?" she asked with a roll of her eyes.

"I hear you," Chappy told her.

"You hear me, but you aren't gonna let me pay for my car, are you?"

"Nope," he said cheerfully.

"You're impossible," she told him with a shake of her head.

"No, what I am is madly in love with you, and I want to treat you like you should've been treated in all your other relationships. It makes me happy when *you're* happy, and I want to make sure your car is safe for you to be driving around in Maine."

He loved the tender look on her face. It was obvious she wasn't used to being taken care of, and he wanted to see her wearing that expression for the rest of their lives.

"Be careful out there. I heard you talking to JJ yesterday about the increased risk of avalanches because of the warmer weather we've had. And the snow isn't all melted off the road yet. If you run off the road, Baxter won't be there to lead you home," she teased.

"I'll be careful, because for the first time in my life, I have someone to come home *to*."

"I love you," she whispered as she went up on her toes to reach his mouth.

He lowered his head and kissed her with all the love he had in his heart. He pulled away long before he was ready. "If I don't get going, I'll never leave," he said, running his thumb over her swollen lower lip. He couldn't help but remember how her lips had looked stretched around his cock. His dick twitched in his pants.

"You're showing the messages and stuff to the chief of police, right?" she asked, biting that lip he'd just been admiring.

"Yes. It'll be fine. Promise. We'll figure out who's been harassing you."

"I hope so."

"We will," Chappy vowed. Because the alternative wasn't even an option.

"I'm hoping maybe he'll give up soon," she suggested.

Chappy didn't answer. They both knew better, and he wasn't going to lie to her by suggesting otherwise.

She sighed. "Right. Well, don't get so upset at the messages that pop up on my phone the moment you get service and end up wrecking. Okay?"

"I won't. And now I'm really going to get going. If you need anything, I'm leaving the satellite phone for you. You can call my cell, or yours for that matter, and I'll turn right back around. And Bob, Cal, and JJ's numbers are all programmed in as well. April's too."

"Baxter and I will be fine. I'm just going to be here working. You want me to make dinner for when you get back? Anything you're in the mood for?"

"You." The word popped out automatically.

She grinned. "I think I can manage that."

"I love you, Carlise. So much, you have no idea."

"I do," she said, her smile fading as she got serious. "I never thought I'd have this. A man who respected me, *liked* me, and genuinely wanted to make me happy."

"I feel all those things and more," Chappy said. He kissed her again, hard and fast, before forcing himself to step away. He was two seconds from saying "Screw it" and hauling her back to their bed. But he needed to take care of her car. Tow it down the mountain and talk to Chief Rutkey. The sooner he left, the sooner he could be back, and the sooner he could have her again.

"Are you sure there's nothing you want from town?" he asked.

"Nope. Just you to get back safely."

Lord, he loved this woman. He was already planning on getting her all sorts of things from the grocery store. Chocolate, the flavored tea she said she liked, strawberries, garlic chips. He'd learned a great deal about her likes and dislikes during their many lengthy conversations. And he liked the thought of spoiling her.

"Go," she said with a smile.

"I'm going."

"Be safe."

"Always." Then he headed toward the door, making a detour to the couch, where Baxter had taken up residence. He ran his hand over the pit bull's fur, nodding in satisfaction when he felt how much the dog was filling out. "Watch after her, boy," he said.

Baxter huffed out a breath as if he understood what was being asked of him. Then Chappy continued to the door. "Lock this behind me," he ordered.

Carlise rolled her eyes but nodded. "I will."

He left the cabin, and every step away from her felt . . . *wrong*.

He wondered if it would always feel like this. He hadn't felt this particular trepidation when he'd left her before, to check the messages on her phone. So why now? Maybe because before, he was only going down the road, and for a short time. Today, it would take him hours to do everything he needed to get done.

He'd hooked the trailer for her car to the back of his Jeep earlier, so it was just a matter of starting the engine and leaving. But Chappy took the time to study the lay of the land. The sun was out once more, and he could see water dripping from the eaves of the cabin and from the trees.

The snow was melting, and he'd lived in Maine and had the cabin long enough to know that JJ's warning was spot on. The rains that had softened the ground before the snow started, the extreme amount of heavy snow dumped on them during the storm, and now the warmer weather . . . it all made for the right conditions for avalanches.

He was confident that his cabin wasn't in any danger. It was close to where slides normally occurred on Baldpate Mountain but not in the direct line of fire, so to speak.

And Carlise wasn't going anywhere. She wasn't a huge fan of the cold—which he thought was somewhat amusing since she lived in Cleveland—and she'd reassured him that she and Baxter were going to stay snuggled up inside until he returned.

Taking one last look around, and seeing nothing out of the ordinary, Chappy climbed behind the wheel of his Jeep. The uneasy feeling stuck with him as he drove down the drive and out onto the road. The faster he got his errands done, the faster he could get home and reassure himself that all was well.

~

Hours later, Carlise was happy about how much work she'd gotten done. Thanks to the quiet cabin and zero distractions, her translation work was going much faster than when she was at home. She'd caught up and was back on track to finish the book by the deadline the author had requested.

She was taking a break, snuggling with Baxter—who'd turned out to be quite the cuddle bug once he'd gotten over his fear of her and Riggs—when a noise outside caught her attention.

Recognizing the sound of a vehicle engine, she frowned slightly. Maybe it was Riggs getting home a little early. He'd only been gone for about four hours, but maybe he'd finished all his errands.

Carlise stood and headed for the window at the front of the cabin. To her surprise, Baxter followed her. He was usually content to stay on the couch, stretched on his back with all four of his paws in the air, when she got up to use the bathroom or get a snack. But this time, he was right at her side, and she noticed the hair on his scruff was actually standing up.

"It's okay, Bax. I'm sure it's nothing."

When she looked outside, Carlise was surprised to see a Toyota RAV4 heading down the drive toward the cabin.

"Who in the world is that?" she asked out loud, despite knowing she wasn't going to get an answer.

Baxter pawed at the front door and growled low in his throat.

The hair on Carlise's arms stood up. She froze, hardly daring to breathe.

Had her stalker found her? How? And when? Had he been watching them? Waiting for Riggs to go somewhere and leave her alone?

She was working herself into a huge freak-out and was about to run to the kitchen to grab Riggs's satellite phone when the SUV stopped, and someone got out.

Carlise stared for a moment in total shock before a huge smile formed on her face. She went to the door and gently urged Baxter aside. "It's okay, Bax! It's safe. That's my friend. Be nice! No—stay!" she ordered as she slid out the door, trying to keep the dog from pushing past her legs to get outside.

She had the door shut and had turned by the time Susie reached the steps of the porch.

"Susie! What in the world are you doing here?"

"I'm hoping that's a happy greeting and not a pissed-off one," her friend said with a smile.

"Yes! Of course it is!" Carlise opened her arms and hugged her friend. Susie was petite, only around five feet four and skinny as a rail, but she had a personality that made her seem much bigger. Her long black hair was thick and gorgeous, and her brown eyes sparkled when she was happy. She never seemed to leave the house without a full face of makeup and the most fashionable clothes, and apparently a road trip was no exception.

She was younger by five years, and sometimes that made Carlise feel ancient compared to her put-together and sometimes-naive friend, but she wouldn't trade her for anything.

"I can't believe you want to stay here willingly," Susie said with a laugh as she looked around. "You weren't kidding about being in the middle of nowhere!"

"Right? How in the world did you find me?"

"I did a lot of thinking after we hung up, Car. I felt really bad about how I behaved . . . but I was still really worried about you. You sounded so out of character on the phone, and with the notes and stuff you've been getting, I just knew I couldn't live with myself if I didn't make sure you were really okay. And I wanted to meet this Riggs guy. So I pieced together all the things you told me about where you were, the roads and the town, and I made my way here. I flew into Bangor and rented this SUV and . . . here I am!"

"I'm so happy to see you," Carlise told her. "I still can't believe you found the cabin."

"I asked around in that small town. Apparently, there isn't anyone else there named Riggs who works with trees and has a cabin. It wasn't too hard to get directions."

"Well, I think it's great. Riggs isn't here right now, though."

"He left you out here by yourself?" Susie asked, her brows shooting upward in surprise.

"It's not like anyone's out here who would want to hurt me," Carlise replied.

"So he doesn't even have neighbors?" Susie asked.

"Nope. And I don't think the animals around here count. Wait here a sec while I grab Baxter." Carlise was a little concerned, actually, because she could hear the dog scratching nonstop at the door. He wasn't barking, but he definitely wasn't thrilled that she was outside while he was stuck in the cabin.

"Is he nice? He doesn't sound happy."

"He's nice," Carlise reassured her friend. "But he's not used to people. He was starving when we found him, and I think he'd been beaten. So he's just wary."

She opened the door, and Baxter almost ran past her. Carlise grabbed him by the collar that Riggs's friends had included when they'd come up with the dog food. "Hang on, Bax. It's okay! That's Susie, she's a friend."

But the dog didn't seem inclined to give the woman standing on the porch the benefit of the doubt. He was growling, his fur still sticking up, and if dogs could glare, Susie would be getting an eyeful.

Carlise frowned. He hadn't acted like this when JJ and the others were there. She couldn't imagine why he was so riled now.

"How about this—I'll hold him while you go inside, then I'll leave him out here for a while. Before you leave, I'll come outside, grab him, and bring him back in so you can get to your car without any worries. Okay?" Carlise asked her friend.

Susie looked petrified and nodded immediately.

Carlise hung on to Baxter as she moved farther along the porch, away from the door, giving Susie a clear path to get inside.

Once she was safely behind the front door, Carlise scolded Baxter. "You aren't being very nice. That's my best friend, and you'll probably be seeing a lot more of her. I'm not leaving you out here forever, just for a while as we visit. Then I'll bring you back inside, okay?"

To her relief, Baxter turned his head and licked her face. Carlise laughed. "Off with you, mutt. Go find some bunnies to chase and snowballs to eat."

She let go of the dog, and to her surprise, he immediately sat instead, staring up at her.

"Oh, don't make me feel guilty. It's not even that cold out here," Carlise told him.

Baxter merely blinked.

Steeling her heart, Carlise stepped to the door and slipped back inside. She turned to see her best friend peering around the cabin with curiosity.

"One bed, huh?" she said after a moment, smirking at Carlise. "You left that part out on the phone."

Carlise chuckled. "Yeah, you already weren't thrilled with the situation, I didn't think it would be good to spring that on you."

"This is literally a romance book come to life. The damsel in distress needing a place to shelter in a storm, and—surprise—there's only one bed, so I guess you have to share it."

Carlise giggled. "Heroine in peril," she said.

"What?"

"'Heroine in peril.' I think that sounds better than 'damsel in distress.' Less needy. Less pathetic."

Susie rolled her eyes and laughed. "Whatever."

"Besides, the first three days, he was so out of it with a fever that there was nothing romantic going on, believe me," Carlise said.

"Wait, did you have to hold his dick while he pissed?" she asked with wide eyes.

Carlise burst out laughing. "Oh my God, no! Jeez. He was alert enough to walk to the bathroom with my help, and then I left him to do his thing. There was no willy holding while he was sick."

"But there is now," Susie said knowingly.

Carlise couldn't stop the smile from forming on her face. "Oh yeah, there's lots of willy holding now."

The two women laughed together.

"You look good for someone who was terrified just weeks ago," Susie observed when they sat on the couch.

"I *feel* pretty good. I mean, don't get me wrong, I'm still scared of Tommy, but Riggs has promised to help me figure out who's bothering me and make them stop."

"How's he going to do that?" Susie asked.

Carlise shrugged. "I'm not sure. But I trust him."

"There's that trust again," Susie said, sounding unconvinced. "You don't even know him."

"Actually, I do," Carlise countered.

"How can you? You met him only a couple of weeks ago."

"It's hard to explain. We've been together twenty-four seven for weeks. I *know* him, Suz. He's a good man. Hardworking. Loyal. His friends are amazing. And he went through hell while he was in the military—"

"So he has PTSD and could snap at any moment?" Susie interrupted.

"Maybe he does, but I've seen no signs of it. And no, he's not going to snap. He has great self-control. Lots of it."

Susie tilted her head to look at her friend. "Are we talking BDSM, because . . . gross. And if you tell me he ties you up or uses handcuffs, I'm dragging you out of here right this second!"

"No!" Carlise hurried to say. "If anything, he's always asking for permission to touch me. It's . . . nice. He just has control over his emotions. What he does. What he says. He's not going to hurt me, Susie. I wish you could see that. Actually, I'm sure you will when you meet him. He's the best thing that's ever happened to me. I love him, and now I realize anything I felt in the past was just a poor facsimile of what I feel now. So much so, it's almost ridiculous."

"Ridiculous? You said you loved Tommy too," Susie said in a tone Carlise couldn't interpret.

She opened her mouth to answer but heard Baxter whimpering and scratching at the front door. "Crap. I can't leave him out there. I feel awful. Do you mind if I bring him in? Maybe he'll be better now that we're sitting, and he'll see you aren't going to hurt him."

"I don't know," Susie said nervously.

"Maybe I could put him in the bathroom?" Carlise mused. "I could put his bedding in there and maybe even his food. That should keep him busy."

"I guess that'll work," Susie said. "The door is sturdy, right?"

"Yes. He'll be fine in there. Hang on." It didn't take long to get Baxter and bring him inside. But instead of the dog relaxing when he saw Susie on the couch, the hackles on the back of his spine rose once more. It took a little bit, but eventually Carlise got him settled in the bathroom. He wasn't happy, but thankfully he didn't try to get out of her hold or attack Susie.

"There, that's better. What were we talking about?" Carlise asked as she finally sat back on the couch with her friend.

"How much you love this guy you just met, even though you said you loved Tommy," Susie said, almost accusatorily.

Carlise sighed. "I want you to like and get along with Riggs, Suz."

"And I can't do that until I meet him. When is he getting home?"

Looking at her watch, Carlise said, "I don't know exactly, but according to his estimate when he left, maybe another forty-five minutes or so—"

Susie stood abruptly, and Carlise looked up at her in surprise. She blinked in confusion . . .

Then her eyes went wide when her friend reached into the pocket of the coat she hadn't bothered to take off, pulling out a gun—and pointing it right at her.

"Get up," Susie said in a voice Carlise didn't recognize.

"What?" she said, struggling to understand what was happening.

"*Stand up.* I need you to get a piece of paper. You're going to write Riggs a note—and we're leaving."

Carlise laughed incredulously. "You're kidnapping me? I think that's going a bit far, don't you?" she asked. "And can you please not point that gun at me? It's not loaded, right?"

"Oh, it's loaded. And I'll absolutely use it," Susie said. "Now get the fuck up and get a piece of paper."

At that moment, she realized this wasn't some really poor joke. Fear instantly flooded Carlise's veins. "Susie?" she asked as she slowly stood. "What's happening?"

"You're so goddamn stupid," Susie scoffed, shaking her head. "First for dumping Tommy. You'll *never* find a man as good as he is. You hurt him—and you didn't even care! Well, don't worry about that part. I stepped into your shoes. The only problem is, he still thinks about you . . . which is unacceptable."

"What?" Carlise asked, her brain swirling in confusion as she tried to keep up with what she was saying. "You're dating *Tommy*?"

"Yes. *And* we're going to get married."

"No," Carlise whispered, shaking her head. "You *can't*, Susie. He's abusive! He's going to hurt you!"

"No, he isn't!" Susie screeched loudly. "He's *mine*! I've *always* wanted him! When you two started dating, I tried to be happy for you. I really did. But you never deserved him. And you're a *bitch* for leaving him like you did! I comforted him after you snuck your shit out of his house without warning, and one thing led to another. He loves *me* now. Regrets not choosing me in the first place.

"But every now and then, he still brings you up . . . said he regrets hurting you and making you leave. He even admitted he had hopes of patching things up with you before we got together."

Susie barked out a deranged laugh. "But that'll *never* happen. You dumped him. Accused him of terrible things! And since we're friends, you'll keep coming around, like a bad fucking penny. The only way to help him realize how much he loves me is to get *you* out of the picture once and for all. Then he can concentrate on me—and *only* me."

Carlise shook her head. "But . . . he's yours already. And I have Riggs. I'm hoping to move here, to stay with—"

"But that's not enough!" she interrupted, ranting. "People are talking! Saying bad things about him! When the cops delivered the restraining order—*at his workplace*—it got him in trouble. They automatically assumed he's a dirtbag, and he almost lost his job! You've ruined his reputation by spreading your fucking lies about being abused. He was never going to hit you. Your screwed-up childhood just made you see something that wasn't there. You're a *liar*—and you'll never get him back!"

Carlise wanted to tell her friend that she didn't *want* him back, but she didn't get the chance before something unbelievable occurred to her. "Wait . . . was it you?"

"Was what me?" Susie asked.

The woman in front of her *looked* like her friend, but the gun pointed in her direction and the angry words were *nothing* like her best friend. "The notes. The texts. My tires."

Susie smirked. "Yup."

"Why?" Carlise asked, truly shocked and appalled.

"You tried to *ruin* Tommy! That wasn't fair. I thought it was only right that you got some payback. Didn't you say this Riggs guy would do anything to protect you? Well . . . I'm doing the same for my man."

"I was *terrified*," Carlise said, trying to wrap her mind around the fact that the woman she considered a sister was the person who'd been threatening her for weeks. "I confided in you."

"And Tommy and I laughed about it," Susie said, her smirk turning cruel.

She was deranged. Carlise couldn't think of another explanation for why Susie would act like this, why she'd do *anything* she'd done.

"But then you disappeared, and I couldn't have fun anymore, and it pissed me off! It's a good thing you called when you did because I was all set to have a little *chat* with your mom . . . use a little physical persuasion to find out where you were hiding. I was actually in her parking lot when you called." Susie flashed another evil smile. "But when you were saying all that ridiculous shit and sounding so happy? Well . . . I couldn't have that.

"I need you to *suffer*, Carlise. Like you made Tommy suffer! I tried to get you to come back to Ohio, but you were too damn stupid. So I did what I had to do . . . and here I am. Now—*get that fucking piece of paper!*"

Susie emphasized her point by pulling the trigger on the gun and firing at the floor.

Carlise jumped so badly at the loud noise, her entire body immediately began to shake. Her mind, though, was still frozen. Still thinking of everything she'd just heard.

She couldn't believe her best friend had actually planned on torturing her *mom*.

Baxter growled in the bathroom. Loud, vicious growls that made the situation all the more terrifying.

"Now!" Susie screamed.

Moving quickly and trying to figure out how the hell she could get out of this, Carlise went over to the pad she used to take notes while translating books and tore out a sheet. She held it out to Susie. But her former friend merely shook her head.

"Write," she ordered. "I'll tell you what to say."

Carlise didn't want to, but at the moment, she had no choice. So she picked up the pen that was next to the notebook and began to write as Susie dictated.

She was crying by the time she'd finished.

When Riggs read the note, he was going to be pissed. But not at her. She had no doubt that he wouldn't believe anything on that piece of paper. They loved each other. Truly and deeply. There was no way he'd turn his back on her because of a note.

Not to mention, as soon as he reviewed the cameras, he'd learn what had happened.

She hadn't been so sure about the cameras, had thought more than once of taking him up on the offer to turn them off . . . but she trusted Riggs. And now? She was eternally grateful for them. If Susie hurt her, Riggs would know what had happened—and who was to blame.

"Now pack," Susie ordered. "And hurry up. We need to be off this godforsaken mountain before that asshole returns."

With little choice, Carlise began stuffing her things into the backpack she'd worn when she'd first set out into that storm. When that was full, she put the rest of her things into the suitcase his friends had brought to her after finding her car. She was crying nonstop now, not sure what to do, how to escape.

Susie. She never in a million years had suspected her *friend* was the one who was terrorizing her. Now, it made glaring sense why she'd never been able to catch a glimpse of her stalker. Hell, she'd told Susie everything she was doing, where she was going . . . how badly the messages and gifts were scaring her.

And the person she'd thought had her back was actually *laughing* behind her back the whole time. Enjoying the fact that she was frightened and constantly looking over her shoulder.

Now she had a loaded weapon pointed at her—and seemed to have no problem using it.

Had she ever really known Susie? Apparently not.

"Now what?" she asked tonelessly when she'd finished packing.

"Now we leave," Susie said.

"And?"

Her former best friend smiled again. A grin so malicious, it made the hair on Carlise's arms stand on end.

"You'll no longer be Tommy's problem," Susie said. "And he and I can live happily ever after. I won't have to worry about you being a pain in my ass or coming back to try to seduce him away from me. Now *move*. And don't even *think* about going anywhere near that bathroom door. I'll put a bullet through that dog's head before he can get close to me."

Baxter was still losing his mind inside the small room, his snarls and growls loud and continuous. The thought of him being killed was more than Carlise could bear.

As she shuffled toward the front door with her suitcase and backpack, she took a deep breath, and her tears stopped flowing. She needed to clear her head if she was going to survive whatever Susie had planned for her. And it sure wasn't bringing her back to Cleveland and pretending none of this had ever happened.

She had to get away. She'd watched enough crime shows to know that if someone bent on doing harm got you into a car, you were done for. And they both knew Susie couldn't navigate the snowy winding roads and keep the gun pointed at Carlise at the same time. As soon as she was in the SUV, it was likely Susie would shoot her and find a place to dump her body in some desolate forest area on the way to Bangor to catch her plane back to Ohio.

Anger swam through Carlise's veins. No. She'd just found Riggs. She didn't want to leave him. Leave Baxter.

She wanted to get to know JJ and Bob and Cal. And find out what the deal was between April and JJ. She'd seen the look Riggs's friend had aimed at the administrative assistant when she'd almost fallen in the snow, and it definitely wasn't one of mere concern.

She wanted to see her mom again. Wanted to make her a grandma by giving Riggs as many babies as he wanted.

Carlise had too much to live for. She wasn't going to let Susie take everything away from her. And for what? Jealousy?

She still wasn't even clear why Susie had turned on her, why she couldn't just go back to Tommy, leaving Carlise in Maine to enjoy her life with Riggs. But she supposed, at the moment, it didn't matter. All that mattered was getting the hell away from her.

"Riggs isn't going to believe that note you made me write," she said as she put down the bags and reached for her jacket hanging on the coatrack beside the door.

"Sure he will," Susie countered. "This was a fling. You've come to your senses, and now you're going home."

Carlise shook her head. Susie was the stupid one. How was Carlise supposed to get off the mountain? It wasn't as if she had a car, and Susie certainly didn't let Carlise mention her visit or use her name in the note. So apparently, she must think Riggs was going to believe she'd levitated away from the cabin or something.

She wasn't about to point out the flaws in Susie's plan. Even without cameras, Riggs would eventually figure out who'd taken her, and he'd know that Carlise wouldn't have left voluntarily. He had to.

"He's going to come looking for me," she told her firmly. "People in town will remember that a woman was asking where he lived. They'll track down the rental car . . . did you put it on your credit card? Use a fake name?"

Susie looked surprised for a moment, like none of that had even occurred to her—and clearly it hadn't—before pressing her lips together and frowning.

Bingo. She'd always thought her friend was smart, but apparently, she was just a good actress.

Her stupidity worked to Carlise's benefit at the moment. Susie had screwed up. Big time. She might as well have left a huge neon sign pointing straight to her. With her mistakes, and the cameras filming her every word and action, Susie would be caught quickly, whether she killed Carlise or not.

It was currently the only positive about this extremely screwed-up situation Carlise had found herself in.

"It doesn't matter," Susie finally said with a shrug. "I'll claim ignorance. Tommy will be my alibi."

She wanted to roll her eyes. As if he would ever make a convincing alibi. Carlise knew him. Knew he'd throw Susie under the bus in a heartbeat if it meant saving his own ass.

Susie had acted impulsively by coming out to Maine to find her, and doing so would be her downfall.

"Hurry up, or I'll shoot through the bathroom door at that damn dog," Susie seethed.

She had no doubt she'd do as threatened, so Carlise hurried to tie the laces of her boots, then stood. "I'm ready."

And she was. Ready for the first chance she had to run.

She'd go into the woods. Riggs and Baxter would find her. Of that she had no doubt.

Susie gestured with the gun, and Carlise opened the door. She exited the cabin where she'd been so happy for weeks, not looking back. She'd see it again. She had to believe that, otherwise she'd be a basket case and wouldn't be able to do what needed to be done.

She walked toward the SUV parked by the cabin and calmly put her bags into the back seat as Susie ordered.

"Get in," her former friend told her, pointing toward the passenger door with the gun.

Carlise's heart raced. She slowly opened the door and sat on the seat. Susie slammed the door shut, just missing Carlise's foot. She kept the gun pointed at her as she walked around the front of the car toward the driver's side door.

This was it. Her only chance to get away. Even though they were literally in the middle of the Maine wilderness, Carlise knew if she left with Susie, her chances of survival were zero. She'd rather be lost in the woods than dead.

Susie reached for the door handle on the driver's side of the SUV—and Carlise made her move.

She wrenched her door open and ran.

She heard Susie scream for her to stop, but she kept going. Heading straight for the trees, in the general direction Riggs had taken her when they'd gone for a walk.

The sound of a gunshot behind her echoed loudly in the peaceful tranquility of the forest. Carlise's body jerked, but she kept running.

She could hear Susie running after her, and she tried to go faster. But she knew she wasn't going to outrun her former friend. Susie actually *liked* to work out. She went to the gym almost every day. She prided herself on staying slender and fit. While Carlise wanted to be healthy, she wasn't a fan of exercise. Hell, she sat on her butt most days, working on her computer.

She was huffing and puffing as she frantically looked around, trying to figure out a good place to hide. Since it was winter, the trees were mostly bare. And the few evergreen trees she spotted wouldn't conceal her for long.

"You better fucking stop!" Susie shouted from way too close behind her.

Carlise didn't bother to answer. One, there was nothing she had to say to the psycho who'd pretended to be her friend while terrorizing her—and laughing about it with Tommy. And two . . . talking was almost impossible with how hard she was panting.

"Where do you think you're going? There's nowhere to hide! Just stop, bitch!"

Susie was catching up. Carlise's heart rate, which was already high, skyrocketed even further as she panicked.

The sound of a second gunshot didn't help. Then another shot a millisecond later—and pain bloomed in Carlise's shoulder.

She stumbled as she ran and almost fell but caught herself at the last second.

Susie had shot her. *Shot her!*

Anger and terror had her running at a pace she didn't even know she could manage. She was literally running for her life.

Carlise heard an abrupt thud, then loud crunching behind her, and she risked turning her head to see what was happening. Susie was sprawled on the forest floor. She'd obviously tripped over something.

This was Carlise's chance.

To get ahead.

To hide.

To *live.*

She tried to run even faster—and was suddenly surprised to realize she knew where she was.

Ahead of her, less than twenty yards away, was a group of pine trees that looked completely out of place, as there weren't any others in the immediate area.

Against all odds, she'd run to the very spot Riggs had brought her to the day of their walk. She sped up even more as she headed straight for those trees.

Glancing at the ground ahead of her, Carlise felt relief racing through her veins, making her body shake almost uncontrollably. The handle to the bunker door was right there! The snow surrounding it had melted considerably, and the earth Riggs had dug up to clear the edges of the hatch was a beacon in the otherwise undisturbed forest floor.

She came to an abrupt stop, leaned over, and yanked the handle upward. To Carlise's immense relief, it opened without any resistance whatsoever.

Sending up a heartfelt thanks to the doomsday prepper who'd installed the bunker, she quickly turned to go down the ladder.

"No!"

At the shout, Carlise looked up—and saw Susie about fifty yards away and closing in fast.

She almost didn't recognize her friend. Her normally elegant hair was spilling out of the neat ponytail it had been in when she'd arrived at the cabin. Snow and dirt were caked all down her front after she'd face-planted into the ground.

But it was the look of loathing and fury on her face that made Carlise freeze for a split second.

How could this be her friend?

The woman whose shoulder she'd cried on when she left Tommy. Who'd listened to her deepest hopes and fears. The woman who'd laughed and cried with her, who'd supported her.

The loss of her friend was almost as painful as the throbbing of her shoulder.

More gunshots exploded, and Carlise instinctively ducked—until another noise, unfamiliar and chilling, suddenly echoed around them.

It sounded like thunder . . . but the sky was blue—there wasn't a cloud in sight.

Reaching up for the handle of the hatch, Carlise paused for one last glance at her ex-friend.

Susie had stopped and braced herself to shoot, but she was no longer looking at Carlise. Rather, she was staring at something beyond the bunker. Her eyes were huge, and her furious expression had morphed into one of shock and fear.

Carlise had no idea what she was looking at, but there was no time to find out. Any second now, Susie would shake herself out of whatever trance she was in and try to kill her.

She slammed the door to the bunker and fumbled with the locking mechanism. It was pitch black in the bunker, but Carlise had never been so grateful to be out of the sun as she was right at that moment. She was pretty sure the door had to be bulletproof because no self-respecting prepper would build a place like this and make the mistake of not having an entrance that was able to withstand any enemies trying to get inside.

"Let me in! Holy shit, *let me in*!" Susie screamed from outside. Her voice was muffled, but Carlise could hear her just fine. And there was no way she was unlocking that door. If Susie thought there was a chance in hell, she was delusional.

"The mountain's falling! *Oh my God!* Please, Carlise! *Please!* It's coming toward me! I'm gonna be buried! *Let me in, let me in, let me in!*"

Carlise heard her former friend pounding on the door, but instead of responding to the absolute terror in her voice, she backed away from the hatch, slowly scooting along the floor toward the back of the bunker.

"It's an avalanche! Can you hear me? If you don't let me in, I'm gonna die!"

The thunder she'd heard must have been snow and ice breaking away from the mountain.

Carlise felt physically sick . . . but she couldn't open that door.

Susie had *shot* her. She was bleeding, and her shoulder hurt worse than anything she'd ever felt in her life. Her ex-friend had threatened her for months, making her think she was being stalked. She'd hooked up with her ex for some insane reason, and now she had it in her head that Carlise needed to pay for dumping him. She'd fully intended to kill her and leave her body somewhere in the Maine wilderness.

Nothing made sense right now, but the one thing she knew was that if she let Susie inside that bunker, only one of them would ever come out. Since Susie had the gun, it didn't take a genius to know it probably wouldn't be Carlise.

It took every ounce of strength she had to ignore Susie's increasingly desperate pleas. She heard a sound like a train barreling through the woods, and the bunker walls shook. Susie let out a piercing scream that was abruptly cut off . . .

And then, Carlise heard nothing beyond the loudest, scariest thunder continuously booming right over her head.

She half expected the door to the bunker to explode inward, letting in the tons of rocks and snow that were currently sliding down Baldpate Mountain. But the door held. The sound went on and on as the avalanche seemed to last forever.

Carlise was relieved she was safe from being shot again . . . but only for a moment. Then guilt swamped her. Susie had been outside in the direct path of an *avalanche.*

There was a chance she'd survived. Carlise read about people living through them all the time. But without anyone around to dig her out, her friend was likely gone.

Dead.

The reality of her own situation hit Carlise. She might have been safe from the path of the slide, but she was underground. The avalanche had surely buried the entrance to the bunker. And it wasn't as if she had any provisions down here. The metal shelves were empty.

She'd been buried alive just as surely as Susie.

A whimper left Carlise's lips before she could control it. She backed up until she was leaning against the wall of the bunker but cried out in pain the second her shoulder touched the surface. Not only was she buried, but she'd been shot, the hole for air had been covered, and Riggs would find that damn letter and think she'd left him!

Taking a deep breath before panic could overwhelm her, Carlise shook her head.

No. There were cameras. Susie's car was still parked in front of the cabin. With her bags inside and probably both doors still open. And she had no doubt Baxter was still going insane in the bathroom, probably trying to scratch and bite his way out.

Riggs would try to find her. She knew it.

The only question was . . . how the hell would he do so? How deep was the snow above her head? Would he even search so far away from the cabin? Would he assume she'd been buried while running? Even if he did think to check the bunker, how would he find it with all the snow covering everything? With the door buried beneath so much debris?

The odds of her being found before she starved to death or suffocated were slim to none.

A tear rolled down Carlise's cheek. She'd finally found the man of her dreams, only to be ripped away from him in the cruelest way imaginable.

"I'm sorry," she whispered. Her words seemed to echo around the metal box. Now that the avalanche had stopped, everything was quiet. Too quiet.

"I'm here, Riggs," she said out loud. Hearing her own voice was preferable to the oppressive and scary silence. "I'm here."

Carlise pulled her knees up and wrapped her arms around them, trying to ignore the pain in her shoulder. That was the least of her worries at the moment. Her head dropped to rest on her knees, and she let go of the tears she'd desperately been holding back.

Chapter Fifteen

Chappy frowned as he pulled down his drive. A vehicle, with both front doors standing wide open, was parked haphazardly in front of the cabin, but he could see no one inside.

Who the hell was here, and why were the doors open?

He noticed the Maine license plate, but he didn't know anyone who drove a RAV4. He immediately went on alert. Ever aware that Carlise had a stalker, he reached into the glove box of his Jeep and pulled out the weapon he carried with him in case he came across a random bear or moose who wasn't inclined to give him some space.

Walking quickly, Chappy headed for the RAV4—but a familiar sound stopped him in his tracks.

He'd only heard an avalanche once, but the deafening noise had been imprinted on his brain. It sounded like distant thunder, and the closer the hundreds of tons of snow and rocks got, the louder the thunder became.

Every muscle in his body tense, Chappy stared in the direction of Baldpate Mountain. His cabin was out of the slide zone. His brain knew that, but he still fought his body's instinct to run.

The avalanche sounded close. Really close.

Chappy forced himself to skirt around the SUV and up the stairs to the cabin. Even if there was a slide happening right that moment, he was safe. He wanted to reassure Carlise that they were fine right where they were. That he'd done the research and made sure his cabin would be clear from any slides that might happen.

But the second he opened the door, Chappy knew she wasn't there. Wasn't just in the bathroom. There was an empty feel to the cabin that had previously been filled by Carlise's presence. She'd brought light and love to his world and into this home away from home. Both seemed notably absent now.

Then another sound, coming from the bathroom, had his heart in his throat.

Baxter, growling in a vicious way he'd never heard from the skittish dog before.

He opened the bathroom door, expecting to see Carlise, but only Baxter flew out of the room. The dog ran around the room, his nose to the ground, before he went to the door and barked loudly, over and over.

The dread Chappy felt was almost overwhelming.

Carlise missing, Baxter shut up in the bathroom, the unfamiliar car out front with both doors open . . . And now that he thought about it, he thought he'd glimpsed Carlise's suitcase on the back seat.

Shit. She was *leaving*? Had she called a car service to come get her?

No. She wouldn't leave him. He knew that down to his bones.

Baxter scratched at the door and continued barking. He looked back at Chappy as if to say, "What are you waiting for? Open this!"

Adrenaline swam through Chappy's veins. He noticed his satellite phone sitting on the kitchen counter and dirty dishes in the sink. Carlise never would've left them like that. Like him, she was kind of a neat freak, and even if she had gone out for a walk or something—which he highly doubted she'd do on her own; she'd said her plans were to stay inside and work while he was gone—she wouldn't have left the cabin with dirty dishes sitting around.

There were also papers on the table and a pen that hadn't been there before. Something he normally wouldn't question, if not for the fact that Carlise was fastidious about packing all her things when she was done working. She was kind of anal when it came to her notes.

As he looked around carefully, he realized quite a few things seemed out of sorts. The blanket on the couch wasn't folded, which Carlise habitually did when she got up. A towel she used to wipe Baxter's feet after potty breaks was lying on the floor instead of hanging on the coatrack.

He had to check the cameras, see what had happened before he'd arrived home.

He ran outside, forcing an unhappy Baxter to stay in the house, his heart thumping frantically as he started up the generator. Looking down at his cell phone, he swore. The Wi-Fi wasn't working. *Again.* And he didn't have time to fiddle with the antenna to try to fix it.

He needed help and he needed to find Carlise. She clearly wasn't anywhere nearby. Whoever owned that SUV wasn't here, either, but the vehicle itself told him they were both still in the area, somewhere on his mountain.

Chappy shut off the generator, then hit a preprogrammed number on the satellite phone he'd grabbed on his way out of the house, waiting impatiently for JJ to answer. Baxter barked once more from inside the house as he returned to the porch. "Hang on, Bax. I need to get help on the way before we let you outside."

"Hey, you just left here. What'd you forget?" JJ asked, chuckling over the line.

"I need help," he said without beating around the bush.

"What's wrong?" JJ asked, all humor gone from his tone.

"When I got to the cabin, there was a car I didn't recognize in front of the cabin, Baxter was locked in the bathroom, and there's no sign of Carlise or whoever owns that car."

"Shit. You think her stalker found her?" JJ asked.

"I have no idea, as I can't get the damn Wi-Fi to work so I can't check my cameras, but I'm guessing yes."

"Shit! How?"

A horrible thought struck Chappy then. "The only people she's talked to are her mom and her best friend."

"Could Carlise have emailed anyone? Been tracked through her phone when you checked her messages?"

"Possibly. But Carlise wouldn't have opened the door to someone she didn't know or her ex-boyfriend or her dad."

"You're thinking . . . it's the friend?" JJ asked, catching on to what Chappy wasn't saying.

"I highly doubt her own mother was stalking her. They seem close. While I don't know what she talked to Susie about, I'm guessing she probably told her enough for her friend to have a pretty good idea where she was."

"I don't know, Chappy," JJ said skeptically. "Your cabin is in the middle of nowhere."

"I realize that, but it's still findable. There's something else," Chappy told his friend.

"What?"

"I heard a slide as I was walking toward my cabin. To the east."

"Fuck."

"Yeah. And both front doors on the car in my driveway are wide open."

"What are you thinking?"

"I'll check the cameras when I can access them later to confirm, but I think the friend came here, and Carlise let her in without a second thought. Something happened while they were talking and . . . maybe the cat was let out of the bag? Maybe she found out Susie's her stalker. The woman must've tried to force her to leave with her, considering both car doors are open. But if the vehicle's still here, that has to mean Carlise ran."

"Possibly straight into an avalanche," JJ said grimly. "It's the most likely direction she would've gone, since your place is surrounded by so much scrub brush in every other direction."

"I need you and the other guys," Chappy said, his voice hitching. "She could be buried! I need help."

"Already on my way. I'll call the others. We're coming, Chappy. But if this woman was stalking Carlise, she's probably dangerous. Don't let your guard down."

Chappy had assumed the same. "I won't. When you get here, I'll already be out looking."

"We'll find you. She's going to be all right," JJ stated.

"You don't know that," Chappy said weakly, the words burning like acid on his tongue.

"I know that you've been through hell along with the rest of us. There's no way you found the woman who was meant to be yours, only to lose her now. She's smart, Chappy. She knew enough not to let anyone get her into that car. She knew her best bet was running. Those are *your* woods up there. She knew you'd find her."

Chappy took a deep breath. Damn straight, he'd find her.

Baxter barked loudly.

"Wow. Was that Baxter?"

"Yeah, he wants me to get off the phone and let him outside—bad."

"He can track her," JJ said.

Chappy blinked. He hadn't even thought of that. Baxter adored Carlise. His gaze followed her everywhere, both inside and out of the cabin. And he clearly hadn't been happy to be locked in the bathroom.

His friend was right, Baxter probably *could* track Carlise. Hell, he'd found her in the middle of that snowstorm, then led Chappy straight to her. He could do the same now.

"I have to go," he told JJ.

"Go. We're on our way. Be careful. I don't want you to have survived those assholes overseas, only to be taken down by some woman who's not right in the head."

"Ten-four. Later."

JJ hung up without another word. Chappy tucked the phone into the inner pocket of his jacket and headed for the door. "Find her, Baxter. Find Carlise." Then he opened the door.

The dog leaped outside like a shot. He frantically sniffed around the cabin, obviously trying to pick up Carlise's scent. He headed for the SUV parked in front of the cabin and put his front paws on the passenger seat.

Then he jumped down and took off into the woods.

"Shit! Hang on, Baxter! Wait for me!"

But the dog wasn't waiting for anyone. Chappy ran after the pit bull, catching glimpses of him as they weaved in and out of the trees.

The silence all around him was eerie. Usually there were birds chirping, the wind blowing through the trees, some sort of noise. But after the thunder of the avalanche, it was as if the forest was holding its breath.

The lack of sound felt like a heavy blanket on Chappy's shoulders. He'd rather hear Carlise shouting for help. Something. *Anything* indicating she was still alive.

"Carlise?" he called out as he ran.

The only thing he heard in return was more oppressive silence. As he followed Baxter through the trees, he prayed the dog knew where he was going.

He'd been running for several minutes when he finally saw them—footprints in the snow. Because of the warmer weather, a lot of the snow had melted, but not all of it. The prints in the snow lifted his spirits. Carlise *had* gone this way. He'd bet his life on it.

Was betting *her* life on it.

He saw two sets of prints, and based on the spacing, both people had been running. He assumed Susie had been chasing Carlise, and his resolve hardened. Best friend or not, she was going down. He'd make sure Carlise pressed charges and the woman was put away for as long as possible.

He wouldn't even entertain the idea that Carlise wasn't all right. That her friend might have done something drastic.

Chappy ran until the prints stopped. He lost their trail when the relatively flat area he'd been running through changed drastically. There was now a mountain of snow in his path. Snow and rocks from the avalanche.

Carlise and her pursuer *had* run straight into the path of the slide.

His gut twisted as he stared at the tons of snow that had fallen down the side of Baldpate Mountain.

He heard a bark, and Chappy looked up. Baxter was standing on top of the snow, staring back at him.

Chappy could take out a terrorist at fifty yards. He knew how to kill someone with his bare hands. He'd been tortured and hadn't let even a moan of pain pass his lips. But this . . .

Knowing his Carlise had possibly been caught in an avalanche was more than he could handle. He couldn't have fixed this, even if he'd been by her side. Couldn't have held back tons of snow to protect her.

And right now, he couldn't do anything but pray she'd somehow been far away from this position on the mountain when the snow had come crashing down.

Baxter barked again, repeatedly this time.

If the dog wanted him to follow, that's what Chappy would do. It was possible Baxter could lead him over the snow to the other side, where he'd maybe pick up Carlise's trail again.

The massive snowbank was as tall as Chappy, and he grunted with the effort it took to haul himself to the top. He followed Baxter . . .

But to his utter dismay, the dog stopped about halfway across the wide swath of snow—and began to dig.

"Shit!" Chappy cried, going to his knees beside the dog, digging with his bare hands. If Carlise was under the snow, he needed to get to her as soon as possible. She could be suffocating!

"No," Chappy said out loud, digging faster. His hands quickly went numb. The rocks and ice tore at his flesh, but he didn't feel the pain. All he could think about was getting to Carlise.

He didn't know how long he'd been digging, but it had to have been thirty minutes or more when he slowly sat back on his haunches and blew out an anguished breath.

It had been too long. If Carlise was under there, she was dead. There was no way she could survive without oxygen for as long as he'd been digging.

"Baxter," he said brokenly.

The dog ignored him, still trying to dig deeper into the snow.

"Stop, Bax," he tried again. "She's gone."

But he didn't even pause. His paws were bleeding, just like Chappy's fingers, but the tenacity of the dog never waned.

Not wanting him to hurt himself any more than he already had, Chappy reached out to grab his collar. To his surprise, Baxter growled.

Chappy immediately let go, not wanting to get bitten on top of the hell that had already become his reality in the last hour.

As soon as he released the dog's collar, Baxter went right back to digging. They'd made some progress, the hole they'd been working on was a couple of feet deep now, but from what Chappy could tell, they still had at least four feet or more of snow and ice and rocks to get through before they reached the ground.

He sat back on his heels and watched Baxter for a moment longer. Then he tilted his head back and stared up at the blue sky. Tears filled his eyes, and he let them fall.

He'd never felt as helpless as he did right that moment. He'd promised to protect Carlise, to keep her safe, and he'd failed. Big time.

When she'd needed him most, he hadn't been there. If he hadn't made that last stop at the lumberyard—he'd picked up some lumber to make Baxter a doghouse—he would've been at the cabin when

Susie arrived. If he'd been faster at the police station, if he hadn't had that cup of coffee with JJ, if he hadn't spent so much time at the grocery store . . .

So many what-ifs. So many regrets.

"Chappy?"

He heard his name being called, and for a split second his heart soared. Carlise! She wasn't under the snow. Baxter was wrong! He was digging for nothing.

But then his brain kicked into gear. The voice he'd heard was male. It wasn't Carlise.

"Here!" he yelled back.

"We're comin'!"

Chappy recognized the voice now. Bob. His friends had come. Had made damn good time getting up to his cabin. He had no doubt they'd driven way too fast and recklessly to get here . . . he just didn't think it would be enough.

Turning, he looked across the snow and saw Bob, Cal, JJ, and Chief Rutkey jogging toward him. The rocks and uneven snow kept them from moving very quickly, but they were here. Even better, they were each carrying a shovel.

"JJ told us about the avalanche, and we figured these would come in handy," Bob said, his grave expression no doubt mimicking Chappy's.

"Shit, mate. Your hands," Cal said with a frown after the men had scaled the tall snowbank.

"I'm fine," Chappy said quietly, holding out his hand for one of the shovels.

JJ shook his head. "We've got this. Move."

Chappy was about to tell his friend off, but Alfred, the police chief, took hold of his arm and hauled him to his feet, pulling him away from the hole Baxter was still frantically trying to dig.

"We've got this, son. Hold the dog so we can widen this hole and find your woman."

This time, Chappy took hold of Baxter's scruff and pulled him away from the hole. Surprisingly, the dog let him. Chappy knelt by his side and held his breath as his friends threw snow and rocks away from the hole. It widened and deepened quickly as they dug.

But still, there was no sign of Carlise.

With every shovelful of snow and debris they took out of the hole without finding her, the lower Chappy's hopes sank.

"Are we sure this is the right spot?" Bob asked.

"Yes," Chappy answered before anyone else could. "Baxter came straight here and started digging. She's here somewhere."

The threesome dug a little longer before Chief Rutkey said, "Damn, there's a pine tree doubled over. We'll have to dig around and free it before we can get to the snow underneath."

Something about his words clicked in Chappy's brain—and for the first time in almost an hour, hope soared inside him once again.

"The bunker!" he exclaimed, going over to the hole and looking into its depths.

"What? What bunker?" the chief asked.

"There's an old prepper bunker out here," JJ told him.

"Oh yeah, that's right," Alfred said. "That old guy who owned the cabin that was swept away in the last avalanche we had out here. He was a paranoid son of a bitch. Not friendly in the least. I only found out he had a bunker when his wife got locked inside and he needed help to get her out. Came to my house personally and swore me to secrecy. By the time we got her out, she was a wreck but physically just fine. I'd forgotten all about it."

"The pine trees," Chappy said. "That's the landmark I use to locate the bunker when I'm out and about. They're the only ones around here. The bunker was at the base of them."

"The trees we're digging around could've been swept down the mountain," Cal warned.

But Chappy shook his head. "She made it to the bunker. I *know* she did. I showed it to her last week. And before the footprints were wiped away by the slide, she was headed right for it. And Baxter led us here. She has to be down there!"

"And the friend?" Cal asked, one brow raised.

Chappy met his gaze, instantly knowing what Cal was thinking. "I don't know. Maybe . . . maybe they're both in there."

"Damn," JJ said and started digging again, a little faster now.

Minutes later, the men had reached the forest floor. The hole they'd dug was at least six feet deep and several feet wide, and the tops of their heads just peeked over the edge. They'd uncovered the door to the bunker, right under where Baxter had first started digging.

JJ pulled, but it wouldn't budge.

"It's stuck," he said in frustration as he tried to pull harder.

"Move," Chappy said. "Let me down there."

He and Alfred helped pull Bob and Cal out of the hole, making room for Chappy to jump in. "It's not stuck. It's locked," he said, relief nearly making him collapse.

It could be locked only from the inside.

"That's right," Alfred said from above, reading his mind. "After the guy's wife got stuck inside, he reconfigured the door to make it easier to open, but as a safety precaution, it could only be locked from inside. The last thing he wanted was some scavenger—his words, not mine—coming along and trapping them in there."

Chappy went to his knees next to the door and leaned down. "Carlise? Are you in there? It's me, Riggs! Unlock the door. You're safe. The avalanche is done."

When there was no immediate response, he tried, "Susie . . . ?"

All five men held their breath as they waited for some indication that someone was alive in the bunker.

~

Time had no meaning in the dark bunker. Carlise shivered as she huddled against one of the walls. She hoped it was her imagination, but she felt as if it was harder to breathe now than it had been when she'd first entered. Though . . . she had no idea how long ago that may have been.

Her mind wandered to places she didn't want to go. She wondered if it hurt to suffocate. If she'd claw at her throat, trying to get air in that wasn't there, or just fall asleep.

Her feelings swung wildly from being grateful to have found the bunker and escaped the avalanche to sorrow and anger at Susie's betrayal. She'd managed to not think about Riggs for what felt like forever . . . but she couldn't stop herself from thinking about him now.

Shifting so she was lying on the cold floor, she curled into a ball, swearing when the bullet hole in her shoulder made itself known once more. She'd taken her coat off a while ago and balled it up, leaned against it on the wall to try to stop the bleeding, but she didn't have the energy to put it back on.

She thought about how lucky she'd been to come across Riggs's cabin. About how worried she'd been when he was sick. How peaceful he looked when he slept, how handsome when he smiled, and how he could turn her on with a simple laugh.

She'd miss the way his calloused hands felt against her skin. How strong and masculine he looked while chopping wood. How he baby talked to Baxter to coax him closer so he could pet him. How protective he was.

The way he felt inside her, how his eyes had sparkled when he'd admitted he wanted four kids.

She'd miss literally *everything* about the man.

It wasn't fair that she'd been able to get away from Susie, find this bunker, and survive a freaking avalanche, only to die from lack of oxygen.

She didn't want to die. She wanted to live. She wanted Riggs. Wanted to explore Newton. Wanted to see his apartment in the small town.

Tears fell from her eyes, and her stuffy nose made it even harder to breathe.

Carlise sat up. She wanted to be like the kick-ass heroines in the romance books she translated. She wanted to be able to find her way out of this situation on her own and show Riggs that she wasn't helpless. That she could make it in the rugged woods of Maine.

But instead, she was going to die.

God, she hoped it wasn't Riggs who found her body when the snow melted. She didn't want him to have to go through that after everything else.

Sighing, Carlise grasped her updrawn legs, ignoring the twinge in her shoulder, and closed her eyes, resting her cheek on her knees. Breathing was definitely harder now. And she was so woozy. Maybe from blood loss.

She could almost hear Riggs's voice in her head. Telling her how much he loved her, how proud he was of her. How brave she was.

It was official—she was dying. There was no way she could hear Riggs's voice. Her brain was playing tricks on her. She was hallucinating for sure.

A second later, she lifted her head, going perfectly still.

No—she *could* hear Riggs's voice!

It was muffled, and she couldn't understand what he was saying, but it had to be his voice!

She dropped her arms from around her legs, got to her hands and knees, and started crawling in the direction she thought the door was.

She slammed her head into something hard, making nausea swirl in her gut.

"Don't puke, don't puke," she admonished herself out loud. It felt weird to hear her own voice. She'd stopped talking to herself shortly after entering the bunker. But somehow, it gave her strength. She wasn't dead yet, and she'd fight for her future with everything she had.

Putting her hand on the wall, she felt the metal shelves that lined one side of the bunker. She vaguely remembered what the space looked like from when Riggs had shown it to her the first time, and slowly, she made her way toward the end where the ladder was located.

That was when she heard it again—Riggs's voice for sure.

"Carlise? Are you in there? It's me, Riggs. Unlock the door. You're safe. The avalanche is done . . . Susie?"

She opened her mouth to reply, but suddenly, she couldn't speak. It felt as if there was no oxygen left at all.

For a moment, she panicked. If she didn't get to that door, she'd die. And she was so close to seeing Riggs again! To feeling his arms around her.

She had to move. She couldn't come this close to being rescued, only to fail now.

She started to stand with the help of the ladder, her shoulder aching. It felt as if it took every ounce of her strength just to lift her leg to the first rung, but determination rose within her. She could do this. She had no choice.

Carlise thought about her mom. How strong she was. How she'd survived for years in an abusive relationship. She wanted to make her proud. Wanted a chance to tell her how much of an inspiration she was.

Her shoulder screamed in pain as she stood a couple of rungs up the ladder and stretched her arm toward the lock. She couldn't quite reach. She'd have to go up one more rung. She braced carefully, giving herself the leverage she needed to slide the lock.

She grasped the dead bolt and attempted to move it, but her arm was so weak and sore, and she was so light-headed. She couldn't move it.

"Riggs," she whispered, almost overwhelmed with despair. He was so close. Just on the other side of that door, and yet he might as well be miles away.

She wasn't sure if he'd heard her weak voice or not, but she could hear *him* as easily as if he was standing right next to her, without a bulky door between them.

"Open the door, sweetheart. You can do it. I know you can! All you have to do is move that piece of metal a few inches. I'll do the rest. The guys are all here, and Baxter. He led me straight to you. You're safe. Do it, honey. For me. For our kids. For our friends. *Please.*"

Feeling as if she was two seconds from passing out, Carlise didn't think she had the strength to try again. But her hand moved without thought from her brain.

And just like that, the door was unlocked.

The second the dead bolt moved, Riggs was there. The sunlight was blinding after she'd been in the dark for so long, and Carlise immediately slammed her eyes shut. She felt herself falling for a split second, then Riggs had her. Holding her so she wouldn't fall backward, his arms clasped around her upper chest.

She inhaled deeply, blessed oxygen filling her lungs.

Then she cried out as Riggs lifted her up and out of the bunker, her shoulder screaming in pain.

"Fuck, where's the blood coming from?" JJ asked.

"I don't know. What hurts, honey?" Riggs asked, sounding frantic.

But Carlise couldn't speak. She was too busy trying to get as much air into her lungs as she could.

"Turn her. Her back's covered in blood," JJ said in a calm tone, which somehow reassured Carlise, despite his words. She could still be bleeding to death, but his even, soothing tone kept her from panicking.

"Riggs," she croaked.

"I'm here, sweetheart."

She opened her eyes into slits so she could see him. The worry and love in his gaze almost stole her breath again. "I wasn't leaving you. She made me pack and write that note."

"What note?" Bob asked from somewhere above them.

But Carlise kept her gaze on the man she loved. She wouldn't have blamed him for doubting her when he read the note, but she could admit that it would be a blow.

"I didn't see a note," Riggs told her. "But even if I had, I would *never* think you'd just leave me like that."

Carlise took another deep breath and nodded.

"Hand her up so we can get a look at that shoulder," Cal said from above them.

"Hang on," Riggs said.

Before Carlise could even brace herself, Riggs was clutching her waist and lifting her.

"Careful," JJ warned as she was suddenly airborne.

Before she could process what had happened, she was standing on top of a huge snowbank in the sunlight, supported by Bob and Cal. Her eyes began to adjust, and Carlise looked around in awe. The area looked nothing like it had when she'd gone into the bunker. It looked like a snowy, rocky wasteland. The trees she *did* see were sticking out of the snow at odd angles, as if they had been snapped at their bases as the snow roared down the mountain.

When Riggs emerged from the hole, he immediately pulled her into his arms, holding her firm and steady.

"I'm gonna lift her shirt to take a look at her back," JJ said quietly.

"Eyes on me, honey," Riggs ordered.

She braced as she felt JJ carefully grab the hem of her shirt, but she did as Riggs asked, looking into his beautiful eyes.

"I love you. You're amazing."

It was obvious he was trying to distract her, but she was keenly aware of the cold breeze against her skin as JJ lifted the shirt high enough to examine her shoulder. "Did you find Susie?"

"No. She didn't go into the bunker with you?"

Carlise dropped her gaze, but he wasn't having that. "Honey, please . . . look at me."

She did.

"What happened?"

"It was her. She was my stalker. I told her a little bit about Newton, and that was enough for her to find me. She said she asked around town about your cabin and got directions. I guess she was jealous of me . . . or . . . something? I don't really even know. But apparently, she loved Tommy, and they started dating after I broke up with him. She somehow got it in her head that I needed to be punished for leaving him, for telling people he was abusive. It makes no sense, Riggs . . . If he was hers now, why would she care that I left him?"

She inhaled a shuddering breath and shook her head. "Anyway . . . she had a gun. Was going to shoot Baxter. Made me write a note saying I was leaving. I knew I couldn't get in the car, so I ran. I figured you'd find me in the woods, even if I got lost."

"Damn straight I would," Riggs said.

Carlise cried out when JJ probed the bullet wound in her shoulder.

"Be careful!" Riggs growled.

"Sorry. Looks like the bullet's still in there. It's gonna have to come out."

Carlise began to struggle. "No. Not here! Please! It hurts—"

"Easy, sweetheart. He didn't mean *he* was going to take it out. We'll take you to the clinic in Newton. If they can't do it, they'll send you to a bigger hospital. You'll have the best drugs, and you won't feel a thing. I promise."

Carlise nodded and tried to calm down. Of course JJ wasn't going to perform surgery in the middle of the woods. She'd simply panicked.

"Can you carry her?" Cal asked. "We can take turns to get her out of here."

"I've got her, but thanks," Riggs said.

Before Carlise could protest and try to be brave, tell them that she could walk—even though she wasn't at all sure she could—Riggs had carefully lifted her into his arms. She rested her head against his shoulder and wrapped her good arm around his neck. The other lay limp in her lap as she tried not to move it much. Every jostle sent pain shooting down her back.

JJ draped his jacket over her, and Cal and Bob stood on either side of Riggs, clutching his arms and helping him climb down the steep mountain of snow from the avalanche.

Baxter barked, and Carlise jerked. "Was that Baxter? Is he here?"

"Yeah, it's him. He led me straight to you," Riggs told her.

"I had to put him in the bathroom because he was acting really aggressively toward Susie. I didn't understand then, but I guess he was trying to warn me. I didn't listen," Carlise said sadly.

"Don't blame yourself," a man Carlise didn't know said from behind them. She lifted her head to look over Riggs's shoulder.

"I'm Alfred Rutkey, chief of police. Chappy came by today and explained your situation. I was going to look into it, but obviously didn't get a chance."

Carlise nodded and put her head back on Riggs's shoulder.

"How'd you get shot?" JJ asked.

Carlise sighed. "When I was running from Susie. She was shooting kind of wildly from behind me. One of her shots got lucky, I guess. She tripped, and I was able to get into the bunker right as we heard the avalanche. I locked it before she could get in." Her voice lowered, and she sobbed as she said, "I wouldn't let her in. She was banging on the door. *Begging*. Telling me she could see the snow coming toward her. But I ignored her. I killed her!"

"No!" all five men exclaimed at once.

Carlise might've found that funny if the situation wasn't so solemn.

"She was going to kill you. She *shot* you," Cal said fiercely.

"She deserved what she got," Bob growled.

"If you'd let her in, you'd be dead right now," JJ agreed.

"Guess I need to arrange for a search for her body," the police chief mumbled.

But the only opinion that mattered was that of the man who was holding her in his arms. "Riggs?" she whispered. "Do you think about me differently now?"

"Yes," he said without hesitation.

Carlise winced.

Then he went on. "I admit I'd thought you were a bit of a fish out of water out here. You're a city girl. I wasn't sure you could hack living in a small town in Maine, even if you were willing to try. But I underestimated you. You're stronger than anyone I've ever met. You kept your head in what had to be a terrifying situation, and you did what you had to do in order to survive. You could've gotten in that car with her. But you didn't. You protected Baxter. You got away from her. Outsmarted her. Remembered the bunker and got yourself inside."

"I think the shots triggered the avalanche," Carlise admitted. "They were so loud, and they echoed all around us."

"That's a real possibility," Alfred said. "The conditions were definitely right, and all it can take is the right stimulus to get it started."

"Do I think about you differently now?" Riggs continued. "Yes. You aren't a fish out of water. You were born to be mine. To be here, in Maine, with me. You'll be a fierce protector of our kids, of our future pets, of our friends, of our mountain retreat. You proved that you can take care of yourself when the shit hits the fan . . . and while I never want you to have to go through anything like that again—*ever*—knowing that you'll fight the grim reaper himself to stay alive makes me love you even more."

"Riggs," she whispered, overwhelmed.

"Your only job right now is to get well. I'll get the footage from my cameras to Chief Rutkey, so he'll have the evidence he needs against Susie, in case she somehow survived the avalanche. There will be absolutely no doubt as to who was harassing you. You're free, honey. You can go anywhere you want, do anything, *be* anything."

"You want me to go back to Cleveland?"

"No. I want you to come back to our home—the cabin—to recuperate. I want you to move in with me back in Newton, marry me, have my babies. I love you, Carlise. So damn much."

"Yes," she said on a sigh.

"Yes? To what?"

"All of it."

Riggs stopped dead and studied her face. "Yes?" he asked, as if he hadn't quite heard her correctly.

"Yes," she told him with a smile.

"JJ, Cal, Bob . . . will you guys stand up with me when I get married?"

"Hell yeah!"

"Wouldn't miss it."

"Of course."

"When?" he asked Carlise.

"Maybe you shouldn't ask her when she was just rescued from near death and is probably a little loopy from pain," Chief Rutkey said dryly.

Carlise ignored him. "Whenever you want."

A gleam entered Riggs's eyes, but he only nodded.

Carlise had a feeling she might be Mrs. Chapman before the week was out . . . which was perfectly all right with her. "But I want my mom there," she said a little belatedly.

"I was going to call her as soon as we got cell service on the way to Newton," Riggs reassured her. "She'll want to know you're all right and what happened."

Carlise nodded, her eyes feeling extremely heavy. Suddenly, she could barely keep them open.

"Sleep, love," Riggs murmured. "I'll take care of you."

"I know you will," she told him, before she let the stress of the day and the pain take her under.

Chapter Sixteen

"I'll be back as soon as you give me the word that you're getting married," Carlise's mom said, doing her best not to let the tears in her eyes fall down her cheeks.

"I will, Mom," Carlise reassured her. Her arm was still in a sling, but she was feeling pretty darn good, all things considered.

The doctors at Newton's clinic were top notch, and they'd immediately gotten to work removing the bullet from her shoulder when she'd arrived with Riggs. Luckily, because of the distance between her and Susie, it hadn't gone too deeply into her flesh. They were able to extract it without the need for any kind of major surgery. But they'd still used some heavy-duty drugs to knock her out, and they'd completely numbed her shoulder before they'd started.

When she woke, she'd been in quite a bit of pain, but Riggs had taken it on himself to make sure she didn't downplay her discomfort, that she took the pain pills she'd been prescribed.

Her mom arrived not too long after she'd woken up in the clinic, and they'd both been pretty emotional about what Susie had done. It was a rough day or two for Carlise, but with the support of Riggs and his friends, she'd managed to put what had happened behind her pretty quickly. For the most part. She knew she'd have bad moments for a long time to come, but with Riggs at her side, she could deal with just about anything.

The cameras in the cabin had been all the proof anyone needed as to what had happened, and that Susie had arrived to kill her former best friend. It still didn't make a lot of sense to Carlise. Until Chief Rutkey told her that he'd dug deep . . . discovering that Susie had kept a lot of secrets.

Her birth name wasn't even Susie. She'd spent most of her childhood in and out of psychiatric hospitals. She'd learned to cope amazingly well for years, but apparently, she'd stopped taking her meds sometime after Carlise began dating Tommy, and she'd slowly spiraled downward.

The entire thing made Carlise extremely sad. Especially the fact that she'd never really known her friend at all.

Carlise's mom had stayed in Newton for four days, enough to make sure her daughter was really all right, and to meet Riggs and all his friends. JJ was driving her back to Bangor in a few minutes so she could catch her flight to Cleveland.

"You love him," her mom said.

Carlise smiled. "So much. You aren't worried we're rushing things?"

"Not at all. Anyone can see just by looking at you two that you were meant for each other. But with that said, if you ever decide you need more time or you change your mind, don't hesitate to say something. I made the mistake years ago of going ahead with a marriage I didn't want because I couldn't bear inconveniencing anyone."

Carlise wanted to reassure her mom that there was no way she'd ever feel that way about Riggs, but she just nodded instead. "Okay."

"I love you, and I'm so happy that this stalker business is behind you, and you can get on with your life."

"I wish you'd consider moving here," Carlise said a little sadly.

But her mom chuckled. "I'd never make it here. I mean, I love you and all, but Newton is a little small for me. Rest assured, I'll be happy to come and spend weeks at a time visiting my grandkids."

Carlise felt her cheeks flush as she smiled.

Her mom leaned in and hugged her, being careful not to touch her bandaged shoulder. "Again, just say the word about the wedding, and I'm here," she said.

"It's not going to be anything huge or fancy," Carlise warned. "In fact, Riggs has already requested we have Granny's Burgers at our reception."

"Sounds good to me," her mom said with a grin, not looking upset in the least. "As long as my baby's happy, it doesn't matter what kind of wedding she has."

"I love you, Mom," Carlise said.

"I love you too. I'm going now, before I ruin my makeup by crying it all off."

"Call when you get home," Carlise ordered, doing her best not to cry as well.

"I will. Bye!"

Carlise watched through watery eyes as JJ took her mom's arm and led her to his Bronco. She felt a cold nose nudge her hand and looked down to see Baxter sitting by her side, looking up at her with concern. "I'm okay," she told the dog.

She saw his gaze dart to the left a split second before she felt Riggs's arm come around her waist. She leaned back into him and waved with her good arm as JJ drove out of the apartment building's parking lot with her mom.

"You okay?" Riggs asked.

Carlise nodded.

"You'll see her soon."

Carlise nodded again.

"How's your shoulder? You need a pain pill?"

"I think I'm okay until later." She turned in his arms.

They were standing on the landing outside his apartment door. The building he lived in wasn't fancy, just two stories, and all the apartments had outside doors. There was a set of stairs leading up to the second floor and a small parking area. She'd already met most of his neighbors. They'd all been appalled to hear what had happened to her and had gone out of their way to make sure she and Riggs had everything they needed so he wouldn't need to leave her side while she was healing.

"How're your hands?" she asked.

She'd been alarmed the first time she'd noticed his damaged hands on the way to the clinic. He'd shredded his fingers trying to dig through the snow and ice to get to her. They were bandaged now and healing well, but she hated that he'd been hurt in the first place.

"They're fine," he said. "And before you ask, Baxter's paws are also fine. The vet said to keep him out of the forest for a while, and he'd be good as new in no time."

Carlise knew that, but she still worried. She looked down at the pit bull with a tender gaze. Baxter hadn't moved from her side, his gaze still locked on her. Riggs hadn't been wrong earlier when he'd said that Baxter was her dog. He was completely devoted, and the feeling was definitely mutual.

"April's coming over later and bringing a casserole," Riggs told her.

"Another one?" Carlise said with a small laugh.

"Yup. JJ's jealous as hell about it too."

"What's going on with those two?" Carlise asked. "I mean, they can't keep their eyes off each other, but as soon as one knows the other is looking, they pretend they weren't just staring wistfully."

"I think it's complicated," Riggs said with a shrug. "She's our employee, and he's still dealing with what happened to us while we were POWs."

"I could talk to her," Carlise offered.

But Riggs shook his head. "Don't. Until he's ready, it won't do any good. And if you talk April into making a move, and he rebuffs her, we'll lose the best admin assistant we've ever had. They'll figure it out sooner or later."

"How can you be sure?"

"Because if it's meant to be, it'll be. Look at us. Somehow, against all odds, we're here, safe, madly in love, and getting married. Speaking of which . . . we need to set a date."

Carlise chuckled softly. "You that worried I'm going to change my mind?"

"No. When you find the best thing to ever happen to you, you want the rest of your life to start as soon as possible," Riggs said, making Carlise melt into him. "Besides, when I get you pregnant with our first child, I want to be married. And neither of us are getting any younger. If we're having four kids, we need to get on that."

Carlise's belly clenched. She couldn't wait to give Riggs babies. She pulled out of his arms and turned to the apartment door. "Come on," she said breathlessly.

"Where?"

"To bed. If April's coming over, we don't have a lot of time."

"Your shoulder—" Riggs started, but Carlise shook her head and interrupted him.

"Is fine. You're just going to have to be creative. I need you, Riggs. Inside me. It's been days. And we're finally alone. All this talk of babies and being yours has made me extremely horny."

He chuckled, letting her lead him into their bedroom. Baxter, seeing where they were headed, went to the expensive dog bed Carlise had bought for him to take a nap.

"Help me get this shirt off," she told Riggs.

He carefully grabbed the hem and leaned down to rest his forehead against hers. "I love you," he said softly.

"I love you too," Carlise said on a sigh. "And to answer your question . . . soon. I'll marry you as soon as I can arrange it."

"Good."

Then there were no more words as they used their bodies to prove exactly how much they loved each other.

~

Later that night, Chappy was glad he and Carlise had taken the time to make love when they had. Because not only had April shown up with a casserole, but the rest of the guys had been right on her heels. JJ reported that her mom had gotten to the airport just fine, and they were celebrating the fact that both Carlise and Chappy—and Baxter—were safe and everything had turned out all right.

His friends were sitting on the floor around the coffee table in front of his couch, everyone playing a cutthroat game of Uno, when Chappy got up to refill drinks. He stood in his small kitchen and watched as Carlise threw her head back and laughed at something April had said.

It was amazing how well she was doing. Of course, she'd had a few nightmares, and he'd held her while murmuring into her hair that she was safe and brave and how proud he was.

What had almost happened to Carlise made him physically ill whenever he thought about it, which was more often than he wanted to admit. He'd never forget the moment when he'd opened that bunker door and seen her. Lips blue, gasping for air . . . she had literally been minutes away from dying. He had no doubt of that.

Baxter had saved her again. And she'd saved herself. He was prouder than he could ever fully articulate. And he'd hated to take his eyes off her ever since that moment. It had been excruciating to leave the room while the doctors dug the bullet out of her body. And even though his friends and the doctors and nurses had all tried to convince him to go to his apartment, take a shower, and get some sleep, that Carlise wouldn't even know he was there, he couldn't make himself leave.

He'd almost lost her.

Had come way too damn close.

It hadn't helped that it happened the first time he'd left her alone by going to town. It was going to take a while for him to get over that.

He was grateful business was slow right now and he hadn't had to leave her alone since.

It would take *Carlise* a while to get over the fact that her best friend had been the one terrorizing her. But together, they'd make it through.

She'd agreed to marry him. To have his babies. To stay here in Maine. He'd never felt like a particularly lucky man, but now he felt as if he was the luckiest person on the planet.

"Hey," Cal said quietly from right next to him, making Chappy jolt in surprise.

"Sorry, didn't mean to scare you," Cal said. "You good?"

"Yeah," Chappy said, keeping his voice low. "Thanks."

"How's she *really* doing?" his friend asked, motioning toward Carlise in the other room with his head.

"Amazingly well," Chappy said. "The doctor said there wasn't much damage from the bullet, and she'll be back to normal in no time."

Cal nodded. "They found her friend."

Chappy blinked. "They did?" The last he knew, the search was still ongoing.

"Yeah. Her body was swept down along the front of the slide, and the searchers found her earlier today."

Chappy was relieved. The last thing he wanted was to have to think about Susie's body being out in the wilderness for the rest of winter, revealing itself only after all the snow had melted. He'd wanted her found for Carlise's sake. For both their sakes. They needed to move on. He dreaded having to tell Carlise and potentially bringing all the bad memories to the foreground. But she'd be all right. He'd make sure of it.

"I appreciate you letting me know." He looked over and saw his friend staring off into space, as if something was on his mind. "What's going on, Cal?" Chappy asked. "You've been quiet tonight. Are *you* all right?"

His friend sighed. "Not really. I have to go to DC for a while."

"What? Why?"

"Family."

Chappy frowned in sympathy. Cal's family dynamic was . . . complicated. The relationship between him and his parents seemed pretty solid, but as much as they'd willingly shielded Cal from the politics of their home country—allowing him to have little to do with the bureaucracy—he was still expected to be loyal to the crown. He was rarely asked to make an appearance in Liechtenstein, but every now and then, he felt obligated to do his duty . . . and comply with a request he might prefer to avoid.

And his lineage meant Cal being a POW was still huge news, even three years later. There had been enough stories about his scars and injuries to sour Cal on any kind of media attention for life.

No matter how much Chappy, Bob, and JJ told him that his scars wouldn't matter to someone who loved him, they all knew the man was still extremely sensitive about his appearance. He wore mostly long-sleeved shirts and pants, even in the summer, and when he caught someone staring for too long, he'd completely shut down.

"What do they want you to do?" Chappy asked.

"Babysit."

"What?" he asked with a frown.

Cal sighed. "There's this woman. She's befriended one of my cousins, and he talked the family into getting involved in her so-called problems. They like her. A lot. I think his parents have visions of her marrying into the family. But apparently, she's in some kind of trouble. No one will give me any details until I get to DC. Because of my military service and discretion, they want me to deal with the situation."

"Can you say no?"

"It's complicated," Cal said.

"Can you say no?" he repeated more firmly. "They *do* know you aren't a bodyguard, right? That you've been out of the military for years? That you chop trees for a living?"

"They know all that, but they still think I'm their best option. My cousin is . . . unpredictable. And they don't want any more media attention on the royal family than we've already had in the last few years . . . which is mostly my fault. I *could* say no, but it would make my life and dealing with my extended family awkward. Trust me, it's easier to just do what they want. The sooner I go, the sooner I can come back."

Chappy scowled. He hated that he felt unable to help his friend. "You need one of us to go with you? Have your back?" To protect him from his family . . . which he didn't say out loud.

"No. My plan is to take care of this as fast as possible and get back to Maine."

"Okay, but you know if you need anything, all you have to do is call."

"I know, and I appreciate it."

"I *do* expect you to be here for my wedding. And word of warning, I'm not waiting long."

"Wouldn't miss it for the world. I'm pretty sure I can take a weekend trip back here without an issue, if it comes to that."

"Good."

"I'm happy for you," Cal said. "Carlise is one of the good ones. Don't let her go."

"Not planning on it," Chappy said firmly.

Cal nodded. "All right. Let me know how she gets on. I'm headed out in the morning."

"Cal?"

"Yeah, mate?"

Chappy wasn't usually one to butt into his friends' personal business, and he never would've even considered saying what he was about to say before he'd met Carlise . . . but meeting the woman who he knew down to his bones was meant for him had changed things. Changed *him*. He wanted to see all of his friends just as happy and content. "Keep an open mind."

"About what?" Cal asked, frowning.

"Women."

Cal rolled his eyes. "Here we go," he muttered.

"I'm serious. I'd written off getting married and having a family. I mean, we live out here in the middle of nowhere. There aren't exactly a lot of choices when it comes to dating. But then Carlise appeared as if she was destined to be here. All I'm saying is, don't ignore what's right in front of you. I feel as if we have a split second in life to recognize our other halves, and if we ignore that pull, discard the feeling, it'll never come back."

"No one's gonna look twice at me, Chappy," Cal said. "They want the fairy tale. The handsome billionaire prince—and we both know I'm anything but."

"You're one of the best men I know," Chappy said soberly. "Money isn't everything. Neither is being famous or having smooth skin. I value your loyalty. Your strength. Your steadfastness. And I know there's someone out there for you."

"She's not going to appear in the woods like some kind of nymph, like Carlise did for you. I'm okay with being single. Not everyone wants to be married and have kids."

Chappy knew deep down his friend was lying. Cal wanted that as much as, or more than, he did. He just wasn't willing to admit it because he was afraid he'd never find the right woman. It was easier to pretend not to care when in reality, he cared all too much.

"Be safe," Chappy said after a moment, knowing Cal wasn't willing to listen to him any longer.

"I will."

"You know if you need to bring this chick back to Newton, you can. We'll all help out."

"I appreciate it. I'll let you know once I get the lay of the land. I guess the woman is some kind of model. She lives with her sister and mother. I need to see what the actual situation is before I decide the best course of action."

"Are the sister and mother in trouble too?" Chappy asked.

Cal shrugged. "No clue."

"All right, do what you need to do and get your ass back here. Don't think we're gonna let you off the hook for your shifts. The trees around here won't cut themselves."

Cal chuckled, and Chappy was glad to see it.

"Right. And you're gonna be busy with your new wife, yeah?"

"Damn straight," Chappy agreed.

"I really am glad she's all right."

"Me too. And call us, Cal. I'm serious," Chappy said sternly.

"Yes, Mom."

They both chuckled. "That's JJ's title," he told him.

Cal nodded, then clapped him on the back before heading back into the living room.

Chappy watched as Carlise stood up and headed his way. "You need help with the drinks?" she asked.

"No, I've got them, sweetheart. How are you feeling?"

"I'm good," she said. "I heard some of your conversation with Cal. He's leaving?"

"Yeah."

"He's gonna find his Cinderella," she sighed as she leaned into Chappy.

"What?"

"He's gonna come back with his Cinderella. I just know it," Carlise said. Then she straightened, kissed his cheek, and went back into the other room to continue the game.

She constantly amazed him. It was obvious she was keeping an eye on him as much as he was on her. It felt good to be looked after. He wasn't sure why she was so certain Cal would find someone, but he hoped to hell she was right. He deserved to find a woman who loved him for who he was, rather than for his title or how much money he had in the bank or how he looked.

"You afraid to get your butt kicked?" Bob called out. "Get over here, Chappy, so I can crush you with my Uno skills!"

Chappy grinned and balanced the cans of Coke he'd taken out of the refrigerator, making his way back to his friends. As he sat next to Carlise and passed out the soft drinks, he couldn't help but say a silent thanks for his friends and his woman. He was definitely a lucky son of a bitch, and he had no plans to ever lose his newfound happiness.

Juniper Rose ran a hand over her sweaty forehead and inspected the freshly mopped floor with satisfaction. She'd been busy all day, preparing for the member of the Liechtensteiner royal family who would be coming soon. She wasn't exactly sure what was going on, since her stepmom and stepsister never told her anything, but from what she could glean from their whispered conversations, Carla, her stepsister, had told a friend she'd met online that she was being harassed and threatened.

Which was a lie.

Anyone who got to know Carla wouldn't bother with her, period. While she was beautiful on the outside . . . inside, she was a horrible, awful person.

June was bending to grab the bucket of dirty water when the door to the backyard opened, and she heard toenails clacking on the floor. She turned to yell "No!" but it was too late. Her stepsister's two spoiled-rotten corgis ran into the room, leaving muddy footprints all over her previously clean floor.

"Oh, dear," Carla sighed in the most insincere tone June had ever heard. "They got the floor all muddy. Guess you'll have to stay up late to deal with it. Come on, Pookie and Snookie. Time for bed." And with that, June's mean, equally spoiled-rotten stepsister swept out of the room, her two dogs at her heels.

June blinked fast to keep the tears at bay.

She lived in a big, gorgeous house, and from the outside looking in, she knew it might seem she had a perfect life. If only people knew. After her father died when she was fifteen, she'd been devastated. She'd assumed her new stepmother and stepsister would feel the same, that she wouldn't grieve alone . . . but instead, they'd seemed almost thrilled.

The money from his life insurance had immediately gone toward all the material things they hadn't been able to buy when her dad was alive.

June didn't care about cars, clothes, or designer handbags. All she wanted was her dad back. He was the only person who'd ever loved her for who she was. A slightly awkward, plump, shy woman who'd rather stay home and read than socialize.

In the years since, she'd turned into her family's maid more than a daughter or sister. She cleaned, drove Carla to her modeling appointments, maintained the bills, cooked, and generally did whatever she was told.

She was a real-life Cinderella—and she hated it. She hated that fairy tale, because no rich prince was going to swoop in and save her from her dismal life. She'd have to work up the nerve to save herself.

June had been hoarding money. Money left over from grocery runs, the odd bill here and there as she cleaned the house. Soon, she'd leave. She had no idea where she'd go, but wherever it was, she wasn't going to be anyone's poor relation ever again.

Prince Charming?

Bah. He didn't exist.

Find out what happens when Cal heads south and meets June in the second book in the Game of Chance series, *The Royal*. You know he's gonna get knocked on his butt! Read the first chapter below and pre-order the book now!

THE ROYAL

Game of Chance Series, Book 2

Chapter One

Callum "Cal" Redmon pulled his Rolls-Royce Cullinan into the Greens' driveway on the outskirts of Washington, DC. Traffic had been terrible, and he was in an awful mood. His back hurt, his knees were throbbing, and he had a horrible headache. Ever since he'd been a POW and had been relentlessly tortured, his body hadn't been the same. He felt as if he was at least twenty years older than his thirty-seven years.

The last place he wanted to be was here. He'd told his relatives that he wasn't a bodyguard. That ever since he'd gotten out of the military, he didn't want anything to do with weapons, being covert, or any kind of security. And yet . . . here he was.

Being part of the Liechtenstein royal family wasn't easy. Even though he hadn't grown up in the tiny country, and even though he barely knew the queen and king, he was still expected to be loyal. Still expected to drop everything to do their bidding when they asked. So when Carla Green had told his second cousin—whom she'd met online—that she was being stalked and was scared, his cousin had reached out to Cal to see what he could do about it.

When Cal, being Cal, had told him he couldn't do *anything* about his latest online model friend's personal life, that she should call the local police, his cousin had dug in his heels. He'd talked to his mom, who'd talked to her sister, who'd spoken with the queen. She, in turn, had called Cal's parents . . . and the next thing he knew, he was being guilted into driving to DC to "investigate" the situation.

Cal wasn't qualified to do a damn thing about Carla's problem. Yes, he could shoot, was a damn good shot, in fact. But that didn't necessarily make him qualified to be a bodyguard. He could barely handle his *own* body.

Most days, his very bones hurt. The beatings he'd received as a POW had screwed him up, bad. Torn ligaments, broken bones, pulled muscles . . . those were just the tip of the iceberg. Technically, all the injuries he'd sustained had healed, but the effects were ongoing, and his scars—inside and out—were many.

Not only that, but Cal didn't particularly like people. He was grumpy on the worst of days, and standoffish on the best. He'd seen the worst humanity had to offer, and he much preferred to hole up in the house he'd bought in the small Maine town where he and his friends had settled after they'd gotten out of the military.

Thanks to his royal lineage and parents who'd invested their family money carefully, Cal never had to worry about the size of his bank account. No one would know simply by looking at him that he had over a billion dollars in his portfolio. Most days he wore jeans and long-sleeve T-shirts, and he definitely didn't flaunt the fact that he had money, and lots of it.

Yes, the Cullinan he was driving was obnoxiously expensive. No one needed a Rolls-Royce SUV. But he hadn't been able to resist. It was sleek, had all the bells and whistles, and most importantly, was excellent on the snowy roads of Maine. Most people would think the vehicle was just another SUV like the thousands on the road. It was covered in dirt and looked more like a work truck at the moment than a three-hundred-thousand-dollar vehicle.

Cal drove his SUV around the back of the fairly large house sitting on five acres and parked. He took a moment to reach for his phone to text JJ and let him know that he'd arrived at the Greens' safe and sound.

He'd call his friend later and let him know what he'd found out after talking with Carla, but for now, he took a second to enjoy the silence that surrounded him. Closing his eyes, Cal took a deep breath. What he really wanted to do was turn around and drive right back to Maine. To sit in his quiet house and be left alone. But he hadn't been able to say no to his mom.

He and his parents had a complicated relationship with the royal family back in Liechtenstein. His mom and dad had left the country after she'd been knocked over by a member of the media when she'd been pregnant with him. They hadn't been trying to take pictures of her but rather the queen and king, and his mom had simply been in the way. That had been the last straw for his dad, and he'd moved them to England.

The queen and king hadn't been happy, but it wasn't as if his dad was ever going to be king. He was so far down the succession line, it would be nearly impossible for him to rise to the top. They'd lived a peaceful life in London, only going back to their home country now and then for official functions.

Cal had joined the British Army, becoming intrigued by a team of Delta Force Operatives he'd seen in action while overseas. Strings had been pulled, agreements made, and not long after, Cal had found himself in the US, training to become a Delta. It was hard work, grueling at times, but he'd done it. He was assigned to work with Chappy, Bob, and JJ.

Cal had never clicked with anyone the way he had with his teammates. The men became inseparable, and when they'd made the decision to get out of the military after being taken hostage, there hadn't been any question in Cal's mind that he'd go wherever the others did.

They'd settled in Maine—after Cal had won a game of rock paper scissors—and had established Jack's Lumber, a tree service. And while the work was difficult, especially with the relentless chronic pain Cal suffered day after day, he had been satisfied and mostly content for three long years.

Opening his eyes, Cal sighed. He was stalling. He needed to go inside and talk to Carla Green and her mother. Get some facts, see what kind of evidence she had, assess how serious the threat was. His cousin Karl had always been an overdramatic kid. When he'd stubbed his toe, he yelled and cried as if someone had chopped it off. When he'd gotten an A minus on a test, he'd expected everyone to treat him as if he'd just cured cancer. He fell madly in love with each of his girlfriends and went into a monthlong sulk when they broke up.

Cal didn't know if Karl and Carla had truly only met on the internet, but he was mostly certain his cousin was simply being overly dramatic once again when he'd gone up the chain of relatives to get him to do his bidding.

Wiping a hand over his face, Cal took another deep breath before leaning over and opening the glove box. He shook out two aspirin and swallowed them dry, praying they'd make a dent in the throbbing in his head.

He reached for the door handle and climbed out of his SUV. He arched his back, trying to stretch out the kinks from sitting still for so long. Wincing at the way his movement pulled against the scars all over his torso, Cal sighed.

Every day, every movement, reminded him of the hell he'd been through. His friends had done what they could to turn their captors' attention to themselves, but once they'd realized who they had in their clutches, they'd been positively gleeful. They'd laughed as they cut him, as they'd beaten him, as they'd turned on their video cameras to show the world how low a real-life prince had fallen.

Forcing his thoughts away from the not-too-distant past, Cal started to head back around toward the front of the house before movement caught his attention.

A woman exited through a side door of the house, carrying a trash bag and heading toward a bin directly opposite. Cal instinctively took a single step back, concealing himself behind the house as he studied her. She was small, perhaps a full foot shorter than his six-foot-one frame, and full figured . . . with the kind of curves Cal loved. Probably because he'd grown up around the opposite—skinny women who did whatever was necessary in order to fit into designer dresses, to resemble society's version of what a pretty woman should look like.

Regardless, he'd always been far more attracted to women who carried some meat on their bones. He loved how they felt against him, under him, how their full tits jiggled and bounced, how their thighs and rounded stomachs were so soft in his hands. A Rubenesque woman was the epitome of sexiness.

Cal would take a curvy woman over a stick-thin one every day of the week.

Curves aside, there was nothing particularly notable about the woman he was watching at the moment. She was wearing an oversize T-shirt that she'd tied into a knot at her waist, her brown hair pulled up into a ponytail at the back of her head. A pair of well-worn, faded jeans hugged her thighs, and she had no makeup on her face, as far as he could tell. But there was something about the full effect that had Cal watching her with fascination.

She pushed the lid off the bin and grunted as she lifted the obviously heavy trash bag. After throwing it in, she wiped her brow on the sleeve of her shirt, then sighed deeply and turned her face upward to the sun, closing her eyes.

She stood there for a long moment, her head tilted back, a small smile on her face, as if feeling the sun on her skin was the highlight of her day.

Cal was entranced. He hadn't even said one word to the woman, and yet he could tell by the way she was enjoying the simple pleasure of the sun on her face that this was someone he wanted to know.

The first time he'd stepped outside after being rescued, he'd done the same thing she was doing now. He'd taken a deep breath, closed his eyes, and lifted his face to the hot Middle Eastern sun. It had actually hurt, the blazing sunshine burning the cuts and bruises on his skin, but nothing, even three years later, had felt as good as that first breath of fresh air.

And for some reason, Cal had a feeling this woman was feeling just a little of what he had that day. As if by standing out here in the sun, with the birds singing around her, she was free. Free of her worries and troubles.

"Juniper!"

The shrill voice screeching from inside the house made the woman jerk in surprise, and she turned her attention toward the door she'd exited. The small smile on her face disappeared, and Cal watched as she removed any expression from her face and headed back toward the house.

"Juniper! Where the hell are you?" the voice from inside called out again.

It grated on Cal's nerves, the pitch high enough to exacerbate the throbbing in his head.

"I'm coming!" his curvy angel said calmly, as if she was used to being yelled at. And Cal supposed she probably was. She was most likely hired help for the household; it made sense if she was taking out the garbage. Cal's family had certainly had their share of maids, gardeners, cooks, and other staff over the years. But he couldn't remember his mom ever speaking to any of them as disrespectfully as the unseen woman inside the house, whoever she was.

Juniper. Cal smiled. It was a beautiful name.

He watched as Juniper reached for the door handle that led back into the house. She turned and looked up at the sky for another brief moment, and Cal could clearly see the expression on her face. It was no longer blank.

The longing, sorrow, and frustration he saw there spoke to his heart. But as soon as he caught a glimpse of the emotions, they were gone, as was she.

Cal's heart beat fast in his chest. He wasn't sure what just happened, but he'd never felt like this before. He wasn't a believer in love at first sight, like what happened in the fairy tales. Yes, he was a prince, but he wasn't going to meet his Snow White, Cinderella, or Sleeping Beauty and fall madly in love at first glance.

But . . . he couldn't deny he'd never experienced a draw toward a woman like he'd felt with the mysterious Juniper. It wasn't just her looks, although her body was exactly what he preferred in his lovers . . . it was the peacefulness that exuded from her as she'd turned her face to the sun. And an underlying strength.

Shaking his head, Cal rolled his eyes. He was being ridiculous. There was no way he could've seen all that from a woman who'd simply been taking out the rubbish.

Yet he had. He knew it.

Cal had no idea who Juniper was, but he knew he wanted to seek her out. Talk to her. Maybe that would bring him to his senses. She'd say something annoying, or find out who he was and act like so many other women had . . . she'd simper and flirt and do everything in her power to try to make him fall madly in love with her.

Wasn't going to happen. He was immune to love.

But that didn't make his curiosity disappear.

For the first time in years, Cal found himself looking forward to the hours and days ahead. Yes, he had to meet Carla Green and assess her stalker situation, but now he had another goal . . . find the mysterious Juniper, and see if the draw he had toward her was a momentary blip. Or if it was more.

The story his dad told him of the day he'd met his mom popped into Cal's head. How he'd taken one look at her and known she was the one. He'd told Cal that was how love happened for everyone on his side of the family. They met the person meant to be theirs, and the stars aligned, the birds sang, and that was that.

Cal had always rolled his eyes and secretly thought his dad was making up the stories about their relatives. That he was doing what he could to perpetuate the "royal" Disney myth about soul mates and love at first sight. Now, for the first time in his life, he wavered in his long-held assumptions about how his parents had gotten together.

Shaking his head, Cal continued toward the front of the house. He was actually eager to get inside . . . because on the other side of the door was the enigmatic woman who'd caught his attention without even trying.

Juniper "June" Rose wiped her brow on the sleeve of her T-shirt for what seemed the thousandth time that day. She was exhausted. She'd been going nonstop for hours. Her stepmom and stepsister had been in a tizzy for days. Ever since they'd gotten word that a real-life prince was going to be coming to the house.

From what June had been able to figure out from the bits and pieces of gossip she'd heard while cleaning, overhearing Elaine and Carla's excited whispers, Prince Redmon, from some small European country, was coming to the house to talk to Carla about her "stalker."

June snorted out loud. Stalker. Yeah, right. No one was stalking her stepsister—it was just another made-up story so she could get attention. June had never met a meaner, colder, more self-centered woman in her entire life. All Carla Green was interested in was being famous, like the Kardashians. Everything she did was toward that goal. She wanted to be rich, famous, and adored.

The problem was, Carla was truly awful. She actually enjoyed making people cry. To that end, she certainly did everything she could to make June miserable. She was eight years younger than June and acted more like fifteen than her actual twenty-four.

But Carla was also gorgeous. She was six feet tall and slender, had long blonde hair and big blue eyes, and when she wanted to, could be extremely charming. June assumed that was how and why she was able to sweet-talk the man she'd met online who knew Prince Redmon.

June had accidentally interrupted her stepsister one night when she was FaceTiming with the man, Karl—and had been appalled to find Carla naked from the waist up, holding her DDD boobs aloft for the camera.

Of course, Carla had gone to her mom and accused June of spying on her, and June had to endure an hour of being yelled at and called "ungrateful" and "jealous." Which was ridiculous, but of course, Elaine didn't give June a chance to tell her what really happened.

June had thought about leaving more times than she could count. She was thirty-two. She wasn't chained to the house. She could walk away at any time.

But in years past, every single time she worked up the nerve to leave, she'd look around and see the chair where her dad used to hold her in his lap and read to her. Or see the marks on the wall of her height throughout her childhood. He always made a huge deal when she grew a fraction of an inch, though at five-three, she'd always been the shortest kid in her class.

She'd remember her dad kneeling with her in the garden out back as they pulled weeds and laughed about something or other.

Her dad had adored this house. He'd scrimped and saved in order to be able to buy it, to give his daughter a better life, not the cramped apartment he'd lived in during his youth. Things had been tough, but he'd always managed to pay the mortgage, even if they had to eat hot dogs and ramen noodles for weeks on end.

And throughout all their struggles, they'd had each other. They'd played on the five acres around the house and laughed together, and he'd taught her how to cook. Cleaning never seemed like a chore when he was doing it with her.

Everywhere she looked in the house, she saw her dad. It was all she had left of him.

It was hard to believe he'd died so long ago. Throughout the years, her stepmom had slowly but surely moved the things her dad had loved so much to the basement or the attic. The rooms looked nothing like they had when it had been just June and Dad.

When he'd lain in the hospital dying, he'd told June that he'd left the house to her. That he knew she'd love it and care for it as much as he did. And she'd promised to do just that. To preserve their happy memories.

When he'd died, she'd been devastated. Hadn't been able to think straight. At first her stepmom had been her rock, had kept June from falling apart. But looking back, June now knew the woman had been grooming her. Building her up, only to tear her down. Somehow, she'd even convinced June that college would be a waste of time and money, because she'd never been academically inclined and her dad would want her *here*, taking care of the house.

She'd had a moment of clarity when she'd been in her early twenties and started looking into ways to kick Elaine and Carla out of the house as they removed every vestige of her father . . . only to find out that she'd inadvertently signed away her rights to the home her dad had loved and cherished.

One day, right after she'd turned eighteen, Elaine had brought a bunch of papers home and explained they were legal documents June needed to sign for her inheritance, now that she was of age.

She'd stupidly trusted Elaine, had signed page after page without reading . . . and had ended up giving ownership of her beloved house to her stepmom without knowing what she was doing.

Without any options, June had stayed. Partly because she had nowhere to go, had no money to rent her own place, and didn't have any marketable skills to get a well-paying job. But mostly she stayed because this was where she and her dad had been happy.

He'd met Elaine when June was fourteen and Carla was six, and within a year, he was dead. It wasn't fair, and every day, June missed her dad terribly.

But now, with each year that passed, June's stubbornness to stay the course, to not leave the house where she'd lived with her dad, was waning. Carla was a bitch, her two corgis were horrible and just as nasty as their owner, and Elaine had a calculating look in her eye that June didn't trust.

She'd been squirreling money away, bills she found around the house, change in the washer that Elaine and Carla had left in their pockets, and leftover cash from running errands.

It wasn't enough, not really, but June had finally reached the point where she knew she had to leave. She didn't have any friends to help her, because Elaine had skillfully isolated her long ago from the kids she went to middle and high school with. And for years she'd been kept busy working, doing all the cleaning, shopping, cooking, and other errands.

When she was just out of high school and still deeply grieving the loss of her father, and when she still thought Elaine had her best interests at heart, June had been glad to help out. To do her part to help raise Carla and keep the house running as smoothly as possible.

But now she realized how stupid she'd been. For too many years, she'd been Elaine and Carla's slave—and she was done.

She'd miss the house, but the happy memories with her dad had been replaced by humiliation and degradation. The house was no longer a cherished safe space—it had become her own version of hell.

June didn't know where she'd go or what she'd do, but *anywhere* would be better than here. She'd been researching the best places in the country to live, the cheapest places, and hadn't decided exactly where she wanted to head yet. Somewhere far from Washington, DC, that was for sure.

"Juniper!" Carla shouted as she burst into the kitchen.

June hated how Elaine and Carla insisted on calling her by the name her beloved father always had. At first it had been comforting—it felt intimate and was a reminder of her dad. But now her full name on their lips was grating and made her skin crawl.

"Yes?" she asked as she turned away from the pot she was stirring on the stove.

"He's here! Finally! He's gonna stay in the room next to mine. You need to get up there and change the sheets. Make sure he has a clean towel—and make it one of the small ones." Her stepsister grinned with a mischievous glint to her eye. "Because I'm gonna *accidentally* walk in on him, and I want to see how big his dick is. Can't do that with a huge beach towel wrapped around his waist. Oh! And spray some of my perfume on his sheets. I want him to associate my smell with being in bed."

"Right now?" June asked innocently. She wanted to roll her eyes at Carla, tell her she was disgusting and far too desperate, but she knew better. It was much easier to fade into the background, to do what she was told, than to disagree. She'd learned that from experience.

"Of course, right now! Duh! You're so stupid."

"Okay, but the dinner might burn if I do," June told her.

"Shit! That won't do. Fine, after you serve us, after the appetizers and before the dessert, when we're eating the main dish, run upstairs and do as I said. Oh, and make sure that door between our rooms is unlocked too. How else will I be able to accidentally catch him naked?" Carla cackled. "Have you seen him?" she asked.

June shook her head. She wanted to ask her stepsister when the hell she'd possibly have had time to spy on their guest when she was busy doing last-minute cleaning, like sweeping dog hair from the entryway floors, taking out the trash, and cooking the four-course dinner Elaine had insisted the prince would be expecting.

"I've heard he's covered in scars. Karl actually warned me not to make a big deal of them, but I went online to see what he meant, and he's *hideous* without his clothes. I'll have to close my eyes when he's on top of me because . . . gross! But luckily his face is fine. I mean, his nose is crooked, and he's missing part of one of his ears, but I'll make sure he grows his hair long so it covers that up. As long as he has a big dick, I don't really care what the rest of him looks like. Anyway, we'll be beautiful together. I've already started looking at wedding dresses. I want to rival any other royal wedding that's ever been televised! I'm going to be a princess—and I can't wait!"

June felt a pang of pity for the prince. He had no idea the vipers' nest he'd walked into. Had no clue Carla was planning their wedding, all while calling him "hideous" and "gross" for things he'd had no control over.

Carla stared at June for a long moment. "Well?" she finally demanded.

June knew what she wanted to hear. "You'll be a beautiful bride," she said woodenly.

With a fake smile, Carla nodded. "Of course I will. Mark my words—Prince Redmon is going to be my husband within three months. No one can resist me. I haven't had all those plastic surgeries for nothing. I'm going to be a princess!" she declared again. Then she glared at June. "And don't be late with our dinner. Keep your mouth shut—and don't even look at the prince. He's *mine*, and I'll do whatever I have to in order to have him. Understand?"

June nodded immediately. "Yes."

"Good. God, you're so pathetic. As if he'd ever look twice at a fat cow like you." Then Carla turned and flounced out of the kitchen.

The second she left, June let out a breath. She'd stopped letting her stepsister's insults get to her years ago. She knew she was overweight, but she didn't care. Her dad had been plump, and she'd seen pictures of her mom. June definitely had the Rose genes . . . she would never be tall and skinny, but she was all right with that. While she didn't work out like most people did, working around the house and in the yard kept her muscles strong and her stamina up.

Turning back to the pot on the stove, June heaved a deep sigh. She really did feel bad for Prince Redmon. Carla would be relentless in her pursuit of him, and like most men who got caught in her snare, he'd be hooked before he realized exactly what kind of woman her stepsister was.

But it was none of June's business. She'd tried to warn some of the men Carla had dated in the past, and it hadn't gone well for her. Inevitably, Carla or Elaine had found out what she'd said and made her life extremely miserable for weeks afterward. It was easier to just keep her mouth shut and let Carla's suitors find out for themselves what a bitch she really was.

June shook her head at the thought of Carla becoming a princess. She'd ruin Liechtenstein's reputation for sure. But again . . . it wasn't her business. When she left, she'd be free of Carla and Elaine Green for good. She wouldn't look back. Her time was coming, and June couldn't wait.

Pick up book 2 in the Game of Chance Series today!
The Royal

About the Author

Photo © 2015 A&C Photography

Susan Stoker is a *New York Times*, *USA Today*, and *Wall Street Journal* bestselling author whose series include Badge of Honor: Texas Heroes, SEAL of Protection, and Delta Force Heroes. Married to a retired US Army noncommissioned officer, Stoker has lived all over the United States—from Missouri and California to Colorado and Texas—and currently lives under the big skies of Tennessee. A true believer in happily ever after, Stoker enjoys writing novels in which romance turns to love. To learn more about the author and her work, visit her website, www.stokeraces.com, or find her on Facebook at www.facebook.com/authorsusanstoker.

Connect with Susan Online

Susan's Facebook Profile and Page

www.facebook.com/authorsstoker

www.facebook.com/authorsusanstoker

Follow Susan on Twitter

www.twitter.com/susan_stoker

Find Susan's Books on Goodreads

www.goodreads.com/susanstoker

Email

susan@stokeraces.com

Website

www.stokeraces.com

Printed in Great Britain
by Amazon